5/98

98
1

the voice of the turtle

GAYLORD MG

98

the voice *of* the turtle

AN ANTHOLOGY OF CUBAN STORIES

Edited by Peter Bush

Grove Press

Published simultaneously in Canada
Printed in the United States of America
First published in Great Britain by Quartet Books Ltd. in 1997

FIRST GROVE PRESS EDITION

Library of Congress Cataloging-in-Publication Data
The voice of the turtle : an anthology of Cuban stories / edited by
  Peter Bush.
     p. cm.
   ISBN 0-8021-3555-2
    1. Short stories, Cuban — Translations into English. 2. Cuban
fiction—20th century—Translations into English. I. Bush, Peter
R., 1946–   .
  PQ7386.V65   1998
  863'.010897291—dc21   97-38169

Grove Press
841 Broadway
New York, NY 10003

98 99 00 01   10 9 8 7 6 5 4 3 2 1

Contents

INTRODUCTION

I sought out the songs of the Cuban turtle for this anthology, driven by particular experiences of *cubania*, the favoured contemporary word for Cubanness. On visits to the Island during the 1990s I met young writers who are the children, if not the angry young men and women, of the Revolution. Their lives have been shaped by the twists and turns in the policies of Fidel Castro's government as it responded to the United States boycott, the collapse of the Soviet Union and its Eastern European satellites. As I made my gringo way up the staircases of various tenement blocks to their bedsit cubbyholes, from an open door would come the voice of the Committee for the Defence of the Revolution: 'Who are you going to visit?'

The work of writers who had lived or live in exile or whose island literary presence had been more or less silenced – Calvert Casey, Lezama Lima, Virgilio Piñera, Severo Sarduy and Guillermo Cabrera Infante - was always a point of discussion, a specific literary tradition giving a context for new writing. Their books were casually displayed on plywood coffee tables bought from the second-hand booksellers who set out their cardboard boxes full of treasures and trash every morning on a cobbled square in Old Havana. I hunted down the books of Carlos Montenegro, the author of *Men Without Women*, the 1930's novel of prison sexuality: one eager dealer biked off to return ten minutes later with Montenegro's despatches from the Spanish Civil War and two first editions of his short stories.

I attended literary gatherings on poet Reina María's roof terrace, listened to readings and heard about the opinions and publishing projects of a group of writers who met regularly with Reina, Jorge Yglesias, and Rolando Sánchez Mejías. At the Cuban Writers' Union forty writers turned up to discuss the projected anthology. Stories appeared from everywhere; on threadbare paper, in thin anthologies, magazines, faded photocopies, barely visible typescript. Writers apologized for having no copies of their best-known stories and rehearsed the difficulties and possibilities of being critical from within, or getting into print in an economy starved of paper.

In Miami I found Uva de Aragón whose mother remembered Madrid meetings with Galdós and Lorca, and story-writers from the Mariel exodus in a city of Spanish speakers that would soon be the home for two writers I had met in Havana. In London, I attended the launch of Cabrera Infante's autobiographical *Mea Culpa* which was greeted with almost unanimous hostility by radicals who retained an enthusiasm for the Revolution. They had no time for bitter irony or self-doubt in that public arena of debate.

We all bring our pre-conceptions of the Cuban or the Caribbean to these stories. The confrontation that took place at the Institute for Contemporary Arts on the Mall leading to Buckingham Palace reminded me of other mismatches of hopes and realities in relation to Cuba. There was the night when an English provincial theatre did its best to recreate the atmosphere of Havana's top tourist Tropicana night-club. 'Cuba comes to Northampton' ran the poster of rumba-rhythmed mulattas. Three coach-loads of pensioners from Kettering and Wellingborough sat on the edges of their chairs. The Friday-night-is-music-night olde-tyme dancers were joined by a dozen local lovers of the Revolution. Fevered excitement of anticipation soon turned to disbelief as the curtain rose to reveal a bearded, ringleted and ear-ringed combo of Cuban new-wave jazzrockers: not a maracas, not a bared black thigh in sight. The people's musicians blasted away and the county's elderly responded by making the most of an unexpected revelation from the Caribbean. Nobody walked out.

There were those October days in 1962 when Cuba was on everybody's mind. We cycled home from school wondering what would happen, passed notes round the back of biology lessons - what'll you do first if war is declared if the H-bomb is going to drop? Why should we fear a small island that has fallen to Communism?

In Madrid 1964 I walked past buildings and lampposts festooned with flags and banners celebrating '25 Years of Peace' under the rule of Franco who kept the peace by jailing students and trade-unionists. I had left behind a home dominated by talk of strikes, time-and-motion, overtime pay to live in dingy back-rooms and cheap flats shared with Peruvians or Cubans sent by parents from Lima or Miami to get an education in the mother-country. Their diplomas were issued by late-night bars, washed down with rum-and-cokes called Cuba libres: accompanied by fleeting references to the triumvirate of military chiefs, Peruvian Velasco, Cuban Castro and Spanish Franco but really lost in the selfish fun of being alone for the first time, Godless, parentless, vino tinto at 15 cents a glass, and the girls from Latin America who could stay out late as against the madrileñas who had to be back at home at ten before the night-watchman locked the door.

This was a prelude to three years at Cambridge University where Latin American literature only warranted a sideways mention as a foot-note to lectures on Spanish literary achievements. While García Márquez was picking up his pen to dazzle the West with butterflies and Buendías, a whole continent's fiction, poetry and drama was silenced by Calderón's avenging husbands, Lorca's gypsies and the noventayochistas.

The 1898 generation was all the rage. There had been this war in the Caribbean. Spain had lost Cuba, its last colony in a war with the United States. For frenetic months in the middle of 1898 the Madrid newspapers ranted as a century later the British press would bellow for the Falklands. Spanish monarchs organised charity balls, the rumour ran that the USA was going to invade the Canary Islands, but los yanquís were victors and Spanish bourgeois families yielded their grip on lucrative sugar plantations to Uncle Sam. Spanish intellectuals desperately searched their souls for solutions to national decadence and the demise of empire, called for national regeneration, pitted Spanish Quixotic spirituality against European love of science and technology. There was hardly a word about Cuban feelings and no reading of Caribbean reactions to the new dependence on North America. The war in Cuba was taught exclusively from a Spanish point of view. It was in those turn-of-the century years that the Platt amendment enshrining the USA's right to intervene in the island was made in Cuba's constitution, and the US military base in Guantánamo was established. How come that base survives to this day? we might well ask/have asked.

Yet there was an insular history and culture of Taino Indians before the Spanish conquistadors arrived and killed them off in an act of genocide in the early years of imperial expansion after 1492. Then over the centuries hundreds of thousands of African slaves were shipped in, coolies from China and poor migrants from the Peninsula to suit the economic interests of Spanish sugar plantation owners.

One year after those lectures on 1898, a professor was despatched by the university to Latin America to begin to fill in the literary gaps just as the Cuban Revolution led by Fidel Castro became a burning issue, and Che Guevara beards appeared on chins as well as posters on every campus. Discussions raged as to what exactly was the class nature of the Cuban state. More simply, would the revolution spread through Latin America? 1898 was replaced by 1968 as the year of historical significance and many student-minds focused on changing the world rather than interpreting it, hero-worshipping los barbudos, the bearded ones who came down from the Sierra Maestra to liberate their people. Others engaged in intricate debates on dialectics, joined striking dustmen, firemen or carworkers on picketlines, flitted from one left-wing sect to another, eyes on Ho Chi Minh in Hanoi and the General Strike in France. Take your Desires and Dreams for Reality went the graffiti; Cut Sugar Cane for Cuba was the call from Solidarity leaflets, be a New Man; Volunteer Labour for the Revolution and help achieve its goal of a ten-million ton sugar harvest.

There was another side, over the waters in Miami, or in New York, or wherever the exiled went. They came and went in many varieties: gusanos, worms, counter-revolutionary conspirators according to

Havana, the quedados, also in Miami but whose minds stayed faithful to Fidel. Both sides were left with a legacy of hatred and violence, families and friends divided by civil war, expropriation and rhetoric, the historical reality that Cubans lived through. Thirty-six years later the boycott remains, the island economy has been dollarized and some exiled intellectuals and entrepreneurs still harbour dreams about regaining their pre-revolutionary family business.

Why start a book of stories with more stories rather than a narrative of the rise of Cuban fiction? Because this anthology is rooted in particular experiences which privilege the story as opposed to the politics, history or literary theory that could have predominated in this introduction. As readers invest what they read with their own personal histories, so these tales from exile or from the island will possess an added poignancy.

War and revolution, exile and migration are the central and most common experiences of the twentieth century: the jagged edges of dislocation and separation, sharper and more painful than any performative linguistic act currently being staged in the theatres of academia. The experience of exile and isolation, lived inside or outside the country of birth, lived as a holding on to identity, to nationality, wanting to be, to construct the self, identifying, in this case, with cubanía. And the accompanying nostalgia for what was, landscapes of the mind, even the hopes dashed. On the island, the fear of change – after Fidel, the deluge – and the confidence that life in a Havana squeezed by the US boycott is nevertheless better than a Haitian existence.

Cuba has a strong tradition of short-story writing reaching back to the 1920s nourished by literary prizes, newspaper and radio serialisation and oral traditions which may be Afro-Cuban, Creole, Galician, Basque, Spanish or North American, most often hybridized. It is a tradition that has always travelled with the diaspora out of Cuba. The tradition of departing and returning writers began well before January 1959 when Fidel Castro seized power. The turtle of this anthology has a voice but its song resounds in many voices, echoes the exile, the loss, dispossession and diaspora that reaches from before the 1920s to the most recent 1990s. The first story by Hernández Catá is a War of Independence story recounted from abroad less than a generation on. The final story is by Marilyn Bobes, a contemporary writer who lived in France and has since returned. The aim of the anthology is in the first place to give some idea of the variety of that historical and literary experience through a selection of stories worth reading in their own right.

The English-speaking world tends to marginalise Cuban and other Latin American writing by simply ignoring it or reducing it to the exotic. In this anthology you will find a range of styles and stories: with and without plots, surrealist humour, macabre humour, lyrical meditations, the fabulous and the historical. It is necessarily a selection from the wealth of twentieth-century story-tellers available. Not every writer can be here. Three other Cuban anthologies in Spanish have been published recently and have only one story in common with the Turtle. Some writers and translators reside within these pages who would never share a public platform: a limited form of consent to cohabit at least in a literary tradition. In the case of Alejo Carpentier, permission to include one of his stories was not granted.

As an editor, in the interests of heterogeneity, I have opted to retain the North American English of North American translators and the English of English translators. Some writers and translators sent in personal notes on their lives and works and I retained or translated them with all the anger and disillusion with which they were originally written. Why obliterate those personal resonances in a book of stories?

Clearly none of these stories would be available to be read in English if it were not for the translators: a necessary statement of the obvious in an English-speaking culture that likes to downgrade translation as second-best or resist access to the foreign. I have pursued a policy that is labour-intensive but creative and collaborative in relation to the writing: namely, the translations have been read and edited as translations from the Spanish. They have been read and copy-edited as English texts that are translations. These translations will for most readers be read as original texts, and they will accept the strangeness or foreignness as they would accept strangeness in original writing in English. All reading of literature is translation to a greater or lesser extent, even when we read the most canonically English of texts. The translations have also been sent to the authors or their heirs whenever possible as another source of an alternative reading and insight into the text.

The Voice of the Turtle proposes a hopeful recognition of difference, a necessary dialogue between conflicting readings and obsessions, stories of openings rather than closures: words born of ambiguity, confusion, anger and tragedy that can be in turn comic, beautiful, entertaining and disturbing.

Peter Bush

Acknowledgements

Many people have intervened in the construction of this anthology. The idea took shape when I was consultant on a Rear Window Channel 4 documentary, produced by Tariq Ali on the life and work of the late film director Tomás Gutiérrez Alea, *Tales from Havana*. Interviewing Titón, the actors and production team of *Strawberry and Chocolate*, Ambrosio Fornet and Juan Carlos Tabío during the Special Period was the best possible introduction to the recent political and artistic climate in Havana. Amanda Hopkinson got together her London Cuban network at an early informative party and continued to help the project through to the launch. I took the idea to Georgia de Chamberet at Quartet Books, now of Book Blast, who championed it through the vital commissioning stage and took an active interest, following up those contractual ends and accompanying me on one visit to the island to meet writers and negotiate rights with the Cuban Literary Agency, Jorge Timossi and Tania Jiménez. I would like to thank the following for their encouragement, helpful suggestions and insights into recent Cuban history; José Antonio Évora, Guillermo Cabrera Infante, Juan Goytisolo, Andrew Hurley, Suzanne Jill Levine, Carol Maier, Senel Paz and Jesús Vega. The group of translators range from the very established to the very new and all have met their deadlines, been patient in their responses and helped out over questions of rights whenever necessary. My translations have benefited from workshops with students at Middlesex and Sheffield Universities and at UMIST and with fellow translators at a British Council Seminar organised by the Centre for British and Comparative studies at Warwick University. The anthology would not have been possible without funding from the Translation Panel of the Arts Council where Jilly Paver was as helpful as ever. Michael Jacobs got contracts to Cuba via an architect friend in Sevilla. Max Jourdan brought back numerous biographical notes and wonderful photos of some writers in their contexts. Barbara Probst Solomon helped track down Edmundo Desnoes in New York .Colleagues at Middlesex University have tolerated my various absences in Havana and Miami and the School of Modern Languages gave financial support. Julia, Tom and Ruth have listened sympathetically to the wheezing *Voice of the Turtle*, and put up with post-midnight faxes.

Prologue

Poetry As *Eruv*
Octavio Armand

'*Ruins are better for defense than intact buildings.*'
General Frido von Senger und Etterlin

I

There is one dossier I will never forget. It belonged to a Latin American who applied for a teaching position in a Venezuelan university. Among his professional qualifications he had included two that were totally, absolutely new to me: Torture, Exile. Their presence seemed to offer my vision a physical challenge, daring me to join the blackness of a few letters and form those two words on a predictable, boring page. My eyes slid on the letters and could not connect with them, as if the words had been left there like the banana skin that turns up in so many sitcoms. But this was not a case of carelessness; this was a serious joke. The two words blazed like the colophon of a carefully prepared document. I felt sad, amused, sick to my stomach.

For me, exile had always been a decentering experience. I looked desperately for an elusive center that perhaps had been hopelessly lost. As if they were pieces of a puzzle, I joined bits of landscape, tastes, phrases, instants that might permit a semblance of continuity. A possible history. I was determined to construct ruins, and I looked for everything, saw everything in the rearview mirror that was Cuba. People who know me well know that those efforts – those failures – were part of an increasing bitterness.

Exile isolated me not only from the island but from the isolated Cuba-in-exile, and the cowardly aggression and pettiness I encountered increased my solitude. There were, and there are, people who persecute those exiles who do not fit easily into their particular image of the American diaspora. I have a *curriculum* too, of course. Wasn't it Darío who said that everyone among the living has a *vita*? Mine, however, excluded me automatically, because it indicated my date and place of birth. As a Cuban exile, the only discipline available to me was bitterness. Others did not suffer what for many years I have been calling a double exile. This is why some people underline the supposed condition of 'tortured', 'exiled' when they apply for jobs. But how can a decentered being dare to approach the center so boldly? The torture victims I have known do not usually talk about their tortures. Maybe they never learned how to capitalize on them? We are certainly living in pathetic times if to the profession of torturer we can add the no-less-terrible profession of tortured. Exile has also become a profession. After all, here I am, momentarily but absolutely centered, to repeat once again *et campos ubi Troja fuit, etiam periere ruinae, et in Arcadia ego!* I will not do it. I am probably going to disappoint you, but today I want to speak of an appealing illusion: the adventures and advantages of exile. Exile as Arcadia.

II

When I speak of poetry as *eruv*, I realize that I am building castles in the air, for it would certainly be no easy task to undo the work of heavenly bodies and politicians with a poetics. Nevertheless, this must be tried. Poetry could be a cure for some of the ills that afflict our planet. And since we are talking about castles, even though they are in the air, I want to recall a curious therapy whose roots go back to the days when castles were built. This so-called cure was healing by sympathy, also known as magnetic transfer, transplanting, or translation. It was only applicable to movable diseases. Movable or transplantable. Some years ago I spoke to several groups of translators about the five types of cure by *translatio*, since I believed and I still believe, that language – being a movable disease – is susceptible to this treatment. Evidently exile is an even more *movable disease* than language. Consequently I feel obliged to list once more the various types of sympathetic therapies, all of which involve the transference or transportation of an illness from the affected body to another body: *inseminatio, implantatio, impositio, inoratio, inescatio.* According to this doctrine, it is believed that a patient will be cured if the body used as the object of transference falls ill or dies. On the other hand, if the body rejects the illness, there is no hope. For example, in the treatment by *inseminatio,* a seed is sown and watered with a liquid distilled from *magnes mumia,* the remains of a mummy; its growth determines whether or not a cure will be possible. Healing by *impositio* is no less dramatic: a piece of skin from the affected part of the body or some of the patient's excrement is inserted between the bark and the trunk of the tree and then covered with mud. In *inescatio,* a third type of healing by *translatio, magnes mumia* is fed to an animal. A variation of *inescatio* is of particular interest to the theme of exile, of transposition: nail clippings from the patient are tied to a crab that is then thrown to the current. In this case, there is a literal effort to distance the illness. Perhaps we exiles are crustaceans thrown to the current by the millions in order to cure or remove the ailments of our peoples. If this is true, the sacrifice may well be worthwhile.

III

To read Valle-Inclán's esperpentos and Joyce's English after he put so much English on it is to consider the possibility of a tribal revenge: the use of intense caricature, a billiard prose to counter the linguistic models imposed by the metropolis. Grimaces, deformations, defects as effects produced by a rigorous sequence of disrespectful caroms all throw language out of whack, provoking an eccentricity that can sneak Galician into Castilian and Gaelic into English. Exiles are very sensitive to this kind of eccentricity. The distance and time that gradually separate them from their landscapes and their people threaten to ruin their languages, rip their last ties away from them. Language is seen, felt and traversed as territory. Excess and word play are methods for keeping it alive. The fascination awakened by the mechanisms and mysteries of a language reveal a fear of losing it. Exiles turn into Champollions not to interpret hieroglyphics but to create them. Every day they risk burying or disinterring their own tongues. Finally, there comes a moment when they themselves do not know if they are speaking a dead tongue, since exile is a shadowy zone where languages can die, become petrified, pulverized. Exiles fight, play with their languages to keep them from turning into Latin in the hands – and handling – of power. This gives them the advantage of knowing danger in the flesh, of feeling the immediacy of its painful reality. People who have not experienced such an apprenticeship live in a hypnotic state: ideological and commercial propagandas are the poetics of pawnbrokers and jailers. In truth there is no longer a free world.

IV

Recently, we have seen literature, language itself as a living image of human experience, become a clandestine activity. Through the erasures of censorship and self-censorship, which are very routine phenomena for a large part of humanity, we are made aware that what gets expressed barely hints at expression itself, and that expression, which is at times hidden, oblique, latent, is based on simulation, on silence, and on an emphasis dismantled and dissolved by discreet irony. The abyss between what we say we mean and what we mean to say, between the meaning of a particular expression and the meaning it expresses, has never been greater. That abyss reveals one of the state's most radical encroachments, perpetuated on behalf of a new man who has already been duly mummified. As an added insult, the same state that strips words imposes abundant and monstrous catchwords. You must learn to silence what you feel and you must also learn to proclaim what you do not feel.

Exiles enjoy a freedom inconceivable in the landscapes they left behind. They are trapped like the rest of their compatriots, but they are outside the cage and can therefore take notes for an unofficial, heterodox history. This is one of the decided advantages of exile. People in exile are living documents, their very language is a document. Thus the obsession, which grips some as if they were notaries, with fixing an image, a moment. Certain aspects of things Cuban, even of Cuban speech, have been frozen in Miami, Paris, London, New York: as living fossils, they may survive mutations, mutilations and many deaths. In this sense the literature of exile has the ghostly, poignant presence of a daguerreotype. Remember, for example, how Spain has been remembered in the Sephardic tradition, which is still alive. Archaic, conservative like the earth, like language and motherhood, the tradition of the diaspora recovers what history and time itself erase, forget. In 1981 a collection of ballads by Spanish Jews living in New York was published in the United States. Recited in New York and published in Los Angeles, these ballads carry us back from both coasts of English America to the Spain of the Catholic Monarchs. Where we hear or read them, we are in 1492 and Spain is descending on America. Perhaps those of us now in exile were then conquistadors, *encomenderos*, and slaves. Or Jews. History repeats itself.

We no longer enjoy an easy homeland. The millions of Latin Americans in exile are the Sephardics of Spanish America. I recognize the exaggeration: it is hard to compare an experience of years or decades with one of centuries. Nevertheless, I feel as though we were living in 1492, a year of discovery and expulsion. The discovery of America proved that Earth was not a dish. But we twentieth-century Americans have insisted on refuting geography with history, which is certainly not round. We are falling from our landscapes into the abyss of exile. At least for us the earth is a dish. Which is why some of us are gathered here in Colorado, an English-speaking land with a Spanish name. A new language, a new world.

We have repeatedly emphasized the tragedy of expulsion, but we have not dared to throw ourselves into the adventure of discovery, because we are so weighed down by an intense, painful fidelity to the past. In the radical way, however, exile forces us to espouse a difficult but rich and unexpected new humanism. When we encounter new languages, we have no choice but to discover new worlds. A chain of changes and transpositions, the deepest meanings of *uprooting*, recalls translation and its original sense of transfer or removal. For us, the word *translation* still has that flavor, which is why some of us are bilingual, why most of us are a bit schizophrenic. Whether we like it or not, expulsion has made us cosmopolitan in the stoic sense of the word, that is, in the best sense. We can testify to the fragility of borders between peoples and nations: we can testify to the traitorous expiration of documents and papers, those friends of fire; we must submit to laws that are infinitely more human, since at times we are undocumented and we are always outcasts; we know that language itself, the only territory we have left, permits no complacency, that language has meaning only if we are willing to grant it meaning, if necessary placing it again and again on the stone of Sisyphus. After it falls a thousand times, maybe everyone will be able to glimpse the stereotype of the absurd in the lapidary cooing of dogmas.

V

Exile is not only alienation. It can also be a cosmopolitanism, albeit an involuntary and painful one. The experience of transposition, which is deeply related to translation, implies the possible convergence of two unpaired spheres, that of the exile and that of the host. People in exile are never completely dispossessed; like snails, they always carry along their homes: the languages, customs, traditions of their countries. They transpose and translate: they live between two shores. Their homes and landscapes live within them, although they are no longer places of physical dwelling. Seen in this way, exile becomes a staggering enlargement of a landscape's four walls. When people are uprooted, those walls become windows. The exile's very existence represents an endless challenge to immensity and formlessness. A permanent construction and reconstruction of what has been lost, and at the same time a cautious, laborious appropriation of what is discovered, in other words, what is different. Because of the very circumstances of this uprooting, the pressing need to overcome or sublimate helplessness, the poetry of exile could take on, and perhaps fully carry out, a task that Heidegger set for poetry in his essay about Hölderlin: the creation of poetic dwelling.

Heidegger bases his thoughts on the expression *dichtersich wohnet der Mensch*: man dwells poetically. I suggest a different one: *eruv*. In the Mishnah there is a list of the thirty-nine principal types of chores affected by ritual restrictions that absolutely forbid any kind of work on the Sabbath. For example, tying a knot, untying a knot, twisting two threads, separating two threads, sewing two stitches, making a tear so as to sew two stitches, lighting a fire, putting out a fire, writing two letters, erasing in order to write two letters. Another restriction that is perhaps no less surprising to Gentiles forbids the transportation or conveyance of things from one sphere to another, in other words from the private sphere to the public sphere or vice versa. Among Orthodox Jews there is a legal fiction – denoted by the word *eruv* – that permits the conveyance of certain things – a house key, for example – without breaking the laws of the Sabbath. On Saturdays, Orthodox Jews designate an area of their neighborhood as a private sphere by encircling it with a piece of wire. An *eruv* is this wire rampart that enlarges the house and suspends the Sabbath restriction by converging the house into a walled city, into Jerusalem.

When I return to Cuba, that is if I return to Cuba, I will ask Christo to surround the entire island with an *eruv*. I want him to wrap it like a present so that it finally belongs to everyone. In the meantime, the poetry of exile could serve as a rampart. Wire, architecture, dwelling, walled city: J*eruv*salem. Perhaps we can make a sphere of translation itself. At least we can try.

TRANSLATED BY CAROL MAIER

the voice of the turtle

I Sent Quinine*
Alfonso Hernández Catá

They had closed all the windows so that the scene outside would not destroy the illusion and the family, grouped around the table, were preparing to enjoy their lunch, cooked in the Cuban manner. All the courses were served together, thus dispensing with the need for a servant, who would doubtless have spoiled the magic of the occasion with the mocking response that vulgar people reserve for the habits of others. It was 20 May, and in one of those households which fate had driven far from its country of origin the everyday need to eat was about to be transformed into a ritual of patriotic communion.

'I want some plantain chips.'

'I want some beef jerky.'

'Pass me a tamal.'

'Be quiet now! First, you must all have some stew.'

The children were joyously greedy, but the smell of the food stimulated their elders' imaginations more than it did their appetites. From time to time, forks would hover hesitantly above the fritters or the pieces of sweet potato that looked like juicy, blue-veined chunks of marble. Almost all of the children had been born outside their home country and, for economic reasons, had never as yet even

* 'I sent quinine' was an expression used, among other things, to describe the kind of opportunist who undeservedly assumed political office after the war, having played no part in the heroic struggle for independence. It implied that the individual had made only a minimal contribution. In this story, however, the sending of quinine is literal and takes on an added dimension, since it is carried out by a child.

visited it. Their parents tried to make up for this with books and conversation, but there were always shadowy areas impossible to penetrate. Towards the end of the meal, when the guayaba jelly and the soft, white cheese were carried from the sideboard to the table, one of the children suddenly remembered something – some ambiguous phrase gleaned from a Havana newspaper, a thought triggered perhaps by the sweet taste of the guayaba – and he asked:

'Papa, what does "He sent quinine" mean?'

'It means, like so many other such expressions, almost the opposite of what it appears to mean. In the context in which you read it, it will almost certainly have been intended as a sarcastic, insulting remark. And yet . . . I know a story about quinine or, rather, I actually took part in a story involving quinine which, out of modesty, I have never before told to anyone . . . not that I haven't been tempted, listening to the boasts of certain so-called patriots. But I'm going to tell you and then you will understand the meaning of "He sent quinine."'

The circle round the table tightened as everyone leaned forward attentively and this is what the father said.

'I was about eleven or so when the War of Independence broke out in 1895, and I was living in Santiago de Cuba. My house, like many other houses, was a place where two nations met: I had a Spanish father, who was a soldier, and a Cuban mother, born in Baracoa and brought up in Sagua de Tánamo, a Cuban through and through. The call for independence that rang out in Baire was received in very different ways not only amongst the ranks of the two main opposing forces, but also in the bosom of many homes. In my own home, there were whispers to start with and a hint of anxiety; the mortar of affection must have been extremely strong, however, since it did not crack under the strain. All the members of my mother's family doubtless sympathized with the separatist cause, but they also loved and respected my father, who had the liberal sensibilities of a well-travelled man of letters, doubly unusual in someone who was both a patriot and a professional soldier. Only much later did I find out why they playfully dubbed him 'Don Capdevila'. Capdevila was a Spanish officer of heroic honesty who had defended the students so ignominiously shot down in 1871. Whenever we went out with my father and we walked along Calle de San Tadeo, near the Parque de Artillería, he would stop and show us the house where he used to live. The fact is, though, that, with a show of deference rare in a situation arousing such fiery passions, no one ever alluded to the war in his presence. My house, I recall, seemed to me like an oasis; it was a low house with a raftered roof in which birds would nest and with a courtyard where a royal poinciana tree cast the bright shade of its flowers on a malanga bush with giant leaves and peppery sap.

'The subdued murmur of battle reached me from outside. Being at an age when even adverse events seem like fortunate incidents if they break up the monotonous passing of the days, our childish curiosity was tantalized daily by rumours, news, hopes, fears. And although the adults very sensibly strove to pretend that nothing was going on, out in the street we boys would play at being Spaniards and Cuban rebels, acting out with sticks and stones what was being enacted in fire and blood in the countryside. In our innocent mouths, the news took on an edge of passion: "There's been a battle in Ramón de las Yaguas"; "We won"; "Liar, you had to change sides and you ended up in the cemetery"; "Sziwikoski turned tail and ran"; "Santocildes is a brave man"; "Not as brave as Maceo". The opinions we expressed in those clearings in Pozo del Rey, where every battle we knew about was refought in miniature, were always sealed with a few slaps and clips around the ear. When I got home, my eldest sister, older than me by four years, would smooth my clothes or bathe my wounds, saying, "Tell them you were quarrelling over a book." I would do so without quite understanding what that delicate complicity meant. And when my parents remonstrated with me, it was clear that they had both agreed to urge me not to get into any more scraps, and never to enquire into the reasons behind those continual quarrels.

'One afternoon, near the local patisserie, a boy called Setién gestured to me confidingly, then almost shouted out at the top of his voice, "Your uncle has left Gibara and gone into the mountains."

'Everyone knew what that meant. I think now that had the Spanish authorities really wanted to plumb the mysteries of certain houses, they would have done far better to pay more attention to the games we boys were playing, instead of collecting statements and garnering suspicions. For me, the news was like a sad, painful secret. That pale, skinny uncle with the goatee beard and the absurd top hat, who always wore black and used silk handkerchiefs, had gone to war. I had always thought Uncle Álvaro a mysterious chap. I imagined him out there carrying a big machete and still wearing that unlikely top hat. Did *they* know? What would my father say? And what about my mother, who always spoke of Uncle Álvaro as a weak, helpless creature over whom it was her duty to watch? I went to the house of some relatives and, like Setién, blurted out:

'"Uncle Álvaro has gone off to fight with the rebels, Aunt Leonor."

'"You'd best keep quiet, my lad, and don't go poking your nose into grown-ups' business."

'That reprimand was enough to tell me that the news was common knowledge and I did not dare to repeat the same experiment in my own home. No, they obviously didn't know. That day, in fact, my mother and father were both wearing an expression of serene sweetness that made them look rather alike. Now, I am sure that they must have known before, that day when my sister whispered to me:

'"Go out and don't come back until lunch-time," when the news had made the circles under my mother's eyes seem darker and cast a shadow over my father's already deathly pale face.

'Days and months went by. The city suffered various ups and downs. At home, these vicissitudes were greeted in silence or with enigmatic smiles. A high degree of tact – not so much verbal as emotional – and a great deal of affection were needed to ease those difficult moments. I'm sure that my mother must have been wholly on the side of those fighting in the countryside and that my father, whilst understanding the justice of the Cuban cause, must have been on the side of his compatriots, following the instinct that so often overrides our reason and dictates so many of our actions. One night – I can even remember the colour of the sky and the smell of the air – my mother drew me aside and said:

'"Listen, soon you will be a man, and a situation has arisen for which I'm going to need your help, a situation that must be kept secret. It's your Uncle Álvaro. He's up in the mountains somewhere and he's ill . . . He's written to me asking me to send him some quinine and some eating utensils – a knife, fork and spoon. We are to leave the package at a shop in Dos Caminos del Cobre for someone called Miguel, who will come and collect it. They know all about it there . . . For reasons I will explain to you when you're a bit older, this is the one and only thing I will ever keep from your father. It's my duty not to let my brother die and it's also my duty not to compromise anyone else for his sake. If they caught you, you would tell the truth, so would I, and, since you're a child, and it's not after all a matter of . . . not that I think they will catch you. You're too bright for that. Will you do it?"

'My shining eyes must have answered for me. The following morning, I went to a pharmacy owned by an Italian gentleman called Dotta and he gave me four small yellow bottles full of small white tablets. From there I went to the ironmonger's, where I bought the cutlery. I remember that they let me choose it myself and when it came to the knife, I chose one with a long, pointed blade, doubtless because it was intended for a fighter. Proud of having carried out the first part of the adventure, I went home and, going in through the backyard, I handed the package over to my mother. My uncle's letter must have given an exact date for the delivery to take place, because my mother made me wait and did not give me my final instructions for nearly a week. For four days before that, I prepared myself by going as far as Dos Caminos on foot with some friends or on a horse belonging to a relative who was a police officer, Alcolado by name. I had to pass close by the cemetery and that was the part I found most difficult, even by day. No soldier ever stopped me or asked me anything: the dead sleeping beyond the stone gateway bothered me more than all the armies in the world. On the way there, everything went according to plan. When I reached the shop, the man led me into a small room at the back and opened the package.

'"It's just so that we know what's in it, to avoid any complaints later on," he explained.

'The parcel, carefully wrapped, contained the quinine – minus the bottles – the spoon and the fork, but not the knife. I expressed my surprise and the man muttered: "See what I mean?", and we left the back room because there was a mulatto woman in the shop wanting a real's worth of lamp oil. Thinking that the man wanted something more, I waited, and when he realized that I was still there, he said: "Off you go then." It was the beginning of one of those brief twilights that we get in our part of the world, a twilight in which darkness falls the moment the sun sets. I got on my horse and thought immediately of the cemetery. I knew no other route back; I would, therefore, have to pass by that terrifying gateway. Just before I got there, I began singing to keep my spirits up and when the white tombs emerged out of that blue mixture of day and night, my horse, perhaps infected by my fear, began to tremble and wheel about. I was in the grip of a wild fear at least as terrible as any experienced by a hundred heroes. I was heroic too – in a cowardly fashion. I stuck my feet under the cinch, flung my arms around the horse's neck, dropped the reins and in a frenetic gallop, in which my sweat mingled with the horse's sweat, and with my eyes and soul tight shut, I leapt over walls and raced across scrubland. The dead didn't catch me, but by the time I reached my house I was covered in blood. My mother was so frightened that she barely listened to my account of how I had carried out my errand. I doubt that any of the sacrifices I may have made as a grown man for my country's independence were as painful to me as the fear I experienced then.

'Years later, on a trip, my mother, by then an old lady, took a package out from amongst her treasures and handed it to me.

'"Do you recognize this?" she asked.

'I knew what it was just by the touch, almost before I opened it. It was the knife that some mysterious fate had removed from the parcel that I had delivered to the shop in Dos Caminos del Cobre. There was a note attached to the handle, with a few faint lines written in pencil. They were in my father's neat, generous hand, but it was oddly shaky. Those lines read: "I have let the other things go, because he is your brother, but not the knife, which could be taken for a weapon. Forgive me." Those tremulous, handwritten lines spoke to us still of his infinite delicacy, even when the hand that had written them had long been stiff and still upon his chest, beneath the earth.

'They are together now; they both sleep in the same cemetery by the road along which I galloped in a state of near terror. Not that I would be frightened now, no! Now, forgive me, my children, but now, instead of riding past, I would go in through the stone gateway, seek out their grave and lie down beside them and rest, for ever.'

TRANSLATED BY MARGARET JULL COSTA

The Night The Dead Rose From The Grave
Lino Novás Calvo

I

That Captain Amiana! He'd been there for ten years. There were
people in the world who had given him up for dead, people who had
known him. Not the rest of us. We didn't know anybody. Amiana
used to keep a two-master over in Havana when he was busy hauling
illegal immigrants to the United States. Poles, Syrians, Russians,
Czechoslovaks, Germans, Armenians, Galicians, Portuguese, Jews.
From all over. Amiana charged them four hundred dollars a head and
then threw them overboard. Overboard, just like that. He knew the
coastguard was out there somewhere watching, through gunscopes,
and he couldn't put them ashore. That happened sometimes. Then
he was spotted and Amiana had to take off. He unfurled his sails and
disappeared. The papers said the coastguard had nabbed him and
they published his picture. And meanwhile . . .

Ten years before, I mean. A crew went with him and they sailed
leeward due west, and came upon the Island. There he folded his
wings and never again was a bird's cry heard on that island. The ship
ran aground on the way in and he didn't realize it was running on land
until it beached in the mud, where some little branches, too green and
too dry, were growing, spying like vermin, and further on, the
mangroves. The ship was stuck there to the hilt. Amiana gave orders to
lower the topmasts and cut a path inland to the bush. A path to
nowhere. Everything was the same, and there was nowhere to go. It was
like cutting paths in the sea. The bush was low, a little taller than
Amiana, very thick and uniform. It wasn't the jungle, with musical

scales, with undulating terrain. It was the sea, a watery tortoise afloat on other water. To walk through that land men had to go by their inner compass, or by the stars. The men who weren't sailors had to go out moored to a cable like divers; to be able to get back to the beached ship, their only guide. Which is why it all happened after ten years. Because the Island was not alive. It was an apparition, like the undead. One felt that beneath it something was fluttering that did not flutter, that did not have a dead life, that saw things through other eyes. The sea looked at the moon, and vice versa, and they did not see each other. The sea did not foam with whitecaps, nor did it have anything to say in itself, or to hear, and the moon was a bit of stunned sky, a rotting welt in the sky, as the island was a stunned welt in the sea. The island and the moon were two apparitions; the island was as mute as the moon, just as unreal.

But a sailor can sail on shore too. Amiana put his people in the bush and there he opened a clearing, founded a city. This was the City, and that was all there was. It was a half-mile from the sea, when I saw it, made up of the houses of the batey, a compound of wooden buildings seated on pontoons, like a lake village. The soil was soft and things were sinking, even the trees. Something was pulling from below. The house of the commander, Amiana, was higher, painted red, and those of his crew pressed in all around. A kilometre away were the barracks and the batey, where the slaves were. To the right and left, between barracks and batey were the cemeteries, one for freemen and one for slaves. They looked alike from the outside. They were natural stockades of trees joined by crossbeams. Inside, no. The one for slaves was bare, except for grass. Amiana wasn't concerned with this. He had other things on his mind.

II

He had his buccan and his coal and the salt and the fish. These were his industries. Nobody knows how it began. Nobody knew this island existed, not even those who bought his products. Amiana would load a lugger and send it to the coast of Cuba, around Oriente, or to the coast of Santo Domingo, and he smuggled the things in. He had correspondents there. He told them the products were coming from the Windward Islands, and that was all. It wasn't important. The lugger unloaded, set sail and sighted land again by midnight. Amiana went along at first. They would drop anchor on a shallow shore and move inland, eight or ten men, with snares and revolvers, not knives. The cane cutters wouldn't have surrendered to steel blades. Revolvers meant something to them: not the fear of bullets, but rather the eyes of gun barrels, the snouts of dogs that were gun barrels to those runaway slaves, who would then be stampeded. I'd been in the country. The cane cutters in the barracks believed that revolvers killed the dead as well. When one died in the barracks, someone would have to shoot into the roof to frighten the dead man's soul, and everything that was ruled there was ruled by the revolver and rum, not by machetes. These cane cutters were Haitians and weren't afraid to split open a body with a machete. They came in crews in the sugar-making season and wandered through the countryside, cutting a field of sugar cane here and another there, wherever it looked best to them, taking their money and moving on. The barracks were free; anyone was welcome there. At night, they hung their hammocks inside and started a blaze to warm up the drum, and they boiled water to mix it with rum and these things: water, rooster blood and rum, rum and drum and moon in the canebrake, also dead, also unreal, stunned welt of earth like that island in the water or the moon in the sky. Dead and yellow soul in the country night. In the middle were the barracks, a long way from the bateys, where the drums howled at night. Amiana's men got their bearings from them, and moved forward cautiously with ropes and surrounded the barracks. The Haitians' drums went silent. The men's eyes froze before the snouts of the revolvers. Sometimes these snouts began to grumble earthward so the villagers would hear as they herded unwilling and grumbling prostitutes before cracking whips. Amiana and his men would tie up the Haitians in pairs and drive them through the brush to the sea. Nobody could have found out about it in Cuba. The Haitians moved in nomadic crews and weren't registered anywhere. There was no one to stand up for them. Men and women. Amiana put them on his boat and took them to his island to work, as slaves.

And not just Haitians! There were still other men about the sea who were pursuing Amiana's former profession. The only difference was that some of them didn't throw the immigrants overboard. Amiana had once communicated with one at sea and had offered to buy the immigrants from him at a dollar a head. I was sold for one dollar. But those who sold them didn't know where they would end up. Amiana didn't want anybody to discover his island. The deals took place on a key far from it. Amiana would tell these men they were going to work in the Virgin Islands and it was all the same to the sellers. They charged three or four hundred dollars a head for them, and then a dollar more. As they approached the key, they would surprise them in their sleep, tie them up, handcuff them and put them ashore. Amiana had his agents there who would transport them on to the Island. All slaves, men and women, white and black men, white and black women, and from many nations.

The Island was populated in this way. In this way a people, a civilization and a language were born. At first, they had to invent words. The words were for understanding one another. They were for saying something the people knew without its being said, among themselves, among those of each class. It was an odd language, but it made sense, not like Esperanto even though composed of many languages, born with blood in its veins and wounds in its body and claws for fighting. The rest is hogwash. Those people understood one another without talking, but they needed words to link them to their superiors, to Amiana's people.

Of industries and their foremen. At first it was coal and then dried meat and then fish and then salt. Charcoal. Amiana went with his people deep into the bush and began scorching the hump. The Island was a tortoise breeding in the sea and at its centre was a hump. At its peak, two black teats protruded: the piles of coal the men were taking from below ground, some time after burying it, smoky, still hot, I don't know if from the soil or from the fire. It gave off a sooty mist when they took it out, a moist haze that slowly stretched out over the forest, like a sleepy black woman. It would cling to the trees and they seemed to be covered and surrounded by black snow. And the men: some were already black. Those who weren't were blackened by the coal. Amiana had bought a barge somewhere that he used for hauling the flesh from those teats to the east of Cuba, to Jaraguá or Guantánamo perhaps, and nobody knew where that coal was coming from. Round about there were other coal-producing keys, and that was fine. They were within the law. The same went for the dried meat.

Some of the captain's men had buccaneering in their past, as Amiana himself did. But they had never done all of that and couldn't figure it out in their heads and didn't remember how. But something spoke to them darkly, from within. The men who went to sugar plantations to abduct Haitians also went to cattle ranches, to dairy farms, to steal cattle. They put the buccan on the other side of the Island. The buccan was a grid, like the frame of a hut, with a coal fire underneath, where we cured the beef. The buccaneers had cemeteries made for the living and the dead. It was a stockade like the other cemeteries, and they killed there. Men fell upon the cattle with machete blows, like tigers, and quartered them alive. One could see them fall down bellowing, drag themselves along the damp ground where the blood gathered, reddening it. The earth stank there, exhaled stench, asphyxiated. The men took the waste and threw it into the sea, from that side, or into the caves for the crocodiles. All the sharks from around the island mobbed in from that side and all the crocodiles nested in those miry caves, where they putrefied the waste (their method of cooking). This way they didn't approach the batey to threaten people. The coal fire itself frightened the crocodiles, but the sharks clustered together in the water to watch the slices of meat on the grilles. The flame itself perhaps seemed like a living slice of flesh and they looked at it from the sea with their thousand eyes. Sometimes they bit one another, jealous over that slice, and then you would see some of them belly up in the sea: a white belly. The sharks and crocodiles came to be friends with those men who fed them. Little by little they got fat and content, filled with peace within, and many died a natural death: full. The buccaneers salted and cured this meat as well and shipped it from that side in a falucca belonging to Amiana.

They made the salt themselves. Seawater flowed in through a furrow to a reservoir they had made in harder ground, between rock and soil, and it couldn't drain off. The sun would come there and slowly drink it up. But the water never yielded completely; it would hold back reserves for itself, saving up salt and sending it to the bottom, where it congealed. The sun seemed to come only in search of that salt, which it couldn't eat anyway, since its rays are snouts and not teeth, and it saw itself reflected, and the salt laughed, unfolding in white leaven, like snow. From there it went to the salting process in containers, and to the falucca, and adiós. The falucca unfolded its wings like a seagull and went out with the land breeze, when it was blowing. The buccaneers and salt workers were both white and black, but here they were slaves. Amiana had a crew of tough foremen, jackals armed to the teeth with the teeth of the cartridge belt, a bayonet on the rifle, a pair of colts on the hip, and the bullwhip, the billy and the cat-o'-nine-tails. 'Nobody move! Move along! Keep them paws outta sight!' the assistant foremen would say, men who before had also been slaves, blacks and whites, Syrians and Poles. There were also women slaves and women bosses.

And it was that way with the fishing. There was also a crew of fishermen and fishing buccaneers, on another side of the tortoise. They had a sloop to go out in with their nets to trap fish. The spiders, some people called them; and the lawyers. They were the ones who had it best. They would go out, sun and breeze in their sails, and you could see them in the distance, like albatrosses, lying to, hour after hour, men and women, but mostly women. The captain of the fishing boat was a Portuguese woman chosen by Amiana. What Amiana was, nobody knows. He was a lean oak, and it seemed he had dozens of legs and arms and hundreds of huge, bloody eyes, with a lead bullet at the centre. The dried fish, salt and cured beef went together. But not just to Cuba. Amiana did business with Santo Domingo, Haiti and Jamaica. With Veracruz, too, perhaps, but not with Florida. He was once hard put to get away from the coastguard there when they chased him for six hours, exchanging gunfire. That was when he was trying to smuggle immigrants in. That was why he decided to throw them overboard instead of putting them ashore. It was all the same to him. Nobody could ever find out, except for his own people. Mute, squat, wild people, like wild dogs.

III

There was a class system. People constantly climbing up and down the social strata. A hierarchy: foremen, assistant foremen, chief, supervisor, technician and then Amiana's wild pack, made up of the soldiers and the 'harem' staff. The harem was a casino. A large wooden barracks with different sections for gambling, dancing and the rest. Amiana chose these people from those who arrived; he selected the beautiful women and the strong men. Some of the women were with their men and Amiana separated them. He sent the men to work the coal or to the buccan and the women went to the casino. Or the women went to work the coal or to the buccan, too, half naked. Clothing was unnecessary there, except for protection against the sun. The men grumbled, but they couldn't do anything. The grumblers were made to eat dirt. The meaning of that is different now. At first, when there were few people, they were punished by making them eat dirt. The word only had to be mouthed by Amiana and his men understood. Guásima trees, rope and tallow.

Men would wake up hanging from the Guásima trees or from the yards of a grounded ship. From there they went to the crocodile caves or to the sharks. They weren't buried in the cemetery, at first. Later on, yes, after Amiana had two cemeteries made, one for his class and one for slaves, their bodies all went to a holding yard and the crocodiles couldn't get past the fence. Sometimes they moved along it, mouths open, jaws grazing the ground, like tame dogs, sniffing at the dead inside, waiting for the buccaneers to feed them. Amiana's cemetery was guarded by soldiers. His favourites went there, his staff, but there was only one mound for him and his number-one woman and his second-in-command. It was the shell of a lugger covered by a mound of dirt. Only in this way was it different from the other one. Nothing was any different from anything else there, except for the bullwhip and the guns.

And the batey. Only freemen lived here, but they were also Amiana's slaves. The rest lived in the barracks, guarded by the foremen and their assistants. There were always men there who aspired to be assistant foremen, and foremen who wanted to move up to the batey. So they got rough and tried to use the rest as stirrups to climb up to where Amiana would notice. Sometimes they succeeded, informing on somebody, humiliating him in his work, making themselves stand out, fighting fiercely. Amiana arranged fights between them in the plaza on days off twice a month. The assistant foremen picked the cockiest ones and stood them off against each other. Amiana and his court would come to watch. It was a fight between tigers. The men punched, kneed, elbowed, bit and scratched each other. The winner was promoted a grade or maybe he skipped several. Amiana needed reserves. His free people sometimes committed infractions and were made slaves again. This was their punishment. The slaves were given lashes or strung up . . . Some of them had been freed and enslaved several times. People often died and Amiana would have to buy new shipments. The slave cemetery grew fatter with the crocodiles. It made no difference. Nobody there ever thought about living again. Some aspired to be free so they could work on one of the ships that carried the meat or coal, and then desert. But they didn't do it. They would become bosses and that tied them to Amiana: 'Christ! Won't this island ever sink again?' said Viola.

He had been free three times and was now a slave again. He was the first to do that. He started acting half-crazy and wandered around the barracks with stories under his tongue. Not on it. They were like communion wafers imprisoned in unconfessed sins, unconfessable sins, because the assistant foremen stuck an eye into every crack and the soldiers a bayonet. Viola began confessing in his way, speaking to people's fantasy. He could come up with strange stories having nothing to do with this island, or with Amiana, or with anything real in the world. So they let him. Only fantasy itself understood the meaning of those tales, but it never explained them. And the stories began to come between slave and freeman. The slaves began to feel like a distinct group. Viola's tales began first to be a boundary, then a revenge and finally brotherly love. This was the love that already existed among the slaves, because of their closeness, because Amiana pushed them against one another. And so it couldn't exist in Viola's stories when Amiana didn't exist any more, without there being another Amiana. But Viola placed him beyond revenge and that stirred them up and made some of them cry.

Not everybody. Not those who had once been free. Not the discontent among Amiana's people. The others had come to love Amiana and his court. They felt ennobled by him, like puddles by the sun, and hated the ones who were stirring up trouble against Amiana. And there were denunciations, and the repressions began. The word was that the rebels depended on the slaves, and Amiana believed they formed a common enemy. That wasn't it. Amiana had Viola hanged from an arm and at night started a white blaze underneath (fire was white there) that licked the mast with its thick and languid tongues, reaching out for Viola, and scaring the mangy turkey buzzards that would come during the day to writhe around. The others saw Viola hanging there, illuminated by a white night fire without breeze, like fire painted on a board, the sea, and they trembled. The hanged man's ship was mired in the mangrove swamp. The moon came through the sky like a phosphorous sponge, coming to rest on a hilltop to look down with its bleary fox eyes and everybody looked. Some of them got sick from it, with lunatic fever, but that wasn't rebellion. Sometimes they would go out at night to see it in front of the barracks and dance to the drums, like slaves of other times. It was the same. There were always a lot of people in the infirmary. But Amiana never heard their lament, its sound suffocated in the humid stillness of the air. Somebody died every month. Somebody would take them out in a piece of canvas and put them on stretchers and carry them to the slave cemetery. The dead piled up at the entrance there in huge graves, on top of one another. The executed rebels went with them.

There were already many of these. The rebellion began in the batey among Amiana's people because of jealousy. The jealous ones spoke then in the name of the slaves and themselves became slaves again. Then, if they kept it up, they were executed and their bones came to rest with the bones of the others in that ground. Other slaves then took their places, slaves chosen by Amiana or his henchmen for their bravery or for being informers. These were rebels from below against those from below. As they ascended, they would cross paths with those who were descending. This kept Amiana going and fed his ego. He began to take pleasure in the chase, as if scratching a fleabite from inside or squeezing a boil. Everything was that way. One felt stunned, and would imagine the moon scratching its belly or plunging a knife into its bowels, like the Japanese, just to feel something jump. Nothing jumped. Things and people slid or snaked along in search of some kind of trampoline so they could jump and throw themselves against the others. Determined people these, or climbers. Amiana would appear, flaunting himself in a rattan chair, smoking a cigar with his Panama hat and his guayabera, his leggings and his machete and his cartridge belt, in the doorway of his house. This was a red house, made of boards, that could be glimpsed like a glowing coal there in the bush. He kept a few kidnapped women around; from the house he could get over to the casino on a path. Everything was guarded by a stockade of soldiers, miserable cardboard figures, worse than Amiana. In the casino there was always laughter and music that hit the barracks like balls of clay and awakened rebellion in those who heard it. There were already many. Amiana's people wanted to seem deserving in his eyes, so they would invent plots and discover rebels where none existed. But then they did. Amiana would order them to the barracks and they would resent it and begin stirring up trouble among the slaves. These slaves were quick to get the idea: you get out of here by denouncing the new arrivals from the batey, by sending them to the cemetery with the rest. 'Pretty soon it won't hold any more!' said Skinny.

Skinny was the new boss of the coal workers and Viola's lot would soon fall to him. There were fewer and fewer people, and these were forming factions. As the population of the batey increased, in the barracks it was dwindling. These two heads watched each other through informers and spies . . . Most of the slaves had already passed through the batey at some point in that pendular movement and now delirium had set in. Men devoted themselves to chasing one another up and back and seeing visions of Amiana's collapse. Those who saw it coming cosied up to the rebels or helped them secretly from the batey with arms.

IV

It was then that secret factions were formed, another partisan language came into being and everything else. The people who took the products out of there got embroiled, running machine guns and dynamite and oil for the rebels. The others caught the delirium too. There were three groups of rebels: mine workers, fishermen and buccaneers. They understood one another in that language they wrote on trees where they gathered, on the way to the cemetery. Only the initiated, five or six rebels, knew that code. But in the end Amiana cracked it. There was a traitor. Some of Amiana's people, men and women, became slaves for a few days, pretended to be rebels and found out what was going on. They also had their own language. The others, those the men had brought there from their own countries (more than ten countries), were forgotten. Everything was forgotten, and that's why it was necessary to make history every day, and buy more men from those smuggling immigrants. The new arrivals embarked on war, like everybody else, with Amiana or against him. A war nowhere to be seen. The bombs that exploded around the batey or in it were placed by somebody who could only be imagined. Amiana's dogs claimed they had sniffed out the authors and sent them to the slave cemetery. It was already filling up. But the truth was something else again. They just exposed whoever they got it into their heads to single out, sometimes innocent people. They were killing their own enemies, not Amiana's. Dressed in khaki, whips in hand, they would go escorted by soldiers from barracks to worksite, whipping us as if we were animals. Nobody knew why. The lashes made us remember the dead that had gone before, and passions began to fill the air. It didn't move; it was still, inflamed, and all of us inhaled, and it was like breathing in gunsmoke, or like music reaching into your gut. Everybody was dancing a little. In the casino it was a different song and a different dance. Amiana's people had invented it. Or it had just come into being by itself. At first, each couple danced the dance of their country while the rest looked on. They danced the dances of ten different countries to a single tune that had nothing to do with any of them. They were carried away as the tips of their toes got tangled up in a cascade of notes. Lost in music. Eventually, everybody was dancing something strange, faraway and magical, beyond explaining, and it was the new dance, everybody's dance. It was the *son*, and rumba, and tango, and two-step, and shimmy, and waltz. And others I can't name. The casino had got wilder with the war. The underground struggle relieved their consciences and justified everything. So at night their uproar could be heard from the barracks. Men would get rummed up at the casino and then take off to rove the Island in patrols and force people out of the barracks ('Everybody out!') so they could search for hidden dynamite. Meanwhile, trouble usually broke out someplace else. Naked and trembling, they came outside: 'Death is near,' said Fish-Face.

Another rebel leader. Fish-Face was the one who prepared all the assaults. He was Sicilian and became a gangster to save himself. It was either die soon or let Amiana kill them before their time. Fish-Face started putting together a major campaign. A rosary of bombs would blow up wherever in the batey Amiana had his people, and they would be thrown into confusion. It was the last attack. They had caught and hanged the dynamite runners. Amiana had put trusted people aboard the ships. Fish-Face took off. Spies had uncovered his scheme, as he found out from still other spies. And he stole a boat and rowed out to sea from the buccan at night. At first, its fire lighted his way. We spotted him and lit a huge fire to say goodbye. Sharks were trailing him. Adiós, Fish-Face.

There were still a few pounds of dynamite he hadn't been able to use. Only two or three knew about it, and nobody knew who they were. People were ready to kill or be killed, and it made no difference. No longer did the infirmary hold the sick. They had either killed themselves or done something to get themselves killed, like making attempts against Amiana's people. They said they were sacrificing their lives for the others. Nobody had a life any more, and nobody wanted one. The guásima trees sprouted men at night, and the moon looked on. Fat crocodiles gathered about, as if obeying a dead custom, and fell asleep, as if they were followers of the dead in the guásima trees. They weren't hungry, and there was nothing that could wake them, except the fire that drove them back to their caves. That was when Amiana's tigers came in the late morning – to fumigate the island, they said. Sometimes shots were heard, but the report didn't get far. There was no air to carry it.

And when there was . . . It was October, and to the west one might feel a cyclone pass, but a long way off. Every night driving squalls came through that howled in the bush like owls. Amiana's people stayed indoors, and nobody ever saw him any more. His second-in-command, the ranking boss of them all, was a big Chinaman who had been a bandit and a pirate in his own country. Nobody knew his name. At times it seemed he would walk around the Island by himself, with those beady eyes that pierced your body and gave you a fever. I think he had some witch in him. His bodyguards covered him from a distance, like a halo, and nobody could get to him. You could get to the others, but not the Chinaman and not Amiana. The others were going down one by one. The foremen were being felled. A whistle would sound in the bush, another would reply and then another, and finally a foreman would fall. They were taken to the cemetery of the freemen. Amiana had ordered his grave mound built near the entrance. He said he'd fall one day or another, but would fight for peace until the end of his days. It was on some leaflets they printed on a hand press and distributed in the barracks. These handouts also had the weather and the batey news. Sometimes there were poems to Amiana. Nobody knows who wrote them. But there was nothing about the world outside, beyond the Island, and the dates were figured by counting the moons since Amiana had been marooned there. I don't know how many had gone by. The sheets carried the headline: 'Amiana, Apparition Island, such and such a Moon'. It was written in the Island language with our letters. 'We've got to inform the Cuban rebels,' said Chubby. 'We'll do it without them,' said Curly.

The two current leaders, Curly and Chubby, were foremen who pretended to hunt down rebels. When the dynamite was gone, they brought more. Any informers they found among the rebels they killed and made the Chinaman believe they'd been rebels. 'The day is coming!' said Curly.

He came over to the buccan and went out to the fishing and coal areas, and spoke to the lieutenants he had there. 'We must kill the Chinaman!' said Chubby. Nothing would be gained. The best thing would be to kill the key. The key was what brought forth these men who seemed like Amiana's own flesh. 'We have to kill the Chinaman!'

V

That's what he said. But Curly had something else ready. Chubby had sailed to Jamaica and brought back a quintal of dynamite he was hiding in a tree trunk. Nobody could tell it was there. The bark of the hollowed-out trunk was as smooth as ever. It was just slowly drying out, thinking about when that load near its base was going to blow. Perhaps it would have shot upwards like an arrow, and would reach the moon laughing like that overhead. No more bombs exploded for a month. The Chinaman had cleared them all out, they said. He began to shuffle his trusted men, changing their duty stations. He no longer trusted the spies. He took his soldiers and laid waste. His men fell upon the rebels with whips, breaking both their ribs and their will. None of these could ever again rebel. Only the faithful remained, high and low. Chubby had fallen for want of a firm hand and Curly held on to his position. They readied themselves in silence. Another month passed without attacks and Amiana again stuck out his snout. He went to the buccan, the coal and fishing areas and made speeches to the men. He spoke in the name of peace, and promised to deal more fairly when business got better. He meant more rum in the water and some tobacco perhaps. Curly was on guard duty and looked at Chubby kneeling down, like everybody else, next to a nipple of coal. Then they left. The foremen cracked their whips. And men began to cut wood and chant.

The plan. Curly wanted to do the impossible. He wanted to mine Amiana's grave mound with dynamite, kill the Chinaman and set off the charge while Amiana and his people were all there with the dead man. The Chinaman would be buried in Amiana's grave mound and all of Amiana's people would attend.

'Bravo!' yelled Chubby.

But nothing happened. They had the free cemetery garrisoned with dogs and armed troops loyal to Amiana. Curly tried to plant dynamite anyway and lost everything. The Chinaman saw something suspicious about the way Curly was acting and pumped fifty bullets into him. Then he did the same for Chubby. But the Chinaman didn't find out about the idea. It remained hidden among us and we would nourish it at night and pass it along from ear to ear. We weren't going to do anything. It was our secret about what Curly was thinking. So it was never revealed. Each held on to the secret because it seemed worthless. It was a plan that would not be carried out.

'It must be done!' said Snot Nose.

Snot Nose took it upon himself. He had a dry wit and a long nose and bulging eyes. He had been a musician and a soothsayer and a spiritualist somewhere or another. He was the one who put the fever into everybody. He started talking about secret powers and secret signs in the bush and had us all reeling. Amiana kept him around for that, to stupefy people and make Amiana seem divine. Snot Nose said the boss was assisted by the spirits of the trees and the earth, and that it wasn't time to kill him and wouldn't be time for fifty years, when the Island went under again, with everybody. He said the Island had risen to sustain Amiana; the spirits brought him men so he could take the ones he needed to protect him, so nobody could touch him. That's why Amiana wanted Snot Nose around. We knew, some of us, that Snot Nose was never a spiritualist, that he was on to something else. He had played violin at an open-air theatre, that was all. Now he lived in the bush, hiding out in the brush and the caves he dug, talking to the spirits, he told Amiana. At times he would prophesy things. He had very sharp eyes and could put on twenty different faces and find things out. He knew a little astronomy and had forecast the cyclone. He was the Island priest.

'I'm going to put the people to sleep!' he told Amiana.

And at night he'd go to the barracks with his fables and stories about the spirits. That didn't seem bad to him. He would get people worked up and make them forget their troubles (until 'that day' comes, he used to tell me). Snot Nose. He had a chameleon's soul! He was the only one on the Island who could enter through any door. Sometimes he would go into the casino and grab a violin away from one of the musicians and start playing with that bow of a body. He would shove the violin into his midsection and bend over it, as if possessing it, and it would sound like two or three screech owls in unison. The other musicians shook. One big black fellow there, the band leader, would shake until his teeth chattered every time Snot Nose tore those sounds from the violin. Amiana would laugh. He didn't know Snot Nose was doing it for a reason. To hold the band members in his sway. He ruled them: the musicians were reeling, their souls clinging to Snot Nose like pins to a magnet. Not even Amiana ruled them so. The Chinaman stood in the doorway at attention, fully armed, and never laughed. Casino women would come to him wrapped in silky scales, like snakes. They would slither around him, snaking out the pink tip of a tongue for him to see, licking him up and down with their smiles, past the bullets, through to his beady eyes. No good. He didn't laugh. He would shove past them with great long strides towards Amiana, and then go out. Snot Nose saw him leave and go into the countryside at night to look over the barracks. There was no reason for it now. A peace pervaded the Island, keeping vigil over Curly's death. Nobody had moved since. Amiana laughed. Snot Nose didn't want anybody to move. This was how he was becoming more and more a sorcerer, attracting the barracks people's souls to his secret powers. It was no good resisting them. A huge invisible boat sailed round the Island, in the teeth of a hurricane wind. It was captained by Curly, under sentence from the Island's leading spirit. He had to sail round once a day. Snot Nose always knew exactly where he was and could hear him giving orders. Chubby was his chief mate, Bejuco his pilot and Viola steered. They were all in our cemetery, where freemen rarely entered. At night Snot Nose was at the centre of every group that came together in or out of

the barracks. The moon was overhead. Sometimes a bongo would
begin to growl. It was fine with Amiana as long as it didn't drown out
his band. Barracks people would dance around a fire as assistant
foremen looked on. Snot Nose attracted these men to him as well. He
told them there was a special bush spirit for assistant foremen. There
was a god for each social class. His was the owl. People trembled when
they heard one. They were half naked, wearing only knee-breeches,
unkempt, bearded, squatting near a fire over warm ground beside a
barracks. About twenty or thirty men. Snot Nose at the centre, sitting
Indian-style on the ground, his eyes bloodshot and bulging from the
night before. Even Amiana went to see him once. To see the man who
had pacified the Island with spiritualism, who spoke with the trees,
with crocodiles, boas, gall gnats and wild ducks (gods of the casino
women), and with the dead. And this was what really made people
tremble. Snot Nose wanted to bemuse people so they wouldn't rebel,
so Amiana and the Chinaman would be off guard, and the spies: and
there were fewer of them by the day. The Chinaman got dead serious
and adopted a strict policy with everyone. For him there was no music,
women, rum or anything, only war. I don't even think he ate.

But the real pacifier was Snot Nose, at least for Amiana. The
Chinaman couldn't have finished off the bombs, until Snot Nose
decided to scatter his powder over the souls and thus extinguish all
the fuses. That powder lit up inside, like magnesium flares, and the
masks and skulls of Snot Nose's spirits could be seen etched in the
night, covered in yellow moon dust. And inside things went wild.
The trees in the bush danced and talked as we do, so Snot Nose said,
except he was the only one who could see them. They danced for an
hour every night, and the inaudible signal to stop the dance
sometimes caught them far from home, and there they stayed. So
people sometimes found that the palm trees and the guásimas and
other trees had changed places. They all were witness to that. And
some even said they were beginning to understand the zzz of
mosquitoes and the bzz of wasps and the hss of snakes. The men
always looked from side to side, and their words became more and

more abstract, forever alluding to something that was not reality, that was true reality, and walked as if skimming over the ground. Sometimes strange voices could be heard in the barracks, of men and women dreaming of spirits. When someone died, nobody went to the cemetery, except for the bearers and the gravedigger. Nobody dared go into the cemetery. That was what Snot Nose wanted.

'You'll drive them mad!' said Ruddy Cheeks.

'Shush!' replied Snot Nose.

Ruddy Cheeks, who was now sick, was an old friend of Snot Nose. Ruddy Cheeks didn't believe in spirits, neither did Snot Nose. At one time they had visited the Cuban countryside with a puppet theatre, with a Punch and Judy. Now Ruddy Cheeks was sick and dying. The Island, and the swamps, and the gnats, and the giant ants, and the air, and the plague, and the moon, everything was helping Amiana and the Chinaman to kill. Yet they had stopped killing. But something happened in that peace. Everybody felt Snot Nose's spirits auguring something in that void. They felt them rattling around in him as if they were inside a bongo drum. Snot Nose sank into invisibility sometimes for several days and reappeared looking even stranger, his eyes bulging. The spirits within him pushed them outwards, and all of us men in the barracks now looked like spirits. When he reappeared he went back to the casino and left a spot more powder and sulphur in the souls of the musicians.

'Goodbye, Snot Nose!' said Ruddy Cheeks.

VI

I think Snot Nose poisoned his soul. First he became Amiana's priest, and then he was stricken with a kind of divine thirst. It was as if the spirits he was gathering to himself had seared his soul, making of it an arid plain, thirsty cracks opened to the sky, asking for water. Snot Nose was already looking towards the sky, his eyes rolled up in his head like those martyrs in engravings. Maybe he had even seen one and had read its inscriptions. Snot Nose was going mad. Otherwise, he could never have done what he did: he killed the Chinaman – and things really worked out for him, even though he had to change the plan. Snot Nose could go anywhere he wanted, except for Amiana's cemetery. The Chinaman's word was law there, and he didn't believe in Snot Nose's powers, the only one who didn't. Amiana allowed the Chinaman his whim of keeping the cemetery untouched by any slave, no matter who. The Chinaman went to the cemetery and talked to his soldiers, chosen from his most loyal men. People in the barracks said that wasn't because of the Chinaman, since the Chinaman had brought from his land a cult of the dead, but because of Amiana, who had hidden his money there, in the mound containing the hull of his boat.

So he couldn't do it in the free cemetery. Snot Nose had fifty pounds of dynamite stashed somewhere in the bush. Nobody had any idea so much dynamite was around. Anybody who had known was dead. Snot Nose had always worked under cover of darkness and alone. Now he used others who were able to work in a darkness as murky as in a church crypt. They had already crossed over into the realm of the dead, and indeed looked upon ordinary mortals as if from the beyond. Snot Nose felt he belonged to the other side, and so already his remaining days caused him great sorrow.

'I'll die for them!' he said one day.

Hardly anybody understood.

The men he had chosen were in the infirmary with fever. The foremen didn't guard them there. Snot Nose slipped them out through the back door one night and took them to the slave cemetery. The four men stood there in the cemetery, half naked. Snot Nose was in their midst, like a grisly cross. Only the dead and the gravediggers ever frequented this cemetery. Snot Nose picked the slaves for gravedigging. Snot Nose was the law here. With the spades and coal buckets they had brought along, the men set to work. This went on for several nights. Nobody ever entered here days unless a slave died. Snot Nose didn't want anybody coming there now. When two men did die he had them secretly removed from the infirmary to be buried someplace else in the bush. Nobody should see what they were doing, even though it probably wouldn't make sense to them anyway. They were making a grave mound just like Amiana's. That way, you couldn't tell the two cemeteries apart. You couldn't tell anything from anything else on the Island. One path was like the rest, one tree like all the others. The men hauled dirt and broken limbs and branches and rocks in from the bush to build up that pyramid-shaped molehill. Amiana's was just like it, where they said he kept his money. The dirt was just the same at night or in the day, whether old or new. So this grave mound was just like his, once they had finished it. The men withdrew to the infirmary and he spoke to the musicians in the casino again. Not to suggest anything but to put his spirits in their bodies and lead their orchestra. Sometimes he jumped notes violently or changed melody, just to see if the musicians were following him. They didn't even notice. They played nothing, it was the skeletons of the spirits the sorcerer carried in his eyes. Snot Nose's eyes bulged and bulged, and he ate only garlic soup, drank rum and smoked metre-long home-made cigars. Amiana had also thought of cultivating the Island over time, and the Chinaman was preparing his army, carrying out manoeuvres on the Island and camping in different places. Snot Nose sometimes appeared on the encampment and talked to the soldiers. He exhorted them all to be obedient to the Chinaman and Amiana. Except for one person.

He was Blondie, a black man, the Chinaman's cook. Snot Nose concocted an herb poison and gave it to the cook, who mixed it into the Chinaman's food. Snot Nose didn't get to the cook with spiritualism. The black man knew no spirit lived in Snot Nose, unless maybe it was the same one that lived in him. There was no way to measure time there. It could have been a century or a day.

'Adiós, pal!' Snot Nose told the cook.

The next morning, the Chinaman was dead in his tent and nobody knew why. Amiana came to the campsite and had him taken over to the

chapel in the batey. They laid him out there. Snot Nose followed them
there and started hovering over the dead man, looking at his green
face, as green as green could be, and at his staring, blood-clotted eyes;
he was muttering to himself, as if praying. He said a spell had killed
the Chinaman, but who had cast it, he didn't know. He began to create
a ceremony of exorcism, supervising the casket-building and
appointing the casket-bearers who would carry it to the cemetery of
the free, at night. It had to be at night and when the moon was
hanging low over the bush. The men in the funeral party were to
march straight into the moon, looking it squarely in the face all the
way from the batey to the cemetery as they marched to the sound of
the funeral dirge Snot Nose had composed. It was all to take place on
the day after the Chinaman's death. Snot Nose took aside one of the
men who had helped build the false grave mound and showed him a
hiding place behind the slave-cemetery fence. Nobody doubted for a
minute that the Chinaman would be taken to Amiana's cemetery. But
the two cemeteries were identical now. And the moon would be above
and the men would all follow along behind the dark of night. No
slaves would come along. Snot Nose said the dead man's body must
be kept clear of slave souls so the spell could be buried with him.
'Let's get those barracks closed up!' the foremen yelled. Their
assistants obeyed.

VII

What a burial! I think Snot Nose was already kind of crazy. Crazy
from knowing he was soon to die. He had got hold of a watch and
was counting the seconds as he stood next to the dead Chinaman in
the chapel. Hair standing on end and eyes bulging out like two
bloodied eggs, Snot Nose now seemed even more stooped. The batey
was quiet. The day's work was done. In a shed behind the chapel,
some musicians were sounding a kind of bellow, both funereal and

slow. Snot Nose was there with his violin. He went to the shed, where he would hunch over his violin and look at the others. Their notes harmonized with the wailing of the mourners, hired from among the casino women. Amiana had them dress in mourning from the waist down and gather around the dead man to sob. Chins propped on hands, elbows on knees, they sat on benches, grunting. Seven or eight pretty women, all white. They surrounded the Chinaman, who was laid out in an unpainted, wooden box that had been placed on sawhorses. As if crocodiles had inflated it by blowing air between skin and bone, his face had become bloated, closing the staring eyes. A crocodile hide concealed the Chinaman's body, its snout resting on the chin. That was Snot Nose's work.

For two days his chantings were heard in the batey. Amiana had deemed that he be obeyed in everything. The night before he accompanied two riflemen into the bush for the she-crocodile. Then he skinned it himself in a clearing in front of the chapel, using a knife that had belonged to the Chinaman. First, he placed it belly up just outside the door and ordered all the freemen to file by it. The crocodile left offspring. Her belly was white. The veterinarian drew off fat from time to time for the sick. Now Snot Nose told him to take some and smear the Chinaman's entire body with it. Next, they wrapped him in black cloth and placed the hide over him. Amiana watched. He went to his house and sent for Snot Nose to tell him what to do without the Chinaman. Snot Nose spoke in parables, and he left Amiana to drown in them. He said that there would come forth upon the earth a general who would lift up all men. Amiana trusted Snot Nose and was silent. They were alone in the parlour of Amiana's bungalow: its walls were covered in crocodile skins. From its location at the far end of the batey, one could see the chapel through one window and through the other, the sea.

'The moon rises at eight,' said Snot Nose. By eight, the moon would be high.

It was dark by seven. Between seven and eight, Snot Nose walked through the barracks, looking into men's eyes. He said nothing to them until the end. Some of us could see that Snot Nose had poisoned himself within and, as he approached death, had begun to believe in his own farce. The islanders believed him and he was caught up in that simple faith. He said a lower spirit had taken over the Island and demanded a great sacrifice from him in order to be pacified. He didn't say what it was. At the infirmary he took leave of the sick; he kept glancing out towards the slave cemetery, about a hundred metres from the bush. Then he went over to the cemetery to talk with the man he had hidden out back. As Snot Nose approached the man was on his haunches with a watch in one hand and a match in the other. 'At eight,' said Snot Nose.

The fuse was long enough to burn all the while the burial party was en route from the batey. Only Snot Nose knew they were headed for the slave cemetery. Even the man with the watch didn't know why he was lighting the fuse. He didn't even know the Chinaman was dead. Many were in the dark about that. But Snot Nose had spread the fever throughout the barracks and nobody could sleep. You could see them peering out of their tiny rooms, watching the bush. Silence. A silence that didn't breathe. There was still no moon.

Snot Nose went to the batey once more before leaving. The mourners wailed more loudly as the casket-bearers made ready to leave at eight. The mourners wailed more loudly at eight while the bearers arranged themselves on the four sides of the casket. The musicians were already waiting on the road, just outside the batey. Snot Nose left to join them. The men in the barracks would fire a signal shot when the moon appeared above the bush. The musicians were silent.

'Three more minutes,' said Snot Nose.

Beside Amiana's burial mound his gravediggers were waiting. Snot Nose had put others beside the duplicate in the slave cemetery. He hadn't said why.

'One more minute,' he told the musicians.

VIII

A cannon was fired. Mourners broke into loud shrieks as the band began playing a funeral march in military cadence. Snot Nose took up his place before the musicians, stooping low over his violin. The march began. Behind him followed the dead man, and then Amiana's people. Moonlight washed over the roads, casting sendals of magic shadows that veiled the way. The music numbed the feet that slowly followed it along a path. To its sound the mourners cried, soldiers marched and singers sang. Snot Nose was leading the way . . . everyone thought to the cemetery of the free. Except Snot Nose himself. His violin hooted owlishly – long, low whistles that came from his chest. As he bent over his violin, the bowstrokes sent exorcisms out into the air, between the moonlight and the shadows. Snot Nose's bowed body and the bow of his violin led the way through the bush. The procession was a boa's bewitched body and Snot Nose its head. And only the head knew where it was going. The snake's hundred feet were silent against the soft soil. Only the piercing sound of the violin could be heard; it was like the hiss of a poisoned arrow in flight through the darkness towards Snot Nose and the others. The bush was swallowing them up. The batey was empty and the barracks people were lurking there beneath the night sky, on the cemetery side. The sky was starless, clear. The moon had startled them and they had taken flight like a flock of birds.

This happened as we left. Then some other things rose into the sky. We all saw from the barracks windows, all the slaves. We could hear the passing music, and the wailing women, the groaning men and the hooting without tempo of Snot Nose's violin. We trembled. We were sick with whatever that sorcerer had put in our blood. In the bush something was rotting; something was festering in silence, and it was not of this world. In the barracks, eyes and ears flattened against the sky. We couldn't make out the bush or one another, and even our breathing was imperceptible. Each was alone with his dread.

The music was receding towards the hiding place where a man waited, hunkered down. Only he knew where he was. Even Snot Nose had forgotten him by now. For now his entire soul had moved into his head and was fleeing to God knows where on those shrieks from his violin. The man struck a match, saw it was eight o'clock and lit the fuse. Then he slipped into the bush as he heard the funeral procession moving out and went back to the barracks. Even the sick had got up and were coming to the windows in the barracks rooms, some half crazy and feverish. Most of them didn't know the Chinaman was dead or anything about the silent emptiness that had suddenly invaded the bush. But everybody sensed it. Snot Nose had filled them all with the charge of illusion and quiet dread that was stirring within. That's why some were crazed and feverish. Even the night seemed quietly mad. We huddled together, listening and looking. The fuse was burning quickly towards the false burial mound in the slave cemetery and now every living slave was possessed as if holding within a burning fuse that rushed towards the charge of illusion and dread that Snot Nose had planted.

'We're lost!' Amiana cried out.

Too late! No sooner inside the cemetery he realized his mistake; it wasn't the cemetery of freemen and he shouted out. Amiana was alone in eluding Snot Nose's charm and enchanting music; he didn't believe in witchcraft and was just pretending to. But too late. Even he didn't know how to get out of there. The funeral party had stopped beside the mound and the musicians and mourners and slaves had fallen silent. Only Snot Nose's violin could be heard now, its dead strings crying out in the night to the moon. All the freemen were there, heads bowed, dozing their final minutes. Amiana had lifted his arms to the sky and stood there, transfixed by the moon, screams of terror caught in his throat, as if already frozen by death. Snot Nose was silhouetted against sky and sea, his body standing tall now among the rest. But nobody saw him there. Even he didn't see, and he was deaf to the music he had created, the music of the fuse spreading underneath and racing along on the fuse to raise all the enslaved dead. Ten years of dead slaves. We the living felt them die: the living dead. Then we saw them rise. We didn't hear the explosion itself. Our eyes had melted into our ears and all our senses awaited the night of those dead ten years. Nobody knew anything; they felt it. And they were filled with awe.

The dead rose in that night of terror and ascended towards the moon wearing the clothing of the freemen in the funeral party. We saw them rise up. I saw Snot Nose rise up among them as the mute violin of his soul hissed like hellish coals, or a swarm of bees. Or locusts. A cloud of locusts rising from earth, from sea, dark against the sky. So we ran. The charge dread Snot Nose had planted in our souls exploded, exploded the barracks and we fled in terror, scattering through the bush, towards the batey, the sea and the boats. Towards other islands. And that Island was left alone, with its free dead. That night the slaves rose from the grave and we all fled! Snot Nose! Snot Nose! Snot Nose! That's what the rowers said. I went off by myself.

TRANSLATED BY SUZANNE JILL LEVINE AND
PETER BUSH

Lucumi Dance
Luis Felipe Rodríguez

If you ask the inhabitants of this dark-soiled clod of creole land called Hormiga Loca if they've ever seen a shark, said Marcos Antilla with a wink, someone will probably answer in all good faith, 'Once I saw two of them, a male and a female . . . at school. My teacher showed me them in a book about all the animals in the world.'

Well, now that you know something of the physical and mental limitations of Hormiga Loca, it would be reasonable for you to ask, 'How is it you have a shark around here, when you are not inhabitants of the sea?'

Everyone will reply, 'Our grandparents, who are at rest beneath the earth with Jesus Christ, can answer that. When we glimpsed the first light rise over the Sierra Maestra, that black man, as old and ugly as the Mahdinga, was the shark we call Tintorera.'

Then you won't ask again, happy in the knowledge that Tintorera is Tintorera, as historians are happy merely to record the dubious birthplace of Columbus. With a little imagination, we can see the following scene taking place in the hamlet of Hormiga Loca, where Tomás Cumba, known as 'Tintorera', is a popular character: one day, we don't know exactly when, nature put the finishing touches to our furrowed island, and realized something was missing. She took a fistful of earth and threw it, like a sweet potato, in the foothills of the

Sierra Maestra. Hormiga Loca immediately sprang up, with a local Mayor and cacique, Olegario Machuca, four banana trees, half a dozen dairy cows, a canefield and the indispensable and inevitable sugar mill. The sugar mill which grinds the cane, just as Hormiga Loca grinds down the life and patience of Tintorera. Tintorera thinks of this fertile soil, which produces only one fruit, as simply another juice. Sugar-cane juice, that everyone sees flowing, as its way of life, but nobody, not even its owner, knows where it comes from or where it ends up. Like the twisting coil of the bindweed, separated from the spindly trunk, Tintorera winds his way back and forth, at the mercy of everyone's good or bad humour. They all tell him to perform the tasks that could only be taken on by someone with a dried calabash for a head and a fungus the colour of a used bandage growing sparsely about his mouth. The fish after which he was so aptly named immediately springs to mind.

On Sundays, when the youngsters who love din and dominoes go to Exuberancio Martínez's bar to empty a few bottles of genuine creole liquor, that's where you'll find Tintorera. In this life, where so much is suffering, Tintorera never says no to the sandpaper bite of a hard drink. 'Tintorera, pour yourself one . . . But first dance the Lucumi dance.'

If that's all they ask, Tintorera will dance the dance he brought to this world, as the birds brought their song and the trees their roots. And Tintorera starts to dance the Lucumi dance with all the passion and pain searing through his veins, the blood dripping into a fissure created in the parched earth by the heat of summer. And meanwhile, the nearby canefield shimmers like a river flowing into the sugar plant whose mills, pumps, boilers and triple-action machines have been the life and death of Hormiga Loca to this very day. The liberating revolutions that had given him and other sons of the island colony their freedom had passed before his eyes. But Tintorera never left the dark earth or the canefields. Sometimes when a first flash of bright lightning lit up his head, he would dance the Lucumi dance, making his body feel good and banishing all thoughts from his

mind. The Lucumi dance, grandmother of the *son*, the popular
creole music which brings joy and deception to his uncertain future.
Sometimes, when the flickering of an idea comes to his mind,
Tintorera turns his thoughts to the past. He vaguely recalls that his
ancestor came with him, when he was very small, from a land of
burning heat, where it seemed everything was made from the rays of
the sun. Perhaps it was Zapata Marsh, where he and his father were
flung, like heaps of jerk beef. Since then . . . since then he has seen
only the creole earth and its canefields. He first became acquainted
with cane juice through the engine of the primitive sugar plant,
'Cunyaye'. He saw it transform itself into honey and pan sugar, while
his body bent under the double whiplash of sun and overseer. Then
came the sugar mills to make the sweet crystal, with machinery that
became so complicated, beyond the understanding of this simple
soul, as were the wires at the back, though he was their passive tool.
He arose with the dawn and sunset would find him by the canefields,
while his hand seemed to become a recipient for sound, for the song
recalled today in the popular verse:

Cut the cane,
move swiftly,
here comes the overseer
lashing his whip.

On that Sunday, Tintorera had one too many in Exuberancio
Martínez's bar. It was already night when he left, unconsciously
tracing short flourishes in the air. As he walked by the canefield, from
the shadows of his drunken mind surged a strange idea. Like
someone trying to ward something off, a voice which came either
from God or the devil, he began to dance; but the strange thought
gripped his entire body and soul. It was like a long-repressed revenge
which forges a sudden hatred for the canefields. 'Canefield,' he cried,
with the frenzied impulse of a drunkard or madman finding
something confusingly distressing in the depths of his misguided

mind, 'I'm gonna punish you. Old black man doesn't know what he has, old black man is sad and drunk, and gonna punish you, because canefield gave the black man a lot of leather, work and itching.'

Then, flames of burning alcohol burst from Tintorera's head, and in the startled night the inhabitants of that creole land saw their canefield burning. The flames spread from the rustic cases of green gold while innumerable sparks danced fantastically, the sugar canes cracked like guns. All this time, Tintorera danced the Lucumi dance between the fires, lost in the clouded musings of someone ignorant of the deep reason of instinct and the blind and elemental forces of the ancestral flame. The terrible, purifying fire also danced a symbolic dance among the cane, beyond human instinct and pain.

TRANSLATED BY OLIVIA McDONALD

Daddy Turtle and Daddy Tiger
Lydia Cabrera

When the world was young, Frog had whiskers and rolled his own cigarettes. In the beginning everything was green. Not just leaves and grass and things that ought to be green, like limes and Esperanza the grasshopper, but minerals, animals and man, that Oba-Ogo made by blowing on his own manure.

Things weren't very organized: fish sucked on flowers, birds hung their nests from the crests of waves.

(The seas poured out of snail shells; rivers ran with the tears of the first crocodile to feel grief.)

Mosquito sank his sting into the buttocks of a mountain and a whole range was jolted into motion.

That same day Elephant married Ant.

A man went up to heaven on a rope of light. The Sun warned him, 'Don't come too close, I burn.' The man took no notice. He went too near, he was roasted, he turned black from head to foot . . . He was the first black man, father of all blacks.

(Joy belongs to the blacks.)

Another man went up to the Moon riding a Horse-Bird-Cayman-Cloud-Girl. Moon has a round eye, a circle outlined with charcoal. And inside the eye was a hare going round and round.

This eye is a well of cold, primordial water from the sky. The hare is a piece of ice. Rain lives in the Moon's eye.

Moon was born dead. Neither man, nor woman. Chaste.

When Moon's mother saw that she had given birth to the flat, tinny face of a corpse, she had a nervous attack. Moon's father rubbed her down with elder flowers, baptized her Moon and said, 'Moon, be born, die and return to life.'

Moon came down and rolled around the mountains. She went under the brow of a mountain where Hare was taking fire from a bald Indian. Moon said to Hare, 'Run and tell men from me that just as I am born, die and return to life, so they shall be born, die and return again.'

Hare went off to find men and Moon waited for him in the crest of a tough sugar cane.

On the way, he met his cousin Rat drinking beer. He had stolen a barrel and was already drunk, blind drunk.

'Let me have some,' said Hare. He wasn't used to drinking, the beer went straight to his head and he mixed up the message that Moon had entrusted him with.

When he got back again, Moon asked, 'Did you tell men what I told you?'

'Yeah, yeah. I told them: just as I am born, die and . . . never come back, so you shall be born, die and never come back. And they started digging their graves . . .'

Moon grabbed Hare by the ears and split open his lip with a cane. 'As punishment, I shall keep you locked up for ever.' And she shut him inside her single eye with a good silver padlock, and ever since then he has gone round and round looking for a way out, but has never managed to find one.

The Moon is cold. Cold is white. The man who went to the moon turned white. He was the first white man, father of all the whites. They are sad . . . everything can be explained.

'Let's be brothers,' said Turtle in those days to Deer, 'Hoof of the Air'.

'Fine,' answered Deer.

'We shall never leave one another,' said Turtle.

'Fine,' answered Deer.

They set off together down the same path.

They came to a lake. They fished out the Evening Star with a fishing net. They went to see the king's daughter, Anikosia, and

offered it to her, still damp. The king's daughter was delighted and
hung it on her ear. She was cross-eyed and her belly hung down to
her knees. She had only one very, very long, narrow breast which she
slung over her shoulder for convenience and pulled along. Although
she was still a virgin, her endless supply of milk provided all her
father Masawe's servants with more than enough nourishment. She
gave them gold and ivory, but she didn't care much for the star, that
earring of light . . . What she cared about was blood, Turtle's blood,
that could cure asthma. And Anikosia's eye said (vice versa), 'I shall
make a noose.' And Turtle's eye, which overheard her, said, 'I will
make a knife.' And the eyes laughed, threatening as teeth.

Then the King's daughter said to them, 'Let's run away. I can't go
back to my father's house now that I've stolen his gold and ivory.'

'Fine,' said 'Hoof of the Air'.

'Let's not waste time. The Cock that guards the king's treasure
will run and tell on me.'

And they marched on without stopping, crossing the plaza where
blind people were warming themselves in the sunshine and killing
fleas, which they were munching with relish.

When Anikosia, who was guiding them, felt that she was outside
her father's territory, far enough away and out of danger from the
first explosions of the king's anger – anger that fairly regularly
produced some frightful cataclysm that altered the shape of the
earth – they stopped to rest under a leafy banyan tree.

Anikosia came up and immediately pretended to drop off to sleep
exhausted. Deer lay down at her side and really wasted no time in
falling asleep. Turtle grabbed the woman's breast that was creeping
over the ground like a snake and – one, two, three – wrapped it round
the banyan tree's trunk. Then he seized his machete, which sounded
just like a silver bell with diaphanous daylight inside, and woke Deer
up, shouting,

'This woman has a really ugly face. She needs her head cutting
off!'

With one blow he chopped her head off her shoulders. As soon as the head felt itself cut off and flung violently into the air with no warning, like a grapefruit, it waited a second or two to take in the gravity of the situation, dazzled by the sudden explosion of light and deafened by the wild jangling of bells, hooters and buzzers that were set off inside it when it crashed against a stone. Then, recovering from that terrible, unexpected blow, it bounced back with indescribable rage – its thinking matter was all inflamed – and fell on Turtle, frantically biting the bumps on his shell. And it managed to break its four rows of teeth, which were filed down to points, and to dislocate its jaw.

Inflamed by this new setback – unable to pause and reflect coolly for a second – it struck out with its forehead, its temples, its chin and the crown of its head beating against Turtle's tough, invulnerable armour plating until it destroyed itself and collapsed, overcome by its own fury, like a piece of rotten fruit at the feet of its impassive executioner.

Meanwhile, a new head, with an even more repulsive face and a ghastly expression, sprouted diagonally across Anikosia's neck (all the time the fight had been going on, her two arms had never stopped pulling desperately at her captive breast but had succeeded only in tightening the knot in the noose). And once again Turtle chopped it straight off, exactly at Adam's apple level.

This head had no taste for biting and attacking. It was content to express its more hidden feelings by pulling a series of very expressive faces indicating hatred and by uttering a few particularly vicious words. From its lips flew a swarm of dark moths, horned Giant Owlet Moths, with Anikosia's face alive and staring stamped on to the funereal velvet of their wings.

A third head barely raised an aged, wrinkled forehead. Anikosia's body extended itself and died once and for all with discreet convulsions.

Then Turtle and 'Hoof of the Air' saw the gold leaf of an unknown plant sprouting from the bellybutton of the corpse. Driven by curiosity, they lifted the cover of her belly and found seeds and roots that had never before been planted. The first grain of maize like a grain of sunlight.

They went on in the same direction as the maté fields, navigating by the wind. 'Hoof of the Air' was loaded down with the dead woman's body until they could find a suitable place to bury it, and so it was that they left the green parts of the earth behind and it began to dry out, to break up, to incline sharply until they came to the edge of a precipice and threw themselves off it. But the moths that had been born from the lips and breath of Anikosia's second head flew off to tell the king what had happened and now they came back in their millions, turning the day cloudy.

The walls of the horizon they had left behind trembled and collapsed in silent uproar. Deer thought he saw the huge shape of a hunter; fear made him feel the impatient savagery of a pack of hounds about to dash out of the leaden clouds. His scent was in the dogs' nostrils! Meanwhile, Turtle realized that it wouldn't be long before the volcanoes woke up . . .

The mournful, sluggish flight of the Owlet Moths who kept dying and being born all the time traced the ritual signs of a curse in the sky over their heads.

'"Hoof of the Air", my brother,' said Turtle, leaping on to his horns in a single bound, 'don't leave me, because you are my legs, as I am your brain. You're surely not going to leave me now, just when Masawe is preparing his revenge? The old man has started setting fire to the volcanoes with his tinder, so they will pour their fire over us.'

Deer was fleeing the dogs in the black clouds, unleashed and hungry, fleeing the hunter, remembering what he did, what he looked like – just as all his ancestors used to flee, and now in his fearful heart all those ancestors came alive again – at a speed comparable only to that which Cyclone shows on his famous excursions, and the torrents of liquid fire which the mouths of the volcanoes were spewing forth could no longer catch up with them.

And finally beneath their feet the land came to an end and the clear sapphire sea Kalunga began.

'Great Mother of my race, save your smallest child,' begged Turtle by the shore. And there came towards them a promontory, which was the giant Morrocoy, diving underwater and coming up again with joyful majesty. Wizard of the ocean, who had spent his childhood rocked in its arms, covered with insignias and wearing a robe of rocks and seaweed, he had officiated since the beginning of time in the sanctuary of that lonely coast. But he was old and forgetful, and all he could remember of the ancient liturgical rites was how to bless the waters, so he repeated that with a touching obstinacy thousands of years old.

'Moyumba' cannot cross open water, which is joined to the sky. The venerable mass of Morrocoy swam off with them and, having crossed seven seas of seven different colours and a great gap in the age of the world, left them one afternoon on the shores of a happy island, in the year 1845 . . .

Certain that no misfortune could come to them under that new sky, which was like a caress, they went trustingly into the sweet-smelling forest and eventually they came to large village, walled in by the sea.

The women were like flowers and many of the men looked like women with their smooth hips and dainty feet. They wore white and spoke in sugary voices. Eventually Turtle and 'Hoof of the Air' put down their gold and ivory and the seeds from Anikosia's belly, and since they realized that over there the land did not belong to anyone who took it and looked after it, but to the one who bought it – and with gold, to be precise – they acquired in exchange for their gold a beautiful estate which was later called Ochú-Kuá-Oru-Okuku.

'You see? We're going to be landowners here,' said Turtle to Deer. In addition to two wide brimmed palm-fibre hats, they supplied themselves with a plough and two new machetes. They ploughed a good stretch of land and threw in the seeds. They didn't respect Sundays or any other holiday; if anything, they doubled their efforts and went on ploughing and sowing different seeds. And everything grew fantastically, incredibly and flourished wildly.

Long years went by, during which Turtle and Deer looked after
their farm with the grace of God and enjoyed it. Deer lived in the
extreme north, in a hut of bricks and tiles. Turtle lived in the south
and from his house a permanent scent of bougainvillea and jasmine
wafted across the roadway, along which squeaking carts and peasants
with their livestock passed every day. And they were as close as the
fingers of a hand; you probably couldn't have seen one without the
other.

As he came out of the sea, Turtle had brought along some
witchcraft hidden in his pupils, the art of healing with herbs, sticks
and chanting.

One day Deer fell ill.

For some time Turtle, who had been working hard on his sowing
and harvesting, had not been feeling very comfortable about the way
the world was going. Now it happened that having climbed to the top
of a hill looking for certain herbs that he needed to prepare a potion
to cure his compadre, he stayed longer than he should have done and,
to the misfortune of Deer, contemplated the amazingly fertile
expanse of Ochú-Kuá-Oru-Okuku. Then Turtle experienced an
extremely strong, totally new sensation.

'To possess this for ever, to be lord of everything and not just half
of it,' was what that landowner came to reflect on there at the
summit. Below his feet the palm groves stretched out, the still-virgin
forests of cedars and mahogany trees, the cultivated fields, the
golden maize fields, the flowering cassavas, the rice already turning
yellow in the distance in the glittering lagoon. The hunger for land
was born in his breast, grew vast as the day. He thought greedily, with
a painful kind of avarice, of the thousands and thousands of fruits
that were ripening at that very moment on every branch on every tree
in the orchards. And he wanted all of it for himself, the avocado
trees, the guavas, the plum trees his brother had planted. The
honeyed oranges famous throughout the region, the mangoes from
which you could drink warm melted sunlight. And the little
pathways of sumptuous purple, the colour of black women's lips,

and the medlars whose sour skin encloses a heart so sweet that the memory of its taste softly flooded his mouth. And the mameys and the scented custard apples that were now in season bent branches double with their weight, swollen and white like the breasts of pregnant women. Yes, all that was Ochú-Kuá-Oru-Okuku, of which only half belonged to him. Swept by breezes up there on the summit, Turtle breathed in the lemon-scented air with delight, drinking in and counting every exhalation from his lands, and gave up letting his conscience speak clearly and firmly to him . . .

He decided to abandon the trail of the herbs he had been looking for that could drive back the fever demons – even Burukú* – by closing up the pathways of the blood. It took a lot of skill and cunning to capture them, because they could change shape and move from place to place at the slightest sound. All they needed was a glance without the presence of Ifa[†] for them to dash off and hide in a crack in a stone, or camouflage themselves in the undergrowth or fly higher than a scavenging vulture. And in inexpert hands that had not been initiated by a true witch of the night or by a son or grandson of descendants of Babalú,[1] they could change into air. Turtle raised a fervent litany of curses to the skies. The idea that his faithful friend might die of exhaustion at that point refreshed his heart with a sensation of pure joy, and instead of life-restoring juices, as soon as the palm groves began to redden and the singing of birds faded away into the sweetness of the dusk, Turtle sent to Deer, who was waiting impatiently for him, trembling in his hammock, three 'chicherekús', wooden dolls or very old, still-born children. They had smooth, vacant faces with no eyes or noses, just greedy mouths with curved white teeth. Flourishing clasp knives or clubs of lignum vitae, hurling themselves about or jumping out of shadowy corners, mocking, inexhaustible, badgering and struggling to show

* Burukú: a demon that produces convulsions and kills by smallpox.
† Ifa: the great oracle and adviser to humans and gods.
[1] Babalú: the caring deity for sufferers from smallpox, venereal diseases and other skin infections after a career as womanizer. The son of Naná Burukú.

off their teeth at close range: 'Daddy, Mummy, look at my toof!'
They tormented him all night long with their grating voices from the
edges of hell, occasional piercing screams, knife slashes out of
nightmares in the arteries of his temples. From precipice to
precipice, far beyond dreams, they lashed at him until the sun – they
are children of darkness – made them flee in terror to the cavern
from which they had come, to die again at Conanfinda* in the breast
of Agayu,† who engendered them, or with the 'Lady Mistress of
Evil Things'.

Deer spent more than a week feeling that his tongue was a slug
trailing through the dust or a whole dusty road that he never stopped
swallowing. About to die, with an aching in all his bones from the
blows which the 'chicherekús' rained down on him, when his body
lay inert and his soul abandoned it he could hear splashing in his
belly a heavy liquid warm with rotten sunlight that was so heavy he
could not stand on his feet.

Turtle did not appear with the medicine, and all the locals were
quacks, so if Deer hadn't vomited up the water in which the fever lay
like the root of an iris, along with a black cat, and if he hadn't been
wearing his amulet that his mother had given him and had a good
Eleddá¹ over his head, he would have died then and not when his
hour was finally up.

Nevertheless, he recovered quickly and completely, with eggs and
chicken broth.

Convinced that Turtle must be ill too and that this was the reason
why he had been left to himself, once he was back on his feet he
saddled his pony and crossed the estate at a steady trot, anxious to
hear about his friend. He found him blooming with health on the
roof of his porch, smoking a cigar . . .

When Deer saw him looking so well, he was deeply wounded in
the depths of his soul, but he said, 'Good morning, compadre. I

* Conanfinda: a cemetery.
† Agayu: a powerful awesome giant and the owner of a river that rushes down
  from on high.
| Eleddá: a guardian angel.

nearly died of a terrible fever.'

Turtle not only didn't return his greeting as though he didn't exist, but he turned his head away disdainfully and spat, the way you spit when you want to make a point of being offensive rather than merely suggesting it.

'Hoof of the Air' could not explain what Turtle's disconcerting behaviour meant, but what filled him with outrage and hurt him most of all was that deliberate spitting, which he felt in the most sensitive corner of his heart.

'What have I done to my brother?' he asked himself, and since he was not a very confident man, he was inclined to blame himself for things he couldn't remember, so he insisted worriedly, 'Compadre, good morning. Good morning. I am saying good morning to you because we used to share the same bed . . . What have I done to deserve such treatment?'

Then Turtle stretched his neck out as far as it would go with its black and yellow stripes and condescended to reply in the same scornful manner that could have been inferred previously from his silence: 'Shouldn't you be greeting me as the boss, and showing me due respect?'

'But . . . what the devil for, compadre? Me . . . you . . .'

'Because the devil knows things haven't been as they should be up to now. I had never really thought about you, for all sorts of reasons that I don't propose to discuss with you. The first is that I, Sir Turtle-Turtle, am worth more than you are.'

At this statement of self-admiration, 'Hoof of the Air' protested feebly: 'No, that's . . . I don't agree . . . .'

'You have to recognize that I'm the boss.'

Not knowing how to argue with him, Deer stammered, 'Well . . . no.'

'And from now on you do as I say.'

'No, I shan't.'

'Right,' said Turtle, standing smugly and firmly on both feet and rolling up his trousers, which were always too big for him, 'let's see which of us is the best man and who gets to be boss.'

But they did not come to blows as the mocking bird, sitting on a custard-apple branch, thought they would. It even interrupted its warbling to pay more attention to what was going on.

Turtle proposed, 'Let's each clear a slope. The one who finishes the job first will take over the whole estate and there'll be no further argument . . . That means he'll be the only one in control of this land. The only one!'

'Fine,' said 'Hoof of the Air' sadly.

It was Sunday, the day when the two friends used to put on their striped duck trousers and show off in town their shirts of embroidered cheesecloth and their rich silk scarves. Instead of falling in love with girls peeping at them out of windows, or playing cards or fighting their splendid cockerels in the pit, they sharpened their machetes and went off to clear scrub from their respective fields. Compadre Turtle chopped and hacked and Compadre Deer chopped and hacked too. For fifteen days they cut and cleared and finished work at exactly the same time.

'Neither you nor me, Compadre Turtle.'

'Neither you, or me. Compadre Deer.'

Faced with this, Turtle decided, 'Next we'll burn the stubble: when my field is on fire I'll step into the flames and stay there until it's all burned out . . . If I burn like a branch, then you will be master by right. If God consents to let you burn, then by virtue of your death I shall make what's yours mine. And in peace. I can't see any other way of resolving such a delicate situation.'

'But who goes first?'

'Me, naturally,' answered Turtle arrogantly, 'and while the blaze lasts I shall sing in the middle of the flames and you can answer from your nice cool corner.'

This solution seemed fair and proper to Deer. He set fire to the land Turtle had cleared and watched him disappear calmly into the tangle of flames. Turtle, who knew the land well, crept into a cave, carefully stopped up the opening with a stone and the fire rushed past his head backwards and forwards, crackling and destroying everything. Quite safe in his hiding place, he sang:

'Bibiribiriquiá, bericó,
Bibiribiriquiá, bericó,
Bibiribiriquiá, bericó,'

The fire went out and Turtle came out of his cave. He dragged the stone that had hidden him so well to the middle of the slope and stretched himself out on it, face upward.

Smiling, with his arms crossed behind his neck, he greeted Deer without a burn on his body, as though he were waking up from a siesta, a pleasant nap in the freshest hollow of a simple bonfire of wild raspberry canes.

'Well, as you can see, this is where I passed the test. A river of fire ran over me, my saliva tastes like live coals and my whole body stinks like a bonfire . . . I can see redness . . . but I haven't been fried . . . Come on, compadre, now it's your turn to burn a bit . . .'

And 'Hoof of the Air', who ran confidently into the fire, was surrounded and encircled by flames. He was trapped and soon he was nothing more than a flame among flames. When Turtle sang ironically:

'Bibiribiriquiá, bericó,
'Bibiribiriquiá, bericó,
'Bibiribiriquiá, bericó,

only firewood answered him, hissing and spitting.

Then Turtle looked for the burned body, the carbonized body of his friend.

'Oh, "Hoof of the Air",' wept Turtle, '"Hoof of the Air", my caravel, my brother! When you came into this world, you came with nothing . . .'

He said a Paternoster over him and cut off his horns, which the fire had licked but not consumed.

With his friend's horns, he made a musical instrument. Every afternoon, just before sunset, he would play it on the flat roof of his house. One person who heard that music was paralyzed with the pleasure of it. It was an Ox, named 'Butterfly', who was going slowly down to the village on a matter of great importance. The music was coming from the home of Turtle, who lived on his own. Ox remembers letting himself be carried away by the rhythm, and in a daze he found himself face to face with Turtle, whose bright eyes were half-closed and who seemed to be in another world, as he clutched a rare instrument in flames, from which came the sounds that had enchanted him.

'I'll give you whatever you ask, Turtle,' said Ox, 'just give me that instrument.'

Turtle returned from the heights of ineffable sweetness and was silent for a long time, considering in a melancholy fashion the huge, excited and beseeching mass of the quadruped.

'Give me that music, Turtle.'

'Well, friend, your hoofs are very strong and my legs are quite short . . . It might happen that you'd take my music so far away that I couldn't catch up with you, old and tired as I am.'

'Don't insult me, Turtle. There are some things we oxen never do.'

'So you oxen say . . . but nobody can escape from an evil inclination. I can't grant your wish, so off you go!'

But Ox went on begging him to let him hear just one more time 'that' divine tune that had made him tremble with emotion like a leaf, that had drawn tears from the depths of his soul, even more than the 'Bogguará arayé' of midnight funeral chants. And Turtle ended up saying, 'Keep calm, comrade, I'll make you happy . . . but first let me warm a drop of coffee.' And he put a pot full of tar on to the fire.

'Here,' he said, holding out the horns that were silent and still now, crossed with a single blue thread like a vein. 'In the warmth of a hand and by virtue of blood, the music plays by itself.'

So as soon as Ox touched it, everything was flooded with music.

And he thought he was dancing among the stars and that his body, which sometimes felt so very heavy, was as light as a breeze. It was as though he were made of nothing at all, of something even lighter, even subtler than the scent which a jasmine gives off. His winged feet never touched the ground. Now the most gracious and light of all creatures was dancing, happy with a boundless happiness, suspecting nothing. And like someone who pauses midway through a particularly wonderful dream so that the dream will last longer, so Ox thought, 'I'm not giving this marvellous thing back to Turtle for anything . . .' And he started to take off, ethereal and ungraspable as the music that was making him immaterial.

The tar in the pot began to bubble . . .

From the regions of the inexpressible, 'Butterfly' Ox fell heavily to the hard earth, recovering amid dreadful stinging pains the sense that his body was a crushing weight and, with his back covered by sticky boiling tar, he escaped as best he could, dragging his weight and with one horn less, 'To remember this by,' said Turtle.

Another time it was a dim-witted horse, who was going sadly up a hill to the wake of his beloved, and just as he crossed the path between the sugar cane and the coffee bushes he heard Turtle play. Weeping and swearing that even if he were hungry he wouldn't steal so much as a crumb, nevertheless, in a state of trance, he tried to steal the music that made him whinny with joy and think he was in the pastures of heaven . . . Turtle threw the tar at his head, which left him blind in one eye, then with his pruning shears he cut off an ear and his threadbare tail that used to scare off flies . . .

Almost every day some animal appeared, drawn by the same magic, to ask him to lend them his instrument. Thanks to his cunning, which apart from his horny exterior was the only thing he had inherited from his ancestors, and the effective splattering of tar on every state of ecstasy, Turtle went on cutting off horns, tails, paws, ears, never bothering exactly what he cut – 'You can't be bothered with details when you've too much to do' – and recovered his miraculous music from the covetousness of everyone, for even those who least suspected it had a trap set for them: not only the Magpie, who is a thief by profession, but even an honourable matron like the Sow, so highly respected, so distinctive and set apart from all frivolity by her stoutness and her saintly behaviour, who was really interested only in her continual pregnancies and enviable deliveries. She slipped in one night to Turtle's home and, having trained herself to be so skilful that she could sneak in without being noticed in the dark, she stole the dreamed-of instrument.

If she hadn't grunted to herself when she fell into the pit when the door hinges creaked, which she hadn't anticipated, Turtle wouldn't have caught her with the evidence of her crime still in her hand.

Because he was dealing with a lady, Turtle didn't use the tar, which was bubbling away on the stove as usual as a precaution. However, he thought it was only fair to land her a violent punch on her hindquarters that made the matron squeal, her dignity more wounded than her opulent flesh.

'Oh, sir, Turtle! The rear of a lady is sacred! Who do you take me for?'

As the news of Turtle's music spread throughout the region – though when people praised it they never went so far as to confess why some significant part of their anatomy was missing – Tiger, our great nobleman, who was about to celebrate his name day with dancing, a banquet, fireworks and speeches in his honour, also took a fancy to it and turned up at Turtle's house at crack of dawn one morning. Turtle received him with the honour that befitted a Great Animal who has power in his teeth and holds on to it with his teeth. He gave him the best of his produce: he ordered the six fattest hens in the flock to be brought so that he could prepare him 'a little picnic basket' with fruit and meats to take home to his family as a token of esteem . . .

Then the Boss explained to Turtle that the object of his visit was to invite him to the party on his name day and to ask him to lend the instrument which, from what all the cripples who had heard it said, was worth more by itself than all the best orchestras in the capital and in the civilized world.

'You do me honour. That instrument, Señor Compadre, is the comfort of my old age. I call it "Cocorícamo".* I made it, as they say, with my heart good and bad. It's been my only entertainment since I realized that my youth had left me! One day you open your eyes – that is, you close them – you look inside yourself and you see an old man . . . that's what women make you understand by looking unenthusiastic and asking for money. Oh, Your Honour, lending is losing, and if you say you gave it to me, then I don't recall that. But even though it's you, the great man, the most important man, the most upright, the most carnivorous, the saviour of our country – and that's the truth – however much it costs me because of the affection I hold for you, I am not going to give you "Cocorícamo".

Grin, Grin, Grin
Grin, Grin, Grin,
Grin, Grin. Grin,
Bongo Monasengo, Si Kengó!
Bongo Monasengo, Si Kengó!
Grin . . . Bongo Monasengo, Si Kengó!'

The music, rising imperiously from the stool, prevented Tiger from arguing . . . A tickling – grin, grin, grin – from the nape of his neck to the tip of his tail, and then the 'Cocorícamo', a pleasure so intense, the pain of pleasure without pause, made him lose all judgement and all sense of his own importance. He rolled about, he turned over and over, he wriggled, he spun round, howled, rolled around face upwards, like a mad street cat drunk on a roof with love and moonlight. The powerful Compadre, who held the will of a whole people in his claws with a bearing so terrible and so majestic, was no more than a big writhing cat, covering himself with ridicule.

* Cocorícamo: the imponderable, according to Fernando Ortiz, *Catauro de afrocubanismos.*

When, instead of the powerful roaring that made people tremble from one side of the island to the other, there came from his glorious throat a sound equivalent to a particularly contemptible 'miaow', Turtle demolished him by pouring over his head the contents of the pot of boiling tar. And Tiger couldn't escape that fiery porridge; it stuck to his flesh and scalded him all over. And so it was that Turtle came to cut off nine claws and half his whiskers, and as if that were not enough, he added a beating, calling him 'Pansy!' at every blow.

Tiger went home tied across his own horse in a very sorry state, with his 'picnic basket' and his six chickens as a gift trotting behind him insulting him all the painful way home, going 'cheep, cheep'.

When his poor wife, who had washed her hair that day, saw the blood pouring from her husband, she fainted dead away into the arms of two helpfully robust slaves. His daughters also managed to faint in their turn, once they were convinced that their father was going to pull through. His sons – already of an age to avenge an insult with just one bite – begged him to tell them who had reduced him to such a state, who had injured him, wounded him, crushed him and cut off his whiskers.

In a savage silence that nobody could rouse him from, wrapped in bandages and poultices of spider's webs and oil of musty scorpion, Tiger slowly got better.

Deep in his guts, he harboured resentment. One word beat incessantly in his brain: 'Pansy!'

'Who knows!'

Five years went by, five years (and quickly too) during which Tiger looked at his mutilated paws and secretly planned his revenge.

It so happened that his closest pal, Rabbit, had gone off to see the world and one morning, when nobody was expecting him, he turned up in the yard. 'God has sent you to me, compadre!' cried Tiger, opening his arms. He spent the whole afternoon with him, shut up in his bedroom. Without raising his voice – because walls don't only have ears, eyes and memories, they also have tongues, viperish women's tongues – he told the true account of his nine missing claws, the gap in his beautiful set of teeth, the lumps and scars on his back, omitting nevertheless a few useless details, the memory of which embittered him more than everything else.

Rabbit took a bag and a drum and set off around the locality.

'Sandemania, sandemania
Eleuro kengueeré, kangara ulrimakanga obbá . . .
Sandemania, sandemania.'

An edict from the king summoning all landowners to a public meeting . . .

He beat his drum and announced the Royal Command at the property of a widow, a small land-owning Cow, whose lands adjoined Turtle's.

'If you see Turtle, Madame Cow – that will save me having to go and look for him – tell him he must not miss this meeting.'

He said the same thing to Donkey and to Spotted Bull, neighbouring tenants, who hurried along to tell Turtle that the king had sent them to call him.

'To increase taxes, obviously,' grumbled Brindled Cow, who smeared herself with herbs, hurriedly put on shoes of canary yellow satin, pulled on a dress of sky-blue muslin with wide frills of fancy embroidery and, thus bundled up and suffocating, but happy to be able to show off her earrings and necklace of French gold, set off down the village street mounted on a mule. A little later, Turtle heard the drum beating merrily on his doorstep.

'Are you still here, Comrade Turtle? Down there in the village the meeting has started and you and I are the only ones missing.'

'What meeting?' asked Turtle. 'I heard something, somebody mentioned something, but I didn't pay any attention. I can't hear very well these days . . .'

'The king, the king has summoned us all urgently . . . on a matter of greatest importance.'

'And maybe I thought I'd heard my friend Cow say that Tiger was running this meeting with the king?'

'Compadre Turtle! You're dreaming! Tiger! Holy Mother of God. Let him rest in peace and may God keep him in His glory! He died a good two years ago . . . I went to his funeral, which was very grand. A bell-tower fell on his paw, he got night dew in his wound and within a few hours gangrene had set in.'

'What's this you're telling me, comrade? First I've heard of it . . . True, we weren't very close, but I respected him and esteemed him for what he was worth. And even though he is no longer with us, this news affects me. Gangrene in a paw? Seems impossible!'

'Huh! Nobody escapes death, not even if he's Tiger.'

'True, true. That's why they say that once death is hungry . . .'

'Come on, comrade, don't let's dwell on it. Put your hat on and let's go. I'll tell you all about it on the way. If you like, I'll take you in this bag.'

'In a bag? Better to go on foot,' thought Turtle, and he set off happily with Rabbit, who was a charming fellow and a good conversationalist.

But after a while Rabbit finally said, 'At this rate we'll never get there at all. I'd be in town already if it weren't for your blessed slowness. Come on, Turtle, get into the bag. I tell you, you don't weigh much and I'll be off like a rifle shot.'

'It just doesn't seem appropriate, compadre, to turn up at a public meeting as a landowner and for people to see me arrive crated up like a chicken.'

'As soon as we get to the village I'll let you out, so nobody will see you.'

Turtle got into the bag and Rabbit started to run.

'Are we nearly there?' asked Turtle, pushing at the top of the bag with his head when he thought an hour was up.

'Still some way to go.'

(Dadum, dadum, dadum.)

Another hour of bumping and jolting went by.

'Compadre Rabbit, I can't stand this much longer, I'm feeling sick.

Is the village in sight yet?'

'There's a fair stretch still to go.'

(And dadum, dadum, dadum.)

With his stomach and his frozen intestines hanging out of his mouth, Turtle began to plead, pushing open the bag: 'How much longer, compadre?'

Finally the bumping, the nausea and the sickness came to a halt . . . Turtle found himself face to face with Tiger, surrounded by his entire family.

'Now I think the meeting is complete!' And he pulled his head in straight away so as not to watch his own death.

With sentences of stone, Tiger sent off for a plantain root.

'Get your head out,' he roared. 'Get your head out or I'll flatten you, shell and all! Look at this plantain root! Look at it closely, you swine! I shall plant it this very day, Saint Isidro Labrador's day. When it starts to fruit and the plantains ripen, I shall eat you in a stew with plantains and okra. I'll drink your blood in a zambumbia.* But before that I'm condemning you to the torment of thirst and hunger. I have spoken.'

He shut him in a trunk and ordered it to be put on top of the barbecue with no further ado.

Later on, Tiger was so profoundly satisfied that he felt like playing a game of cards. That day he didn't only pardon all the slaves who were due for punishment, but after he had eaten he asked his wife to play 'La Paloma' and 'La Monona' on the piano, which hadn't happened for five years.

And when the plantain grew a splendid bunch of fruits, Tiger bought a pot and invited his friend Rabbit, who had taken on the lucrative task of being President of the Supreme Court and Chief Fireman with exceptional aptitude.

Exploiting the absence of their father, the littlest tigers went out to the barbecue and opened the trunk. Inside, totally dried up,

---

* Zambumbia: a drink of fermented sugar cane, with red-hot pepper.

parched and blackened, Turtle was in his death throes: the painful sound of the lock made him recover consciousness, only to be reminded that his final hour had come . . . and by mistake, instead of grieving, he started to dance. His dancing when they thought they would surprise him delighted them. The fresh air, the bright small day that opened into the trunk after a year of darkness slightly restored his strength. One of the tigers – the one who was three minutes older than his three brothers – applauded: 'Bravo, Turtle. You're a really good dancer!'

'Oh, no, your father dances much better than I can,' he answered in the far-off, vacant voice of those who have died a good while before dying.

'Since a herd of elephants and five lions attacked him, which he fought off single-handed, Dad has been lame.'

'Oh boys,' sighed Turtle, making the most of a flash of lucidity. 'If you throw me in a basin full of water, then you'll see what dancing really is! Dryness just doesn't suit me . . .'

Impelled by curiosity, the tigers rushed to put ladders underneath and hurried back with a brimming basin.

Water! Blessed be! Turtle's whole being, body and soul, revived delightedly when he saw that adored water so near to his mouth and drank it passionately with his eyes in anticipation.

'Pongueledió, el bongué,
Pongueledió el bongá,
Pongueledió, el bongué,
Pongueledió, el bongá.'

And he danced before the enraptured tigers, a thanksgiving dance, for love of water and thirst appeased.

'Yippee, yippee! More, Turtle . . . faster!' they shouted in chorus round the basin, as the rhythm took hold of them.

'Oh,' answered Turtle, 'but I can hardly move in here. If only we could go to a stream . . .'

'Yes, the stream! To the stream!'

In the stream. Turtle did no more than suggest a few movements, crooning:

Pongueledió, el bongué!

'My boys, what a shame there isn't a river nearby!' Now the tigers couldn't think of anything except dancing. They took him down to the river. And in the wide, free current, Turtle danced with such frenzy that the tigers were unable to follow the speed of his movements, and in their confusion saw not one but one thousand Turtles, one thousand Turtles like a miracle!

'What if we took him down to the sea?' But the eldest tiger, who was afraid of witchcraft and feeling that he was going to lose his head and lose count of so many Turtles when there should only be one, said, 'God spare us! It's getting late. If Dad finds out we took Turtle out of the trunk, he'll wallop us, like the day when we covered his chair in glue.'

And they shouted, 'That's enough, Turtle! Come on, remember today's the day my dad is going to eat you with plantains and okra.'

'I'd almost forgotten! I'm here, son,' answered a thousand Turtles, and Turtle once again stopped dead. 'Just let me go down to the bottom for a minute and say goodbye to the river.'

He chose a stone the same size as himself, covered it with mud, gave it his shape and used a nail to engrave the signs that nobody had ever been able to decipher on his shell.

Muddying the water, he pushed it gently towards the bank, where the tigers picked it up and dashed off homewards . . .

When Tiger with his jangling silver spurs came back with his friend Rabbit their saddlebags full of provisions, the tigers were playing peacefully on the porch.

A tooth for a tooth, an eye for an eye! The friends went out to the barbecue and forced open the trunk. There was Turtle, exactly as they had left him one year ago. Hiding his head in shame and terror! In the same position and at the same despairing angle.

To announce his presence, and because he could no longer contain his hatred, Tiger gave him a blow with a machete and the blade split in two . . .

'Pain certainly does harden a body!'

They put him through a series of frightful, humiliating tortures. By the end, he was nothing more than a stone. Tiger couldn't get one single drop of blood out of him to drink in his zambumbia as he had sworn to do. Nor a shred of flesh to flavour the stew. But no matter! They had him now, at the bottom of the pot . . . His punishment had been exemplary!

And Rabbit felt it was his duty to say to Tiger, who waved a fork at him by way of a sign, 'You eat him yourself, Compadre! Your honour has been avenged.'

TRANSLATED BY SUSAN BASSNETT

Truants
José Lezama Lima

It was no stray breeze, nobody swam on the breeze. We forgot the confines to its colour, till it was like compacted sand our breathing laboriously admitted. It rained and rained, and between rains a soaking wind managed to impose itself, isolating us, entangling us in the columns, or made us look at the men passing by as all the same on many days and in many different bodies. There was a dry spell which Luis Keeler turned to his advantage and hurried schoolwards, stopping nevertheless to watch how the slowest trickle of water over the letters on a shield advertising a jeweller's shop had curled round towards the last letter, seemingly to stagnate there, before it acquired a weary hue of green, turned in on itself, twisted timidly round, avoiding the slide round the edge of the sign, where it would have to wait for the breeze to head – it might well take another route – straight for the shield, whose musty letters now surged against the levelling imposed by wind and rains, and finally the drop of water after running over the shield's fortifications and faded deserts jumped off, disappeared.

Armando Sotomayor had also turned the dry spell to his advantage and headed to his school, a drab sight, as if teacherly voices had formed a moist scab that separated the wall from people's gazes. Reminder of the rain and sickly water streaming off houses on to the saffron-coloured ground, where it was gradually erased, as if shoe-soles cleaned away the unlikely faces etched on the mushy asphalt. It was as if an idea, intent on identifying the object it confronted, met the green, scaly-yellow of the school walls and dived into the sea to erase itself.

Luis and Armando looked at each other. Armando observed how at the same time as he began to feel the watery dampness evaporate from his navy blue jacket with its white stripes greying in the distance he saw how they also stood out in fresh colours that dried slowly, as if they'd had to think hard about it, and left on the queasy walls fly-legs, old faces that almost crumbled. Armando no longer looked at the damp, queasy walls, as if the rain had whiled away the time stretching taut deer skin over the walls, blown on stars, traced in a faint cartography of constellations. Armando's eyes swung slowly round, fell on the approaching Luis. He didn't say hello, only, 'Don't let's go in, the waves are raging against the Malecón and I want to see them.'

Pleased by this first word from Armando, the more youthful Luis greeted him first with concealed glee, then quickly responded, 'Come on.'

The dampness persisted, more evident on Luis's sweaty face than on his damp shoes. The last droplet lingered on the jewellers' shield, finally fell so rapidly that the absorption of the earth cried out. Luis seemed to be pondering the danger of another downpour, and the excuses he would make at home if his parents discovered their improvised walkabout. Although any question from Armando came too abruptly, he didn't look him in the face, like someone enjoying the presence of a misty mirror, imagining the lunar atmosphere as dense or relishing the baby food on his tongue. His strong feeling about skiving off school was too important to keep looking at Armando's face, although it's almost certain it showed in his eyes. However, each word from Armando was a look, and we might almost think he spoke so his words would culminate in Luis's eyes, rather than in any necessary response. We should, he was thinking, only go to school in the mornings, all else is excessive. It's true mornings are almost always damp, so that they soften things up, render words useless. When I see my aunt arrive oleaginously white and damp in the morning, her eyes screwed up and her clothes pulled roughly over her immobile body, I think I see her riding up on a cow and very slowly – as if we removed the sweaty covers from a plaster statue –

dismounting from the morning globe. To contemplate our morning cup of coffee is to create voluptuous rivalries, reduced almost to nought when schoolboys penetrate their academies. A rich taste penetrates each resistant pore, a pigeon dies colliding with a column of cigar smoke, seaweedy waters wash up the corpse of a blind sailor whose hands hang limply down, his tattooed nostrils revealing an effort of will to survive in waters muddied by spit and soggy scraps of paper.

At last they had reached their desired spot, gazed upon waves, then came a desperate emptiness rapidly filled by clouds. The landscape wore a distinctive appearance according to the style or distinctive manner of their gaze. Steely blue waves swirled round a fist on loan from a ferrous, seaweedy skeleton. The predictable audience assembled as ever in a city being blasé over a blazing fire, or lighting up an oil-lamp in a deluge. Somewhat distracted, Luis and Armando had reached the waves, all that did not seem their final purpose. It had served momentarily, but a more slippery secret pounded within them. Skiving school is the inner voice of crisis, of something we are casting off, of a flesh that can no longer forgive. They had missed an afternoon of school, and now they let their hands dangle down, tilted their heads, everybody was running, and Luis let his shoes get wet, never lifted his gaze from the next wave. He realized that it was a grey day, that they had truanted from school, that Armando was by his side occupying a magic space, doubly enclosed, a rhythmic space, because now and then his hand lifted to his hair wanting to force it into an unreal, shifting shape. His hair disobeyed him, escaped, as if that was not the right place for it to dream, refused the mastery of a hand it did not recognize as his. Luis imagined a few drops made little difference to his shoes. He had not heard the cries, the whitest scraps of paper which, as he escaped, he threw at the wave, which later graciously returned to forget and pick them up. The curving sweep of the waves, one wave's obscene assimilation of another created a vaporous mist cleansed of memories. As if the clouds converged above them, converting the truanting children

into damp archipelagos. A boat gently beats against them, and sees
itself slowly rejected by the hands of a clock. They changed direction,
the final purpose uniting them vanished imperceptibly. The words,
which bound them together became more tense, were to become
more arcane. Both began to turn inwards, to be unaware of the other.
They moved away from the waves, thought how tired of riding the
strand they would lose themselves in a more compromising
adventure. Rather than looking at the waves they had imagined them
entering the watery atmosphere they abandoned, a distant noise
reached them, one wave pushed against another, setting off curved
sounds tapering down to penetrate the cottony bays of inner ears. By
now they had decided to go for a walk. Their first excitement had
turned into the tolerable tedium of having to go for a walk. Armando
stared at one of the two buttons hanging from the white-striped blue
of Luis's suit, invariably he thought one was different, then began,
his pleasure renewed, to discover that they were identical. He no
longer waited on the next wave, but on the changing attraction of the
bluey buttons, the same, yet not the same, appeared, were
submerged. The wave spreading out, and then one button's
certainties and the other's improbabilities. This aqueous gaze
elongated asphalted fish. As if a crane, a complaisant bird were
absorbed by the demanding asphalt which could thus show off its
new brand of asphalted crane. All so diffuse, you couldn't say the
crane shield on the asphalt, like the one lingering over the raindrop
on the jeweller's advertisement. Luis shook, as if he'd collided with
a cloud or just been woken up. A deeper voice, less infused with
dampness, spoke out. He felt terrified, as when one discovers that of
the exquisite escaro fish only the intestines are edible. Luis felt the
invisible damp on his walk with Armando. No fixed point could
compel it: any line of illumination was so elongated it died in
electrified water. Marsh moon green, vibrant verdour of moon-lit
reeds. Carlos suddenly appeared – his name a compulsion, an
enslavement to comma and full stop – older than Armando, telling
him imperiously, the word Luis didn't utter, which he felt he heard

tearing him apart: 'Didn't we say we'd go to the cinema?' 'There's still time.' Drily, without looking at Luis, who has paled into insignificance, Armando says, 'Goodbye, I'm off.' Drily, without a decisive look, without a final attempt to identify the distinctive colour of the buttons on his white-striped blue jacket. New snowy birds lower their beaks upon mandolines that spell out numbered elegies. The dream thickens in the memory of that last wave which turned definitively to marble. The wave is the monster seeking out the alabaster cup when two wandering hands decide to disembark at the same time.

His gaze followed the curve of the seemingly futile breakwater, for the blurred waves stopped at a preordained place, traced on the crest of the wave and the seagull. He also saw how its arm whirled round, was lost, until it fell asleep, slowly curved round, driven on by the whirling seagulls which described invisible and not so invisible circles, for when he went to stretch out his arm he felt the spider-fish bite, and looking upwards he saw the seagull hide at a geometric angle, or fly into a large bowl of blown glass like an albino arrow. He could no longer isolate the memory of the spider-fish, or the gently curving swoop of the gently compassionate seagulls. He could not separate the matches from the needles in his chrome alloy trinket box. Nor the book of questions from honeysuckle answers, from clusters of corals, or from the rottenest anemones. The clouds swiftly parted to reveal a bleeding castle. The weaned clouds turned that mother-of-pearl death agony a slightly deeper shade of pink. In the wake of the circling seagulls a dozen adolescents appeared, hiding their creamy flutes in the sands, leaving their buried ears as souvenirs. At the centre of the goldfish bowl float a dozen tiny Roman warriors.

He sat on the wall, the water no longer washed back from the stones. It headed stealthily for the inner ears, washing against the castle, with no bell or hunting dog to cleave that damp, to enliven the opportunities in the secret rush of waves. He saw how marine monotony opened out in sleepy eddies, sighted a tired strip of seaweed green, pearly grey, a frozen intuition, an ebbing secret. A wavelet appeared, created by the matted reeds, guided only by the sound of fish twisting around to peck each other on the neck; it seemed that once alerted, the seaweed began faintly to hear its name, went to lace itself to the stone. A moment of frustration and the seaweed separated out, rather queasily, settled back in the same spot. Luis Keeler felt the fixity of the seaweed, also felt its invisible race towards the mossy breakwater. Seaweed holding there, like a crown descending to the foot of the castle that was bleeding over the river. Seaweed clamouring for the kingdom of unending sleep. Between the traces of the quail and the root of the castle, the photograph delicately taken from the shadow of the noisy swell could guarantee a surging array of seaweed strands.

As the seaweed washed for the last time against the crumbling stone, Luis Keeler descended into sleep. A light sleep, surrounded by seaweed, cottonwool, by hands lightly touching a bag of sand and lace. Letters from Persia, quails of domestic service, goldfish bowls overturned after the crime. In its desire to find the last word and the level of the dream, the quail tugged desperately at his lips. In paradise water flowed once more and heaven is created. The line of the breakwater lengthened, and he too was being stretched, thinned out. He felt the thought escaping him, the way he had felt the traces of the quail, to occupy the centre of that renowned, different seaweed that could show off its pride and wilful promenades. The unsatisfied touch could no longer be prolonged in the look or in that last fragment of his lips. Dreamed densely as if by someone able to talk with their mouth full of water. An absolutist seaweed separating out the mirror of wandering thoughts from memories and from clouds.

He crossed over a marine line that had been drawn by the reeds before they had turned into humming-birds. The last one spread over Luis Keeler's body, also falling asleep in the leafy foliage of his nerves. One of his eyes, transfixing the porcelain globe, now brought together with the drill for the garnet stones, focused on the fingertip of the nimblest of bandits. And was victorious, a little wheel ran the distance that separated the look from the ashen object.

Afterwards the other eye stared at the decorations left by the carapace of boiling waters, of lavas and stings. Now he stood up, the seaweed departed and the boundary of the breakwaters erased, and the night soaked his entrails, grew like a tree shaking the ink from its branches. It would have been right to shout out, but at that moment the cinema cages were emptying and from the clamorous lives of the seaweed arose an absolute system of illumination. Shouting out would have meant breaking a foot, intuiting the final flourishes of the seaweed or the way blood circulates in garnet rock.

TRANSLATED BY PETER BUSH

Twelve Real Beauties
Carlos Montenegro

Plácido, the cock-breeder, pretended to doze off. The colt he rode was already resigned to doing likewise. And so they crossed town. Until they'd left behind the barracks and crossroads by La Pastora, they'd be play-acting. Plácido said it was a trick he'd learned from dogs which take to the centre of the street, their tails down and heads bowed, when they enter unknown territory, some – with the most savvy – even limp along. Their performance was saying, 'Respected doggy brothers, with your permission I'll go my way, I'm old, tired and half lame.' The 'respected doggy brothers' know all the tricks, because they've worked them in their own time, and allow a free passage, simply warning them not to leave their visiting cards on electricity posts or street corners. Now, it's a doggish tendency to infringe this rule, but not all dogs are brave enough to lift a leg; whence – we assume – that most vulgar of utterances, 'So-and-so is the biggest piss-artist.'

Once past La Pastora, horseman and steed were transformed. Plácido sat upright; gathering the reins in his left hand, he pressed on his spurs and dropped his right arm by his side in a statuesque pose, as the colt cantered sprightly off, its legs weaving fretful filigrees. They no longer needed to pretend they were not in a hurry or had nothing to fear. From being naturally lethargic, they now acquired a typically rebel profile.

On this occasion we will relate an incident that honours both Plácido and all the anonymous figures who helped give us a land without foreign masters. That day Plácido, the cock-breeder, had additional reasons for playing it cannily: his saddle bags were full of loose salt for the insurgents, as well as two yarey palm-leaf hats, a

thick roll of bandaging and a drop of quinine. The 'wurst' was the
salt, because there was so much, and it annoyed Plácido; and the
yarey hats annoyed him even more. 'They risk their hides in the hills
yet give themselves airs as if death in a new hat were less painful and
wild rat meat didn't fill your belly, however tasteless. The spoilt brats!'
A bag of nerves in the streets by the barracks, Plácido saw it this way:
'I don't mind them being desperate for a *paraguayo*, for no way can a
soldier fight without a machete. The same goes for the lead for their
shotguns; and bandages, there's always give and take; and quinine,
'cause malaria is no believer in ideals, though everyone knows it prefers Spaniards. But, hell, if our compadres have decided to risk their
lives for freedom, why do they need so much salt, let alone so much
yarey. Can't they leave their favourite things for later?'

Don Cipriano, the owner of La Pastora, had a 'nephew' who was
another of the reasons why Plácido wasn't completely at ease. As he
fetched and carried for the insurgents, to put on a front and catch up
on the gossip he had gone into the store ostensibly for an early-
morning drink. That was only a week ago. While the nephew was
getting a glass for his rum, he said, 'The sergeant's after a fellow who
passed through with a new yarey and came back carrying only an
empty bag.'

And Plácido, putting on a brave face, immediately retorted, 'So
what? Do only rebels wear palm-leaf hats?'

'Look. They say the fellow takes messages for the insurgents. The
fact is, the sergeant ordered us to add yareys to the list.'

There was no one else in the store. Plácido gulped down his drink,
thinking, 'Just as well this retarded shit-bag's tongue is bigger than
his brain . . .' That wasn't all, way back Don Cipriano had really
wound him up. Knowing he was reputed to be a loyal son of their
land, Plácido risked buying a bag of loose salt. When Don Cipriano
looked enormously suspicious, Plácido let slip an excuse he had
ready: 'The bandits killed one of my steers and I need some salt to
cure the leather.' And he thought he had clinched it with a 'Long live
New and Old Spain!' Plácido's only known passion was for fighting

cocks. He was a living Bible on the subject. Nurturing that credit balance and concealing his other great weakness, which came from his creole spirit, he'd no problem meeting up in the pit with the sergeant, whose rank never got in the way of such gifts from God: he never missed a fight. Outside the pit, he was all hatred and cruelty towards the 'traitors'. Anyone brought into his presence suspected of favouring the rebels went in fear and trembling, and never left – if he did leave – as he had gone in. That – and everything else we've mentioned – buzzed round Plácido's head as he pretended to be asleep riding through the town. To calm himself down, he imagined he was at the pit the previous Sunday where he'd lost a cock that was a 'real tiger'. Despite its reputation and a winning run of five fights without losing a feather, Plácido had had doubts about the cock. He was less than convinced by such facility. In the first skirmishes, he pressed savagely in, put his opponent against the boards and, in a single flurry, gouged and beat his enemy to the floor. Sure, he was 'classy', but not 'top class'. He had yet to show how he'd react to punishment at the moment of truth. And that moment came last Sunday: Plácido's bird was all shiny and preening while his adversary, a mangy specimen, made the best of a bad job and went for the plumage of the odds-on winner, hacking away with his talons until Plácido's bird stopped dead in its tracks, raised a bewildered head and looked for an escape route from such a savaging.

The sergeant bellowed above the hullabaloo, 'Get up, rooster, you're from Jerez!'

In seconds Plácido's bird stretched out like a broody hen, lay its head tamely on the sawdust and offered itself up to the slaughter.

'Pick it up. Plácido, it'll make a good stud! ' shouted one Creole.

In the tense silent moment that followed, all eyes turned to the Bible, who muttered, 'Brute strength. Otherwise, he's as "soft as sweet potato". . .'

That was last Sunday and, now trying to lose himself in his pretend nap, fretting over his kilos of loose salt and yarey hats, Plácido wondered whether he wasn't also 'soft as sweet potato'. It was so easy to just to snuff it! Half consoled by the idea of his advancing years, he thought he heard someone call out.

He didn't turn round until the shouting drew nearer: 'Hey, you . . . Are you deaf?'

A soldier was coming towards him, his gun slung over his shoulder. 'The sergeant wants you. I've been after you all morning.'

It wasn't the usual tone for arresting people, but Plácido had too much evidence in his saddlebags not to feel up against the wall. Right then he thought he wasn't in the same class as his late lamented fighting cock. Old, lean, lanky, used to rushing in, a mulatto go-between, ever ready to turn round and give up. But what could he do if his moment had come? He looked tense as he asked, 'Why does the sergeant want to see me?'

Plácido reduced all experiences to lessons he'd learn with his fighting cocks. Not only did he defend the theory that brute strength wasn't enough, since it didn't prevent what he called being as 'soft as sweet potato'; he had another which was quite contrary – what he used to say when a scheming bird left his 'tender care': 'It knows too much to play clever.' They rush in, parry with their head, like it was a sword, run off, suddenly turn round, hit out and kill. He'd had more than one like that. But one unlucky day they escaped, flew off, cock-a-doodled, missed every target and ended up in a pot of rice. That's fate. Needless to say, Plácido knew nothing about philosophy or the golden mean; but learning about fighting cocks he'd discovered it wasn't about being very brutish or being a know-all. Both kinds are in danger of being killed by a 'rat'.

The soldier didn't know why his sergeant wanted to see Plácido. 'He said to me, "Do you know Plácido, the cock-breeder?" And, no, I didn't know you. "All right," the boss added, "ask around and tell him to come and see me as soon as possible. Be as friendly as you can." That's all he said.'

Hell, if only he hadn't got the salt, the darned hats, the bandaging, the quinine . . . what else was he carrying? . . . Then there was the gossip, he couldn't exactly fly out of the pit like an escaping cock. If the soldier had bumped into him at the cockfight, on the outskirts of the town, no way could they have 'pulled' him in . . . He slowed his horse down, all he could think of was throwing out handfuls of salt, and making sure the soldier didn't see him. The fact is, man is the most brutish of brutes. One day at the cockfight, they'd been talking about animal brain-power. Somebody said horses were really clever. The owner of a saltpan used to weigh one down with sacks of salt. It was a long haul and the horse reached its destination worn out. A once- or twice-weekly event. Once, when the horse was crossing a ford, it slipped and fell into the river. After they pulled it out, the animal realized its load was lighter and decided to slip up again. The third time it happened its owner beat it soundly and sold it to a sugar mill, where the wretched animal died going round and round the press. Too clever by half! Plácido could draw no comfort for he wouldn't have a third chance. The sergeant would cut him dead first time.

While he was remembering the story he took a handful of salt and threw it over his shoulder as if to fend off misfortune; the soldier saw him and asked him what he was doing. The breeder of fighting cocks smiled sourly: 'You know, soldier, it's a clean-up.'

The soldier didn't understand. When they reached the barracks, Plácido was barely rid of any of the salt. The soldier's words sent a chill through him: 'Take the horse inside. It might be a long job.'

What could he do! In the sergeant's office Plácido's hadn't the glimmer of an idea. The beast was shut up there, pacing up and down. Fists like hams. When he heard him, the sergeant lifted up his head and everything seemed to change.

'You finally got here; I was losing patience.'

He stood up, placed his big hands on Plácido's shoulders and stared him in the eye. 'I want the truth. Be straight . . . Come on . . . A sip of good creole coffee for our fellow countryman.'

Plácido felt his insides turn liquid. The things men go through! The whole truth and nothing . . . The only truth Plácido had at that moment, and this isn't a snide remark, was a soft hunk of sweet potato.

'I want you to take a look at something and then tell me it straight. This way.'

The sergeant turned round so abruptly, Plácido almost put his hands over his face in order to ward off the blow. He followed the sergeant into an inside yard. Twelve big birdcages were lined up there. The sergeant stood and stared at Plácido as if he were the Virgin Mary. 'Well! What do you think? Ever seen anything like it?'

Without belittling his high ideals, Plácido was first and foremost the King of the Cockfight. Lots were in the other business where he was only a 'carrier pigeon'. But he was king when it came to the big cages. And a cock's great qualities always included Plácido's 'tender care'. He was a patriot because he was born a Cuban and maybe because it's a contradiction to dub a cinnamon cock a 'pink'un'. Oblivious to all, Plácido went from one cage to the next, getting more excited by the moment. When he reached the last one, he flung his arms wide and exclaimed, 'Twelve fighting cocks! Twelve real beauties!'

With tears in his eyes, the sergeant split his sides laughing and asked, 'What? What do you mean?'

He could have gone on asking that question for the rest of his days.

'So they're twelve fighting cocks?'

'Real beauties!'

Plácido opened a cage and took a bird out. His hands cradled it soothingly, rocked it and, once the bird was quiet, he put his fingers between its shanks, lifted it up to see its profile.

'What a bird! . . . The kingdom of Spain is his for the taking!'

The sergeant looked at the king, in ecstasy.

The coffee arrived, which Plácido gulped down, thinking it must be cyanide he was shaking so much. Opposite was the passage that led to the sergeant's office. On the table were his saddlebags – and the yarey hats! Those handsome specimens had left him speechless. He looked at the high walls around him. He couldn't have flown over them even on the wings of twelve fighting cocks. As he watched the soldier coming along the passage, he didn't hear the sergeant say, 'One will be yours. Nobody can match you and with my twelve fighting cocks you'll be king of the world . . . What's the matter? Don't you feel well?'

He seemed the more anxious of the two. A moment before he'd been the happiest man on earth. His habitual cruelty was a professional hatred he had acquired; this joy over his twelve fighting cocks was innate, elemental, that of a simple son of the glebe, the furrow or the sea.

'Out with it. What's the matter? You've gone a deathly pale.'

The soldier was a few steps away, deferential, wanting to pass on news of the find. His sergeant rebuffed him violently. 'What do you want now? Leave me in peace!' But the soldier walked over, whispered in his ear. Plácido felt cornered. His moment of truth had come. He felt the enemy's spurs driving into his skull. Fuck! Was he going to surrender without lifting his feet off the sawdust, showing he was as 'soft as sweet potato'? The sergeant bore down on him, raging, shouting, 'Idiots! . . . You're all idiots!' Why right now? For the first time in his life as a colonial soldier, the prospect of crushing the enemy made him see red. Hell, if they don't need looking after any more, let them sort themselves out . . .

Plácido didn't run for it. He knew he had to move quickly and make up for lost time. He leaned his arm on the sergeant's muscular shoulder. 'You realized what was the matter?'

The sergeant nodded imperceptibly. He heard him sigh at the line the wretch was taking. 'Tricks of the trade. You have to hide them or they get blown. I just saw the salt on your table and thought my secret was out.'

A distant glimmer of hope calmed the sergeant's rage. Didn't this sad case know he'd just been told the whole story, even about the jobs Don Cipriano did for him, the storekeeper, the leader of the 'volunteers'?

Plácido saw the hesitation on his face. He had to make a quick move. 'Tell me when you want to fight them. Wait. This is what I should be telling you . . . First, don't clip them; make sure you ease them in and they don't feel exposed. And not a word to anyone.'

He put his hand to his mouth, realizing he was going to ask him about the salt. 'Let's make a start. Bring me a big handful of salt.'

He lowered his voice to a whisper: 'As they're a Jerez breed, some smart-arses feed them peppers when it's their blood pressure that needs to be down. Every morning a dose of coarse salt so their blood won't boil and leave them as defenceless as roasting chickens.'

He was interrupted by the sergeant's guffaws. Fruit of his reviving spirits, they flew along the walls of the passage, where the soldiers couldn't believe their ears. But he was still something of a colonial sergeant. 'And what about the yarey palm leaves?'

'Oh, that's common knowledge. It's the only way to transport them; sacks harm them. And as for the quinine – don't mosquitoes bite fighting cocks? And the bandage protects their feet when they're tied up.'

'Hah, hah, hah! I'll have those swine marching every day. And old Don Cipriano can stay behind his counter. They nearly spoilt the show . . . Really, how was I ever going to work out a Jerez fighting cock needed so much salt!'

Plácido spent the whole day inventing whatever needed inventing for the 'tender care' of his Jerez birds. Two bottles of cognac were uncorked. At dusk they hugged each other and said goodbye. 'A last word of advice. For heaven's sake, don't ever again call a cinnamon a "pink'un".'

And Plácido was helped on to his colt, which, scenting so much soldiery, decided to leave at a resigned trot. 'No, my son, get cantering. Let's get to the pit in the jungle, 'cause the one in town will soon be a cemetery for the Jerez cocks. I'm sorry for their sakes. They are twelve real beauties.'

TRANSLATED BY PETER BUSH

A Conciliar Discourse
Virgilio Piñera

Nobody could know beforehand what time the council would begin. The Pope had said in no uncertain terms that it would begin when it began. After all, if it were such an important event, why worry about fixing a definite starting time? The most important, most dramatic things in life, the Pontiff seemed to be affirming, should be marked out by being improvised and surprising. When one imagines life will explode from pressure or welter of incident, one soon realizes that it won't and that events take their course uninterrupted.

Something like this happened with my selection as cameraman for the *World Papacy News*, which was, I think, the chanciest of chances. When my boss informed the Pontiff that the chosen one was our leading cameraman, the Pope sent a cablegram rejecting the man designated precisely, he said, because of the designation, asking for someone to be sent not expressly chosen for the occasion.

A product of this papal prerequisite, I found myself in the *Città Eterna*. Apparently like everything else in life, eternity is born, grows and dies. And so dead was the *Città Eterna* where I paced that I smelt the stench of mummification. In vain did my feet trip the light fantastic over the dead slabs of the Appian Way. There was nothing to be done: I couldn't summon the past into the present, and the present mockingly surveyed the past. Then a bird sang: the mechanical movement of my hand to my chest, and the thought transforming the current warble into an identical trill from the reign of Augustus disabled today's bird, which was struck down from its branch on high. Executed by the poison of eternity.

The council would be celebrated in the Palazzo de la Signatura. As I went in, Cardinal Gaetano huffed his way towards me and whispered that His Holiness would quiz me about the enormous poster hanging down the façade of the palazzo. I should respond sarcastically; deny that any such poster existed. The Cardinal went off.

'Don't you think it's deserved? The best bit of redundant Latin I could think of. We must bring the Church down a peg or two.'

And the Pontiff pointed to the flashing neon letters: Roma finita, causa locuta.

'Of course! For ever and ever, amen,' I replied with a handshake that shook him from head to toe.

'If we carry on like this, I think that the famous, much-trumpeted eternity of Rome . . .' and he went quiet for a moment. Then asked ironically, 'How does it feel to be in finite eternity?'

'Eternally ephemeral.'

The Pope smiled. He stared at me.

'We have so many distractions,' he said suddenly. 'I want to make the Church a circus, a stadium. We must get supporters. I'll pay one dollar twenty per convert. Now shut up. I can sense you want to be polemical.'

I had gestured in astonishment. He continued, 'Being and not being polemical amount to much the same thing. Why not waggle your big toe or scrump the apples of paradise? Why not open a can of frankfurters? Why not show a shoulder, or hide a hand? Or listen to this kind of dialogue? "How's culture doing?" "Very culturally?" "And the Navy?" "Very navally." "And the fodder?" "Very fodderily."'

I interrupted him to ask, 'And what about the onions?'

'No deal. There are no onions. You won't buy an onion in Rome for your own weight in gold. On the other hand, we can hunt butterflies, the beautiful butterflies whose myriad hues glisten amongst nature's imperfections. Oh, the darling butterflies pitied for being in jail, and the little dears applauded for being in jail. No, there are no onions; only butterflies, as round as eternity and as dead as eternity. Where can my soul be?'

Outside not a single curious bystander. I found that strange. The least eternal aspect of all this eternity was the eternal bystanders, beings who gather by palace entrances or chancellery exits, in a midwife's chambers or opposite a fairground magician. I couldn't see them anywhere. In its infinite eternity, the majestic entrance to the Palazzo de la Signatura seemed free of eternal bystanders. The night, with its bonfires and cries of the newly born, was also ephemerally eternal. Where can one find the eternal bystander, who can tell one something is forbidden, sealed off, concealed? I felt triviality was beginning to threaten that finite eternity.

It was two a.m. when hot chocolate, concocted according to the Vatican's secret recipe, was served. They call it *Chocolat à l'Éternel*, in a subtle allusion to eternity.

As he sipped, the Pope confided that he was party to the nature of both the assassin and the assassinated. 'Just imagine, cameraman, eternity is born from such a mixture. All those cardinals expect a miracle, think the dagger will sink between my seventh and eighth ribs. Or equally think, with the old modes of thought they suffer from, that I'll flourish a cardboard weapon. Then they will rush to the world's press to announce that the Holy Father, a suicide, is at the same time murdered and alive. Such is the rubbish that prospers and is propagated.'

He was silent for a moment. Finite eternity continued gyrating around his axis. 'What's more, I belong to the Opefaf and the Opifaf.'

'I'm in the Opefaf,' I said, showing him a small armband I extracted from a jacket pocket.

'Very funny. From now on you also belong to the Opifaf,' and he handed me an armband bearing the motto: 'We Opifafs will overcome.' 'You know, the approach that reduces everything to the absurd: if you belong simultaneously to two hostile organizations, you end up neutralizing the lethal power of both. Our aim' – and his voice acquired a ridiculously resonant timbre – 'is to show the best films that deal with the Opefaf and the Opifaf. There's no world market yet, but we have high hopes of this council meeting.'

At that moment, one of the loudspeakers, set up in the left corner of the vast hall, began to emit brief calls for silence. To encourage people to shut their mouths, the announcer recommended exercising the muscles of lower and upper lips. By the time he was beginning to doubt the workability of the exercise, I'd barely had time to synchronize my lips; the entire hall was engaged in the pleasurable exercise of opening and closing theirs. Nobody could refuse to open and to close. What else, at such a moment, could replace the fascinating exercise? An intellectual's delusion, his mirage, arises from the trifling fact of his own intelligence. Why not follow the impulse of the moment and, on the contrary, insist on the best method, on the finest pedigree, a well-fitted shoe or a well-made-up face?

Then the loudspeaker announced that a gentleman wanted to tell a story. A man emerged from a mass of women to say, 'The man who is going to die by the noose tells the tyrant who is sentencing him, "The only thing you can't do is die for me on the beautiful scaffold you have built."'

The narrator's final words were greeted by vicious cat-calls. At once people bellowed out that the story was boring, insipid or straining after clever-cleverness. 'Be silent for the rest of your days,' some people shouted.

Straight away, sobbing their eyes out, they approached the narrator and bombarded him with tears. The man defended himself with roars of laughter, but when these were drenched in tears, he had no choice but to beg for mercy.

'The tyrant sentences the man, who dies sentenced by the tyrant.'

'Less rhetoric, less polish, less tyrant, less man and more noise.'

The narrator exclaimed, 'Paf to paf. One paf to stop another . . .'

Delirious bursts of applause. And exclamations: 'Brilliant! Not at all boring, so limpid.' The ladies embraced the narrator, the gentlemen kissed him on the cheeks, and he hugged ladies and gentlemen. As in a supreme offering to that trivialized multitude, he opened and closed his lips five times, so skilfully, so precisely and cleanly that the trivialization penetrated deeper into the intimate folds of their souls and brought forth what is commonly denominated the music of the spheres.

Such a thought – a sky-blue vision of unfettered melodies – led me by the hand to old ideas of roundness, circles, heavens. As thought's only value is its movement, I began to think about my camera lens, which is also round. That's why thought is the only antidote against the poison of time. After all the complications, serious faces, profound reflections, universal soulfulness, the world's striking simplicity floated to the surface. This was borne out by the fact that anyone could be happy and admired in life just by uttering, let's say, the word 'bun'. This word could contain the thoughts of brainy philosophers, poets and novelists, of that whole self-important crowd. And 'bun' was the equal of the vain philosopher's complete oeuvre.

Just as a fingernail rescues a finger from a splinter, something totally unexpected came to my aid. I felt myself being touched on both shoulders at the same time. A hand on each shoulder. But they belonged to a single body. Man's guile is so limited! I had thought that one hand belonged to the Opefaf and the other to the Opifaf. How obsessed I was with particular schema! Couldn't I see that those organizations were commercial products, every wit the same as pharmaceutical goods or ladies' wear? Why continue that foolish masquerade of respectability, of the right word, of saying 'no' because I'd just said 'yes'? What would happen if I switched products? Nothing, a billion times, nothing. Those hands which belonged to the same body had just taught me the supreme lesson. To what heights of thought was the devil of disputation sweeping me. The height of randomness, of knowing that very soon, perhaps right now, my camera lens would stop working for me. For a time, photos would be objects of infinite repulsion.

'Let's go,' the Pope said, clasping both my hands.

'To heaven, Your Holiness?'

'Neither heaven nor hell; those are allegories in paint. No, let's conspire and deconspire,' he elaborated jocularly.

'I would like to know if the conspiracy and deconspiracy offices are very far apart. I don't have much time; besides, the council may start any moment. You know there's no set time.'

'No,' he said in the same jocular tone, 'no offices at all . . . The Opefaf and the Opifaf have bypassed the old methods. D'you see that over there? D'you see that human ball, undulating, concertinaing, swelling out and turning inwards; d'you see that centripetal, centrifugal ball? That's where we're heading.'

Mechanically I followed in the Pope's footsteps. The human ball wasn't more than twenty metres from where we stood, but it must have been warned of our imminent arrival. Before I could attach myself, half an hour passed by. It moved like a starfish or a leaf floating on a rippling stream, and its very movement contained a sarcastic definition of life. It didn't drastically avoid contact, but, at the same time, what a ridiculous tilt to its rump, what a grotesque intensity to its to and froing! A revelation: the ball communicated its rhythm to me. I stopped my normal movement to follow the rhythm of the ball. I soon became aware that its strength resided in the infinite desire to imitate which it infused. It became like one of those infusory species of animals, endowed only with a mouth and an anus, whose pathetic contracting and retracting rule out exegesis, purity and impurity, eternal laws, predestination, the consolations of religion, military magazines, literary sects, maturity and immaturity, conventional lies and truths . . .

But the ball also grew with successive accretions. I soon realized the whole gathering was following the ball's capricious movements. As it bounced along, all those in the council assembly hall attached themselves to its mass. Here's the rub, the secret reason: we were all dancing its dance. Till then we felt proudly in possession of our own steps, our *sui generis* dance, our inherited castle . . . but the blessed ball levelled us, made little balls of us all – little meat or moth balls – alas, both faceless and characterless.

Suddenly the ball undulated my way, and I stuck to it like a fly to honey. Newly born to the maelstrom of the trivial, I was surrounded by Opefafs and Opifafs, by daggers, by tonsures. It was an orgy of identification, where you can't look me in the face, for you'd see your own; no, don't speak to me, I'm already speaking to you, like that, our thoughts colliding in the air – little balls shooting off at the speed of sound, bang! That's right, the ball's called Bang, everything it hits turns into a ball. How could one know, for what reason, to what end, with what solid arguments, what constituted Opefaf and Opifaf, what you don't say because of what I'm saying, air or water, wisdom or sarcasm, a parallelepiped or an ellipsis, solipsism or tomato sauce, Procrustean bed or heavenly music?

The ball was implacable, but stupid as well. It got fatter and fatter . . . One could be equally above or below, eat or not eat, for it ate for everyone, fattened, inflated, dilated, expanded. Now it was touching the ceiling; now the lamps were balls, the columns were balls, sparrows and the roundness of eternity were formalized. The ball was an invasion by leaps and bounds, was irresistible. Very soon the hall in the palazzo was but a plaster mask of the ball, a species of bell jar against the impact of the dialectic.

Then the ball, putting on a Betty Boop voice, exclaimed, 'I declare the council open.'

A thousand voices were heard repeating the word. 'What is a council? Why not a cincil?' A real shouting match ensued. 'If it's not a cincil, we don't want anything to do with it.' Others suggested a councol. The hubbub was infernal. The Pope ordered silence. The ball went quiet.

The Pope brandished a coin and spoke in stentorian tones: 'Heads or tails!'

Suddenly new cries of rejection rose up.

'Heads? What is heads? What is tails?'

The Pope put the coin away and ordered Cardinal Gaetano to explain both words.

'Well, heads is heads and tails is tails.'

The ball burst out laughing. The globular lamps shone so brilliantly that flesh became translucent, fleeting as time, like a carriage silhouetted in the fog with its horses and charioteer.

'I cannot declare the council open.'

Unrestrained, torrential, sick-making, haemorrhaging laughter. Now the ball revealed a mysterious transparency.

He kneeled down.

'I can't do it like this either.'

He sat down.

'I can also do it sitting down.'

He lay down.

'Or stretched out.'

He sat astride the cardinal; he stood up, his legs apart, his legs closed, he lifted his hands, lowered them, crouched down, twisted round, straightened up, put his hands in his mouth, sang, whistled, laughed, cried, but he couldn't; he just couldn't.

But equally he could.

'I can.'

Unrestrained, torrential, sick-making, haemorrhaging laughter.

He kneeled down.

'I can do it on my knees.'

He sat down.

I can also do it sitting down.'

He lay down.

'And lying down.'

He sat astride the cardinal; he stood up, his legs apart, his legs closed, his eyes closed, his eyes open; he raised his hands, lowered them, crouched down, twisted round, straightened up; he put his hands in his mouth, sang, whistled, laughed, cried; he could, he just could.

The ball booed and cheered.

'I can and I can't,' shouted the Pope.

Abysses, cesspits! Dachshunds barking out of tune, elephants bellowing, frogs croaking, trains hooting, sighs freezing on lips, unheard-of violence, at this 'papal can and can't', the eternal, conflictive, rehearsed, glossed, melancholy, suppurating, chryselephantine doubt of Hamlet. In this contrast one perceived the whole horror of eternity, of fame, the infinite, the pathetic battle that is joined to inject beauty into the soul of the beautiful and ugliness into the soul of the ugly. We hold up a mirror in order to be reflected, and think that what we see is our own image. Seeing oneself reflected through psychological truths, eternal truths, the truths of religion and the truths of the people. And perfection hovering over everyone like a prettified atom bomb!

There, on the contrary, nothing would be engraved in letters of gold, nothing would conspire to be the butt of sufficiency, appearance and flight . . . *Passed away!* A new being, not at all eternal, quite corruptible, who would always be welcomed with hoots of laughter. Give me a spin and I'll support the world!

As there were no protocol formalities, they proceeded to a free examination of the three eternal themes, whose comic potential could not be revealed, still held in theology's millenary thrall.

How happy, content, radiant the doctrines of grace, transubstantiation, hypostasis now revealed themselves! Everyone applauded, quite moved. Grace so gracious, transubstantiation so transubstantiated, hypostasis so hypostasized! This triggered some delightful sneezing.

The mistake arose because they had been taken seriously for centuries. Yet like the god Janus, they were serious and amusing. And like a turtle, the council had turned them over to make them an object of ridicule.

Then ten theologians dressed entirely in black came forward and stood to the right of the Pope. Immediately, the same number of anti-theologians, dressed in bright red, stood to the papal left. The free examination was about to begin.

Theologians and anti-theologians fused in such a tight embrace that they assumed the shape of the ball. At the same time, their movements were so rapid that one could see only black and red stripes. A little later, their speed was so vertiginous that one's sight could appreciate only whitish expanses, like an array of saltpans. Two objects unequal in themselves equal to themselves as a result of the effect of speed or . . . the absurd. One spin! Now it was impossible to distinguish theologian and anti-theologian in the ball. And yet – how distressing! – the effect of the confusion was to reach pinnacles of harmony, empyrean melodies. How can one possibly go on living after the horrible sensation caused by the clash of ten theologians and ten anti-theologians? And, nevertheless, one does, and it is precisely this sensation which is behind truth and life.

At that moment the following words came up on the illuminated screen:

INFUSION, FUSION, REFUELLING,
FUELLING, PROFUSION, SPINFUSION

The screen went blank. The theologians swapped their black clothes for the red of the anti-theologians. The latter went from papal left to papal right, and the former, from papal right to papal left. Once more they fused in tight embrace. One could see black and red stripes; then only white stripes; whitish expanses like an array of saltpans came to mind. Then nothing came to mind. They'd finished their number.

They repeated their little number, and by dint of repetition it stuck in everyone's mind, like a dagger. Nobody asked for it, nobody meditated on it, no spectator would comment to his neighbour in the ball whether he thought it a good or bad number. Everyone was the number, carried it within himself; it was second nature and no spectacle. Now the tension became so powerful that the ball threatened to explode.

Cardinal Gaetano went over to the Pope. 'Your Holiness, it's four a.m. It's time for the sufficiency test.'

As if absorbed in deep thought, the Pope let his gaze wander across the hall and, raising his right hand as if to deliver the *urbis et orbe* blessing, he said, 'At four, the sufficiency test; at five, my assassination; at six, the sun . . .'

The cardinal put a cane in his hand. The Pope was now a schoolmaster. Two servants brought a blackboard; another brought chalk; one left a boardrubber; a fourth, a globe of the world.

'Your attention,' said the Pope. 'The lesson is about to begin.'

He wrote the following revealing words on the blackboard: 'What is the Holy Mother Catholic Church?'

A thousand voices repeated the question loudly, softly, screaming, laughing, amid bouts of coughing and convulsions.

'Top marks to everybody,' said the Pope proudly. 'I can see you are all on top of the subject. So the Holy Mother!'

And the question 'the Holy Mother?' set off a Gregorian chant. The papal method was to answer question with question. Soon one would see the same happening with the reply. With a movement of the lips, the reply was repeated in the form of a question. Give me a spin and I'll support the world!

The Pope tapped abruptly twice on the edge of the blackboard. The class continued.

'Struggles between the pontificate and the empire,' wrote the Pope.

Struggles between the pontificate and the empire?' replied the flock.

The effect was reaching its climax. The Pope rubbed his hands and even drew some cartoons. There was the blind alley, a congested cart, a gladiator fallen on the sand, a gagged theoretician . . . How strange! The topic suggested needed only those two little tails, two little fly legs that make up question marks, to become the wall most resistant to disquisition. How is it possible, mother nature, battered image of solemnity, funereal vision of infallibility, that by turning the subject into a question and the question into laughter hours of exposition, vinegary visages, sly jabs, convoluted minds and subtleties of sacred texts could be invalidated?

The Pope wrote down in the form of a question 'Struggles

between the pontificate and the empire?' *Ipso facto*, the ball turned it into a subject and immediately offered it up as a question. A vicious circle and ecumenical guffaws resulted.

A general recess. Animated little groups. The chitchat that followed created the curious effect of the tick-tock of a watch. Let's take a look at the situation.

OSWALD:	I'm thinking of buying a bicycle.
ANTHONY:	They say prices have rocketed.
DARIO:	Mine's ten years old.
PAUL:	I like a bicycle with good handlebars.
PETER:	My father owned a bicycle shop.
AMALIA:	They say they're expensive.
JOHN:	Apparently, there's a shortage of raw materials.
EUGENIO:	Adolf, do you remember my yellow bicycle? It lost a wheel.
THOMAS:	And what are you thinking of doing?
ERNEST:	I take the children for a ride on mine.
CLARA:	It was so funny the day you fell off with the children!
AURELIA:	What a day that was! Everybody in the mud.
ALEXANDER:	No need to exaggerate. If you can handle a bicycle properly, there's no real danger.
CARLITOS:	Did you see what the guy in the circus did on his bicycle?
MANUEL:	Weaved in and out.
ROSENDRO:	Right, he spends the whole day pedalling!
EULOGIO:	I reckon a bicycle is very useful.
CONRAD:	But also very tricky.
ISMAEL:	Like women . . .
IGNATIUS:	Do you remember old Conrad's bicycle? A very big wheel and one tiny one.
JOSEPH:	And have you got a bicycle?

He slightly raised his voice as he directed the question at me, because he was a good way away. I shouted that I had and that I'd worked in a bicycle workshop. The bicycle conversation was infinite, was renewed imperceptibly, broadening out in such style that nobody could be remotely aware of its innumerable components. As one wave gives birth to another, and one bicycle to another, the bicyclical exchanges propagated themselves. And the exchanges obliged one to sit comfortably, to roll cigarettes, to enjoy the gentle breeze mysteriously invading the hall, through either the skylights or the ventilation slits. Bicycles led to relaxation, distension, fusion and spinfusion, but relaxation, distension, fusion and spinfusion did not lead to the subject of bicycles, as one might have thought. I was fascinated by the exchanges and was about to complain that because of the ball's special configuration, it would be impossible for me to catch the fine detail of these memorable dialogues when, as I turned round, resigned to my fate, to insert myself in other conversations, I heard the word *bicycle*, gleaming, spinning powerfully. In front or behind, next to me or wherever – the sad notion of destination had been lost – and everybody was talking about bicycles.

A sort of chubby dwarf was telling his wife, 'When I was a kid bicycles were more expensive but the bicycle was no motorbike and it was real fun I didn't ride but stood on one and people should remember Fidencio riding on his old bicycle pulled by a bicycle boy inside the repair shop lots of bicycles tomorrow I'm going to see some new bicycles let me tell you about Matilde's bicycle it was a woman's but one of her inner tubes burst she probably fell ill because the bicycle wasn't mended in time when I walk through the repair shop I can see a whole row of them and a red one I really like and . . .'

He shut up. The Pope was standing on the conference table, staring upwards, getting ready to deliver his bicyclical summing-up: 'Let us hope that bicyclical production is speeded up as quickly as possible, in order to bring well-being and happiness to the huge biking congregation. We must recognize that the bicyclical calms the agitated spirit and activates the circulation of the blood. Moreover, I

can reveal, a bicycle can carry the Father, the Son and the Holy
Spirit. With this in mind, bicycle factories are now manufacturing
them with good rubber, hard-wearing handlebars. I have been invited
by the head of one of the bicyclical trusts to immerse myself in the
complex manufacturing process of these magical artefacts. I have not
forgotten that you all have a secret desire to own an OK bicycle. No,
dearly beloved brethren, these bicycles will not be like bishops *in
partibus*. They will rush to be of service. I am deeply moved when I
imagine the marvellous spectacle of a whole people riding bicycles.
Think of it as a second nature being added to your innermost nature.
On the other hand, I assure you that it isn't the history of the bicycle
that interests us, but it's bicycle . . . Who knows the meaning of a
bicycle? I ask you who would waste their precious time researching
such a derisory notion? "That's a bike!" we would say, as it sailed by.
How much time does the human mind need to take note of something
which wants to take it into empyrean fields, limbos and ethers. And
that something is the bicycle. Start discussing it and you'll see it is a
never-ending conversation. Where does an exchange about bicycles
take us? Nobody worries. What is undeniable, deeply beloved, is that
the bicyclical conversation takes us, takes us for a ride . . . The
movement is what fascinates: you move, the bicycle moves, you move
it, it moves you; you shake, it shakes, you shake it, it shakes you. Can't
you perceive the movement? With a bicycle one cannot not move.
Everybody, for example, will start talking about hell or paradise. The
conversation will languish. Why, dearly beloved? Very simply, heaven
and hell have no wheels, go nowhere, nobody can jump on and ride off
. . . Once I listened to two distinguished theologians in the thick of a
controversy. I won't bore you, just to say that they came to blows,
kicked and thundered at each other. The supreme shame of it! The
failure of two wheel-less bodies! The controversy had to be ended.
The polemic dried up. And the theologians, cut to the quick, at the
end of their tethers, dry-mouthed, their arteries furred could no
longer return to their topic, were felled by cardiac arrest. That night
there was a wake for the fulminated bodies of the two bicycle-less

theologians. (*Applause.*) O bicycle who art on earth, Paraclete of man, visit these your sons with your precious form! Beseech your wheels to help this your flock to move with you. You are the consonant of man and the pedal of his soul. Your wheels turn man into a ball and you carry him hither and thither, in a free-wheeling flurry. (*Applause.*) What better thing than a bicycle can we desire in this vale of laughter? It leads us away from apostles, prophets, the wise and the perfect, it bangs its pedals against the heads of the saints and knocks them over. Bicycles suppress life after death, free us from *terror mortis*, invalidate the oracle, hurling it into Mount Etna or Chimborazo, pinch intellectual bums, bite blue-stockinged rumps, ulcerate contemplative livers, avoid duels to the death, propagate lack of definition, penetrate temples, the cradles of the newly born, nuptial beds, the couches of the dying, tell us we are all abysses and ride on, on, on . . . Give me a bicycle and I will move the world! *Item bicleta est . . .* '

He gave the *coram populo* blessing. The ball received it on its knees, but ever undulating. Suddenly, His Holiness took out a dagger. 'The murder,' he exclaimed.

The ball now floated in a sea of papal blood.

'I want to murder you,' His Holiness said.

The ball burst into laughter.

'I don't want you to let me kill myself,' the Pope replied to himself. 'Well,' he said, 'that doesn't seem a contradiction in terms.'

'Well, of course,' the Pope responded to himself, 'you say, I say, I say that what you say is what I say . . . The wind of life buffets us like dice in a shaker and confusion reigns. I flourish my dagger, I lower it. Nothing happens.'

I realized that murder would be impossible. For it to take place, the parts would have to be agreed – a willing sacrifice – or the parts in disagreement – a propitiatory victim. But what could agreement and disagreement do when faced by the terrible onslaught of the trivial? What did it matter that each part had its project, sinister or not, confronted, embedded in each other, in such a way, so icily cold, that it would have been impossible to restore them to their pristine state?

Give me a spin! I am the educated, elegant, very knowledgeable product of a university, a manufacturer of precision instruments and reader of Plato. At night I contemplated the mystery of the stars. Ho-ho! Ho-ho! Give me a spin! I am a solitary, proud, individual soul, with my camera and my studies on the polarization of light. Ho-ho! Ho-ho! Give me a spin! I am bored to tears, saying my life was the triumph of patience over the devil of indeterminacy. Ho-ho! Ho-ho! Give me a spin! I am studying myself studiously in studies of the cesspits of life. I am, am, am . . . Dapper and discreet. 'No, don't say that, say this . . . Have you handed in the proofs of your manual on the propagation of light?' Give me a spin! I am newly born into the maelstrom of the trivial, naked, riding a bicycle, I'm starting a new life. Like this: Ho-ho, ho-ho.

I shouted at the top of my voice, 'I've got a green bicycle!'

The impact was immediate. As if the cap had released its charge of nitroglycerine, the bomb exploded: 'With headlamps and a good set of tyres?'

I relaxed my muscles deliciously. A warm thrill went through me. I looked up: the sun was beaming down. It was six a.m. But already they were handing me a bicycle and telling me to get on. Three hundred versts or ten kilometres or five miles away, I could make out the Pope pedalling along. He was followed by his bicyclical flock.

TRANSLATED BY PETER BUSH

Tobias
Félix Rodríguez

Things can get nailed in our heads or in our hearts. It hardly matters which, for once there they become ours, belong to us. There is one small difference though: the things we get nailed here in our heads, where God's light turns into words that help us make some sense of the world around us, can come loose in the dampness of time, like prints on a wall. An open window with a wind blowing outside, a speck of dead dust coming loose, and the print falls down, or we forget what had seemed so firmly fixed. It would be crazy to think this is either good or bad. And crazier still to say so, because that's the greatest folly of all: saying things and believing they might be of use to others because just then they're so right for us.

What have we got to guarantee anything?

It's there that the difference lies between the things we get nailed in our heads and the things we get nailed in our hearts. Because the heart cares nothing for reason, nor has any use for words, but is made of something surely akin to what was fashioned on the world's brightest morning, the only flesh worms cannot pollute – that of God himself. Take a good look and afterwards say what you will, but it won't alter a scrap of what I'm saying. That's another of our follies: believing one man's words, his alone, can somehow be changed into different words that will contain the light of God in someone else's head. But we won't go into that now. The fact is there's a difference between the things nailed in our heads and the things nailed in our hearts, and the nails driven into our hearts bend at the point into hooks. And as there's no dust, except that from the pure substance of God's flesh, things can't fall away, unless it's when our hearts allow themselves to sway this way and that until they become still.

That's what happened to me with old Tobias's story. It got nailed in my heart, hooked itself there, and will remain fixed within me while my heart leans this way and that until it becomes still. And I really don't know. Perhaps even then, when what I am now starts rotting away down there, where roots look for their path to the juice that turns them into flowers and fruits, perhaps even then what old Tobias told me will still be hooked in there, who knows for how long.

It was in that stinking jail, San Pedro Sula, back in '26, a bad year for my bones. It had been one thing after another, and I'd been stumbling around as though with my eyes closed, getting kicked in the backside. You can't imagine. A kick in the pants always makes you feel bad inside and like doing some damage. The sting fades though and you add it to the list of life's injustices. There's no bile inside and you keep smiling. But when you get a kick where the last one hasn't stopped hurting, on top of it another and yet another, you feel it to the quick and then you know for sure whether what's inside you is a mangy dog, a snake or a tiger.

At first I'd come to think I'd got one of those mangy dogs that even runs from its own shadow inside. But another couple of boots unleashed the tiger in me and before I know it out comes my knife in old Ambrosio Esquivel's gambling dive. There was a man in front of me, may God forgive him his sins.

That's why they'd got me there, waiting to transfer me somewhere or other. It was like a hole between four walls, bare earth underfoot, an awful stench in the air. The only light was the burst that fell through the high, barred window when the sun was in the middle of the sky. So it would be day in one half of the cell, while in the other half it was like night. Then the other way round.

There were two Indians who huddled together in a corner, hours on end, heads buried in their chests, as though that feeling of being alive together gave them the strength to go on. Now and again they held hands and looked at me. That was all.

Then there was Tobias.

It's hard to know whether a man is worthy of the name until the wheel of suffering has passed over him. Stories can be made up and told, told so well even that everybody's left believing the speaker a man. But somebody who's been in that stinking San Pedro Sula jail and known Tobias doesn't swallow any fairy-tales. That much I know.

The guard, an Indian with a goatish face and frayed pants, drunk as a skunk, gave me a shove that landed me in there on all fours. When I looked up I saw Tobias. To be more exact, I saw his eyes, because that's what struck you about his face when you looked at it: two tiny blue coins partly obscured by the eyelids habitually half closed against the smoke of his cigarette. Two tiny blue coins, as though seen through the slot of a poorbox. If asked just then I couldn't have said why, but the fact was I liked him immediately. After talking to him at length for three months, I understood why. But right then, when I was picking myself up from goat face's shove, there was no reason for me to like him. The fact was, though, I did. With a small knife he was working at something on a scrap of wood from Campeche. It was later – much later – I saw it was a sailing ship with two masts, a bowsprit and rigging, the whole thing no bigger than the palm of his hand. For Tobias couldn't survive long far from the sea, and there in the cell in San Pedro Sula jail that was the only way he had of feeling close to it. But I didn't find any of this out till later, and with stories, as with everything else, you have to take things one at a time if they're to make any sense. I learned this too with Tobias.

'No sooner are we born than we begin to die. Fifty, sixty, eighty years, full of pain, dying bit by bit, like a bar of soap being worn away yet remaining intact. Suddenly there's a spray of suds and it stays there. These are our memories. They're nowhere, have no body or soul, nobody can see them, and they're hard as iron. If we want to know what stuff we're made of, we have to look at ourselves in them, as in a mirror.' That's what Tobias said, and he added, 'It's because of who we were, we can be. If it weren't for memories we wouldn't be here, nor anywhere else. The travelled path is the true path. The one we're treading now is but a patch of earth beneath our feet.'

He told me this on my fourth day in San Pedro Sula jail, when he'd finished securing the anchor to the ship with the point of a safety pin. I was lamenting the incident in Ambrosio Esquivel's gambling dive, though not because of the dead man, who after all wasn't my brother, nor could ever have been.

'A dead man would just be somebody who's left the dance and doesn't come back,' said Tobias, pushing the sailing ship out on the palm of his hand to see it better. 'He'd be merely that, if it weren't for the memories which remain circling in the empty space he's left in the air. The problem lies there, in those memories that can't be killed. It's then you realize what a man is. You were thinking he was just a head with what's inside reflected in the eyes, a couple of hands moving around like spiders in front of him, and a pair of feet to let him get a change of scenery. But no, there was more, because while all that soon turns to rotting meat, the man lives on in people's memories, smiling, hungering, his simple ways of saying he's cold or likes to smoke before breakfast. While that man's children are still abroad in the world, you can't kill the way he'd place his hand on their heads, nor the way he'd hold a cigarette between his lips, which his wife can still see, as if he were there now, smoking.'

'Well, Tobias,' I said, 'that's all very well, even if it is a bit over my head. Doesn't bring the dead back from the grave, though, does it?'

'No,' he answered, as though from afar, 'no, of course not. But what I'm telling you about doesn't go into the grave with the dead. It stays outside and lives on.'

My head filled with strange ideas because that devil Tobias had a way of talking that made it seem as though he were using brightly coloured words to paint a picture whose images danced before your eyes. I thought I was very clever when I answered him.

'But if that were the case, Tobias, the world would be a bit cramped to contain all the dead who aren't dead. Just think, from Adam to now. How could it be?'

'Lie down on your back in a field some starry night and think about everything you see. Think about the clouds, the stars and the

great empty space above you and see whether you come up with a
better answer.'

I felt like an empty barrel they're trying to squeeze a last drop of
brandy out of and could only mumble, 'All right, Tobias, you win.'

'If you want to straighten out all those wires under your skin, first
you need a pair of pliers. You're wasting your time trying to do it
without the pliers. That's what I was like when I was a cabin boy on
the *María Victoria* and we went out to fish in the Gulf. And then
when I became a proper seaman and got my arm tattooed for the first
time, same thing. I had no pliers and those wires got into a devilish
tangle every time I wanted to explain something to myself.'

He started touching up the boat's mast, scraping at it with his
small knife, and I thought that was that. I still didn't know that even
when he was silent the words never stopped hatching and joining
together to create something in Tobias's head. In a moment I
understood.

'One day, I don't know why, I got to thinking about this business
of memories. I gradually realized that when it came to seeing the
things that matter I was blind. The sea helped me a lot in that
moment and in all the moments which came after. Did you know
there are books out there claiming the first man was a sea animal, tiny
as the tip of a fly's leg? I expect it's why the sea attracts us so much.'

I laughed and the smoke from my cigarette went down the wrong
way and made me cough.

'Honestly, Tobias, I'd never thought my grandfather was a squid.'

'Your grandfather was your grandfather and has nothing to do
with this. I'm talking to you about a time way before Adam had even
got into Eden. But look, we have to take things one at a time if we
want to see, even if it's only to catch a glimpse. And I'm getting
carried away here. I wanted to tell you about when I was a sailor on
the *María Victoria* looking at the sea, when it came to me that no one
dies completely, but not like the priest says, because the soul leaves its
wardrobe, gets hung up, labelled and given a ticket for that cloakroom
of souls up in the sky, but because it remains in memories and

perhaps some other way I don't know about, hovering around the empty space its body left in the air when they buried it under six feet of dirt.'

'OK, Tobias, but what about the pliers? I don't really get that bit.'

'That was the way of seeing things, the pliers. You don't see the same from one side to another. You have to learn to set your eyes right to look. Even if you choose the wrong side it doesn't matter. The thing is not to go racing around trying to take on more, because then you're forever treading water. When it came to me that a dead man was just someone who leaves the dance never to come back, then I'd found a crack to put my eyes up against. All the rest came later, over time.'

He started to take bits of wire out of his threadbare jacket and twist them into the rigging for his sailing ship. His words kept buzzing in my ears as I tried to put them out of mind to think about what they were going to do with me on account of the man killed in Ambrosio Esquivel's gambling dive.

'Listen' – suddenly he was talking again – 'if it hadn't been so, I wouldn't be here now, twisting the rigging of this sailing ship.'

It hadn't occurred to me to wonder why Tobias was in San Pedro Sula jail and I told him so.

'Because of a death,' he said.

I stared at him in consternation. He hadn't said, 'I killed a man' or 'I killed a woman.' He'd said, 'Because of a death.' It meant the same, but it sounded so different to my ears that it was as if he'd said something else. Because of a death. It distanced the dead man, erased him, obscured his form and left only the death, as though it were a death without a man at its centre. But I thought all that later. The first thing to come into my head was a sense of confusion: the nuts didn't fit the bolts, the shoe wasn't right for the foot. How to picture Tobias, sitting there measuring with half-closed eyes his ship made from Campeche wood, how to imagine him leaping on a man with a knife in his hand and murderous rage in his heart. It jarred in my mind and I couldn't connect Tobias with what he'd just told me.

But Tobias was already talking again.

'I was on my way to the coast after a few months inland. I was in no hurry and went along drinking in those fields of maize. They were lovely, and the sky above, smooth as a sheet of blue paper, was restful and made me feel happy. Yes, I was happy. It must have been midday when I arrived in front of Villalba's shack. He was a small, skinny old man, as though worn out by living. The only sign of the Indian blood running through his veins was in the eyes that slanted up towards his brows. He welcomed me with a blessing and immediately set about preparing some tortillas, like someone who knows that when a man comes to the end of his journey he's bound to be hungry. I had only to glance into his shack to tell he lived alone in the middle of his field of maize. When I heard him talking to the mocking bird, twittering in a cage that hung from a rafter by the door, I was sure of his solitary existence.'

' "You've come from Tegucigalpa, perhaps."

'After the welcome and the offer of tortillas, this was the first thing he said to me. So what, eh? But those words that weren't even a question contained his whole life.

' "Well, no," I told him, "not from so far. I've come from the ranches in La Estrella." I was working there.'

' "Ah, from La Estrella!"

'He didn't say the words sadly, didn't say them one way or another, but even so I realized I'd upset him. It's incredible the impact words spoken from the heart can have. I looked at him without speaking, for fear of hurting him again in a way I didn't understand.

' "I always ask the same question, you know. Travellers come from far afield sometimes and one of them might turn up from Tegucigalpa."

"Is there something there that interests you?" I ventured.

' "Well, yes, I've got Gilberto there."

'It seems unreal but I didn't need to ask him to know Gilberto was his son. He'd said 'I've got' and that was enough for me to understand straight off. In that moment I read in his eyes nostalgia and tiredness and something that was like sadness, but not entirely.

'"It's almost ten years since he left. He was coming up to twenty when he told me wanted to study and escape the drudgery of the maize fields. Don Saurez's son, Remigio, put the idea into his head, going on at him about Tegucigalpa. Who was I to say no if he wanted to get on in life? What do you think?"

'"Yes, of course," I said.

'He sat down on the mat by my side, having put the plate in my lap.

'"It would have been wrong of me to stop him. I would have ruined his life because I didn't want to be alone. Just because you plant a seed, it doesn't give you the right to place a stone over it to stop it growing up and flowering, does it? That's what I thought, anyway."

'"I'm sure you did the right thing," I told him. With the right intentions what's best is always done."

'"That's true, isn't it?" he asked cheerfully, his face lighting up. "The proof's in that he made something of his life and did me proud by becoming a gentleman there. I don't see him and it's ages since I've had a letter, but he won the battle, studied, and is a very important man today. Dr Villalba! Can you believe it?"

'He seemed to swell with pride.

'"Of course I'm here all alone and would love to give him a hug and talk to him a bit before I die, but I understand. A doctor is an extremely busy man! He doesn't have time to write letters, but I know he hasn't forgotten me and one fine day I'll hear from him and he might even come to see me."

'Listening to him I thought about Dr Villalba, about Tegucigalpa, so far from those maize fields, thought how I'd like to have him in front of me to tell him in no uncertain terms he was the seed and his father'd broken his own heart to avoid placing a stone over him and stopping him growing up into the air to flower. But of course I said nothing of this. We went on talking for quite a while about that son who wasn't there but all the same filled the shack, covered the maize field, occupied the vast space between heaven and earth like the wind. We were talking when the door moved, allowing a strip of sunlight in and that man appeared. Just looking at his eyes and the way his lips moved as he asked Villalba for something to eat was enough for me to dislike him. He said he was on his way to the coast and had been travelling for days. There's nothing wrong with asking when you're in need, but there are many ways of doing it. And he did it as though he were down on his knees, asking to be pitied. He didn't actually ask that, but that's how it was. Villalba did as he'd done with me. He fixed him a meal with what was left in the pan and straight off asked if by chance he'd come from Tegucigalpa.

' "No," that man told him, "I've come from Santa Barbara. I had a spot of trouble there and they banged me up for three months. Bootlegging. But I was in Tegucigalpa about a year ago."

'The sparkle of joy that came into the old man's eyes was so bright he suddenly looked like a twenty-year-old again.

' "Oh," he said, "then you must know something about him. Everyone in Tegucigalpa must know him."

' "Know who?" the man asked.

' "My son. Dr Gilberto Villalba. He's a famous lawyer and very well known there."

'I've got this way of sensing things I've never been able to explain to myself. It's as if someone inside is telling me what's going to happen. So when I saw that rat's face as the old man explained and tried to prompt his memory by describing his son, I felt something bad was going to happen. And I wasn't mistaken.

' "Gilberto Villalba," he said, smiling. "Gilberto Villalba. Yes, I knew someone of that name, and it must be the same person because in jail they called him the Doctor."

'The old man's voice broke as he asked, "In jail?", but he recovered immediately and smiled again.

' "No. That can't be right. My son is a very well-known lawyer. In his last letter he told me he was even a friend of the President."

'I started to tremble inside and would have happily died if by so doing I could have shut that man's mouth. But what we want and what actually happens are two different things.

' "It must be the same person," said the man. "Must be. It's not a common name and anyway, I've told you, he was nicknamed the Doctor for being as smart and as sly as a lawyer."

' "Look, my friend," I interrupted him, "Villalba is a common enough name in Tegucigalpa and the man you're talking about can't possibly be this gentleman's son."

' "Perhaps he's not," he said, smiling, "but it's not true it's a common name. And for him to be called the Doctor would be too much of a coincidence."

' "It can't be Gilberto," the old man protested weakly, "it can't be."

'I made a desperate effort to put things right.

' "All right," I said, "just supposing it was him, lots of men end up in jail because of politics. Anyone worth anything has enemies."

'I said this looking at the man's shoulders and put everything I felt inside into the look so he'd get the message, but he replied with a guffaw, "Politics! That's a good one, my friend! The Doctor was inside for killing a man, his third. And it came out in court he had a record as long as my arm – robbery, fraud, bootlegging, illegal gambling . . . I'm telling you, the Doctor's a real character!"

'He recounted the list with such relish that my last hope of putting things right faded. But it was too late anyway. By now old Villalba looked as though he'd turned to stone. There he was, smaller and more drawn than ever, dulled by the pain. D'you see? When I come across men like that I can't believe man started as some sea animal, tinier than a fly's leg, but think he must have come into the world fully grown from the filthy bowels of a tiger. Nature can't have gone to such trouble to create such a thing. Anyway, my blood was boiling with rage when, with a smile, he gave the dagger a final twist.

' "Look, let's get this straight once and for all. Does your son have a birthmark as big as a centavo, just here on the right-hand side of his neck?"

'Villalba didn't have the strength left to reply with words but nodded in affirmation.

' "See! It's him all right!" he said, his laughter rising. "Well, well, here I am with the Doctor's old man! If I meet up with him again in some other jail I'll tell him all about it."

' "No, I burst out, the knife already in my hand, "you're not going to say anything to anyone, you damned son of a bitch! You've already said more than you'd any earthly right to." '

Tobias fell silent and went back to working on the ship's anchor with the safety pin. I watched his hands caressing the bit of wood from Campeche and felt serene inside. It was like the first day of being able to eat after two weeks of sickness. That's how I felt inside.

'His name was Juan Aguinaldo,' said Tobias after a while.

'Who?' I asked.

'That bastard,' he said. 'I can't fathom it, because it's such a beautiful name for someone like that filthy scum who came into Villalba's shack with the sun. Don't you think so?'

'You're quite right,' I said, 'you're quite right. Juan Aguinaldo is a beautiful name for a pig like that.'

'Well, he doesn't use it now,' Tobias concluded, attaching the last strings to the bowsprit, 'not any more. And perhaps one of these days someone who'd never think of coming into an old man's shack and stomping all over his beautiful dreams with dirty boots might take it up.'

It's hard to know whether a man is worthy of the name until the wheel of suffering has passed over him. Stories can be made up and told, told so well even that everybody's left believing the speaker a man. But somebody who's been in that stinking San Pedro Sula jail and known Tobias doesn't swallow any fairy-tales. That much I know.

TRANSLATED BY JOHN McCARTHY

A Taste Of Love
Calvert Casey

Monday

Last night I sat for ages in the Philosophers' Park. Nobody knows that the park where Luz Caballero meditates, elbow on knee, opposite the Avenida del Puerto, the far side of Saco's bust and the near side of Father Varela, is the Philosophers' Park. The way nobody knows the park with the amphitheatre is called, or should be called, the Greeks' Park, because of its paths for meditation and statues. One fell down or was removed: anyway, it's gone. Only the empty pedestal stands there, but I really like the place. Nobody knows because in fact nobody knows anything. The way they don't know that behind the park there was a promenade called Valdés's Curtain, or that a hundred years ago the house with pointed gables was home to a sect. But it is only logical people don't know because, as I just said, nobody knows anything.

I reached the park out of breath. I had walked round the whole of Old Havana. All the benches were occupied by couples. I rested for a moment in a space on one of the benches, then crossed over the amusement park they've built opposite. I had an unexpected, very pleasant experience. Quite by chance, I got into conversation with two girls. They weren't pretty or ugly, just nice. They were heatedly discussing the quickest way to go to Casa Blanca. I sorted that out, but to keep sight of them I persuaded them Casa Blanca was totally uninteresting. They looked doubtful and, as I hadn't anything else to say to them, nor apparently had they to me, I invited them to ride on the dodgems. I rarely do this kind of thing, but I suddenly thought how often the best things in life start out like that, with an invitation to ride on the dodgems. Then they accepted a fresh lemonade because that's all they ever sell in amusement parks. And finally we climbed into those little cars which make contact up top with metal mesh and bump into each other for a laugh or a fright, though nobody is ever frightened. As the three of us couldn't squeeze in, they started to row over who was going where until I intervened again, put my arm round the fatter one, guided her into a car and immediately began bumping and shouting so the row would be forgotten. As it was a narrow seat, I put my arm round her shoulder and she said nothing. The other, much slimmer girl climbed into another dodgem on her own and seemed to be enjoying herself. I realized I should have chosen her, but it was too late, I could only watch her from where I was, laughing to herself when she crashed violently into the other cars and flashing her small teeth. In one of the collisions, a long strand of hair caught in her mouth and sent her into fits of laughter. A youth tried to get into her dodgem but was rebuffed energetically, as suddenly she put on a serious face. It was then I realized, before she moved off again, that she was much prettier than she had seemed at first.

As I get sick, I refused to get on the Flying Chair, which they both decided to ride on and I stood and watched them gyrating, screaming through the air, holding on to their skirts, clinging to the chain so as not to fall off. One lad started to frighten them by violently rocking on the chain as it turned at top speed and it looked as if the chair would break loose and hurtle him into the bay.

Everything was going well but when I invited them to sit on the shadowy side of the park they said they had to go. I told them it was still very early, that we should go and relax in the park, but the best I could get was the promise they'd come back tonight.

After they'd gone, not wanting to go straight home, I sat on a low stone wall behind Father Varela. The benches were full of couples making passionate love. I heard the sound of scissors behind me. An old woman surrounded by cardboard boxes and sacking was cutting up dry bread and throwing it to a dog. They looked set up for the night. I tried to get a good look at the old woman. That was difficult in the dark. She was sitting with her back to the fairground. When the bits of bread stopped coming, the dog stretched out between her packages. The old woman looked inside the crate next to her, but took nothing out. She stayed like that for a long time. Then she wrapped herself in a jute sack, held her legs tight and rested her head on her knees. I thought I should give her money for some food. I toyed with the idea but in the end decided not to.

Tonight I must get to the park early.

Tuesday

My luck was in, the much slimmer girl came. Very late, but she came. Accompanying her was an older and much less pretty girl. I'd been waiting for them a long time, walking up and down opposite the amusement park. I tried to remember whether I'd made the date over here or in the park, or on the wall in the Avenida. Thinking they wouldn't show, I sat down in the shadowy part, where the couples sit. As it was Monday hardly anybody was there. I arrived very early. Behind the bench, in the same spot as the night before, I saw the old woman from Sunday, but without her dog. She was slowly eating something greasy her dirty hands extracted from a piece of newspaper. She took an eternity to swallow each mouthful. I had to turn away. I noticed her hair wasn't white but yellow, perhaps from the dust in the park.

Esther and her little friend arrived shortly after. I suggested going on all the rides in the park, since it was empty and nobody would bother us. Esther said no, we should sit on a bench on the lit-up part of the pavement, and anyway she had to go soon. I ignored her. Women always say they have to go when they turn up for a date. Where we sat, the streetlamp shone right in my face. She was a bit in the shadow. I so much wanted to see her in the light and close up.

(This morning, for example, I'd got no clear recollection of her.) The light was hurting my eyes but I didn't want to say we should move. She'd probably remember she had to go. Shortly after her friend said she was going to look at the boats and disappeared.

I soon realized that Esther isn't pretty in a vulgar, obvious sense, but in a vague, almost subtle way. She looked at me rather sarcastically, but that must be because I started to pour out whatever came into my head. When I stopped to let her say something she stayed silent. She has this habit of looking at you, of giving you a big toothy grin. I asked her if we could see each other again there or wherever she wanted, her house if she liked. She doesn't act like a park hooker though she'd come back like that, late at night, with me a complete stranger. And I just can't take my eyes off her. Her skin is so smooth. I imagine the skin over her whole body is smooth, pressed down under the dress that clings to her thighs, forcing her to take short steps.

Wednesday

She didn't come last night. Perhaps because it was drizzling. It drizzled, then cleared and at about nine o'clock started to drizzle endlessly. By that time I knew she wouldn't be coming. But even so, I walked round the parks getting wet and irritable. The amusement park was in darkness. I walked down the streets towards the Avenida. As usual, I turned down Cuarteles, and went up Peña Pobre, hoping to bump into her, though I try to avoid walking that way ever since they demolished almost the whole block to make way for one of those horrible parking lots. I didn't see her. I arrived back at the park exhausted and sat on the wall where I'd sat on Sunday, the day we met. I don't know why I felt drained and still do today. I've been unable to do anything. As if I'd walked from one end of Havana to the other.

Thursday

Just as well Esther came last night. She turned up by herself. In fact, I didn't want her to come. You start giving these things an importance they don't deserve.

I told her as much last night jokingly when we met up. As usual she stared at me and seemed amused. We had to talk about something. To make sure she doesn't leave straight away I talk at her non-stop. She laughs and looks at me. What can she be thinking when she looks at me? We sat on the bench where she insists on sitting, under the streetlamp. I give in after a bit of an argument which she always wins, though the light does irritate my eyes. For example, to make these notes in my exercise book today I've had to bathe them in oleander-scented water. I don't believe in such things, but the cleaning woman spends her whole life singing the praises of the oleander and leaves me a saucer of scented water outside so I can wash before I pick up my pen. And to avoid falling out with her I wash because I know she's watching me.

Esther didn't stay long. I suspect she's there against someone's wishes. She's no other reason to be so reticent.

Friday

My God, she is so pretty. Last night I was able to gaze longingly at her in the 'Coffee Pot'. She finally allowed me to buy her a coffee. I came through the park and saw her on the street corner, waiting for me. Perhaps she wasn't waiting for me and had come for some fresh air, but I know I felt that way, that she was waiting for me. Everyone's eyes were on her and I had to look serious, because at the end of the day she was going out with me. She has small hands. She bites her nails, and hides her hands so I don't notice. I act like someone who knows nothing. Last night I told her her hands were very pretty and immediately she tucked them under her thighs on the seat. The skin on her arms is very smooth. The light fell on her brown hair as it lifted in waves above her forehead, and which she is constantly smoothing down. How I'd love to sink my fingers into her hair. Last night I noted something about her I hadn't seen before, something extraordinary. She has some small, exquisite moles on her forehead, the smallest on her temple, almost hidden in her hair. Her forehead is really beautiful. I think of the expression on her always half-open, slightly mocking lips. Last night, perhaps because of the heat, she was wearing a dress that was very open at the shoulder and you could see the start of her breasts.

Saturday

I try remembering what we talked about last night and can't. I felt so relieved she'd turned up. I was so afraid she wouldn't come. A few minutes before she got up to go, I put a hand on one shoulder. Suddenly she leaned back. The only thing I told her when we said goodbye was that I'd be there, waiting for her. I can't say for certain how long we talked

As I got there, I saw the old woman with the dog, asleep on the pavement. It was very late by now. And had started to drizzle. The drizzle must have woken her up. She came over to where I was, under the tree, and threw a blanket round her head. She gave off a sickening smell. Other shapes that were asleep on the grass, and which I hadn't noticed, got up as well. I saw them looking for shelter under sheets of newspaper or sacking. A bus's headlights spotlighted the old woman. Her skin was blackened and wrinkled. Her body, a bag of bones covered in jute sacking and rags. I have never seen such an old face. The earth caked on her face has hardened as her sweat dried and the rain and her wrinkles have turned into a solid mass. That kind of tramps' dormitory hidden under the trees is depressing.

Sunday

Last night I didn't see Esther. Most terrible of all is the thought she was there close by and I didn't get to see her. Though, on reflection, if I didn't see her, she could not not have seen me. In the afternoon I decided to buy some dark glasses. I never go out in the afternoon because it's very hot and I use the time to read or write, but I realized I needed dark glasses to keep my eyestrain out of sight. When I looked at myself in the mirror I saw they suited me. Perhaps Esther will approve the change. But it was so dark now I'm not sure whether she came. As I couldn't see clearly, I ran after two women who looked like her, but they weren't. I decided to wait for her and not to stray from there.

The old woman was back in the park, in her usual spot. To pass the time of day I started to wonder as I watched her what filthy wretches like her lived on. If she's with the others, they never say anything to each other. They laugh or talk to themselves like her, or dig in their bags for something. As I watched her, she laid a newspaper on the grass and stretched out to go to sleep.

Tuesday

I saw Esther last night. I wish I'd never seen her. Sunday night she didn't come. I spent two hours waiting for her in the usual place. The old woman decided to hang her clothes from the trees because it had rained and they were soaked. She came over and asked me for a cigarette and I quickly went elsewhere to avoid contact with her, though·not too far away. I thought Esther would probably look out for me from a distance away and if she couldn't see me she might leave. I stayed in the park till very late. I'm sure, absolutely sure, that she didn't come.

Last night I left home early because I thought I'd probably have to spend a long time looking for her. I walked round and round hoping to see her coming from one direction or another. Exhausted, I walked down Cuarteles and saw her. She was with her young friend from that first night, who didn't recognize me. They were heading towards the park, but with two lads, not by themselves. The younger had his arm round Esther's waist. Esther was wearing the same tight dress she wore that first day, the one that clings to her thighs.

Thursday

Last night I got ready to go out, but at the last minute, when I was all dolled up, I decided to stay home. The weather was rough and anyway I'd been going out a lot. I feel rather upset.

Saturday

Thursday I decided not to go to the park, or last night. The weather was still bad. Every night it's been raining. There's a damp in the air that does no one any good. I felt better yesterday afternoon and finally went out. I realized I should go to the barber's. It always cheers me up. That barber, who's always pushing raffle tickets or hairgrease or tints, in the end sold me something. Of late I've not felt like arguing with anybody. He not only sold me some but gave me a demonstration. Before I realized, he'd dyed my hair, a German patent according to him, telling me dark hair goes best with dark glasses. If I don't like it, the effect'll wear off in a few days. Perhaps he's right. At least you look a bit different. To make sure I get no peace, he also sold me an eye pencil – he says so my eyebrows don't look out-of-sorts with the glasses or dark hair. I ended up buying the whole lot, I was so impatient to get out of there.

Before going to bed I went out again. I quickly walked through the park, not looking around much, for I was sure Esther wouldn't come and I didn't want to build up my hopes. I stopped in the café for a moment and drank a coffee. Just to spend some more money, I bought some cigarettes, a thing I never do because I don't usually smoke. After I'd bought them, I stood and pondered what to do with them. I suddenly thought about giving them to the old woman who'd asked me for one the other night. I crossed the street and saw her in her usual spot. I went over but she didn't see me. She was asleep. I sat down next to her for a moment and waited to see what she'd do. Seated on the grass, to get a better view of her, I watched long and hard. I shouted to see if she woke up. She slowly stirred from her drowsiness. When she saw the cigarettes, she fell on them. There was something so mean about her that I decided not to give them to her. I pocketed them. Mean, that's the word, mean.

Sunday

Something awful has happened. I wish I'd never met Esther. Last night I saw her in the park again. I think it was the worst night of my life. I haven't been able to sleep. I sacked my cleaning woman because I don't want her to see me like this. Besides, she's always interfering. Esther and I were together a little more than half an hour. She was sitting there when I got to the park and greeted me as if nothing had happened and we'd seen each other the night before. I couldn't think what to say. I sat down next to her. It was very noisy because they'd switched on the amusements and a terrific din was coming from the amplifiers. I had to shout the same thing at her repeatedly. Just once she leaned over so she could hear. She laughed because I breathed in her ear when I spoke to her and that tickled her. Her ear brushed against my mouth. An ear covered with an almost invisible down. The music stopped but I was saying something to her and though the music had stopped I still spoke into her ear. All I remember is kissing her on the neck and under the arm and what happened next was awful. I think Esther suddenly got up because I fell to the ground. The people with never anything to do, who are always everywhere, began to gather round us. I heard her shout and say awful things to me, but I can't remember them. All I know is that last night was the most wretched night of my life.

Monday

Last night I sat in the same spot. I wasn't expecting anything, but, as it's better than staying home, I ended up at the usual place. It was very late, well after midnight, I paced the streets, stopped in front of lots of houses. The silence was so deep you could hear the breathing of the people who slept near the street. Perhaps Esther sleeps near the street. It's so hot! Perhaps she sleeps naked to enjoy relief from the little breeze there is. I looked through a window, tried to penetrate the darkness. Perhaps she sleeps near the street. Perhaps she sleeps naked. I'm very tired.

Tuesday

The worst mistake was not giving her my address. If I'd given her my address, perhaps she'd try to see me, but I didn't. That was my worst mistake. If there was a ring at the door to break this silence . . . She didn't come last night either. Though I knew she wouldn't because it was very drizzly, I sat in the same place and wrapped myself up in newspaper.

Thursday

I think the old woman is ill. Last night I spent a long time by her side. She didn't move at all. She was sitting against a tree, her eyes shut and her head leaning back against the trunk, not in her normal position. I've noticed that whenever she nods off she buries her double chin in her bosom, her body tilts forward and then her head falls on to her knees. Last night a thread of spittle hung from her lip. Perhaps she's dying or not quite. But the fact is, when someone's in her state they're no use to anyone. I spent most of the early hours there. In any case, being at home is difficult.

Friday

This morning something extraordinary happened to me. I woke up in the park. I'd sat all night thinking through each moment of my life. I must have dozed off. There are many hours in the night and I can't have spent them all thinking. The trees started to turn blue and then green. It began to get light. Then I did fall asleep. When I opened my eyes the sun was shining on my face. All night I'd felt hungry. When I woke up, the pangs had gone. I came home because the sun was too strong and I went to bed without any breakfast.

Saturday

Esther and I bathed naked in the water from a spring. As it was night-time, the perfume of the ylang-ylang tree spread furiously from the depths of the jungle.

Sunday

Esther hasn't come, but I'm sure she will. The worst thing would be for her to come and not to find me. Or come one night very late. Hunger doesn't let my thoughts flow easily. The old woman gave me something to eat and some newspapers to wrap round myself. I fell asleep despite all the din from the amusement park and from that whole rabble. Tonight I must bring myself something to eat.

TRANSLATED BY PETER BUSH

Where I Stand
Edmundo Desnoes

I

I can't. Sebastián looked at Paco's flushed face and an awkward smile spread over his own, making him look slightly less ill at ease. *I hope they don't think the songs bug me. My idiotic grin. I just can't do it, I can't sing, I simply do not know how* . . . He rubbed his face with his hands, and his fingertips, soft and pink, glided over the thousands of bristly whiskers of his one-day beard. He wouldn't shave in the country. *How long will my beard grow in two weeks? The Bay of Pigs fortnight. The Bay of Pigs month. The Bay of Pigs year. Harvesting the sugar cane is also a means of defeating imperialism. One son for the cane, a priest in every family, like Spain.*

'Yo vivo en el agua,' sang the gruff voices and the out-of-tune voices and the in-tune voices, sweetly,

'como el camarón
y a nadie le importa
como vivo yo . . .'

I am not the only one, thought Sebastián upon seeing Orlando with his hat over his face and his head leaning against the window; he looked toward the countryside. He couldn't focus on anything, the palm trees, the thatch-roof huts, a fence, the stones, a cow, the bienvestidos in bloom, even the waves all undulated before him like never-ending sheets being shaken out. Just three or four shades of green from the landscape prevailed and were repeated in his eyes. *That's probably what it looks like from high up, only smaller. From* far away, from up there. Isolated from it all, up in the air; clean, alone. Bet pilots and cosmonauts have a great time. From a rocket ship the island must look like a skinny alligator, like a green blot speckled with clouds . . . clouds darkened by the sky.

'Attention! Your attention please!' Orlando boomed, straightening up. 'We are at this very moment crossing into Matanzas province. Last chance for those wishing to return to Havana!'

Boisterous laughter, smiles and the sudden beating of timbales.

'I'm serious,' he said, flapping his hat around, 'there's no turning back now, this is the point of no return. We're done for . . . No, don't laugh.'

'Who got me into this in the first place?'

'Where are they taking us?'

'You really think you're going to cut sugar cane? Do you know what we are all doing on this bus together? My dear sirs, the purge of the intellectuals has begun.'

'Doesn't surprise me, I've been expecting it for ages. Getting screwed is what intellectuals and writers and painters are born for.'

'You jest, but soon enough you'll see. Some day the revolution will eliminate every writer and artist from the petit bourgeoisie. We are shaped by the capitalist society we knew before the revolution, nothing we can do about it.'

'Writers and artists are all faggots.'

'Give me Cuba or give me death!'

'We shall overcome!'

The bus lurched over a pothole and then sped up after crossing the deserted railroad tracks.

Before his very eyes, up front, across from the bus driver, between the back and the bottom of a seat, Sebastián saw the bulge of shapely buttocks squeezed into a pair of pants with a purple and yellow and orange flower pattern. He raised his head and was hit by a shock of very black, blue-black, dyed, feathered back hair, and a bit of tight, olive-colored skin and a thin nose. Bet she thinks those flowered pants are totally amazing, really . . . Fantastic. And Sebastián looked at his shiny black boots and ran his hands over the soft, supple leather. Hope I don't get blisters. No, they fit fine. The problem is when I have to walk a lot, walking . . .

With his hairy arms up above his head, Paco danced in the aisle while Brígida, her lips shining with a trickle of saliva, writhed around, hardly moving at all, brushing against the seats. Ay, why doncha come on over here, baby . . . she sang, the veins in her neck bulging. Paco bit his lips and moved his feet awkwardly in the heavy boots. Sebastián raised his head and smiled. His fingertips bounced over the leather. *Don't put your hand on my shoulder, don't look at me with scorn in your eyes.* Brígida moved her shoulders and closed her wet mouth.

'Attention! We have before us one of the most beautiful views in Cuba, and therefore in all the world, the renowned Viñales valley, immortalized in verse by so many illustrious poets . . .'

'That's not the Viñales, Orlando, it's the Yumurí valley . . .' Ramón broke in sadly, tilting his daintily featured, enormous, nearly bald head. 'The knolls . . .'

'All landscapes are the same.'

'How beautiful is my sweet Cuba!' cried Paco.

'Paradise.'

'I don't see anything. Where is it?'

'Down there."

'That's the famous Yumurí valley?'

'Everything looks so small down there: tiny palm trees, tiny horses; like one of those Chinese landscapes . . .'

'Culture, culture, too much culture.'

'Do you have any band-aids over there?' asked Paco, limping and holding himself up on the chrome rail next to the door.

'What's the matter?' asked Sebastián, 'you need first-aid already?'

'No man, these boots are really pinching me. They're not mine, see, I borrowed them.'

'You're off to a bad start,' and he quickly grabbed the olive green

backpack, dug around among the soft objects and finally pulled out
an almost transparent plastic bag that looked milky inside.

'You're well prepared,' said Paco, swaying back and forth on one
foot, while holding his other one, bare, up in the air.

She turned around; Sebastián saw her knees in the tight, floral-
print pants and raised his head; he smiled and saw his smile returned
on her dark, fleshy lips.

'Don't you have any other shoes?' he asked, as Paco adjusted the
white corners of the adhesive strip on his heel.

'Yeah, I brought some old shoes in my backpack . . .'

'And what do you have there?' she asked from above, pointing to
the bag and then biting the nail of her index finger.

'In here, I have a little of everything: iodine, band-aids,
mercurochrome, aspirin, cotton wool, hydrosulfide, cortisone,
rubbing alcohol, a tourniquet, meprobamate, paregoric . . .'

'You couldn't fit all that in there.'

'Oh no? Well, what do you need? Do you want a meprobamate?'

'No thanks, I don't need anything. I'm as healthy as an apple.'

So I see, thought Sebastián. When I'm attracted to a woman all I
can do is think rude thoughts. Sometimes it's better to be rude than
to be quiet . . . No. An apple. He put the backpack back under the
seat.

'So, your name must be Eve,' and he looked up at her pointy chin
and fine nostrils.

'No, Diana,' she smiled. 'See you later,' and she turned back
around toward the front of the bus.

Sebastián rubbed his eyes and saw Diana's chin and hair and eyes
on his eyelids. Together the entire fortnight. On the sugar-cane
plantation; working the whole time. Then at night . . . Stop
bullshitting. Nothing is gonna happen. We slipped into the cane
fields. I was sweating. I tried so damn hard. That was ages ago. Yep,
fourteen years. My old lady found us and kicked her out. We even
took a dip together in that stinking spring water. Martín Mesa, close
to Mariel, or to Guanajay, rather. It was all because we went into that

sulfur spring together. It looked like milk. We rolled around in the cane fields . . . What a vacation that was! Then the old lady said that poor Juana was a loose woman, a scheming so-and-so; that she had corrupted her son. That I was going to come down with something. On top of newspapers in the canefields.

'Any of you got the time?' asked Orlando, stepping down onto the sidewalk.

'I left my watch behind on purpose, I was just going to look . . .' answered Sebastián, clenching and unclenching his fists. Two days from now they'll be swollen, he thought, and ran his thumb along the pads of his palm. I have to do something, toughen them up somehow. If it comes down to it, I'll urinate on them. If it does the trick. Definitely.

'Let's go eat.'

'What if they leave?'

'Did the political commissar say we could eat now?'

'Watch it, he's right there, he's going to get pissed off . . .'

'Oh, but that title is an honor.'

'Power always corrupts.'

'You already said that.'

'Yeah, old man, Marino said we should go now and eat quickly. But even if we take awhile they'll wait for us. They're not going to go without us. There's a lot of us. You must always count on the masses.'

Four, seven started walking down the middle of the street. The white building fronts, chipped, yellowing, crooked, painted and repainted, rose up and fell away on the sidewalk. A black railing was the only thing that separated the clean, dark, almost empty rooms from the street baking in the sun.

'It looks like there's something over there,' exclaimed Ramón, and they all walked across some planks splashed with reddish mud that were laid like a bridge over a deep ditch, which continued on and then went around the corner.

'What do they have to drink?' asked Sebastián, taking a place next to Diana.

'Order me a mamey milkshake, go on.'

'I'll pay for both of them,' Sebastián said for the second time, putting down his empty glass, lined with a pink film.

'Come on,' suggested Diana, nodding her head toward the door.

'Where to?'

'Are you afraid of me?'

'Petrified.' They crossed back over the sagging boards and headed out toward the railroad crossing. 'Y estoy aquí, aquí para quererte,' came and went through the air from a jukebox in a distant bar, 'y estoy aquí, aquí para adorarte.'

'Here,' said Diana as they reached the corner.

'What's this?'

'Empanadas. There aren't enough; if I'd taken them out there in the café there wouldn't have been enough to go around . . .'

I'm not hungry, thought Sebastián, biting into the meat pastry and looking toward the corner. Three women, dressed in bright blue and white and pale blue, were waiting next to two suitcases tied together with cords. Their tense, impassive faces stared at the deserted railroad tracks.

'Do you work in a candy store?'

'No.'

'Do you live off of Urban Reform?'

'No.'

'Do you write poetry?'

'No.'

They kept walking and stopped by an old wooden house, with a sign that read LONG LIVE SOCIALIST UNITY, and was two stories high, the only two-story house in the whole area, and abandoned. They sat on the curb.

'What do you do?'

'I paint . . . don't look at me like that. You've never seen my work. I haven't exhibited very much. Well, if you really want to know I'll tell you the truth: I've never exhibited anything.'

'What do you paint?'

'Flowers.'

'What kind of flowers?'

'I don't paint horrific things like Antonia Eiriz. I don't burn canvases or make dolls out of crutches . . .'

'Flowers are horrific too, they look like red and yellow wounds, like pus, or like purple, rotting flesh.'

'You're unbearable, you really do say the most idiotic things . . . My flowers are flowers.'

'Van Gogh's flowers look like people, that's what some old dyke named Gertrude Stein said.'

'Van Gogh's sunflowers are sunflowers, period.'

'Doesn't one thing ever remind you of another?' and Sebastián nervously ran his hand over his face.

'Personally, I find psychology boring. Don't you want another empanada?'

'And what don't you find boring?'

'I don't know,' Diana replied, shrugging her shoulders and staring fixedly at the empanada like a crab between her fingers. 'I never know what I like or don't like. One day I think one thing and the next day I think something else. Is that bad?'

If only it were possible, thought Sebastián raising his eyes, squinting into the venomous sun and looking toward the red roof-tiles of a house that some stubborn fool borrowed money to buy on the corner, if only we could walk away from here, turn the corner and find ourselves suddenly on Sixth Avenue, on the subway grills, and feel the hot air lifting her skirt like Marilyn's and hear the racket of the train going by and then turn on to 53rd Street. If only I could take you to the Museum of Modern Art and see once again Van Gogh's cheap, starry night and Cézanne's cold apples and show you Redon's flowers, Matisse's piano lesson, the sensual, decorative nudes of Modigliani with their amazing skin and all their hair, the *Guernica*. Hug you and kiss you right there, in some corner of the museum, feel everything smoldering inside me, like Pollock's veins and nerves, weaving all the colors together and exploding.

'Nothing is bad,' said Sebastián, looking at her eyes, the skin on her face and her mouth free of lipstick, the almost purple edges of her lips, and her hair, 'if you can do it without suffering, without getting caught and punished . . .'

Diana swallowed the last bite of the last empanada and licked her fingertips.

And then to forget about the paintings and the dumb museum and to tour the city, just you and me, no obligations, no one watching us, no one knowing who we are; away from it all, alone on the streets full of dark, indifferent buildings; everything from the outside, how I've always lived; alone, in the autumn, when Central Park is empty, rolling around in the grass with the leaves crackling and getting stuck to your skirt and to my jacket and the ground has another smell, a foreign smell, it is not our land, and we'll feel strange, abandoned, and we'll have a little room and the wood floors will creak beneath our bare feet and you'll tell me your secrets, your childhood, and we'll eat together and sleep together and walk together and we'll never get bored because New York is the world, you never see it all nor do you find all the best spots, it is infinite like the universe, and sad. Jews, Americans, Germans, blacks and Puerto Ricans shouting, *Ay, bendito!*, speaking Spanish like us, and bad English, *el building* and *el job* and *el furnished room*. Sebastián grabbed the empty paper bag, blew it full of air and popped it on the curb. Diana didn't say anything, just blinked, and Sebastián, seated there, again felt the desire to hug her curled legs and rest his hand on her hard, ample thighs.

'We better go or we'll miss the bus. It must have been at least an hour. Maybe we can get a seat together.'

They picked up the pace and Sebastián became aware for a moment of her breasts bouncing as they pressed forward beside him.

'Why can't they go?' And three, four carefully got down off the enormous bus. 'They told me in Havana . . . If I knew that I wouldn't have come.' 'Comrades, I already brought this up . . . in the Party . .

I discussed this . . . ' Marino, on the sidewalk, gesticulated, justified himself in the midst of questions and exclamations. 'Well, then, I'm off . . . ' 'We must be disciplined, we cannot . . . ' 'We men are more sorry than you.' 'Why?' the men asked with their hands. 'Does it increase the output of the masses?' 'No, we are simply not in a position to give the women separate lodgings. Sugar cane is a tough business.' 'We're not prepared yet, next year . . . ' 'I'll give credit where credit is due, as the grocers used to say.' 'Fine.' 'Yes, I know that.' 'OK, let's get their things off the bus now, the women's things off.' They got on the bus. 'What about the food?' 'We'll have to split it up.' 'Eggs and the condensed milk.' 'Equal, separate but equal.'

'That is retrograde, Victorian morality,' exclaimed Orlando, 'I believe in Marxism-Leninism and in free love, like in the first years of the Russian Revolution . . . If we can imitate the Russians in other things, why can't we imitate them in that too?'

'Nowadays, no one ever imitates the Russians in Cuba, we have the right to make our own mistakes now.'

'And then they say that we're bourgeois.'

'In socio-economic terms, and politically speaking, this is a very revolutionary revolution, but the customs are conservative. Personal relationships are still dominated by the bourgeois mentality, hypocrisy and what the neighbors will say . . . '

'You can't have everything.'

'They're gone. Let's go to the Ritz Hotel.'

'They are fostering homosexuality.'

'The queens must be happy. You can't please everyone.'

Ramón blushed and smiled. 'I want to buy myself a hat, I don't have one. My head is burning up, this sun; remind me . . . '

Such is life, thought Sebastián, holding his breath. He flushed the toilet. One starts off imagining great romantic adventures and ends up in a stinking toilet. He smiled. Brilliant. Nothing was going to happen anyway. But what if I had suggested going back to Havana together? I'm sure she would have shaken her head. She really did turn me on. That mulatto skin, those plum-colored lips, flowery thighs, eyes the same color as cockroach wings . . . Nobody wants to take risks anymore. People separate, they break up with the people they love the most, die and that's it. Shit, what a fucking life!

He inhaled deeply as he passed the kitchen: the smell of fried fish and smoke and sweat and chopped onion and hot grease and sacks full of rice, chickpeas and sweat.

'I don't feel like eating, I already had some empanadas . . .' Sebastián announced, sitting down across from Orlando. 'Isn't there anything sweet? I feel like something sweet.'

'Well, the apple jam is good, it's very good,' and he sipped the last of his beer from a thick glass mug. 'It must be Bulgarian, in Havana they sold out right away.'

Sebastián dipped a cracker into the jam and lifted it gingerly to his mouth.

'This is our farewell to civilization,' Marino declared. 'This time tomorrow we'll be eating on red dirt . . . We who thought women would cook for us and bring water and coffee to us out in the sugar-cane fields . . . '

'Even if it was just to look at them.'

'I personally have already learned to be obedient and disciplined,' proclaimed Orlando. 'It's more convenient that way. In order to survive one has got to be submissive . . . I'm not one of those writers who put in their biographies: he always defended the poor and fought injustice. Mine would be say: his pen was never raised to defend a just cause . . . '

'That's very good,' said Sebastián. 'We should invent the decalog of the submissive man. We could start off something like this: Ever since he was a little boy he understood that his parents were not right but they were strong, and he acquiesced.'

'And: an original thought never once crossed his mind.'

'He forgot everything except orders.'

'I got a good one. The motto of the submissive man is: always on the side of power, but going down humbly.'

'That's a double entendre.'

'Do you realize that a few hours from now we are going to be cutting sugar cane exactly, I mean exactly, like the slaves did a hundred and fifty years ago?'

'Slaves worked sixteen hours a day,' maintained Eusebio, with a white cigarette between his nicotine-stained teeth and thick, dark lips. 'Are you planning to work in the fields sixteen hours every day? All of you planning to work on the plantation the rest of your lives?'

'I just remember the orders.'

'Underdevelopment can sink anyone. Just about the entire population is thrown into agriculture, the whole island out in the crops, and in advanced countries, in the United States, that imperialist shithole, something like eight per cent of the population is enough to solve the problem of feeding everyone; and to top it off *they* used to rob *us* . . . '

'It's easier not to think about it. Let them invent! as Unamuno used to say.'

'Cybernetics will solve all the problems,' exclaimed Sebastián, 'machines are the solution.'

'Do you know how long it will take to automate Cuba?'

'In the United States thirty-five thousand people lose their jobs to automation every week,' Marino reminded them, spinning an empty beer bottle on the marble tabletop.

'In the Soviet Union the same thing is happening, they're automating production, but without unemployment.'

'What about us?'

'Don't think about it. If you keep talking like that you won't cut one single cane of sugar,' said Marino, lighting a cigarette. 'We'll get there, one day we'll be communist.'

'I don't know how! We sure won't get there cutting sugar cane, even if we manage to cut a billion tons,' Sebastián commented, looking at two of the guys around the table, one fingering a hard, ripe pimple and the other grabbing the back of a chair and rocking it back and forth.

'I just remember the orders,' repeated Orlando, feeling the attention on him. 'I am a submissive man. Who ever said civilization was good? We must maintain the innocence of primitive man.'

'That's like being a beautiful animal in a cage. I want to be a civilized guy, no hair, no muscles, but industrialized. Yeah, even if I live in alienation and they drop the A bomb on me. It's a risk we have to take, as Fidel said, to get a place in history. Even if they rip your balls off, it's the only justification. Man is nothing more than an aspiration, the desperation to get somewhere, who knows where . . .'

'That's all very abstract.'

'Well, think about tourism, all the tourists who used to come to Cuba to lie around, with the natives in the background, entertaining them with all that steamy music and all those big-bottomed women and those pictures of black Superman in the brothels, how many inches was he, do you remember?'

'I don't know, about fifteen . . . '

'Che was right. Developed socialist countries have to pay a price for bringing us out of the cane fields . . . '

'That's not how politics works,' Sebastián remarked, leaving his plate of solid jelly unfinished. 'It's I got mine, Jack.'

'You think so?'

'We've talked enough shit. Come on, it must be late.'

'Who are those two?' asked Ramón, gesturing toward the beardless and pimple-covered faces.

'I don't know, I believe they're novel writers,' said Orlando smiling. 'I think one is named León. The other one, I reckon, is a painter. They're even more fucked than we are. At least we were able to travel and see museums and experience things and read whatever we felt like.'

'They don't need any bourgeois freedoms now. They have a country, we had a colony, a factory. I would have preferred to be young now,' and Marino took the band off a cigar. 'They have something concrete to make sacrifices for, a reason to have a hard time . . . l had a hard time for the sake of it . . . they're building socialism.'

'You are so full of shit . . . You would not want to be in their shoes.'

'No, I'm being serious. I'm a miserable sod, I know.' The sugar-mill chimney, narrow and yet wider than the three palm trees next to the railroad switch, spewed out smoke that broke up the sky with a thin, gray cloud. It was the sole point of reference on the landscape, the only thing that registered the kilometers going by as the bus changed position. Everything else was green; square sugar-cane fields went by again and again all along the highway, blocking out the mill.

'All that sugar cane has to be cut? One generation passeth away and another cometh but the cane abideth forever . . . '

Two heads turned towards the voice, but no one responded; just a grunt.

They turned in opposite a huge white fence announcing in black letters 'Free Cuba Farm'; the bus slowed down. Some houses, low to the ground and scattered like plastic models among the cane fields and the red ground, had rose bushes in their gardens. The flat, monotonous landscape swallowed up the houses.

'Well, in terms of masonry, this farm is ideal. Do you reckon the bathrooms might have bidets?'

'And bars.'

The rider moved the reins slightly and the horse took the path next to the road. The horse was all skin and bones, but the farm-worker had a rifle lying across his legs; he nodded his head by way of a greeting.

The bus passed an empty cart, pulled by a small tractor with enormous wheels; it turned down a dirt road between one field of sugar cane and another of yucca. Finally it stopped next to a long and narrow hut, their living quarters, with a dung roof and a dirt floor. Through the stanchions you could see a banana plantation, a few palm trees and now a pale patch of sky.

'Let's go get the hammocks now, it's getting dark. Where are the hammocks?'

'Over there, they're sacks . . . '

'I'm going to the bathroom.'

'What bathroom?'

'Those banana trees,' and he held up a strip of toilet paper that unrolled and flapped in the breeze.

'These sacks are rotting.'

'Get another one.'

'You know, a hell of a lot of people are going to be cramming their asses in here at night.'

'I brought my own hammock,' Orlando quipped, extracting from his backpack an olive-green canvas with wide slips at either end.

'Let's all set up in here.'

'No more hammocks will fit in here, there are seven already. You guys go to the other bedroom.'

'What bedroom?' asked Sebastián, pointing to the uneven red dirt, the vertical beams supporting the roof.

'Well, what is it then?'

'Don't ask me, but it's not a bedroom. It's an open space between two posts. In my vocabulary there are no words for this new experience. My vocabulary is very poor and besides, I only have urban words, from the city.'

'Where did you get that machete?'

'They're giving out machetes over there, do you see that big mulatto guy . . .'

'And gloves?'

'Them too.'

'Come on, Eusebio, let's go and collect our work tools.'

'My ancestors already cut cane for me,' and Eusebio smiled with a cigarette between his teeth. 'I have nothing to worry about, my account is more than settled. Now it's you whities who have to cut sugar cane.'

'They appear to be taking this sugar-cane business quite seriously,' Orlando exclaimed. 'I thought this was all a game. I've been deceived!'

'I just got here,' said Sebastián, 'and I'm tired already.'

II

ON YOUR FEET! ON YOUR FEET! it's pleasant and unpleasant a sudden blast of bitter cold screams shakes defenseless twisted bodies in the quivering hammocks unpleasant because it is still dark out and cold and all change irritates annoys and it's a dirt floor and your feet lethargic toes unenthused search for your boots and your boots weigh a ton and pleasant because after hearing ON YOUR FEET! you can always spend a few more minutes in the precarious hammock and revel in it and dream about saying to hell with it all and keep sleeping and move your arms sensually rub your legs against the rough canvas stretch carry on a few more minutes a few more seconds conscious of being asleep and awake and getting up with a stiff neck an aching back all twisted up warped like wood and anyway what does it matter if you slept poorly you were so damn cold the cold air snuck in under the hammock all around if you moved you fell and if you pulled up the covers your toes stuck out your ass your shoulders if you pulled the blanket down and it is so cold at night so bitterly cold that you cannot sleep you wake up it causes pain frostbite in Cuba from night to morning the cold is unbearable and waking up is not unpleasant because you slept curled up in a ball like a dog the same bed as the indians the same house as the indians hammocks and thatch-roof huts time stuck does not advance and to sleep ON YOUR FEET! ON YOUR FEET! you shout yourself now heavy bodies cough spit scratch mosquito bites clear throats yawn blow absorb emit mucus and you roll up the blanket bang into the posts and the boot leather digs in to your ankles go out into the early morning and your member frozen stiff and would you like to serve yourself the woman asks the almost old man to his wife before going to the bathroom each morning truth or just a story it is possible and satisfied urinates looking at the sky the shadows the shrubs and always some palm tree always some palm tree on the horizon the palm tree does not exist it is photographed painted drawn a hallucination it is the Cuban coat of arms and some unbearable joker screams again now from inside our barracks ON YOUR FEET! and it is a bad joke and yet you have to smile you cannot help it is man always a bit stupid and very brave in his stubborn persistence ON YOUR FEET! and he thinks of urinating on his hands and does not he decides to endure it to wait until later and two days go by and on the third he urinates on his hands his blisters his wrists and now ON YOUR FEET!

The sugar cane defiantly grows there in the plantation it is persistent monotonous interminable and only violence can chop it down only obstinacy can fell it insanity can insist the body worn down hands covered in sores back aching raise the machete lower the machete sugar cane is always the same and the sun but first the dew in the morning wet boots walking down the road or in the truck or on the tractor down the road the boundary lines at dawn still cold although you cannot see in the dark the sugar cane is there the plantations become visible in the shadows the mist and you see yes really the sugar cane at the side of the road and then your constant furrow and you have to take a shit first and you have to slip in behind the arum trees and move your bowels the first days stopped up terrified your body closed down nothing all of them did you go or not and did I go or not and how many times is it another victory and your buttocks covered with dew and one feels unclogged and goes back to the constant furrow to the stalk against the sugar cane the obstinacy against the sugar cane rage against the sugar cane the dew has evaporated the sun swallows it up the slightest wave sucks up the slightest thread and Góngora is sucked up by the sun is lost dissolves the sugar cane we cut with our souls and now sweat falls on the pointed leaves and the shirt hot and soaking your body is wet and the sun and the sugar cane and there is always another stalk and water drink water and thirst longings choke obstruct the water falls in a trickle from the canteen down your chin and your neck and you wipe

it dry with your sleeve full of millions of stickers the stickers from
the sharp sugar-cane leaves the cane always overdue indifferent
passive stupid and you crave an enormous machine and gigantic
knife as wide as a plantation cutting down stalks and more stalks and
in one fell swoop and you twist your ankle and cut and get a song
stuck in your head y estoy aquí para quererte y estoy aquí para
adorarte y estoy aquí aquí para decirte AMOR AMOR AMOR y estoy aquí
para quererte and you do not want to keep singing and you sing and
you do not want to keep cutting you raise the machete and you are
afraid your hands already stiff afraid the machete might go sailing
off and cut off a head a hand and the sugar cane scorched scorched
and soon you hurl yourself into it you race along do not have to
winnow just cut and when the sun is up everything is filled with ash
the ash gets into your eyes your nose your neck and your pants in
your hair ash and around your waist your prick your ass and it is no
longer nice even to sit down and suck on the sugar cane the cane
tastes better when cold early in the morning but so anxious you are
so desperate that you take no pleasure and everything dirty sticky
hands and you think you cannot take anymore and keep on and no
longer any energy and you walk and cut and walk in the plantation
the stubborn sugar cane dirty sweet rural vegetable the sugar cane
insistently grows there on the plantation.

And to wash to wash in the afternoon the sun going down to turn
over on top of cold water naked defenseless like a plucked bird and
soap and cold water and filth at your feet foamy gray filth and then to
flop down clean on the hammock eternity is midday the breeze
stretched out in the hammock reading the paper if a five-day-old
paper comes it does not matter here it is always yesterday news
deforming reality the world isolated and to move a little in the
hammock and to feel your aching muscles and the breeze and some
friend passes by offers a candy has come from town from the store a
cigar because those barracks are a tribe and the enemy the one in
charge and the field boss the country people who go by on horse the
sullen farmers who ask for more volunteers every year and they

ought to field work is mule's work more volunteers look and smile at each other and pass by the barracks with the cart and shout at the oxen commander admiral and at times son of a bitch volunteer from Havana the guilt of many of our intellectuals and artists resides in their original sin they are not genuine revolutionaries goes down like a bomb in the barracks the *Granma* paper arrived with Che's letter about the new man and silence people scratching swollen mosquito bites read out loud and what do we have to do in order to be considered revolutionaries integrate with the people six years the revolution Bay of Pigs the October Crisis die have you to die and be born again and you cannot go down on all fours what else can you do and you have to laugh and keep on here obstinate cutting sugar cane clearing it and you eat voraciously and snore and a disturbed night finally falls in agitation the last night and you do not sleep and you do not cut sugar cane the hammocks are cut down forced laughter strained hysterical laughter sharp cries threats of the machete's hack you sleep finally you close your eyes stalk after stalk a sea of green sugar cane passing like a school of fish through the green water stalks and sugar cane and to wash ON YOUR FEET!

III

'Don't you notice anything odd?' asked Orlando, staggering to one side and smiling. 'The town of Jovellanos could be Havana, London, Paris . . . '

'No, I mean, doesn't it seem strange to be walking here?'

'Yeah,' exclaimed Sebastián, 'we don't know how to walk down a street anymore, you just keep waiting, your legs wait, your muscles wait to find the furrows and the clods on uneven dirt roads.'

'I was noticing that my legs were limp,' and Marino ran his hands over his thighs, 'and that's it, that's exactly it.'

'The world beneath our feet has changed.'

'It's not that big a deal, friends,' smiled Ramón, 'it's not that big a deal, all we did was spend a fortnight in the canefields.'

'Each day was a year.'

'When I get back to Havana I'm not going to leave the air conditioning,' said Paco, 'I am going to spend a week locked in my study wearing shorts and listening to Bach and Mozart and asking Irene to bring me big glasses of iced tea and lemonade . . .'

'What I want to do is get in a bathtub full of hot water,' suggested Sebastián, 'soak in a tub of hot water. Although I think that after being stuck in the cane fields you can no longer enjoy civilization. It's been spoiled . . . Now I'll keep thinking of the plantation at eleven in the morning with the sun on the back of my neck . . . I'm permanently fucked up now, I'm not bourgeois or revolutionary anymore. I'm a rebourgelutionary.'

'You'll get over it,' said Orlando, 'a week from now you won't remember a thing.'

'Shall we go eat at the Ritz?'

'Do you think it's still there? What I want to do is get back to Havana fast.'

'We'll be here awhile,' said Marino. 'They told me at the Party that we all had to go back to Havana in a convoy, so we have to wait here until everybody from the surrounding areas arrives . . . '

'All go back in a convoy, what for?' asked Paco.

'We are heroes of the socialist project.'

'What I want is to get home fast.'

'Besides, when we get to Havana no one will even notice, a bunch of busses is like nothing, like listening to rain . . . Eusebio took a train back, he already left.'

'You're right,' said Marino, 'after we eat we can go talk, bring up the matter. Discuss it at the Party.'

'I'm a bit short of cash,' said Orlando.

'I've got some, I have ten pesos left from the expenses money, there are ten pesos here, whoever is short I'll pay for.' 'I have a few pesos,' said Sebastián, grabbing a five-peso bill and two twenty-cent

coins with his awkward fingers. 'I can't even feel the money in my
hands, I hardly have any feeling in my fingers.'

'I still can't make a fist, it really hurts . . .'

'It's a pleasant kind of pain,' said Ramón, 'you can and cannot
clench your fist.'

Sebastián ran his hands across the clean white tablecloth.

'When you stroke your wife you're not going to feel anything,
Orlando.'

'It will be a new feeling, an agricultural feeling.'

'Well, I haven't felt anything with my wife for years,' remarked
Marino, lighting a cigar, 'I've been married more than fifteen years.'

'When you get back, it'll be different.'

'Doubt it, but I have a mulatta on the side too . . .'

Ramón rubbed his calluses under the table, in the dark, with his
thumb.

'Now is the time to confess, my subaltern patriots, as Roberto says,
is anyone here not a romantic and not living with a colored woman?'

'It's the obsession of white Cubans.'

'We are all black now, whites and blacks, we're all black to the
Americans. Dirty, hungry, backward, colored people.'

'Why won't they serve us here? Have you noticed? We look like a
bunch of peasants.'

'Sebastián looks like an Englishman on his island plantation, all he
needs is the hat.'

'Come off it, we could all pass for peasants, the first time we came
in here they served us right away, they're discriminating against us
'cause we look like local yokels.'

'Psst, waiter!'

'Well, in any case,' said Marino, 'it's been a very good experience,
cutting sugar cane is healthy, here we are complaining, but I'm not
sorry.'

'For the first time I feel really involved in the country, we can't
dream of another life anymore, we're all over thirty now, we can't
just go around criticizing everything like snot-nosed kids; if this all

goes down, you go down with it, and if it floats, you float. This is where I stand until the end.'

'After the sugar-cane experience I find it difficult to speak,' said Orlando. 'I realize that I constantly talk shit. I say the same things but it's just not the same anymore.'

'Why won't they serve us? We've been here almost half an hour. Waiter!'

'It's time for direct action,' said Orlando, slamming his hand down on the table. 'Waiter!' he shouted, and hurled a glass to the floor, breaking it. 'Watch, you'll see how they serve us now.'

Upon reaching the park and before striking a match to light a cigar, Sebastián saw Ramón cross the street and head toward a group of guys, sitting and standing around a bench by the grass.

'Those are the guys from our brigade, they're the new-generation artists,' said Sebastián, 'it looks like something's going on.'

'We're going to party headquarters,' said Orlando, 'you can lie down and have a nap in the hall there.'

'What's the matter?' asked Sebastián, approaching the taciturn group. 'Is anything wrong?'

'No, nothing,' said León, touching his face. 'Stop touching your face, your hands are covered with dirt,' said Ramón, 'you're going to get an infection.'

León lowered his hand.

'That's not right.'

'What?'

'You've already eaten, right?' asked the painter. 'We haven't.'

'Why didn't you come with us?' asked Sebastián. 'With what we had there would have been enough for all of you, too.'

'How were we supposed to go along with the group if no one paid for us?'

'That doesn't matter, Orlando didn't have any money and he came with us.'

'That doesn't matter,' said León. 'You shouldn't have to pay for us, the person in charge, Marino, has the responsibility to see that everybody gets to have lunch . . . He didn't think about the others. Are we going to be here until eight o'clock without having anything to eat?'

'I have a peso,' said Ramón. 'Here, take it . . . '

'And I have two pesos left, come on,' said Sebastián.

'No, it's too late.'

'Why?'

'We're not fucking starving to death or anything. You just didn't behave like comrades, that's all, going off to eat like that and leaving us here.'

'You're right, that's true,' said Ramón, 'but what matters now is that you go eat. Don't be silly. Take the money.'

'We're not going to take anything. Marino always tries to make out like he's the party's oldest communist and then he goes and screws us over like that . . . That's not revolutionary, it's not communist.'

'Yeah, but we already left the barracks behind, we're going home to Havana, it's back to the law of the city now, you solve your own problems as best you can, the solidarity of the barracks is over.'

'That is not revolutionary, then they go and tell you that you have to make sacrifices.'

'No one is perfect, not even the system . . . '

'Yeah, but we haven't eaten, and we all cut cane together, we shared everything for fifteen days,' and he placed a dirty boot on the end of the bench. 'I helped you out many a time with your furrow when you were tired.'

'Nothing can be done about that now,' said Ramón, still extending his arm, holding out the three wrinkled pesos, 'Go on, take them, go and eat now . . . '

'We're not going to take anything and we're not going to eat anything.'

The shoeshine boy's brush was cleaning the dust and dirt from the boots, but leaving the toe scruffy, dirty. Toward the ankle of the left boot there was a gash from a machete, a wound filled with red dirt.

'What kind of work did you women do?' asked Sebastián, looking

at Diana's arm enclosed in the bus window and in the distance the
same palm trees and hills and silk-cotton trees as ever, then and now.
The soft hair on her arm was blond, washed out, golden from the
sun. Diana looked at her broken, dirt-filled fingernails and made a
fist, hiding her fingers. Now the sun was going down behind some
cows, immobile in a field, with their heads to the blue grass, without
sun, distant.

'First we picked tomatoes but there weren't enough so when there
were no more tomatoes they sent us to another farm, where we cut
sugar cane. You should have seen me . . . '

'Didn't they say that cutting sugar cane was too tough for women?'

'Yes, but I was really good at it . . . ' and she smiled. 'We could have
all been together.'

'Yes, we missed all of you a lot,' but Sebastián thought it was
better off as it had been. 'I missed you a lot. What happened to your
tight flowered pants?' he said, looking at her now olive-green thighs.

'They got dirty. I was putting them on at night and I fell into a
mud puddle, like an idiot. We went out one night and didn't have a
flashlight . . . '

It was better that way. She would have seen me all sweaty and in
pain and scratching myself and I would have seen her in a mud
puddle. With no feeling in my hands. The mud and the mosquito
bites with discharge oozing out. Women in pants are not women,
thought Sebastián as they crossed the province of Matanzas and he
focused his surprised eyes on women in dresses, their legs exposed
and their skirt folds fluttering. Hygiene is the anticipation of
caresses, as Dolores del Río used to say. He noticed a wrinkled old
woman with a small veil tied into her dyed hair. She moved slowly,
wrinkled. Have they eaten? He felt guilty, he could still taste the food.
That's not revolutionary, it's not communist.

'Did you cut that yourself?' asked Sebastián, looking at a bundle
of thick canes on the floor, carefully tied together, still green and
stained black at the knots, next to his clean boots with the still-dirty
gash.

'What do you think? I'm taking them to my old lady. Aren't you taking anything back?'

'I don't have an old lady, mine is in the States. Besides, I want nothing to do with sugar cane anymore.'

'Until next year.'

'Yeah, until next year. I left everything on the plantation: the gloves, hat, those pants that are stained from cutting scorched sugar cane. That way I won't contaminate my apartment . . . l want to forget sugar cane and plantations exist . . . Even when I close my eyes, I still see that cane.'

'You are a silly fool.'

'And you are lovely, your skin, your eyes, in spite of the mud and the cane and your dirty broken fingernails.'

'Madrid, qué bien resistes
Madrid, qué bien resistes
mamita mía, los bombardeos, los bombardeos . . . '

they were singing here and there on the bus; Marino sang with a broken voice.

León stood up and, from his seat, conducted the chorus with his hands, smiling,

'De las bombas se ríen
de las bombas se ríen
mamita mía, los madrileños, los madrileños . . . '

sang León and Marino together.

'Don't be silly,' insisted Diana, 'as soon as you get back to Havana, after a week in Havana, you won't remember a thing. That'll be my job. A few days from now, I'll remind you and you won't even believe it . . . '

'Yes, I am silly, stupid. Full of shit. People forget everything fast. I can't,' and he listened to them sing. They haven't eaten and yet they sing, they're angry and yet they sing. They were angry . . . not anymore. I'm getting goose bumps again. I thought they'd started to doubt, they were disillusioned with the revolution and look, Marino and the men together singing songs of struggle . . . They can live with the mistakes and the contradictions without losing their minds. Consistency doesn't matter anymore, just roll with the punches, it's the wave of the future. And on with the revolution. *Y palante con la revolución.*

TRANSLATED BY LISA DILLMAN

The Seven Dead Seasons*
Pedro Pérez Sarduy

I

That night I remember saying lots of things, including two swear words. Mum said if I didn't go to sleep she would spank me twice with Daddy's heavy rubber sandals. That night I also remember I was eight years old. It was the last night we all slept together under the same roof.

II

Once upon a time, there was a 'dead time', when at noon I'd go to Horace's to buy 'squashed black' (a cake filled with guava jam), negrito atropellao as we used to call it in Pueblo Nuevo. Then I'd go off with the bundles of watercress I had to sell and sell so that the next day, when Grandpa paid me a cent for every bundle sold, I could eat negrito atropellao at noon.

III

When it rained the boy's room, as Auntie Nena used to call it, would be very wet; it had a zinc roof which Teebaya, her husband, had bought in the last zafra* (the floor was still earthen) and I would

*After the zafra or sugar harvest, 'tiempo muerto', when before the 1959 Cuban Revolution thousands of seasonal cane-cutters had no work.

listen close to the big drops falling heavily, wanting to be one of those drops myself and, when the sun came out above the mango tree, to turn into steam and evaporate away. But when it cleared up and was night-time and the boys didn't come back till late and I was sleeping on my own, outside in the yard I would hear something going like 'pssst, pssst' . . . and my chest would feel like a big lump of sweet potato. In the morning Auntie Nena told me there were crickets that hissed like that. After that, I never wanted it to rain and then clear up, and even less so if it were night.

IV

Nene, my cousin, and I always went around together, up and down, through the scrub, feeling below the stones to see if we could get hold of snails shells to play with.* But there were times when the next day was Sunday and we would have to steal bottles to sell to the Turk: he paid well – two cents a litre bottle and six for a dozen pint bottles. Or we would look out whatever scrap metal we had collected. 'Tomorrow is Sunday and we must get to the matinée movie,' I'd say to Nene between sighs.

V

I nearly always had stomach ache. Auntie Nena said it was worms. One day in school – I was in fifth grade – I had terrible colic . . . and the big fat white teacher wouldn't let me go to the toilet; I held it and held it . . . but when the class ended and I got up from my desk, the others made fun of me and I cried all the way home, I was so ashamed. I remember how for two weeks I wouldn't go to school.

*Used to be called 'cockfight'. The game was like conkers but was played with empty snail shells.

VI

When it was zafra-time at the sugar mill, Teebaya went off in the early morning and wouldn't be back till late afternoon. Then he'd get the idea in his head to take out his old clodhopper sandals and go down to his vegetable garden. 'Ramoncito . . . Ramoncito, fetch me two buckets of water from the pump! And so, Ramoncito went to the pump for water, again and again and again. There were times when the weight of the buckets nailed my eyes to the path I'd beaten from the house to the pump. My eyes watered from the dirt, from thinking that instead of a path it was an endless ravine.

VII

One Sunday afternoon, one of those hot Sundays full of midges, I hadn't gone to the town centre because I didn't have any shoes. So I stayed home on the porch reading for the nth time a comic magazine after taking a bath. Then, all of a sudden I heard, like when the guije* announces some good or bad omen, a whistle I hadn't heard for two years which made me realize that Daddy was coming laden with parcels around the corner by the big porch to the house belonging to Pastora, the fat old white woman who sold wonderful fruit-flavoured ice cubes for a cent. I laughed, cried, even shouted as I always used to and couldn't stop babbling. Afterwards we went out with my little sister, who called Daddy by the formal usted. I told him everything, really everything, and he said, 'Stop your crying and tomorrow we'll go away together!' When that happened my sister was very little and I remember the 13 May was my eleventh birthday.

TRANSLATED BY JEAN STUBBS

* guije: Afro-Cuban name for a little black goblin or childish dwarf (from Yoruba legend).

Buried Statues
Antonio Benitéz Rojo

That summer – how could I forget it? – after don Jorge's lessons were over for the afternoon and Honorata had pleaded with us for a while, we'd go out hunting butterflies in the gardens around our mansion, which was up on a hill in Vedado. Aurelio and I would give in to her because she had a limp on her left side and because she was the youngest (in March she'd turned fifteen), but we wouldn't give in till she begged us, so we could see her lower lip start trembling and the tears come to her eyes and her fingers start twisting at her braids – though the truth was, deep inside we liked to draw straws for the hunting horn, out at the empty dovecote, and wander through the statues with our butterfly nets at the ready, following the paths through the Japanese garden, which were paved with stepping stones and full of pitfalls under the wild vegetation that grew right up to the house.

That vegetation was the biggest threat to us. It had taken over the fence on the southwest years ago – the one facing the Almendares River, which was the wettest side, the side that gave the vegetation the greatest encouragement. The undergrowth had even taken over the plots that Aunt Esther was in charge of, and in spite of all of her and poor Honorata's efforts, it was battering at the big windows in the library and the French doors of the music room. Since that undermined the security of the house (which was Mother's responsibility), loud arguments that led to impasses would end our meals and there were times when Mother, who got terribly nervous when she wasn't 'under the influence', would put her hand on her head to signal one of her migraines and burst into tears and then threaten, sobbing, to desert the house, yield up to the enemy her part of the joint ownership of the property if Aunt Esther didn't weed out (always within an exceedingly short time) the vegetation that was overrunning the porches and that might well be a weapon deployed by those on the outside.

'If you prayed a little less and worked a little harder . . . ' Mother would say as she stacked the plates.

'And if you stopped hitting the bottle for a while . . . ' Aunt Esther would shoot back.

Fortunately, don Jorge never took sides; he would retreat into silence with his long gray face, folding his napkin, avoiding becoming embroiled in the family's dispute. Not that don Jorge didn't belong to the family – after all, he was Aurelio's father; he had married the sister who came between Mother and Aunt Esther, the sister whose name nobody spoke any more. But be that as it may, he wasn't a blood relation and we spoke to him with the formal usted rather than the informal tú, and never called him 'Uncle'.

It wasn't like that with Aurelio. When nobody was looking we would hold hands with him, as though he were our boyfriend, and that summer was the summer he was supposed to choose between us, since time was passing and none of us were children any more. All of us loved Aurelio for the way he carried himself, his lively black eyes and above all, that special way he had of smiling. At lunch or dinner, the biggest servings were for him, and if you could smell Mother's boozy breath above the odors of the food, you could bet that when Aurelio handed his plate toward her to be served, she would serve him slowly, her left hand grasping his against the chipped edge of the rim. But Aunt Esther wasn't far behind her – with the exact same diligence she fingered the beads of her rosary, she would grope for Aurelio's leg under the tablecloth and kick off her shoe. That was the way the meals went. Of course, he allowed himself to be loved, and if his room was next to don Jorge's, back in what used to be the servants' quarters, totally separate from the rooms we slept in, it was because that's what the Code stipulated – Aunt Esther or Mother, either, would have given him a room on any floor, and he would have appreciated it, and we girls would have loved to have him so close by, to feel that he belonged to us a little more on nights when there were thunder storms, with all that lightning, and the house under siege.

The document that defined each person's responsibilities and listed all the duties and punishments, we called simply the Code, and it had been signed by his three daughters and their husbands back when my grandfather was alive. The patriarchal commandments were set down in the Code, and although it had to be adapted to new circumstances, it was the core and center of our firmness in the face of adversity and we were guided by it. I'll just briefly outline its details:

Don Jorge was given permanent right to inhabit the property free of charge and was recognized as a full member of the Family Council. He was in charge of provisions, military intelligence, resource management, education and cultural affairs (he had been Under-Secretary of Education in the administration of Laredo Brú), and also of electrical and masonry repairs and cultivation of the land adjacent to the northeast wall – the wall that divided our property from the big Enríquez mansion next door, which had been converted to a polytechnic institute since late '63.

Aunt Esther was charged with caring for the gardens (including the park), caring for any young or new-born animals that might need attending to, political agitation, water and plumbing repairs, the organization of religious observances, and washing, ironing, and mending clothes.

Mother was assigned to cleaning the floors and furniture, drawing up plans for defense, doing any necessary carpentry repairs, painting the walls and ceilings, performing medical services, and cooking and related work – which was what she spent most of her time on.

As for us – the cousins – in the morning we helped with the chores and in the afternoon we had lessons with don Jorge; the rest of the day was for recreation. Of course, like everybody, we were forbidden to set foot outside the boundaries of the estate. On pain of death.

Spiritual death, that is – the 'death on the outside' that awaited anyone who crossed to the other side of the wall. The ignominious path which, in the nine years the siege had lasted, fully half the family had followed.

But anyway – that summer we hunted butterflies. They would fly up from the river and flutter above the flowering vegetation, stopping at a petal here and there, or on the still shoulder of some statue. Honorata would say they cheered the garden up, that they 'perfumed' it – always so imaginative, poor Honorata – but it always disturbed me a little that they came in from outside and, like Mother, I was of the opinion they were some secret weapon that we didn't understand yet. Maybe that was why I liked to hunt them. Though sometimes they would startle me and I'd run, pushing the vegetation aside, cutting my way through it with my hands, thinking they were going to take me by my hair, my skirt (like that engraving that hung in Aurelio's room), and carry me off, above the wall and across the river.

We would catch the butterflies in nets we'd made out of old mosquito netting and put them in jelly-jars supplied by Mother. Then, at nightfall, we would gather in the study for the beauty contest – which might last for hours, because we had dinner late. We would take the most beautiful one out of the jar, empty its abdomen and pin it into the album don Jorge had given us; with the rest of them (an idea of mine for making the game last longer), we'd pull off their wings and organize races – we'd bet pinches and caresses that weren't sanctioned by the Code. Finally, we'd put them in the toilet and Honorata, trembling and teary-eyed, would push down the handle that would start the burbling gurgle, the basso rumblings of the whirlpool that would sweep them away.

After dinner, after Aunt Esther had lodged her allegations against Mother – who'd rush off to the kitchen with the irrevocable intention of leaving the house as soon as she'd washed the dishes – we would all go into the music room to listen to Aunt Esther at the piano, where she would play her hymns in the quivering half-light of the single candelabrum. Don Jorge had taught us a little of the violin, and its strings were still intact, but the piano was so out of tune that there was no way to play along with it, so by now we just left the violin in its case. Other times, when Aunt Esther was indisposed or Mother scolded her because she'd fallen behind in the mending, we would read aloud from things that don Jorge suggested, and since he was a great admirer of German culture, hours would pass as we mumbled through stanzas from Goethe, Hölderlin, Novalis, Heine . . . .

It was only seldom, very seldom, in fact, practically never (except on rainy nights when the house would get flooded or on some extra-special occasion) – that we would go through our collection of butterflies, the mystery of their wings penetrating deep inside us – the wings charged with signs and portents of what lay on the other side of the iron lances of the fence, outside the wall whose top bristled with broken bottles; and there we three would sit in the candlelight and silence, united in that shadowy dimness that masked the humidity of the walls, the sidelong glances, the wandering hands, knowing that we all felt the same thing, that we had come together in the depth of a dream as green and viscous as that river seen from the fence. And then that sway-backed ceiling, crumbling away piece by piece, leaving dust in our hair and on our most intimate gestures.

So – we collected butterflies.

My greatest pleasure was imagining that at the end of the summer Aurelio and I would finally be together. 'A disguised priest will marry you through the fence,' don Jorge would say, circumspectly, when Aunt Esther and Honorata were off somewhere else. I thought of nothing else; I daresay it comforted me in those interminable mornings of work; Mother was deteriorating fast (besides cooking, which always took her forever, she could barely handle the washing up of the plates and silverware), so I was the one that had to slosh water over the tile floors and shake out the shabby slipcovers and keep the rickety chair-seats dusted off.

This might be a dangerous generalization, but somehow Aurelio kept us all going – his affection helped us all bear up. Of course, there were also other things at work in Mother and Aunt Esther – but how else explain the gastronomical indulgences, the exceptional attention to the most fleeting cold or the once-in-a-blue-moon headache, the prodigious efforts to keep him strong, neatly groomed, happy? . . . Even don Jorge, who was always so proper and so measured, would sometimes turn into a mother hen. And Honorata! – so optimistic, poor thing, so unrealistic, as though she weren't a cripple. But Aurelio was our hope, our sweet morsel of wishful thinking; and he was the one that enabled us to remain serene inside those rusty fence-lances, which were so beset by enemies without.

'What a beautiful butterfly,' said Honorata on that dusky evening barely a summer ago. Aurelio and I were walking ahead, on the way back to the house – he was making a path for me with the pole of the net. We turned around to look; Honorata's freckled face was skipping through the vegetation as though she were being pulled along by her braids; above her, alongside the spreading branches of the flamboyán tree that stood at the entrance to the statuary path, there fluttered a golden butterfly.

Aurelio stopped. With a broad gesture, he signaled us to crouch down in the vegetation. He moved forward slowly, net raised, left arm stretched out at shoulder level, creeping through the undergrowth. The butterfly dropped a bit, opening its enormous wings defiantly, until it was almost within Aurelio's reach, but then, darting beyond the flamboyán, it fluttered into the allée of statues. Aurelio followed it, and soon they both were out of sight.

By the time Aurelio returned, night had fallen; we had already chosen the beauty queen and were preparing her, to surprise him. But he came in serious and sweaty, saying it had gotten away, he'd been just about to snare it, had climbed up onto the wall and been *that* close – and in spite of our insistence, he wouldn't stay for the games.

That worried me. I could just picture him up there, practically on the other side, the butterfly net hanging over the river road and him

– within a hair of jumping. I remember I told Honorata that I was
sure the butterfly was a decoy, that we had to step up our vigilance.

The next day was memorable. By dawn the people outside were up
at arms, carrying on like crazy, and they went on that way all day –
they fired off cannons and their gray airplanes left trails in the sky;
down lower, helicopters in triangular formation made whitecaps on
the pea soup river and whipped the vegetation into a frenzy. They
were celebrating something, there was no doubt about it, maybe
some new victory – and us incommunicado. It wasn't that we didn't
have radios, but for years we hadn't paid the electric bills, and the
batteries in Aunt Esther's Zenith had turned sticky and smelled like
the Chinese ointment that Mother kept in a special place in the back
of the medicine cabinet. Our telephone didn't work, either; nor did
we get a newspaper, or even open the letters that so-called friends
and traitorous relatives sent us from outside. We were
incommunicado. It's true that don Jorge carried on a trade of sorts
through the fence; without that, there'd have been no way for us to
survive. But he did it at night, and none of us was allowed to witness
the transactions, or even ask any questions about them. Though once
when he was running a high fever and Honorata was taking care of
him, he hinted that the cause was not altogether lost – world-famous
organizations were taking an interest, he said, in those of us who
were still resisting.

That evening, after all the hullabaloo had faded away – the
patriotic applause from the polytechnic people, the military music
that came over the wall and its yellowed shards of glass and drove
Mother crazy in spite of her earplugs and compresses – we
unhooked the horn from the dusty old display of antique weaponry
(don Jorge had declared a holiday) and went out hunting for
butterflies. We were walking along slowly; Aurelio's brow was
furrowed. That morning he had been harvesting the cabbages that
grew alongside the wall, and without the requisite protection he had
heard the clamor of the anthems and the feverish, unintelligible
speeches at noon. He was not himself; he had refused to abide by the

results of the drawing of lots and had usurped Honorata's right to assign us our territories and carry the hunting horn. We went off on our separate paths in silence – there was none of the joking of other times, because the rules had always been observed before.

I had been moving down the path that ran alongside the fence, more or less marking time till nightfall, my jar filled with yellow wings, when I sensed that something had got tangled in my hair. For a second I thought it was the gauze of the net, but when I raised my left hand my fingers brushed against something with more body, like a piece of silk, that bumped my wrist and then was gone. I whirled around and saw, hovering in midair before before my eyes, the golden butterfly, its wings opening and closing just at the level of my throat – and me all by myself with my back against the wall! At first I managed to control my panic; I gripped the pole and swung it; but the butterfly dodged to the right. I tried to calm myself, tried not to think about Aurelio's engraving, and began to step cautiously backward. Slowly I raised my arms, never taking my eyes off the butterfly; I took aim and swung. But the tail of the net caught on one of the iron lances and I missed again. And this time I had dropped the rod in the undergrowth along the path. My heart was pounding so that I could hardly breathe. The butterfly made a circle and lunged at my throat. I barely had time to scream and throw myself down into the vegetation. I felt a stinging sensation on my chest and my hand came away with blood on it. I had fallen on the tin ring the net was attached to and wounded myself in the breast. I waited for a few minutes and then turned over on my back, gasping for breath. It had disappeared.

The vegetation rose all around my body – it protected me, like that Venus fallen from its pedestal that Honorata had discovered deep in the park. I lay there, as motionless as that statue, looking perfectly consciously at the dusk as it fell about me, and suddenly Aurelio's eyes were in the sky and I was looking into them quietly, watching them move down along my almost-buried body and stop at my breast, and then continue down into the stalks, conquering me in the struggle and turning into the long, painful kiss that made the vegetation shiver. Afterward, the inexplicable awakening: Aurelio on top of my body, still holding his hand over my mouth in spite of the biting, his forehead marked by my fingernails.

We went back to the house – me, without a word, disillusioned.

Honorata had seen everything from the branches of the flamboyán.

Before we went into the dining room we agreed to keep the secret. I don't know whether it was because of the looks from Mother and Aunt Esther through the steam rising off the soup, or because of Honorata's sighs all night as she tossed and turned in the sheets, but the sun came up and I realized that I didn't love Aurelio as much as I had before, that I didn't need him – not him or that nasty thing either – and I swore never to do it again until my wedding night.

The morning was longer than it had ever been and when I finished my chores I was exhausted.

At lunch, I passed Honorata my ration of cabbage (as hungry as we both always were) and stared at Aurelio icily as he told Mother that a cat from the polytechnic had bitten his hand, scratched his face and disappeared over the wall. Then came the Logic lesson. I barely heard what don Jorge was saying, in spite of the nice Latin-like words he was explaining: *ferio*, *festino*, *barroco* and some more.

'I'm exhausted . . . My back hurts,' I told Honorata after the lesson, when she wanted to go hunt butterflies.

'Come on, don't be mean,' she pleaded.

'No.'

'Sure you're not just scared?' asked Aurelio.

'No, I'm not afraid of anything.'

'Really?'

'Really. But I'm not going to do it any more.'

'What, hunt butterflies?'

'Hunt butterflies or the other thing either. I'm not going to do it any more.'

'Well, if both of you don't come I'm going to tell Mother!'

Honorata suddenly shrieked, her cheeks blazing.

'I've got no objections,' said Aurelio with a grin, grabbing me by the arm. And turning to Honorata, without waiting for my reply, he said, 'Bring the nets and jars. We'll meet you at the dovecote.'

I felt confused, insulted; but when I saw Honorata walk away, limping so badly it broke your heart, I had a revelation – I suddenly understood it all. I let Aurelio put his arm around my waist and we went outside.

Submerged in the warm vegetation, we walked along in silence, and I realized that I felt sorry for Aurelio too. I realized that of the three of us, I was the strongest, and maybe the strongest person in the whole house. Funny – me so young, not even seventeen yet, and stronger than Mother with her progressively worsening alcoholism and Aunt Esther clutching at her rosary. And now, all of a sudden, stronger than Aurelio too. Aurelio was the weakest of all of us, in fact, I thought – weaker than don Jorge, weaker than Honorata; and now he was smirking, grinning lasciviously, squeezing my waist as though he'd vanquished me, never realizing, poor thing, that I was the only one who could save him – him and the whole house.

'How about here?' he said, stopping. 'I think this is the same place as yesterday.' And he winked at me.

I nodded and lay down in the vegetation. I felt him raise my skirt, kiss my thighs, but I lay there like that goddess, cold and still, letting him do it to keep Honorata's mouth shut, so she wouldn't tell the story that would make them all envious – them so unsatisfied and with the war we were fighting and all.

'Scoot a little more to the right, you two – I can't see,' called out Honorata, astride a branch.

Aurelio ignored her; he unbuttoned my blouse.

It got dark and we went back to the house, Honorata carrying the nets and me carrying the empty jars.

'Do you love me?' he said as he pulled a dry leaf out of my hair.

'Yes, but I don't want to get married. Maybe next summer.'

'But . . . you'll keep doing it, won't you?'

'All right,' I said, a little startled. 'So long as nobody finds out.'

'In that case, I don't care if we get married or not. Although the grass and weeds poke through everywhere – they're awfully itchy.'

That night Aurelio announced at dinner that he wasn't going to get married that summer, he was postponing the decision till next year. Mother and Aunt Esther breathed a sigh of relief; don Jorge barely raised his head.

Two weeks went by, Aurelio deluding himself that he owned me. I would make myself comfortable in the vegetation with my arms behind my head, like the statue, and allow myself to be touched without feeling the pain of the affront. As the days went by, I perfected a rigid pose that fired his desires, that made him dependent on me. One afternoon we were walking along on the river side of the estate, while Honorata was catching butterflies among the statues. The rains had begun and the flowers, wetted down at noon, were clinging to our clothes. We were talking about various trivial things; Aurelio was telling me that Aunt Esther had visited him the night before, in her nightgown, and suddenly we saw the butterfly. It was flying along ahead of a swarm of ordinary colors; when it saw us it made a couple of curlicues in the air and then lighted on the tip of one of the lances. It opened and closed its wings, but it didn't move from the fence-rail – it was pretending to be tired – and Aurelio, stiffening, let go of my waist so he could scale the fence. But this time the victory was mine – I lay down without a word, my skirt up around my thighs, and the situation was back under control.

We were waiting for the man because after the History lesson don Jorge had told us he was coming that night, around nine. The man had been our source of provisions for years, and he went by the name of 'the Mohican'. Since according to don Jorge he was an experienced and courageous combatant – which was hard to understand, since his house had been taken – we would welcome him as our guest after pretending to debate the question. He would help Aunt Esther exterminate the vegetation and then he would cultivate the lands on the southwest, by the river.

'I think that's him now,' Honorata said, her face pressed against the iron bars of the gate. There was no moon, so we were using the candelabrum.

We drew close to the chains that restricted access to the estate, Aunt Esther muttering a hurried rosary. The foliage parted and Aurelio illuminated a hand. Then came a wrinkled, inexpressive face.

'Password?' demanded don Jorge.

'Gillette and Adams,' replied the man in a muted voice.

'That's the password. Permission to enter.'

'But . . . how?'

'Climb the lances there, the lock is rusted shut.'

Suddenly a whisper caught us all by surprise. There was no doubt about it – on the other side of the fence, the man was talking to somebody. We looked at each other in alarm, and it was Mother that fired first.

'Who are you talking to?' she demanded, shaking off her stupefaction.

'I . . . I didn't come alone.'

'You mean . . . you were followed?' asked Aunt Esther, her voice betraying her anxiety.

'No, it's not that. It's that I . . . I brought somebody with me.'

'But good God! Who?'

'It's a young woman . . . she's just a girl, really.'

'I'm his daughter,' an exceptionally clear voice interrupted him.

We deliberated for what seemed hours. Mother and I were against it, but there were three votes in favor and one abstention – from don Jorge. Finally they dropped down on to our side.

She said her name was Cecilia and she walked with a very self-satisfied air down the dark paths. She was Honorata's age, but much prettier and without any anatomical defects. She had blue eyes and golden-blond hair, very strange-colored; she wore it straight, parted in the middle; the ends, which flipped up, reflected the light of the candelabrum. When we came to the house she said she was awfully sleepy; she went to bed early, she said – and grabbing a candle she marched very decidedly into my grandfather's room, down at the end of the hall, as though she'd known him, and closed the door behind her. After saying goodnight to everyone (holding his hand to his chest and breathing as though he were winded, or couldn't catch his breath), the man – because I now know that he was *not* her father – went off with don Jorge and Aurelio to the servant wing. We could hear him coughing every step he took. We never found out what his real name was; the girl refused to disclose his name when don Jorge, who was always an early riser, found him next to the bed the next morning, dead and without any identification.

We buried the Mohican that afternoon out by the well next to the polytechnic, under a mango tree. Don Jorge intoned a farewell to the deceased, calling him 'our Unknown Soldier', and the girl brought out a bunch of flowers from behind her back and put it in his hands. Then Aurelio started to shovel in the dirt and I helped him set up the cross that don Jorge had made. And then we all went back, except Aunt Esther, who stayed to pray for a while.

Along the path, I noticed that she was walking in an odd way; it reminded me of ballerinas I had seen as a girl at the ballet. She seemed very interested in the flowers and would stop to pick them once in a while, holding them against her face. Aurelio was supporting Mother, helping her along (the way she was staggering was sad), but he never took his eyes off Cecilia, and he smiled idiotically every time the girl looked at him.

At dinner Cecilia didn't eat a bite; she pushed the plate away as though it made her sick and then she passed it down to Honorata, who reciprocated by complimenting her on her hair. Finally I decided to speak to her.

'Your hair is such a pretty color. Where did you find the dye?'

'Dye? It's not dyed, it's natural.'

'But that's impossible . . . Nobody has hair that color.'

'I do,' she smiled. 'I'm glad you like it.'

'Could I take a closer look?' I asked. I didn't believe her.

'Sure, but don't touch it.'

I picked up a candle and went over to where she was sitting; I leaned on the back of her chair and looked at her hair for a long time. The color was perfectly even; it didn't look dyed, although there was something artificial-looking about those golden threads. They looked like cool, cold silk. Suddenly it occurred to me that it might be a wig, so I gave it a tug with both hands. I'm not sure if it was the shriek that knocked me to the floor or the shock at seeing her jump that way, but whatever it was, there I lay in a daze at Mother's feet, watching the girl run all over the dining room (colliding with the furniture as she went), head down the hall and lock herself in my grandfather's old bedroom – all the time holding her head as though it were going to fall off; and Aurelio and Aunt Esther pretending to be so upset they were beside themselves, putting their ears to the door so they could hear her bellowing, and Mother waving a spoon around with no idea what had happened, and to top it all Honorata standing on a chair applauding. Fortunately, don Jorge was speechless.

After Mother's blubbering and Aunt Esther's long-winded reprimand, I made an honorable retreat and, refusing to take the candle that Aurelio held out to me, I groped my way upstairs in the dark, my head held high.

Honorata came in, but I pretended to be asleep, so as not to have to talk about it. Through my eyelashes, though, I watched her put the candle-stand on the dressing table. I turned over on my side, to make room for her; her shadow sliding over the wall reminded me of the Games and Pastimes of the *Children's Treasure Trove*, a book by Mother that don Jorge had done the negotiations for four years earlier. Honorata's shadow made huge limping motions; back and forth it went, unbraiding her braids, opening the drawer for the white nightgown. Now it was approaching the bed, getting bigger and bigger, leaning over me, touching my hand.

'Lucila, Lucila – wake up.'

I feigned a yawn and rolled over onto my back. 'What is it?' I said as irritably as I could.

'Have you seen your hands?'

'No.'

'Aren't you going to look at them?'

'There's nothing wrong with my hands,' I said, and paid no attention to her.

'They've got . . . like . . . a stain on them.'

'I imagine they're filthy, the way I yanked on that girl's hair and shoved Mother . . .'

'But they're not filthy that way – they're *gold*,' she said, furious.

I looked at my hands and it was true – there was gold dust all over the palms of my hands and on the inside edges of my fingers. I rinsed them off in the wash basin and put out the candle. When Honorata got tired of her vague conjectures, I managed to close my eyes. I woke up the next morning late, and groggy.

I didn't see Cecilia at breakfast because she had gone off with Aunt Esther to see what they could do about the vegetation. Mother was already drunk and Honorata stayed with me to help me with the cleaning; later, we'd see to lunch.

We'd finished downstairs and were upstairs cleaning Aunt Esther's room – me dusting and shaking things out and Honorata with the broom – when somehow it occurred to me to look out the window. I stopped flicking the feather duster and contemplated our estate: to left and right, the fence along the river bank, its iron lances being swallowed by the undergrowth; closer in, beginning at the orange-flowered flamboyán, the greenish heads of the statues like the heads of drowned people, and the gray shingles of the Japanese dovecote; off to the right, the garden plots, the well, and Aurelio bending over, picking up mangoes beside the little cross; beyond that, the wall, the roof-tiles of the polytechnic and a flag snapping in the wind. 'Who in the world would break the news to the Enríquezes?' I thought. And then I saw it. It was flying very low, toward the well. Sometimes I would lose sight of it among the flowers, but then it would appear again farther on, gleaming like a golden dolphin. Now it had changed direction; it was headed straight for Aurelio, and suddenly it was

Cecilia – Cecilia emerging from the big oleander bush, running across the red ground, her hair fluttering in the breeze almost as though it were floating around her head. It was Cecilia talking to Aurelio now, kissing him before she took him by the hand and walked with him down the path that led through the park.

I sent Honorata off to make lunch and I lay down on Aunt Esther's bed; everything was spinning and my heart was thumping terribly. A while later, somebody tried to open the door – they rattled and shook it for a long time – but I was crying, so I shouted that I didn't feel well, to leave me alone.

When I woke up it was dark outside and I realized immediately that something had happened. Shoeless, I jumped out of bed and ran downstairs; I made my way down the hallway step by step, nervous and scared, muttering to myself that there was still a chance, that it might not be too late.

They were all in the living room, gathered around Honorata; don Jorge was sitting on the edge of the sofa, crying softly; Aunt Esther, on her knees beside the candelabrum, was turning toward Mother, who was flailing around in her chair, unable to sit up straight; and me, unnoticed, leaning on the doorjamb, at the edge of the circle of light, listening to Honorata, watching her act it all out in the middle of the carpet and feeling weaker and weaker; and her giving all the details, explaining how she'd seen them just at dusk walking along the river road, on the other side of the fence. And at that, the wailing broke out – Aunt Esther's prayers and supplications, Mother's keening swoon.

I put my hands over my ears, I lowered my head – I thought for a second I was going to throw up. And then, through the skin of my fingers, I heard the shrieking. After that somebody fell on the candelabrum and everything went dark.

TRANSLATED BY ANDREW HURLEY

A Cheese For Nobody
Onelio Jorge Cardoso

For Holbein López, my old friend

'I must, being within myself,
see myself through myself.'

José Martí

The psychiatrist carried, between chest and back, three fingers' breadth of liquid breakfast prepared from a teaspoon of ground coffee which had been added to the boiling grouts for the third time, three days running.

He then took his seat in front of his work table and looked at the diary. For that morning's first appointment there was a name the full length of which he was preparing to read when two timid knocks were heard at the door.

'Come in,' he said and, as it opened, he finished mentally pronouncing the name on the patient's indecisive face: 'Adelaido Ramírez A. Eight thirty.'

'Right on time,' the psychiatrist said politely. The other started to say something which came to grief amid smiles and stumbles, but the psychiatrist didn't take in the fullness of his smile or the total image of the man, for all his senses were unexpectedly dominated by a single one.

The fresh smell of soft curd cheese oozing with whey, enveloped in tender banana leaves, was invading the psychiatrist's nose in two streams of an inescapable aroma.

'I've just arrived from Cascorro, Doctor.'

But the doctor didn't hear him. Apart from feeling his mouth watering, he was transported back to his childhood as though it was he who was now stretched out and in reminiscent mood on the confessional sofa.

The house. Outside, the farmyard. The wind dispersing the cows' bellows. Aunt's hands taking it out of the mould. The cheese, still oozing. Never produced to sell, but for the household. Fashioned to a size that would provide each of them with a portion that afforded total satiety, until the request for water and the 'no, thanks, I can't any more'. Cheese unique in the world which filled a whole period of his childhood and, having savoured it in its early infancy, the family could now spread across the world, divide into new branches: marriages, births, deaths, divorces, climatic or historical events, whatever. Someone, sometime, among the oldest descendants of that cheese-assisted blood, would recall at the right moment – again in whatever climate or language of some other people – the grace of an aunt, a grandaunt, a great-grandaunt, till the disappearance of the last witness and who knows what after that, breaking the seal of future genes to result some day in the emotional manifestation of a taste for that which is white and plastic, beyond cheese and time. No, there was none like it; not in an eternity, never.

So there it is. Short trousers cut above the knee, head projecting a touch above the table, eyes in a trance, the delicious aroma in the air and the aunt – not yet entered the realm of legends, but made of blood, bones and spinsterhood – taking it out of the mould, looking at it with a pleased expression and then cutting off a piece to give him, to convey it to his mouth, bite into its soft flesh, feel the squeaky rub of the cheese against his gum and the ensuing shivers of pleasure and finally, with eyes closed, to transmit across the whole network of nerves and unleashed libido that period of his childhood which was fixed in the experience of four basic sensations: howlwindfarmyardcheese.

And this is where the psychiatrist was when the patient raised his voice to repeat what he was saying for the third time.

'I say, Doctor, please excuse me for having turned up with this.'

The psychiatrist shook his head to indicate that it didn't matter but refrained from opening his mouth which would have allowed a whole stream of saliva to escape.

'You see, I've just arrived from Cascorro, and, as I didn't want to miss my appointment . . .'

'I understand.'

'Actually, my mother made it for me. I went to see her. She knows about my problem. It's not the hard, round variety, it's a whey cheese.'

'I know,' interrupted the psychiatrist, his mood darkening and lowering his eyes, but he immediately recovered and raised his head again.

'Look, you can leave it . . .' and he broke off while he searched for a place to show him. There was a small table between the patient and himself; the other only had to stretch out his arm, which he was about to do when the psychiatrist unexpectedly stopped him.

'No! Here. Don't be embarrassed. Leave it here, with complete confidence,' and he cleared a space between his diary, the telephone and a glass ashtray in the figure of a boy wearing knee-length trousers and gobbling a bunch of transparent grapes.

Then the forces of good and evil appeared to strike an equilibrium. The patient went and quietly stretched himself out on the sofa.

Adelaido Ramírez A. was very sick. An unexpected affliction which threatened to take him to his grave from starvation had burst into his life as he was approaching forty. One morning at breakfast time, he was struck with terror as he faced his glass of milk. He had suddenly felt the deepest revulsion, followed by an irresistible impulse to crash the glass against the floor, and that was what he did. He could have sworn that death was standing on its hind legs on the edge of the receptacle. Yet death is represented by a dry word like a gunshot or a host of other small symbols, and he would have spoken the word or any of its manifold images had it come to him in some way. Besides, it was neither symbol nor sound, but a hidden reason which could not be defined within itself and could be interpreted only thus: as though it had been balancing on its two hind legs on the edge of the glass.

Then it was the squash, breadcrumb, potato and finally the coconut sweet for which he had always had a special weakness. Until the morning when his wife discovered the clue.

'Adelaido, it's the colour. The colour white. See for yourself: milk's white, the squash too, so's the bread inside, not to mention the coconut sweet.'

And then he went to the psychiatrist.

He had already spent six long months of treatment, attending his rooms twice a week.

'That trip to Cascorro, was it your own choice?'

'It was Mother's Day, Doctor. I went to see the old woman. Over at my house.'

'Isn't your house here in Havana?'

'Ya, ha!' He tried to laugh. 'Force of habit, Doctor. I'm for ever still calling it my house,' and he turned his head to excuse himself also with his look. But the psychiatrist didn't see him. He was leaning his elbows against the table, resting his head in his hands, while his markedly protruding Adam's apple travelled up and down the length of his thin, tense neck, disappearing on its downward journey behind the cheese, as seen from the sofa.

The sick man returned unmoved to his previous position.

'Tell me something about your house, the one in Cascorro. But remember, as though you were telling yourself.'

'Yes,' said the sick man and gave a deep sigh, starting to talk only when the psychiatrist was about to prompt him once again.

'It's always the same. Doesn't change. Never even been painted another colour after all these years. I think mother prefers green for the outside, to all the colours in the world.'

'And inside?'

'A milky colour.'

'White!' slipped out from the psychiatrist, his eyes shining.

'Yes, white,' sighed the other. 'My own room's the same as always: a milky shroud. My bed's over there, and at its feet, on the wall, a portrait of my father. Placed so that whichever way you turn in bed, he's still watching you.'

'Watching?'

'I mean, on the wall, watching everything.'

'When did your father die, Adelaido?'

'I was nine at the time . . . As for the rest, mother's very clean, very hard-working and . . . What else . . . ? Well, I don't think there's any more to say.'

'Did your mother remarry?'

'No. She never remarried. As though my father were still watching from the wall.'

The psychiatrist raised his head. Over the months, he had made a mountain of notes about his patient, but in not a single one had he recorded any significant alteration of mood, given his dreams and confessions. Yet now he was beginning to note certain unexpected inflections in his voice.

The psychiatrist distractedly curved his arms on the table, enclosing the cheese between his hands and his chest.

'And your father, what was he like? D'you remember him?'

'Hard. Stern. He knew it all and controlled everything. But I was nine, then, Doctor. I'm not sure. There . . . I don't know what my father was like.'

'You don't know or you don't want to know?'

The sick man felt shaken up inside but held on to his position. A silence took over. Now one could hear only the murmur of the air conditioning as it came in one way and left through another. Finally, he showed signs of restlessness and swept his hand across his forehead.

'What? Is it hurting you?'

'A little . . . Would you give me an aspirin . . .'

'Presently. First, I'd like you to tell me whether you've had any dreams.'

The sick man took his time again.

'Yes. One. I had one.'

'Go on.'

He was definitely stalling.

'Would you give me an aspirin, Doctor?'

'Yes. After you've told me ?'

'Well, nothing much . . . A bit of nonsense like all dreams . . . I was in a boat fishing with someone else. An older man he was . . . I, a boy. The water, calm and transparent; so much so that one could see right through it, like air. Below there were fish of every colour . . . Nothing much, that's about it, but . . . I was furious.' Then he stopped and looked at the doctor as though something more than a fish had escaped from his hands. This time he did catch the eyes of the psychiatrist, who retracted his arms and settled back comfortably in his chair.

'Furious? Why?'

'Please give me an aspirin. It's hurting me.'

'Go on, please.' There was a fine thread of anguish in the doctor's voice.

'Well, because, as I said, we were fishing. The man – one fish, and then another, while I . . . We never fished at the same time. But if he landed, say, a blue fish, it would go white when it came out of the water . . . On the other hand, with me it wasn't like that. I would catch them any colour, yes, but as soon as I pulled them out, they turned black and he . . . was insulting me, "Idiot! Pull them out white! You fool! Half-wit! White . . . pull them out white!"' He stopped again to turn towards the doctor.

'Should anyone be treated like that? Even in a dream?'

The psychiatrist didn't answer. He slowly got up and walked across to the small cupboard. He opened its glass door, took out a bottle and shook two aspirin tablets into his hand. Then, as he closed it again, he saw through the glass panel a poster at the back, the title of which prayed in beautiful Gothic letters, 'Hippocrates' Oath', and he closed his eyes. Then he filled a glass with water and wine and gave it to the patient with the two tablets.

His eyes were now fixed on the cheese and, when he spoke again, his voice rang with at once such decision and a sense of risk that he appeared to be addressing the victual rather than the patient.

'Who was that man on the boat with you?'

'God knows! I don't, Doctor.'

'Haven't you some idea?'

'No, none. My word.'

'Why do you say "my word"? Are you worried I might not believe you?'

'I tell you I don't know who he was.'

'You know who he is.'

'No, Doctor. I don't.'

'Do you want me to tell you?'

'You didn't dream it, I did . . .'

'That man was your father, Adelaido.'

He didn't say a word, but the rhythm of his breathing started to quicken. Meanwhile, the doctor seemed to withdraw from him abruptly. He stood up; after a while he started senselessly rearranging some papers in the drawer, as it could happen at any moment. He knew it from his experience, even his intuition, or one of the two was telling him. The buried memory might suddenly come up like the fish out of his sleep, and this time it would not disguise the colour but instead light up the patient's indignation, or maybe his weeping, who knows. And, now exposed, the big fish, subconscious and abstruse, finally trapped.

The psychiatrist shuddered. The move from libido to consciousness. The return of taste, independent from colour. Hippocrates. On his tomb, according to legend, a nest of bees produced a honeycomb, the honey of which became a panacea for all ailing creatures.

The psychiatrist was now quiet, remote, dark. And then, from the depths of his gut, rose a sound, growing to a crescendo, betraying him, which made him open his eyes and turn towards the patient.

'Guilty,' he said, and was left dumbfounded.

The sick man looked at him uncomprehendingly.

'I say, Adelaido, excuse me . . . Do you think it's necessary to continue today?'

'Well . . . Whatever you say, Doctor . . . I was only going to tell you that yes, he was my father. I knew it.'

'Of course.'

'But . . . could we decipher it, as you always say?'

'Uh!'

'What is the meaning of those fish? Why was I scolded?'

'Well . . . I think you have made a great effort for today. So it will be better . . . ' But he couldn't finish, because the sick man had unexpectedly risen to his feet, his eyes flashing with insult.

'The cursed wafer! Why did I have to swallow it?'

'Ah!' the psychiatrist said deafly.

'Yes, the body of Christ. That day, what I wanted was to play a game of ball. It was Sunday, but he took me to church. All dressed in white. And there, on my knees, while the priest was giving it to me to swallow, I was crying with fury, and Daddy near the sacristy, looking at him, watching the operation. Hell! Nobody should be treated like that!' And the sick man covered his face with his hands.

The psychiatrist sat motionless, disarmed. Who knows what dark thoughts came and went from his own childhood too, right down to his gut's rumblings. Hippocrates was by his side, handing out the sweetest portions of delicious honeycomb. And that would have carried on God knows until when, had the psychiatrist not charged across with a sudden unmeasured thump to grab the cheese.

'No, that wasn't a father. That was a tyrant. He was a tyrant. I say so.'

A moment later, as the patient was leaving the consulting room, the doctor called out after him in a thin whine of a voice.

'Adelaido, the cheese . . .'

'Leave it, Doctor, you know that I can't . . .'

'You'll be able to next week, the next cheese. You'll see.'

And as the sick man closed the door behind him, the psychiatrist opened his mouth from his forehead to his Adam's apple to swallow the cheese, but he couldn't. It remained in the air with his mouth wide open while Hippocrates continued dividing his imaginary honeycomb and handing out portions of the healing honey.

TRANSLATED BY MIRIAM FRANK

The Founders: Alfonso
Lourdes Casal

Wei wu wei
Do without doing

Great-granddaughter 1

My grandmother used to tell me that when her father was seventy
years old and blind – this was fifty years after his arrival in Cuba – he
would fly into a seething rage if he found so much as one piece of
furniture out of place. He would roam the house like some infallible
guardian of order in the world, setting chairs straight and checking
that tables were in their proper position. Very erect, with his grey
moustache cascading down over his hairless chin, he used his
gnarled hands to see the world and to reconstruct it. Wearing his
inevitable blue espadrilles, he walked with confident step, his
impeccably ironed guayabera loose over his white drill trousers.

Five decades on from the hellish journey and, at last, the dream of
respectability, somewhat modified, it's true, but made real, no doubt,
in the geometric precision of the formal living room: the mahogany
and wickerwork furniture, the piano, the six-foot-tall mirror, the vast
tapestries and the chandelier filtering its unnecessary light through the
hundreds – thousands? – of pieces of carved crystal.

Three excited taps of his walking stick would presage the coming
storm – a chair left at a careless angle or, worse, an unfamiliar object
blocking a path previously left open – followed by fulminations
against the murderous intentions of the other inhabitants of the
house.

Once order was restored, Alfonso López would flop into the armchair in the dining room.

Alfonso 1

You would flop into the armchair and when you felt the familiar pressure of the wickerwork on your bony spine, you knew that everything was in its place. Then, you would close your eyes (or leave them open, it made no difference) and look back, which is all you can do with your eyes closed and/or when you're blind and with seventy years behind you. You didn't smoke – ten years tending the leaves in the fields made you lose your taste for tobacco early on – although you had always lived off those who did smoke and it seemed to you that all the memories you had of your life came to you wreathed in smoke. As if every memorable event in your life had taken place in some small, smoke-filled room.

History 1

The importation of coolies to Cuba began in July 1847 (Zulueta & Co. of London, a Spanish ship, the *Oquendo*, 206 Chinese) and progressed slowly at first, then with great vigour from 1853 onwards, continuing busily and, of course, profitably – there is no need to say for whom – until 1874, the year of the visit to Havana of the imperial envoy, the mandarin Chin-Lan-Pin, investigator-into-the-fate-of-the-sons-of-the-great-empire-contracted-to-work-in-the-empire-of-New-Spain. Alerted by Eça de Queiroz, he decided to leave the deceptive capital and travel into the hinterland. As a result of his report, the trade contract was terminated.

The contract: four dollars a month for eight years. In southern China, during the death agony of the Manchu dynasty, that seemed like a fabulous sum. Besides, Manila wasn't so very far away and Tai-Lay-Sun was, of course, Manila. When the journey went on longer than expected – the voyage to Cuba took one hundred and fifty days – the dreams grew bitter. How many committed suicide? Others resorted to rebellion, only to die having gained control of ships they had no idea how to sail. There are legends, tales, about ghost ships, phantasmal clippers, spotted adrift on the high seas and boarded sometimes by sailors who were met by horrific scenes, the spectral spectacle of between three and five hundred corpses. Freedom and its price.

Alfonso 2

Your father – Wu Liau – had been a follower of Hung-Hsui-Chuan. You had heard him talk about the Kingdom of the Great Peace and about the Way and about Christ and the Revolution, probably in as confused a fashion as you remember it now. When your father was captured along with other rebels, a mandarin from Fukien sold him to Tanco, the Colombian who traded in coolies. Your father committed suicide, hanging himself the night before they were due to set sail. You vaguely remember the hard times that followed. Having six children and being the widow of a rebel was not much help in a country where poverty required so little encouragement, in an empire that was clearly in an advanced state of decomposition. So a few years later, you decided to take the place on the ship rejected by your father. Perhaps Taiping, the Kingdom of the Great Peace, could flower across the seas, in the lands of New Spain. Perhaps you could return one day and be a man and not the plaything of mandarins and other petty tyrants.

Even forty years later, the Spanish expression 'They made a Chinese fool out of you' still rankled. You heard your son Alejandro use it once quite innocently. You were already almost completely blind, but you still had the use of your hands and you clouted him so hard that he fell backwards into one of the flowerbeds in the courtyard. Manila, the Manila that became Havana without you realizing it: months and months of blueness – the Pacific is an inhuman, transhuman ocean-days and evenings and nights of sun and cold and salt seeping into your very bones; days and nights and evenings of pressing your face into the wooden deck to try and escape the stench of five hundred piled-up, half-naked bodies, and always that blueness and then land – which was not, however, *the* land – and the journey by train and then another ship and more blueness and, at last, New Spain.

How many people did you see die by your side? Some were carried off by strange fevers, others by terrible diarrhoea, others simply, silently, slipped overboard. The dream of the Great Peace and the dream of death.

Now, however, that you could flop into the armchair and feel the wickerwork against your bony spine, now that you could prescribe exactly where the table with the vase on it should go, now that your dog came and lay across your blue espadrilles as soon as you sat down, now you finally felt at peace. And if this peace – the peace of espadrilles and of the formal living room, of the courtyard with the flower border and the begonias and the creeper and the penetrating smell of ylang-ylang on light summer nights – if this peace was not the Great Peace, it was at least yours . . . and it was enough.

Guilt? You have earned that peace, now that it makes no difference whether you have your eyes open or closed, for you have seen far too much in your time – too many wars and deaths in the years when your eyes still had light.

Wu Liau – you remember how they brought him and deposited him like a bruised bundle in the middle of the room before your own horrified eyes and your mother's screams. Thus ends the revolution – with a rope around your neck, a filthy shirt and two imperial guards dumping you unceremoniously on the ground without a word, with a hysterical widow and six orphans and you – the eldest son – crazy enough, one day, eight years later, commending yourself neither to

God, the Devil nor to your ancestors, to go off in search of Tanco when you heard that he was back in Canton looking for workers. You arrived in Cuba only to find yourself in the middle of another war. Your owner – sorry, your contractor – could not send you to the canefields (the fields in Oriente had been burned) and so he set you to work with tobacco in Alquízar, near Havana, where it was almost as if there was no war. Now you bore your owner's surname, López; they gave you the same Christian name too, Alfonso. A brand-new name, new and Spanish, for New Spain.

Later, they told you that according to Máximo Gómez: 'There's no such thing as a Chinese deserter or a Chinese traitor.' But then you had only just disembarked and you were terrified by all the sounds and stories of war, and the Kingdom of the Great Peace seemed farther off than ever. Rumours about what was going on in the countryside reached even your field – it wasn't your field, of course, but López's, but let's not quibble over details – even relatively peaceful Havana. Many, many Chinese men fought in Las Guásimas (you didn't know it then, of course, but they began fighting the very day you disembarked, 15 March 1874). Pablo Chang used to tell you that – he was the one who wanted to rebel and take you with him. There are even Chinese commanders, Chang would say seductively, and suddenly you could imagine yourself as a mandarin, riding across the fields of Cuba at the head of hundreds and hundreds of horsemen, you in your embroidered clothes and wearing a cap adorned with glass buttons and a peacock feather. The bruised bundle of Wu Liau weighed too heavily in your memory, though, and by the time you had reached a decision, the war had ended. Later, you learned that Commander Sian used to travel barefoot and was the only one among his troops to own a poncho, threadbare and faded from countless washings. When he died, there was no one to place a coin in his mouth, nor even a coin to place there. And now, no one remembers them . . . People do not even know that any Chinese fought in the war.

So, after a small war and another big war and after mini-wars and after lean years and fat years . . . you have learned a lot. The husband of one of your daughters reached the rank of colonel in the 1895 war and what did he get for it? They shot that handsome negro, Colonel Isidro, in the back . . . No, it certainly would not have been worth your while becoming a commander.

The Chinese men who threw themselves into the revolution obviously still had that Taiping madness going round and round in their heads . . .

History 2

The Empire was 'shaken to its foundations' by the Taiping rebellion (1850–64) or, rather, the Taipings emerged out of the rotten foundations of the Empire. Hung Hsiu Chuan: visionary, prophet, military leader. An obscure peasants' revolt became a real revolution. No to the imperial aristocracy, no to Confucian ethics, no to ancestor-worship, no to the Manchu dynasty, no to private property. Yes to agrarian reform, to equality for women and language reform. No to landowners and mandarins. Yes to a revolutionary millenarianism tinged with a rather odd form of Christianity. The Taipings believed that their mission was to create heaven on earth – the Kingdom of the Great Peace that they solemnly proclaimed in Nanking when they took it in 1853.

The corrupting effects of power diluted the utopian puritanism of those early, difficult years, however; but what finally finished off the Taiping rebellion was the profits from the opium trade, which placed France and England firmly on the side of the Manchu dynasty, the Ever Victorious Army (made up of mercenaries led by an Englishman who called himself Charles George Gordon), and the landowners of Hunan who equipped the army of Tseng-kuo-fan, plus, perhaps, the fact that the rebellion was eighty years before its time. When Tseng-kuo-fan retook Nanking for the Empire, in 1864, it was clear that the extermination of the Taipings was only a matter of time.

Alfonso 3

Stripping the leaves was women's work. That was what Amalia did. Amalia was certainly different; she was a mulatta, none too bright, it's true, but fierce as they come, the daughter of a black female slave freed by her white master-father. Amalia, a worker in what was then Cuba's biggest factory (a corner shop by today's standards) in Güira de Melena, spelled it out to you when you tried to lure her up into the hills: 'Bit of paper, then talk,' she said, mocking you, imitating your pidgin Spanish. And she explained to you how her mother had taught her that you have to be firm with men, which was why she wasn't going to open her legs just yet. 'Not until we're married.' You turned on your heel and marched off without saying a word. Who did that little mulatta think she was! You had two daughters already and no one had ever made you sign a bit of paper before. You thought: 'She can have her treasure; however tightly shut she keeps her legs, it'll just be food for the worms one day anyway,' and you spat through the gap where your left eyetooth used to be. You kicked the lemon tree so hard it nearly toppled over. Who the hell did that mulatta think she was! But you couldn't stop thinking about those prominent eyes, that small mouth and the jet-black hair caught up and held in place by a comb, and that mocking laugh and those hands and that intense cinnamon-coloured skin that burned your eyes and even now burned inside your pants. You gave the lemon tree another kick. You turned around. You threw a stone up at her window. She looked out. 'All right, we'll get married.' She smiled at you. 'When?' she asked. 'Whenever you want,' you said, smiling back.

'Any chance of an advance?' you asked, half-joking, half-serious. The window had already closed again when you heard her laughter.

You shouted: 'See you tomorrow,' and leaped on your horse. That night you rode back and forth four times between her house and yours, unable to stop, your cock irremissibly erect, fighting to get out of your trousers. And you rode and rode; you felt as if you were drunk – and doubtless you were – drunk on Amalia and on the wind and on the doves and you rode until your exhausted horse's legs buckled under him, outside the door to the dairy – the dairy belonged to López, just as you once had – and you got off your horse and lay down on the ground next to him, and the following morning, they found the two of you still lying there, wet with dew, mouths open.

History 3

Between 1847 and 1874, some one hundred and twenty-five thousand 'Asians' arrived in Cuba. It is estimated that about ten thousand managed to return to China. In 1899, when the American administrators completed the census and stopped immigration, there were some fourteen thousand Chinese, most of them 'Californians' – that is, not coolies but Chinese immigrants who had arrived via the United States. In 1862, of the 346 suicides that took place in Cuba, exactly half – 173 of them – were Asians. So, over a period of about fifty years there were one hundred thousand deaths (due to suicides, beatings, wars, fevers and, of course, old age, but how do you catalogue the deaths from sadness?).

Esteban Montejo mentions the Chinese: 'A lot of us were slaves. Blacks, Chinese, Indians and various mixtures. The Chinese were always looking and thinking. The blacks were always moving around, doing something. If the Chinese ever had a moment to sit, they would sit down and think . . . on Sundays or feast days, we would dance and the Chinese would sit and watch us, as if they were trying to work something out in their heads . . .'

Alfonso 4

They said in the village that the rebels meant business. At their head was Colonel Isidro, a huge negro, who could strangle a horse with his bare hands, the scourge of both Spaniards and Creoles. All his men were black, they said, and when they struck at night, they would attack stark naked and machete in hand, in order to blend in with the darkness of the forest. By then, the war had reached Occidente. You remembered the Taipings and gave them tobacco and, sometimes, pigs, but you also remembered Wu Liau's corpse and decided to stay with your family. Amalia had given you a daughter, Carmen – your first child in wedlock – as well as the longed-for son, Sebastián you called him (the name you would have liked, but which they did not give you). Your eldest daughter, Eugenia, had come to live with you too (her mother died in a smallpox epidemic). So you had your family to look after – the peace, the Great Peace begins at home. You had had quite enough problems with your second daughter – Leonor – the one you had with that woman from the Canary Islands who lived in Colón. Leonor turned out to be a rebellious tomboy, very much like Wu Liau and a little bit like you. She disappeared one night on horseback and nearly rode the poor animal into the ground trying to reach Oriente. She didn't make it; instead she joined up with Pancho Peréz's troops near Esperanza, and you had heard nothing since. One extremely uppity daughter and Carmen, who, by some miracle, survived smallpox and now this Colonel Isidro striding about the countryside naked . . . The Great Peace remained as far off as ever, despite the new house which your neighbours helped you build in the twinkling of an eye, despite the small farm – by then yours – where you planted vegetables and fruit trees and raised pigs and experimented with growing rice as they used to in Fukien, despite your cigarette stall which was flourishing, what with the village and the war, which, it seems, encouraged people to smoke more not less.

And now it was the rainy season and, one day, you got home late and found Amalia sitting on the doorstep with Sebastián in her arms, waiting for you, and when you saw her anxious, frowning face, you knew at once that something was wrong. 'That daughter of yours' – she weighed each word, emphasizing the 'yours' – 'you've got to talk to her.' You sat down in silence and waited for her to speak. You took off your hat and hung it on one of the posts on the veranda. 'That daughter of yours takes no notice of anyone and she's as crazy as Leonor.' You shuddered. Leonor was a name that always made you feel as if you had been punched in the stomach and left gasping for air. Things must be really bad for Amalia to mention Leonor. You took off your left boot. 'That daughter of yours, Alfonso, she's only a kid of eighteen and she's already mixed up with men.' You took off your right boot, smiled and said gently: 'Amalia, you were only sixteen when we got married.' Amalia brought her hand down hard on the sill, making the doorframe shudder and shaking the stool you were sitting on. 'Your daughter Eugenia is having an affair with Colonel Isidro.' 'Eugenia!' you thundered. She came to the door. She was wearing a red flower in her hair, a marpacífico. Years later you would often remember this scene and that flower was always the first thing to come to mind. 'Sit down!' She pulled over another stool and set it down opposite yours. She looked you straight in the eye and you saw yourself reflected in eyes identical to yours. 'What exactly is going on?' She held your gaze, as proud as yours. 'I'm engaged, Papa. My fiancé wanted to come and talk to you and I told Amalia so that she could ask your permission, but she just flew into a rage.' You were drumming your bare feet on the floor that your boots had left covered in mud. 'Is it Colonel Isidro?' you asked and Eugenia nodded. You took off your belt and dropped it on the floor, machete and all. 'I don't want you to be a widow before you're even married.' You had rolled your sodden shirt up into a ball and were gripping it in your left hand and punching it with your right. 'No one's going to kill Isidro. The man hasn't been born who could do that. We'll get married when the war is over, and that will be any day now. I just

wanted you to know and to give us your blessing. No one else outside
this house must know anything about it.'

You tipped the stool back so that it was leaning against the wall.
The front legs were in the air and your bare, muddy feet rested on
the front bar. Your daughter was still holding your gaze. 'You're a
fool, Eugenia.' She said nothing, but kept her eyes fixed on yours.
You jumped to your feet and stood a few inches away from her. She
looked up, still with her eyes trained on yours. Amalia thought you
were going to hit her. Eugenia said later that she knew you wouldn't.
You took her face in your wet hands and kissed her on the mouth.
'Tell him to come and see me as soon as he can.' Then you picked up
your straw hat and strode into the house.

History 4

The end of the war did, in fact, come swiftly – the end came with the
arrival of the Americans. And vice versa. That signalled another
beginning too. Many of the remaining Chinese had settled in
Havana, in what later became Chinatown. It began in 1858 when
Chang Ling settled in Calle de Zanja and opened a cheap restaurant
there and Laig Sui-Yi opened a fruit stall.

The 'Californians' had started arriving in 1860 and they came with
a few savings. They were the Chinese entrepreneurs, not just small
businessmen but also illegal bookies and racketeers. By 1873 there
was already a five-star restaurant in Dragones and a Chinese theatre.
In 1878 the first newspaper was started.

Chinatown became fully established in 1913 when the doors for
immigration, closed by the administrators, were reopened. Between
1913 and 1929, thirty thousand Chinese arrived, this time as
ordinary immigrants. The dream of New Spain and of a new Cuba
was clearly a powerful one.

Alfonso 5

It was Carmen's wedding day, the only time in your life when you got drunk. 'You really pushed the boat out,' the neighbours said. She was your last daughter to get married and you felt proud of a job well done. Five children (three daughters) and all of them decent folk. Not like your old friend, Salvador Monleón, the most respected patriarch in all Alquízar, who had so many children he didn't even know their names. He was a good stud was Salvador. He stayed on in the village when you all moved to Havana. No one knows exactly how many children he had, but on his birthday, you counted forty-five at the party, of all colours and sizes, some younger than his own grandchildren. It was Salvador who helped you when your contract had just expired and you almost had to sign on again because no one would employ you. He said: 'I need an honest man who's not afraid of hard work,' and he smiled as if to say that he knew you fulfilled both conditions. That was the day you began to be free. One of Salvador's daughters, Bértila, taught you to read and write Spanish, and it was in Salvador's house that you met Amalia, your wife, his wife's half-sister.

And on Carmen's wedding day when you saw him crouch down to come in through the door – he was a very big man – and saw him surrounded by the mist that was by then your constant companion, you knew with painful certainty that very soon you would never see him again and so you decided to get drunk with him on pure rum, in the name of all the good times you had had and of those that would never come again.

Since they had never seen you drunk, your children made a huge fuss. Carmen laughed hysterically and had such a terrible fit of hiccups she nearly had to cancel her honeymoon. Eugenia was angry and jealous that you should get drunk at Carmen's wedding, whereas at hers you had never touched a drop. Leonor sat down in an armchair beside you and matched you drink for drink – a whole bottle of cheap rum. At that point, Colonel Isidro arrived and said to her: 'You certainly live up to your rank as general' (that's how they always addressed Leonor after the war, although, in fact, she only ever made lieutenant). He joined you and Leonor and you each took a swig of brandy, straight from the bottle. And when Leonor said: 'I could drink you both under the table', you and Isidro accepted the challenge and bet a whole roast suckling pig for the whole family, to be paid for by the first to pass out, and two gallons of rum, to be paid for by the second. When the hour of reckoning came, you and Isidro were both sprawled on the floor and Leonor said: 'You see, you don't need balls to drink,' but when she went to get up, she keeled right over and they left the three of you out in the courtyard because you all stank to high heaven of brandy.

Great-granddaughter 2

Alfonso refused to live in Chinatown when he moved to Havana. He rented a house nearby, though, and sometimes he would go in search of smoked pork and sweet bread and sugar candy and glazed fruits.

Alfonso 6

And now you can flop into the armchair and feel the wickerwork against your bony spine and you can look back and see, through the smoke, that you lived through a lot of bad times, but a lot of good times too. You know that it is 1924 and you never expected to get this far. You stroke the handle of your walking stick and take a deep breath; you can fall asleep without fear now. After all, you have had the rare privilege of surviving and being able to die sitting in your armchair, surrounded by five children, five grandchildren, two dogs and a turtle.

Great-granddaughter 3

Ah, the great bearded dragon with eyes of fire and gaping mouth! Let's dance the dragon through the streets hung with little coloured lights and paper flags. Let's dance the dragon through the fireworks and the rockets. And let's wait for them to award the prize and the greenbacks and, finally, there'll be the party with rice wine to drink. But the dragon, after the parade, after the dreams, the dragon, deflated now, the dragon . . . always ends up biting his own tail.

TRANSLATED BY MARGARET JULL COSTA

Traitor

Reinaldo Arenas

I'll say what I have to say fast and crude, so don't get any ideas with
your little tape recorder there, don' think you're going to make all
kinds of money out of what I have to say, spruce it up a little, stick
in a little something here and a little something there and turn it into
a big fancy book, or I don't know, make a big name for yourself – out
of my hard knocks . . . Although I don' know, maybe if I talk crude
it'll be all the better for you. People might like it even more that way,
you might be able to get even more mileage out of it. Because you –
I can tell – you're somethin'. But as long as you're here, and all
dressed up like that too, I'll talk. A little. A very little. Just enough to
show you that without us, you people wouldn't even *be* here. There's
an ashtray over there, on the washbasin, get it if you want to . . .
Fancy new machine, fancy clean shirt . . . Is it silk? Can you get silk
again now? . . . But you'll either have to stand there, just like you're
standin' there right now, or sit in that chair without a seat in it – uh-
huh, I did hear they're selling seats for chairs again – to ask your
questions.

What do you now about him? What does anybody know? . . . Now
that Fidel Castro is out – whether he fell or got pushed or just got
tired – everybody talks, everybody *can* talk. The system's changed
again. Oh – now everybody's a hero. Now it turns out everybody was
against the whole thing all the time. But back then, back when there
was a Watchdog Committee on every corner – somethin' that kept its
eye day and night on the doors and windows and roofs of every
house, that kept watch on the lights, what time they were off and
what time they were on, and every movement we made, and every
word we spoke, and every word we *didn't* speak, and what we listened

to on the radio and what we didn't listen to, and who our friends were
and who our enemies were, and what our sex life was like, and what
our mail was like, and our illnesses, and our dreams. Because all that
was checked on too . . . I see you don't believe me. I'm just some old
woman. Well, you can think that if you want to. Some old woman, a
little dotty. You can think that – it's prob'ly better if you do. Now
people can think. You don't understand what I'm saying. Don't you
see that back then people couldn't think? But now they can, right?
Right. And that'd be a cause for concern, if there were anything to
make me concerned anymore. If people can think out loud, that
means there's nothin' to say. But listen, *they* are there. *They* have
poisoned everything and they're there – they're around out there
somewhere. And now anything that anybody does will be because of
them – against them or for them (well, not for them anymore) but
because of them . . . What am I saying? Is it true that I can say
whatever I want to? Is that true? Tell me, I mean, say the words . . .
At first I took it for a lie. Now I still don't believe it. Times do change.
I hear people talk about freedom again. Talk – they *scream* about it. But
that's not necessarily good. When people yell that way – *Free-dom!* –
usually what they want is just the opposite. I know. I saw it . . . You're
here for some reason, you've tracked me down, and you're here with
that gizmo of yours. It works, right? I mean, it's running now?
Because I'm not goin' to say this twice. There are plenty of people
out there telling all kinds of stories . . . all those 'testimonies'
nowadays. Naturally, everybody has a story to tell, shout it at the top
of their lungs, *scream*, about how they were all – how convenient! –
against the dictatorship all along. And I don't doubt it. Oh, but back
then, did anybody dare not to wear a political badge on their lapel, a
badge that had been minted, logically enough, by the regime? You
look into that – do you think your father wasn't in the militia? Did he
not go off to volunteer labor? 'Volunteer' – that was the word. Why,
I myself, when Castro fell I was almost sent to the firing squad as a
Castroite. My God. What saved me was the letters I'd sent to my
sister in exile. What if those letters hadn't existed? . . . She had to

send then back to me *fast*, because otherwise I'd've been done for . . .
Me, and I've never set foot in the street again, because something – a
lot – of that was left behind, in history. And I don't want to even
smell it . . . I . . . And now you ask me to talk, to make my contribution, to cooperate – I'm sorry, I know nobody uses that kind of
language anymore – you tell me that with what I know, why, you can
make a book out of it or something, from one of the victims. A
double victim, you'll have to say. Or triple. Or – I know! – a victim-
victim. Or a victim-victim of the victims. You can fix that up. Put
whatever you want to. I've got no need to look over it, give my OK. I
don't want to look over anything. I will, however, take this
opportunity for 'freedom of expression' – is that still the expression
people use? – to tell you that you are a vulture. They've been wiped
out? There's no need for them anymore? Such birds they were! They
fed on carrion, on dead animals, and then they'd rise right up into the
sky. So why on earth were they wiped out? They cleaned up the
island under every regime. Boy, could they wolf it down! . . . Maybe
they were poisoned by eating the bodies of all those criminals that
found justice ('found justice' – what an expression!) at the hands of
you people . . . But listen, push that machine over this way a little bit.
And hurry it up too, because I've got no time to waste, I'm an old
woman and I'm tired, and to be honest with you I've been poisoned
too . . . Back then, back when we're talking about, gizmos like this
one (is it running?) got a lot of use, although people generally didn't
realize when it was being used on them . . . You explain to me what it
is you're going to do and what you've come here for. We talk. And
nobody down on the corner is spying on us, right? And they're not
going to search my house after you've gone, right? Of course, what do
I have to hide anymore. And I can speak *for*, or I can speak *against*, is
that right too? This very minute I can speak out against the
government if I want to. And nothing will happen? . . . I suppose
that's possible . . . Is that possible? Yes, everything is that way now.
Down there on the corner they were selling beer today. There was a
lot of noise. Music, they call it. People don't look as shabby and

unkempt anymore, or as angry. There are no signs on the trees anymore with those political slogans on them. People go out for a walk, I can see that, and people seem to be able to be really and truly sad – with a sadness of their own – a personal sadness, I mean to say. People eat, people breathe, people dream (do people dream?) and you see bright-colored clothes. But I don' believe it, as I told you. I've been poisoned. I've seen . . . But let's get to the point. What is it that you want? There's no time to waste anymore. Now it's work work work, right? Before, the important thing was to *look like* you were working. People have ambitions, dreams . . . The story is simple. I can tell you that. But it doesn't matter – those things, you're not gonna understand them. And nobody else hardly, will either. They're things that can't be understood if you haven't been through them yourself. Like just about everything else . . . He wrote several books – you oughtta be able to find them somewhere. Or maybe not – maybe when the system started to be wiped out they all got burned. Back then – back right at the beginning, of course – people did such things. Bad habits, but they'd come by 'em naturally, you know. Inherited 'em, as it were. It's been hard, I know, to overcome those 'tendencies' – is that still the word they use? All his books – you know this – they spoke well of that system that was being overthrown. And yet they were all lies . . . The order would come – 'To the fields' – and he'd go to the fields. Nobody knew that when he was working most furiously he wasn't doing it out of belief in the system, out of loyalty to the system, but out of hate. You should've seen the fire in him when he was scrabbling at the ground, how he would plant, weed, spade. Those, back then, were major virtues. God! And with what hate he did it all, with what hate he 'pitched in'. How he hated all that . . . They made him – he made himself – an 'exemplary youth', a 'worker in the vanguard'. He was awarded the 'ribbon of valor'. An extra shift of guard duty had to be stood, he stood it; the sugar cane had to be cut, he went off to cut sugar cane. In the military, what could you say no to when everything was official, patriotic, revolutionary – meaning that you couldn't get out of it?

And outside the military, everything was still compulsory. With the additional factor that he was no kid anymore, he was a grown man and he had to live – which means he needed a room of his own, a pressure cooker, for example, a pair of pants, for example. You won't believe me, will you, when I tell you that buying a shirt, getting the *authorization* to buy a shirt, was a question of political privilege? I see you don't believe me. What are we going to do with you? I hope you never lose that innocence . . . Since he hated the system so much, he was a person of few words, and since he didn't talk much, he didn't contradict himself like other people did – tomorrow they'd have to correct or deny what they'd said today. 'Problems of the dialectic', that was called . . . And so, since he didn't contradict himself, he became a man of trust, a man of respect. In the weekly assemblies, he never spoke out. You should've seen the expression of agreement he wore, while all the time he was sailing off somewhere, traveling, dreaming that he was somewhere else, in 'enemy territory' as they called it, dreaming that he'd come back in an airplane, with a bomb, and right there, in the assembly, in the plaza full of slaves, where he himself had so often (so ominously) gone and stood and applauded, he would drop it . . . So 'for his discipline and observance in the Study Circles' (that was what they called the obligatory classes in political indoctrination) he was awarded another diploma. When it came time to read *Granma* (I still remember its name) he was the first one to do it, not because it held any attraction for him but because his loathing for that newspaper was so strong that in order to get it over with (like everything he hated) he would do it right then. When he raised his hand to donate something, anything – because we always donated things publicly – how he'd laugh deep down inside, how he'd be exploding deep down inside . . . Four or five extra hours he'd always do, 'voluntarily' – but if he hadn't, then he'd really've been in trouble! On obligatory guard duty, with his rifle over his shoulder, walking past the building that that former regime had built – the headquarters for its *own* hell – how many times did he not think about blowing his brains out, yelling 'Down with Castro' or something of the sort . . . But life is different now. People are different. D'you know what fear is? D'you know what hate is? Do you know what hope is? D'you know what impotence is? . . . You be careful, young man, don't trust anybody, anybody. Not even now – now less than ever. Now, when everything promises trust, is the perfect time to distrust. Afterward, it'll be too late. Afterward, you'll have to obey. You're young, you don't know anything. But your father was no doubt in the military; your father, no doubt . . . Don't take part in anything – run away . . . Can a person run away these days? That's incredible . . . just run away . . . 'If I could only get out,' he'd say to me, whisper to me, after he'd come home from a day of work that seemed like it would never end, after he'd stood on his feet for three hours applauding, 'if I could only run away, if I could only get out of this hell – *swim* out of it, because there's no other way that's possible anymore – run away and disappear . . .' And I'd say, *Calm down, calm down, you know that's impossible, the fishermen bring in pieces of fingernails. There's an order to shoot to kill on the high seas, even if you raise your hands and surrender. Look at those searchlights* . . . And he himself sometimes had to look after those searchlights, those weapons, clean them, shine them, see to the welfare of the instruments of his oppression. And with what discipline he did it, with what passion! You might say that he tried to keep his real self from peeking out, being visible. And he'd come home exhausted, dirty, and covered with medals and pats on the back . . . 'Oh, if I had a bomb,' he'd say to me back then – or whisper, really, 'I'd already have blown all this to bits. A bomb so powerful that it wouldn't leave a thing. Nothing. Not even me.' And I'd say, *Calm down, for God's sake, stop, don't talk anymore, they'll hear you, don't let your fury make you throw everything away* . . . Disciplined, polite, hard-working, discreet, simple, normal, natural, absolutely natural and *adapted* – because deep down he was the exact opposite of all that – how could they not make him a member of the Party? What job was he unwilling to do? And do fast. What criticism did he not humbly accept? . . . And that huge, huge hatred inside himself, that feeling himself abused, mistreated, annihilated, *buried* – and to be able to say nothing; just silently – silently? enthusiastically! – accept, so as not to be even more abused and mistreated, even more annihilated, absolutely crushed. In order one day to be able to have one's revenge – talk act live . . . Oh, how he would cry, so soft you could barely hear him, at night, in his room, right there, in that room next door, down this way . . . He would *weep* in rage and hatred. I will never be able to count, never be able to tell – if I lived for nothing else, I would *still* never be able to list – the terrible things he said against the regime. 'I can't take it any more, I can't take it,' he would say. And it was the truth. Clinging to me, holding me tight – I was young then too, we were both young, as young as you are, although I don't know, maybe you're not so young – everybody is so well nourished now . . . He'd hold me tight and say, 'I'm not going to be able to take this any more, I'm not going to be able to do it. I'm going to shout out all my hatred. I'm going to shout out the truth.' He'd scream that to me in a whisper. And I would straighten his ribbons and medals and things. *If you do that, they'll send you to the firing squad. Pretend, put a face on, the way everybody does. Pretend more than the next one does – that way you'll be laughing at him. Calm down, don't talk nonsense* . . . And he went on doing his duty, doing the work that was assigned to him, only being himself sometimes, at night, and just for a little while, when he came to me, to unburden himself . . . I have never, not even now when there's official kindliness and encouragement, never heard anyone speak so badly of that system. Since he was inside it, he knew the whole system, knew the workings of it, its subtlest atrocities. The next day, he'd go back to guard duty, or the assembly, or the field, or the hand-raising for whatever it was, but he'd go back in rage, and close-mouthed quiet. His chest was plastered with 'merits', his file was full of 'merits' . . . That was when the Party 'oriented' him – you have no idea what that verb meant back then – to write a series of biographies of its top leaders. *Do it,* I'd tell him, *or else everything you've done up till now, everything you've achieved, will be lost. It'll be the end* . . . He became famous – they made him famous. He moved

away from here. They gave him a big house. He married the woman
that had oriented him . . . I had a sister who had left, who was living
in exile . . . She came, though, to visit me – very circumspectly, with
his books under her arm. She handed them to me and she told me the
truth: they were all monsters. *They* were, or *we* were? . . . What do *you*
think? Have you found out anything about your father? Do you know
any more? Why out of all the people that you could've tried to find out
about did you choose *this* figure, who's so murky? Who are you? Why
are you looking at me that way? Who was your father? . . . Your father.
'The first chance that comes my way, I'm seeking asylum,' he would
say. 'I know there's tremendous vigilance, that it's practically
impossible to live there, that there are lots of spies, lots of their
thugs scattered all over the world – that even afterwards, in exile, I'll
be assassinated. But first I'll have my say. First I'll finally say what I
feel – the truth.' *Calm down, hush*, I would tell him, and by this time
we weren't so young anymore. *Don't do anything stupid.* And he'd say,
'Do you think I can spend my entire life pretending? Don't you
realize, don't you *see*, that I've been a traitor to myself for so long
that soon I'm not going to be *me* anymore? Don't you see that I'm just
a shadow now, a puppet, an actor who never steps off the stage, and
to make matters worse that I always play a part that's *dirty*?' And I'd
say, *Wait, wait.* I – oh, I understood, and I cried too, along with him,
hated it as much as he did, or more – I am, or was, a woman –
pretending, putting on the same face that everybody put on, secretly
plotting in my mind, in my soul, and begging him to wait, wait. And
he did wait. Until the moment came.

The moment the regime was overthrown. And then he was tried
and convicted as a direct agent of the Castro dictatorship (there was
not a shred of evidence in his favor) and sentenced to the maximum
penalty of the law: execution. And then, standing before the
anarchistic firing squad, he shouted, 'Down with Castro! Down with
tyranny! Long live freedom!' . . . And until the report from the rifles
– a flat, muted sound – silenced him, he went on shouting those same
words. Words that the press and the whole world called 'the words of

a cowardly cynicism' but that I can assure you – and you write this down in case that tape recorder of yours isn't working – I can assure you was the only true thing, the only thing that came from inside him, that your father ever said loud enough for anybody else to hear in his whole life.

TRANSLATED BY ANDREW HURLEY

Split In Two
Mirta Yáñez

'They're knocking on the door, this is such a long corridor, it's so hot in December, what a racket those dogs are making, who knows what they're barking at . . .' She didn't have to close her eyes to conjure up the image of the icy hillside in her Galician homeland that harsh winter long ago, hushed and silent after the hungry wolves had stopped howling. The little girl she once was, wrapped up in sheep skins, milking Cinnamon the cow; her hands, cracked with cold and rough patches of skin, clutching the full pail of milk in the snow. She'd love to have a cow now, right here in the yard. 'Off we go. Anchors away and best foot forward!' The four dogs, bustling round her aching legs, were almost preventing her from walking across the dining room, choc-a-bloc with modern furniture. 'It's all so uncomfortable. Most of all, that plywood table, a holy disgrace. They're still knocking on the door. I wonder if the cowshed is still standing there after sixty, no, good Lord, seventy years?' She could hear birds flying around above the ceiling: sparrows' nests and bird dirt on the walls, her home was here now, ever since she'd arrived in this country. A warm country, riotous as the devil, that was the good side. Wasn't this the only home she had? And what about the other one? The outhouse and the one room for eighteen brothers and sisters. The doorbell was ringing now. With a noise like a kick up you know where. She still lingered for a moment in the front room. She counts – one, two, three. Yes, they were still intact, three stained-glass panels, framed in the mustard-coloured glass of the windows: there they were, the coloured fish – yellow, purple, blue, against a darker blue background, so different from the thick, black sea of the crossing with the metal turret-heads of German submarines lurking so near, eighteen brothers and sisters, all huddled up next to a basket of black bread and cheese, no one was sick, though danger threatened everywhere, what would be waiting for the young travellers in the brave New World? Then there was the other view of the sea, a small sailing ship, rigged up with provisions, the hull painted in a uniquely beautiful blood-red colour, Havana's the only place you'll see that red, when a flash of sun lights up the city in the early morning. The third picture was a rural scene, this was her favourite, yes sir, with its mountains, the river winding in the distance, the five straight palm trees, a hut, and a bright-red bird in full flight, the stroke of scarlet which just had to be there, Ah, the bird looks as though it's moving. Riiiiiiing!

When at last she opens the door, the young woman standing on the doorstep doesn't know what to do. Behind the old lady (and her four dogs) she thinks she glimpses a gigantic bronze lamp with twisting arms, still looking from a distance like lots of serpent heads. Only three of its eight bulbs are lit, but that was sufficient to light up the damp, chill front room, which smelt of leather and sickly-sweet wood shut up for a long time. Its welcoming shade contrasted with the burning midday sun in the street. With a stab of anguish, the girl recognized the woodwormed damask armchairs, still with Grandad's cigar burns no doubt, the Japanese tables, the 1953 Philco television set in its dark, old-fashioned cabinet, the picture of the nymph and the chubby angels just about to place a crown of orange blossom on her head, the embroidered silk shawl from Seville pinned to the back wall and, of course, the three glass panels, still intact, with that red bird in full flight, only now shrunken to a size smaller, in Granny's higgledy-piggledy front room.

Until that moment she had been convinced the only memory she had of her homeland was an interminable walk in the sun (that round, yellow, postcard sun), the huge hoarding advertising beer on the airport wall, its golden foam flowing over the rim of the glass, the almost lascivious look of the man who declared, in a speech bubble coming out of his mouth, still moist with the last sip, 'This is Cuba, guys'; the asphalt which seemed to be melting under her little white shoes (her best ones) till she reached the stairs of the flying machine, bigger than the advert. Mummy, I'm scared. Oh, how often had she heard the tale of the lonely little Chinese dog who sadly said goodbye time and again, whenever her mother sang her a song to send her to sleep quickly in the freezing nights of their first apartment in New Jersey, that awful cold.

When the old lady spoke it sounded like Chinese to the girl.

'Bernal won't be back till two. I've already explained to the ideology teacher. But don't worry, he'll be back in time to get the circle ready.'

The young woman hesitated. Bernal was Uncle Antonio's son. She could hardly remember Uncle Antonio's face, the widower who lived all alone in the Miami suburbs. But Bernal. Bernal with his head shaved like a scrubbing brush, and a pair of sweaty spectacles slipping down to the tip of his nose, always climbing up the mango tree in the yard, to hand her down one of those juicy golden fruits that she remembered now like an electric current in the back of her neck.

'All right,' the girl answered, 'I'll come back later.'

What a pickle! How on earth could she say to the old lady, Look, Granny, it's me, Rosie, your granddaughter, from abroad, the one in the North, the one who went away when she was a little girl, when her parents, and uncles, and aunts, that's to say, all your children, Granny, went too. You know, the one who speaks Spanish far too correctly, the one who doesn't drop the 's' on the ends of her words. You, Granny, you haven't changed a bit. And what about me? Do I remind you of your granddaughter at all? The girl who used to steal mangoes with cousin Bernal? No, of course not. So Rosie turned and crossed over to the park. My God, how things had changed, and yet everything was just the same. The fritters stall she'd loved so much had gone; one-peso cones with fried calabash, fried banana slices, crackling. So had the neon sign TAKE MEJORAL. Or the ticket-seller on the street corner, or the fruit and vegetable barrow. There were heaps of that stuff in La Saguesera's store, but, no, it wasn't the same. Standing in the middle of the park, with her heavy overnight bag hanging from her shoulder, Rosie takes a long look at the avenue on the right; then she looks to the left, the fork in the road, Granny's house, the bakery and the clinic. Everything is so drab, so many potholes in the road, only in Havana could you find such cavernous holes in the roads, and 1940s cars still driving around, Holy Mary! So why this euphoria? Why this sudden impulse to start jumping up and down with the groups of children running around in the park? In her park! She sat down sideways on one of the marble benches. From that position she could see Granny's house, with its stained-glass panels (the fish, the little ship, the red bird) and the mango tree in the yard reaching over the top of the roof. Amazing, such a huge tree in the middle of a city, swarms of cats and dogs of all possible colours and sizes, sparrows nesting in the front-room walls. And pigeons, no doubt, yes, pigeons. The same ones Granny used to put in her soups when she or Bernal had stomach-ache. Could the pigeons in the park be the descendants of the ones killed for Granny's hot broth? Her cheeks are burning as if she had a high temperature. Rosie puts the palm of her hand on her forehead. She's probably feverish. Flu? Nerves? Suddenly a grainy sensation rushes to the soles of her feet. She moves her toes trying to remember: boiling hot pigeon broth, the embroidered sheet pulled up to her chin in the varnished walnut bed, and at her feet enormous socks filled with the hot coffee grouts. It's not there now, just the feeling that's come back after twenty years. Those childhood fevers (thirty-nine degrees, oh, it's gone up, forty degrees) that Granny was sure she could cure with red-hot coffee grouts, heaped into white woollen socks that gradually turned brown, placed on the little girl's feet, the little girl delirious in her bed, the distant, frightened look in Bernal's eyes, her forehead burning like it is now. The false feeling in her feet, an illusion brought on by the pigeons and the sight of Granny's hands, soft and reddish, full of wrinkles, the same ones that touched her

feverish brow twenty years ago. She looked at the bag at her side and
suddenly thought of the three jam-packed suitcases left behind in
the hotel room. Her mother had insisted on stuffing them full. What
would Bernal say? What would Bernal think of his cousin Rosie?
Would he also remember the afternoons they climbed up the mango
tree to read *Lulu* and *Toby* comics? She knew lots of girls like Lulu
these days. But what would cousin Bernal be like now? Ever since
Uncle Antonio declared, melodramatically, that Bernal 'had died for
ever', Bernal was cut off from the rest of the family, just because he
stayed with Granny, and nobody over there heard anything about
him again. Although in the photos Granny sent by post,
surreptitiously, he had the same shy, compassionate look, ill-fitting
spectacles, the same warm smile he would wear at the bedroom door
when Rosie's temperature was sky high. Just like now.

Someone knocked at the door again. When the old lady opened the
door the girl was waiting on the step. She looked ill and her forehead
was covered in sweat. Her cheeks were burning, as if she had just run
down the hillside. Cinnamon the cow, liked to hide and it was so
difficult to find her. The young shepherd girl also had rosy cheeks
when snow fell at dawn. And now, this heat.

'Ah, yes, come in, sit down. You look awful. Would you like some
coffee? I've just strained it. It's very sunny, isn't it? Does us all
good. The worst thing is the cold. I can't bear the cold. When I was
a little girl my hands would get all chapped. But who would bring
in the milk if I didn't? We each had our own job to do. I don't think
I told you, but the coldest I've ever been was when the Marquis's
barn caught fire. I'd just got over typhus. Mummy used to take such
good care of my long plaits and then I nearly lost all my hair. Yes,
the barn was burning down and the flames were reaching our
house. They told us all to run! But my legs were still very weak, I
couldn't even walk. First they saved the cow, Cinnamon, then my
older brother carried me to the edge of the wood. And he just left
me there. Freezing cold it was, my dear. Just by chance, the
Marquis passed by, and he must have felt sorry for me shivering

and threw his horse blanket over me. Thank the Lord. My smock was full of bits of ice, I had no hair. I looked frightful! . . . Leave the girl alone,' Granny threatened the dogs, waving her hand up and down, as if she was shaking an invisible liquid, an age-old peasant gesture, thought Rosie. Then the old lady started to serve the coffee from a porcelain jug painted with pink and blue flowers and very chipped around the rim. There was a thorny silence that Granny interrupted.

'I suppose you're a journalist.'

Rosie answered immediately that she was. Because it was easier? What the heck!

'All Bernal's friends study journalism. They spend all their time asking questions. And you're so quiet. Don't you want to ask me anything?'

What a mess! Rosie had hundreds of questions to ask Granny. But now, quite frankly, she couldn't think of anything to say. She looked at the stained-glass panels and she counts, one, two, three, a wonder they're all still there, the red bird in full flight, looks as though he's moving. Granny is waiting for me to say something. Damn the sea and its salt! Rosie opened her mouth and gulped: without warning, from the depths of her subconscious, she'd remembered Grandad's old expression of annoyance. Grandad, of good Iberian stock, Grandad and his Havana cigars, his Panama hat, which he took off only to have a bath (although Rosie didn't know that for sure); Grandad gone native, though he still danced a Spanish jig on Christmas Eve, kept a beautiful wooden model of a Galician granary well out of reach of the grandchildren and obstinately pronounced his 's', thick and resonant. Another unexpected image: his funeral in a leafy cemetery, Granny sobbing quietly, her face half hidden by a handmade lace handkerchief, standing near a huge open grave. Bernal takes the little girl's hand. Rosie was very upset and Granny didn't seem to notice. Ask something, just for the sake of it.

'So you don't like the cold?'

'In my village, where I was born, there was a lot of snow. I bet there's still snow there. My house was on the banks of a river, I can't remember its name. It froze up in winter and it was very pretty. One of my cousins went to sleep in the snow and we never saw him again.'

Granny was thoughtful for a moment, and then she changed the subject. 'In the mountains, I had a little friend, a neighbour, who came with me to look after the sheep. If the wolves came near us she'd take a tin can and rattle it loudly while I would run and get the flock together. Sometimes, when I fall asleep, I dream of her. I can't see her face, I can't remember what her voice sounds like, I couldn't even tell you her name, but I know it's her. The year after that, I came here and I never went back.'

Granny leaned over towards Rosie and murmured, 'Did you bring me wafers?'

Rosie said she hadn't and felt utterly ashamed, though she didn't know why. She remembered the three packed suitcases stuffed with (useless?) things, but not a single one of those mysterious wafers Granny was asking for. Rosie looked away towards the corridor; it was so long, through the back-door window she glimpsed the trunk of the mango tree where Bernal and Rosario (her name was still Rosario then, Granny called her Charito) used to climb to steal the eternally golden fruits. Wasn't this the only home she had? And the other one?

'But, Granny –.' The word came out, though nobody seemed surprised. Rosie's voice was strident, familiar, harsh. 'Don't you miss it?'

'Have you noticed how hot it is in December! Bernal also prefers the heat,' Granny paused. 'Do you like the pictures in the window panels? Mountains are the same everywhere, but look at that red bird, there's no other like him. He's forever flying. My homeland was back there and this one is mine too.'

Granny settled down into the damask armchair, as if she was about to nod off, and then she said, 'A little bit here and a little bit there. Your heart ends up split in two.'

Rosie couldn't bear to lie about the newspaper interview any longer. Her forehead was burning as if a barn was burning nearby, in the middle of winter. She gulped again, and she said, for the second time that afternoon, 'Granny.' Then the front door opened and Bernal came in. Ladies and gentlemen, that just had to be Bernal.

TRANSLATED BY CATHERINE DAVIES

Round Trip
Uva de Aragón

I better wear my jeans – no, not jeans – she's going to think I'm too old for that, or she'll think I'm trying to rub it in, that I've got what they can't have over there. What a fool you are, Esperanza! It's your sister, your own twin sister, we haven't seen each other for over twenty years – she won't even have time to notice what I'm wearing – that blouse and skirt are OK. My God, how different our lives are after starting out so alike! The skirt's a little too short, nobody's wearing them like this any more. She's been the self-sacrificing one all these years, never leaving Cuba, looking after the old folks, never getting married or having any children. I hope I have an easy time parking at the airport . . . Well, her not marrying had nothing to do with the old folks. It was her, waiting for that creep Rubén, who led her on for nearly ten years only to dump her and come to Miami and end up with that miserable tramp. A good thing the traffic's not so bad this time of day . . . Can Caridad have changed that much? She was always so cheerful – and who'd have thought it, her whole life spent in a lousy country where they don't even have toilet paper, in a house that's falling down? All alone with Papa now, after Mama died, him gone blind too – my God, what a man, always so argumentative and so full of life, and now they tell me he's a human wreck. Lucky she's managed to find someone to look after him for a month while she's here, else we'd have both died without ever laying eyes on each other again. Who'd have thought, a year ago, that my Ramón was going to die like that, suddenly? But the heart's like that – no warning. All the better for him, but so hard on me . . . Hardest of all in the morning, when I wake up and remember, and not having anyone to say good morning to. Even if those boys of mine *are*

angels! Bless them, they do look after me, but no way, I wouldn't live
with that American daughter-in-law, not for the world. It would be
different with Maruja, at least she's Cuban, but she's got her own
mother and it's only natural that they should live together, after all,
Hilda does look after her children – frankly, there's no way I'd leave
my job at the store, after the trouble I had at first with that American
boss of mine, now things are going more smoothly . . . I wonder
which way the passengers will be coming out. Yes, we've had our
troubles too, those of us who came over here. You bet, haves and
have-nots all had their share of hard times in the early days of exile.
Over there they think here it's all a piece of cake. No way. You tend
to forget the bad times, but those years were real hard, back then
when nobody had credit cards . . . I'd better ask.

'Yes, ma'am, I speak Spanish. Look, right that way, the passengers
are supposed to come out that door.'

So many people, my God, you don't realize or you don't even
think about it, but we Cubans have been through so much. Will
Cachita have changed a lot? Sometimes I feel kind of guilty. I left,
I've had my own life, my own children. What must it be like to live
without children? I don't know, it must be like dying a little every day.
True, we're none of us going to live forever, but at least – well, I
don't know, when you've got children you know you're leaving some
part of yourself behind. And then there's the grandchildren. When
we were little girls playing with dolls, we couldn't imagine how it
would be, this constant mixture of alarm and the feeling, like warm
waves, when they come to you with their little arms wide open and
throw them around your neck. It's almost a quarter to. The plane
must have landed. Why on earth haven't they come out? Suppose
they haven't let her leave the country. You never know, over there.

But why shouldn't they let her?

'Look, look, there's your grandma, the one with the scarf on her
head.'

'Mama, Mama, this way.'

No matter how hard you try not to, you feel like crying. So many families forced apart. Will Caridad and I be able to talk?

All those nights we used to spend as teenagers, chattering away, with Mama telling us to shut up a hundred times. Wonder what we talked about . . . Such nonsense, and we used to take it all so seriously. Will Caridad remember that song we made up about the school janitor? Now, what on earth made me remember that?

'Esperanza!'

'But, Sis, aren't you tired?'

'Sure I am, Espi . . . but I don't feel like going to bed. It's been such a long time since we talked.'

'And it's been a long, long time since anyone's called me that.'

'What?'

'Espi . . . it's like being a little girl again.'

'Oh, Sis, over there you live – I can't explain, it's like living in the past, nourished by memories.'

'Isn't that funny, Caridad. It's just the opposite here. Ramón, God rest his soul, used to say this is the land of tomorrow, of "Tomorrow I'll do this, tomorrow I'll do that." And you know what – he was right, here you live one jump ahead of yourself. You spend your paycheck before you cash it. You've hardly come back from vacation and you're already planning next year's vacation. In August they're advertising for December's Christmas gifts.'

'Remember, Esperanza, what Christmas used to be like at the house on C Street? Those were the best . . . like the year Uncle Pepe from New York came to visit, loaded down with presents, and we had this huge get-together. How much Papa used to enjoy those reunions!'

'And remember the year I asked the Three Kings for an ice-cream wagon, and Papa had a carpenter make one especially for me?'

'Yes, we must've been about seven or eight years old.'

'And those summers at the beach . . . Caridad, are Cuban beaches still so beautiful, or is it just the way we remember them?'

'Esperanza, everything's so different now. You can't begin to imagine.'

'But, Sis, haven't you ever thought that I've done you wrong, that it wasn't fair for you to make all the sacrifices?'

'No, Esperanza, life isn't really serious about the way it behaves – things just happen and they're nobody's fault . . . I'm glad you've been happy, glad you've had your life. Now, tell me, when will I see my nephews?'

'Tomorrow, tomorrow . . . But see here, don't change the subject – we may not have a chance to talk about this again, and I've always meant to tell you . . . and now I can't seem to get the words right . . . that sometimes, I don't know, I feel sort of guilty, like I left you in the lurch, like I should have insisted that you all come over sooner, when our parents were younger.'

'Don't blame yourself, Esperanza. Be glad you're here. Life is sad in Cuba. Now, with the old man gone blind – sometimes he doesn't even know who I am, he thinks I'm Mama or you . . . can you imagine? – and the house falling to pieces, it's been impossible to get it painted . . . I understand why you wouldn't want to come . . .'

'No, it's not that I don't want to go back – actually, it scares me. Because Ramón was so involved here against the government, and you never know with those people . . . Besides, it's true, Caridad, it scares me to see the house looking like that, to see Papa an old man, sightless. You think of returning, of going back to what used to be. But all that is no more. We're not even the same ourselves.'

'Listen, Sis, I think it's been too much excitement for me, I've like a pain in my chest. Maybe it's my stomach. Do you have some camomile?'

'Come on, Cachita, not camomile, but Alka-Seltzer, or Mylanta . . . But, darling, you look pale, you're sweating . . .

'What could it be? It's like – my arms ache . . .'

'OK, so you go to bed right away – tomorrow we go shopping . . .'

'Oh, Espi, I haven't seen a real store in such a long time . . .'

'Patient's last name, please.'

'Miss, do you speak Spanish? It's that – I can't remember a word of English when I'm nervous.'

'Yes, ma'am, look, you must tell me the patient's full name and give me all the insurance details. You do have insurance, haven't you?'

'Yes, yes . . . My sister has her employee's insurance. She works for Sears. Her card must be in her purse. I'll find it right away.'

See here, Esperanza, you shouldn't be doing this. Hospitalizing your sister under your name. If the boys find out they'll kill me, they're so law-abiding, so American. If one only knew it was nothing serious . . . but here any little thing means thousands of dollars in hospital bills. After all, I've hardly used that insurance all these years, and I pay for it every month . . . I better not call Ramoncito, he'll be furious. I'm sure they'll just prescribe one pill or another and we'll be out of here soon and they'll send in a bill for two hundred dollars . . . I should've grabbed a sweater . . . it's so cold in here . . . why won't they let me see her . . . they're taking ages . . . she was so pale . . . worse luck, getting sick on her first night here, she was looking forward so much to her trip . . . what if they ask her name? I better try to see her and explain . . . My God, what a commotion! What can be happening? I'm going to slip in there, never mind what that sign says.

'Miss, you can't go in.'

My God, all those doctors around her, and they're giving her oxygen, and banging on her chest, and giving her shots, and she looks so white, like Ramón did when he had his heart attack, oh, my God, suppose it's that, suppose it's not her stomach, suppose it's not some harmless little thing, suppose she's having a heart attack, suppose my sister is dying, my twin sister, my sister who's lived the other half of my life so I could have the life I've had, my sister who's the only one that could remember the song we made up about the school janitor, my sister who's the only one that remembers those Christmases at the big old house on C Street, with all the cousins playing the 'American steps' game, my sister Caridad, who's not Caridad any more, who's really me, who's dying under my name, because it's me on that bed, so white, my God, I never realized how like Mama she is, or rather how like Mama we are, because her face is my face, the weightlessness of her body on the bed is my own body's weight. Now you've opened your eyes, Caridad, and you're looking at me with my own eyes, and I can see in their pupils the exhaustion of standing in long lines for food, the endless patience with which you give Papa his bath every morning, the kindness of your hands that never knew a caress or changed a diaper . . . And I know what you're screaming at me out of your eyes, *my* eyes – that you can't die because you haven't finished your task, and life isn't serious even about that, and my Ramón is dead and my sons are grown up and nobody needs me and I'm all alone, yes, Caridad, it's so hard getting up in the morning and not having anyone to say good morning to, and I'm so lonely, and now I won't even have your visit to look forward to, and we didn't even get to do so many things we'd planned, I didn't even get to take you shopping, if you could just see how big the supermarkets are, and you who do have someone to go back to, that poor blind old man who doesn't know who you are, and you don't want to die because of him, and you're so tired and you can't take any more, and you're looking at me with your eyes, *my* eyes, and you're telling me I must go back and take your place, but *could* I do it, dear God? You were always the better one of the two. You're the one who's really known now to love. You, the old maid, living your dull life in that crumbling house in that crumbling country. And now you're leaving me without a chance to tell you all this . . . that I've always looked up to you . . . no, don't close your eyes, look at me one more time . . . forgive me for the part of your life I've stolen from you . . . no, don't cry, you've won. I promise you, sister. I'll go back to Cuba and look after the old man . . . You can go to sleep in peace . . . I promise . . . I promise.

'Flight 407 to Havana now boarding.'

Dear God, I've criticized Miami so much, I've so longed for this return, and really the city looks so pretty from the plane . . . of

course I've got to feel sad . . . I'm leaving my whole life behind . . .
funny, while I was living it I used to think it was something
temporary . . . and now I think, I don't know, that those years were
the ones that counted . . . I'm leaving so much behind, even a grave
marked with my name, but actually, I'm leaving nothing . . .

'I'm sorry, ma'am, I'm a little nervous. You see, I'm traveling to
Cuba for the first time in so many years. Are you visiting too?'

'No, sir, I've just spent some time in Miami visiting my nephews.
Now I'm coming home.'

TRANSLATED BY JUANA MARIÁ CAZABÓN

Threshold
Rolando Sánchez Mejías

The table: grubby with tea and sugar.

The flies weren't as irritating as the music: a horrible confusion of Radio Enciclopedia and the news from another broadcast.

I put the packet from the second-hand bookshop down on the chair.

I opened my notebook and revised the points I'd managed to jot down while going through the streets of Vedado in my wheelchair.

A magazine had commissioned an article on the relationship between de Sade, history and death.

Yes, de Sade was definitely in fashion.

Again.

Nietzsche too.

The eternal return was after all an agreeably beautiful idea.

Perhaps this might have something to do with going through the city streets making spasmodic notes while-the-winds-of-the-forest-whip-your-face.

But the problem of death had faded away.

At least for the time being.

It must have faded when Sartre came to look things over and, on his way back home again, bestowed a fraternal and expansive wave upon us all congregated there for his farewell. (Simone at his side, smiling beneath the white scarf wrapped around her hair.)

At that precise moment the problem of death faded away.

I tried to decipher my scrawls:

Every *maudit* goes to meet his noose or his Bastille in order to write (see 'Broken Bodies' as related by R., my favourite student) and probe the fundamentalism that lies hidden in de Sade. In other words . . . . the body as Origin: the Shattered Tablets of the Law: original chaos. History as a Sadistic Machine.

A possible profile of de Sade in the gloom of his cell

Imagining de Sade: grossly obese in his cell. Scrawling obscene graffiti, suddenly featureless in the profound night of the Bastille.

My apoplexy the product of a dissipated existence: orgies, drunkenness, fractured falls down staircases.

Clandestine relations between Eros and the Absolute.

My neighbour burns his wife with cigarettes and I hear her moans of pleasure through the walls, but ultimately *something* fails between them (or are we Cubans condemned to a failure of the Absolute? [See Fdo. Ortiz]).

The chair in front wheeled away.

A skinny lad with dark-ringed eyes.

He was fashionably shorn.

He stared at my notebook and I at the image stamped on his T-shirt: something like the face of a Saint Sebastian in agony or of a somewhat ruthless guru (with strong, imprecise colours).

He read my thoughts.

'No, he's not a saint. Everyone thinks he's a saint. He's my father.'

I pretended not to understand.

He explained that *he* (his father) was insane.

(On this spot, only a few days ago, I'd bumped into a student from high school who declared she was writing the testament of her insanity. I immediately understood she wasn't insane and that her poetry was pretty bad, a kind of kitchen-sink diary mixed with lyrical broadsides.)

He continued his explanation: 'He's the guardian of the Island.'

'Ah.' (Yes, again the same old business: the Island, always the Island.)

I tried to fathom the joke in his grubbily pond-coloured eyes. (Pinprick eyes of the new generation: ingenuous, perverse and empty.)

He said, 'It's a year tomorrow since he was admitted. I want to buy him a bar of chocolate for when I go and visit.'

I narrowed my eyes in emulation of that astuteness proverbial in mature writers before enquiring, 'Why is he the guardian of the Island?' (apeing his manner of underlining words).

'That's something you'd have to ask him yourself. He's said nothing to me, at any rate. It must be a secret.' (He panted, with the swollen chest of an asthmatic.) 'Also, I don't suppose it's that important to know, at least from *this* side.'

I finished my cigarette.

In these forlorn times it was down to you to make something of anything, of an unlikely tale just as much as a non-transcendent dialogue. I decided to continue my questioning.

'Is your father young?'

'Yes, although not all that young.'

'Aren't you saying that's him in the picture?'

'The image is one thing, reality another. Haven't you studied Kant?'

Even Kant had become fashionable among these self-taught youths!

'Who made the image?'

'I did.'

'Do you paint?'

'More or less.'

He rummaged in his knapsack and pulled out some papers. He deposited them on my notebook: they were pencil sketches of his father's face, all broken into discontinuous lines that dissolved into painful traces.

'They're good. A miracle, given that you never studied art.'

'You don't need to go to art school in order to draw him. Just seeing him is enough.'

'Ah.'

I asked for two teas. The sweets had run out, worst luck.

They brought the tea.

He said he didn't like to drink it too hot and began obsessively blowing into his cup.

'Tell me about your father.'

He looked at me slyly.

'You look like a writer. Don't misrepresent me.'

He asked to see my jottings in the notebook.

I explained my project to him.

He seemed to be quite interested and nodded in agreement from time to time.

I told him about the meeting with Sartre around thirty years ago, in my room in Old Havana, where the original idea had somehow taken shape.

A dingy room crammed with damp, evil-smelling books.

Sartre and Simone had escaped from an official reception.

I asked them if they hadn't been followed this far.

Sartre jovially remarked to me, 'You're paranoid. This is a premature moment, historically speaking, to become paranoid.'

Simone was looking beautiful, cheeks reddened with the wine or a touch of rouge. Not so Sartre. He wasn't looking good. His tie was a mess, his hair tangled. He went straight to the bookcase and said, 'What are the writers up to here? Are they trying to render the culture schizophrenic? Books and more books. Including mine! You should spend your time observing reality instead. You –'

I interrupted. 'Stop.'

(Simone was acting misunderstood, looking at the pictures. From time to time she made reference to some detail or other in the landscape. She said that in general she liked the Cuban landscape. Above all the absolute verticality of the palm trees.)

Sartre didn't stop. No. He just didn't stop. Just like his prose. He said, 'They are living a *unique* moment. It's like living right at the heart in History. In such cases, the majority of books are superfluous.'

I said to him, 'Have you just come from talking to *him*?'

Simone left off leafing through a book and said, 'Paul argued with *him* today. They couldn't agree over one aspect of the matter. Everyone thinks it's all so easy for us.'

I asked them all if they wanted coffee.

The moonlight played around Simone's profile and she resembled a Kabuki actor.

Sartre appeared exhausted, sustained only by some striated energy. He said, 'Have you studied the problems of gold in depth?'

I answered, 'In the manner of Pound?' (I laughed softly.)

He went on, 'No, in general poetry doesn't dig too deep into certain dimensions of reality. And certainly Pound was remarkably confused.'

I told him, 'Yes, I know you prefer prose, everything orderly.' Simone's Kabuki profile vanished, giving way to a simple Provençal face.

'Hereabouts, things get very easily twisted around. That's horrible.'

Sartre pursued his idea.

'Gold. In this country things continue to revolve around gold. All within the ontological vicious circle furnished by gold. And worst of all: the ontology which sparkles from the spectre of gold.'

I set about making the coffee.

I heard Simone's voice: 'During the reception *he* discussed the economic plans. They're gigantic! Perhaps Utopia might be that: what cannot be taken in at a glance. Right, Paul?'

Simone continued talking: 'Paul didn't like your last letter. It was as if you'd failed to properly understand the problematic of labour camps.'

'Ah,' I said to myself, 'labour camps.'

The coffee was boiling, its smell diffusing agreeably.

Sartre spoke: 'If that's what worrying you, then I expect you lot *don't* have labour camps.'

I answered, 'Is that what he told you?'

I served their coffee.

Simone spilt a few drops on to her white skirt. She became alarmed.

I moistened a cloth with a little water and fiercely scrubbed at the stain.

As I scrubbed I asked Sartre, 'Do you imagine the only form of violence is work camps?'

He murmured to himself, 'Violence, violence . . .'

The stain wouldn't entirely disappear. In spite of this, Simone happily announced, 'It doesn't matter. It'll be a pleasant memory when we're back in Paris.'

Sartre spoke: 'Are you people aware that de Sade was in charge of the Lancers' Division during the Revolution? Didn't you know? There are certain very complex aspects to things when they're closely examined . . .'

I interrupted him: 'And they can be definitively clarified thanks to dialectics.'

He paid me no attention.

' . . . It was a failure of communication. Communication through violence. Violence as exercised upon and through the body.'

Now Simone was rifling through my papers, all the minuscule and near-illegible notes I used to pin on to the walls along with all the writings in the pile of papers on my little table. I said to myself, 'Get your hands off my papers.'

Sartre said, 'Have you writers thought of how you're going to confront the machinery of the state?'

I answered him, laughing, 'All right. We'll create a Division of Lancers.'

Sartre: 'I'm referring to a praxis. Or in the last resort they'll get shafted' (this last he pronounced in impeccable Spanish).

Then he spoke in low tones, as though he were thinking aloud, 'Yes, and as a last resort you lot'll be screwed.'

He summoned fresh energies: 'I'm going to tell you a story. A story about myself. One night I was walking on the banks of the Seine. At that time the entire space in my brain was consumed by a single problem: the problem of Evil. Meaning, in order to be more precise: existence as a condition of Evil. If only I could resolve that problem

. . . Do you know what it means to a philosopher when he locates a cog that doesn't function properly within his system? . . . A loose cog trying at all costs to subvert the system. Well, fine. Submerged in my thoughts, that figure surfaced, perhaps from one of those little streets that so inexorably lead to the Seine. He was there, only a couple of metres away from me: somewhat hunched, hands serenely folded inside his enormous black leather coat . . . Do you know what it means to come face to face with a stranger on the banks of the Seine at night? My first move was to pull my hands out of my pockets. I was as on guard as a young boxer fresh from training. Meditation had enfolded I don't know what black hole in my consciousness. No further major problems remained outstanding . . . He stood stock still on the same spot, observing me, his hands quietly in his pockets. An almost infinite span of time passed. Until, without losing any of his serenity, he said, '*Ostraka*,' and threw himself into the Seine, disappearing beneath its definitively dark waters . . . Had I been consistent with my then morality, in those days I should have leapt into the waters after him. But *something* prevented me. *Something* inserted itself between him and me. Do you know what? Simple: it was Evil. What is Evil? Simple again: doubt, hesitation, even thought itself! Fine, in order not to bore you, I spent a while staring at the water, where I expected to see him rise to the surface. But no, only cigarette packets, rubbish, even a dead dog . . . I didn't tell anyone. I returned home and looked up the meaning of the word *ostraka*. Do you know what *ostraka* are? Ceramic mosaic pieces used in antiquity as tools for writing with . . . Two days later I learned that he'd turned up dead. He was a Polish Jew who'd hung about in Paris since the war. A Jew who'd been in Buchenwald. A Jew whose task in Buchenwald had been stoking the ovens. The newspaper gave the story in detail . . . So fine. What did he want to *tell me* through all this? A clue? Or only an unconnected word, engendered by madness or by the arbitrariness adopted by language in similar situations? . . . *Ostraka* . . . *Ostraka* . . . The word reverberated in a peculiar manner inside my brain. In the midst of a thousand metaphysical relationships scheming inside that head of mine, this word inevitably kept sticking out, at times impetuously, at others smooth and lascivious as the silhouette of a naked woman. A solitary word which attempted to break with every possibility, gnawing at my senses like a ravenous rat . . . Perhaps had I let him drag me into the depths of the Seine he could have bubbled his secret to me like a fish. But at the end of the day, I prefer to ruminate by daylight, where the secret unarguably loses its essential gravity . . . Do you have more coffee? I've had one too many daiquiris!'

Sartre slumped into an armchair.

He assumed a thoughtful pose.

Simone began to laugh.

In her hands she held one of my notes. (Go on, take your hands off my writing.)

She said, 'In the last resort you too are the children of abstraction.'

Changing the subject, I riposted, 'Around these parts, they're saying that you two had also plotted a dual suicide.' (This was my private invention.)

Simone answered, 'Yes. It was all going well. Both of us were pulling strings but almost at the end, Paul explained the need for such an act (do you remember, Paul?). He explained it in a tiny thread of a voice, as though he were striving to relate something important . . . What's bizarre is that this all took place before this same death's door –' here she broke into enthusiastic laughter at another of my notes pinned like a butterfly to the showcase door – 'Yes, it was this: *Porta itineri longissima.*'

By now Sartre was snoring.

His spectacles had slid half-way down his nose.

He had kicked off his shoes.

He'd dropped off with his chin still resting on his hand as though he were pursuing his meditations through his dreams.

Simone was now attempting to open the ramshackle door of the showcase. I lifted my hands in a warning gesture.

She managed to open the door.

The puppets began tumbling out, lumps of papier-mâché, scraps of cloth, reels of cord, clay dolls that shattered on the floor . . .

Stupefied, surrounded by the trail of disaster at her feet, she said, 'They had already brought me up to date with your views on theatre and reality. But I honestly didn't think you dedicated yourself to all *this*.'

'To what?' (A terseness came through my voice.)

'Well . . . To the relationship of God with things, I imagine.'

I muttered under my breath so she wouldn't hear, 'Go to Hell'.

The lad smiled at the tale I'd told him. I took out some photos and showed them to him:

Sartre and Simone in the Bodeguita del Medio surrounded by their group: everyone raising their glasses in a toast. Someone seemed to be offering congratulations all round.

Sartre smoking a cigarette in front of some oxen, his eyes straying to some infinite point in the earth.

Sartre pursued by flies as he observes the conversion processes of sugar cane through a window.

Che lighting Sartre's cigarette in the setting of an enormous aseptic office.

Sartre cutting cane.

Sartre and Simone bidding us farewell, Sartre raises his hand and says goodbye. Simone's farewell gesture is virtually indecipherable.

Sartre's body in the darkest depths of the empty spaces of a canefield: as indistinct as a badly etched line.

He returned the photos to me, nodding his head like a drowsy bird.

He said, 'Ah, literature, literature . . .'

He continued, 'You lot all talk about jumping to the *other* side, but never act.'

He took out an inhaler and raised it to his lips, inhaling twice.

I asked, 'And what is this other side?'

Someone hailed him from a table at the far end.

It was a long-haired fellow with a flute. Beside him an Inuit-faced woman in her forties reading something by Neruda.

The long-haired fellow lent him the flute and he tried it out.

The woman giggled a little.

All three of them laughed.

He returned, pleased with himself, and told me, 'All life is a problem of communication.'

I told him, 'It seems to me that the *other* side likewise has nothing much to boast about.'

He responded by informing me that I was a sceptic and an unbeliever like everybody else and that there was nothing to be done with people like me.

He went on, 'He did jump. And one day I might too. There are many ways to get there. The problem is to avoid straying along those leading to death, as the Greeks used to say.'

After a pause he said, 'I'd like to invite you along on tomorrow morning's visit, that way you can see how good it feels to be at the *threshold*.'

The word *threshold* hovered in the air. The scars on his wrists also shimmered.

Both visions dissolved in the act of apparition.

I replied that I wouldn't be accepting the invitation.

He made a gesture of resignation with his hands.

'You see? What a shame. That's the reason why things are as they are.'

He drank his tea very slowly, making little sipping noises. Then he began to distract himself with a fly.

He took a match and stirred a little puddle of tea, flicking it in the direction of the fly, which became riveted.

He explained that flies were physically devious creatures that, unlike humans, had a very finite end to their fleeting existences. Then added, 'Like *him*. He says one has to be prepared. That if you take a false step you'll reach the other side without comprehending anything.'

He finished his tea.

He stopped. He lifted one foot on to the chair and straightened his sock. He commented that he lived out in Alamar and that the buses were impossible. He made reference to my wheelchair, explaining that despite the misfortune it implied it must facilitate my freer movement in a city so lacking in transport.

I asked him, 'Do you have money for a bar of chocolate?' (I pulled a comical face.)

'Anyone can find ten pesos, can't they?' (He mimicked my grimace, wide and torn as a vertical wound.)

I selected a book from my package and gave it to him: it was a treatise on bees.

I told him to take it to his father. That my essay project regarding the occult analogies between our society and beehives could wait.

(Yes. Ultimately *everything* can wait.)

He said, 'He's going to be as happy as could be with his present. He still reads, when he has the time to, of course. For the most part, he is kept fully occupied by his job.'

(I saw his father lifting up the book with chocolate-stained fingers, and with a look of profound absence, and the son breaking another square on to the saucer, the two of them sitting on the grass, people in their white coats passing in the distance and behind them all, the sky red as in those old Polish films of the 1960s.)

I recited a couple of lines to him:

Je suis comme le roi d'un pays pluvieux,
Riche, mais impuissant, jeune et pourtant très vieux.

I translated them for him and he laughed.

He left, his knapsack bouncing on his back.

I shouted after him, '*Bon voyage!*'
I ordered another cup of tea and set to work outlining obscene
sketches in my notebook.

TRANSLATED BY AMANDA HOPKINSON

Why Is Leslie Caron Crying?
Roberto Uría

The Institute of Meteorology said today will be a warm, sunny day. And, after juggling probabilities and percentages of rain, wind and surf, concluded that the maximum temperatures this afternoon will vary between twenty-nine and thirty-two degrees centigrade. It might have been a warm, sunny day, but I woke up feeling cold – that kind of cold that starts in your stomach – and windy, with a wave of panic running through my whole body. I'm practically rainy. Wintry.

After they brought me into the world, there were considerable family disputes over my name. Hector versus Alejandro, Enrique versus Jorge. How about Hugo? How about Javier? In the end, Francisco won out. But all these years I've been Panchito and, on occasion, Panchy (with a 'y' instead of 'i' to make it sexier) . . . Except that I've come to prefer Leslie Caron more than any other name. It's so musical, so European. And besides, my bosom buddies admit that there's quite a resemblance between the actress and myself. We have the same grace, the same celestial quality . . .

I belong to a 'holy' family, just about perfect, the kind you don't find anymore. With a mother, a father, adorable little sister, a dog and lots of plants, it's a close-knit bunch, foreign to me. The house, of course, is the classic little nest, decorated and decorous. So it seems I turn out to be the only gray cloud spoiling the prosperity of an oh-so-blue sky.

Because, it has to be said, the dialectic didn't work well on me, or else it worked so well as to not comply with the imperfections of our time. I don't know. The fact is that the members of my family, like almost everyone, are 'useful beings', 'so-cial-ly-pro-duc-tive', wage-earners of progress and conformity, saints and virgins, bastions of the economy. And I, for my own sad part, feel alone like a butterfly or a snail: I'm a beautiful parasite. I take the time to make myself attractive and happy here and now and don't think about the ever-so-revered tomorrow, which increasingly promises to be atomic or neutronic or I-don't-know-what-all . . .

I quit school because it bores me to tears spending five or six hours a day with specialists, cramming me with diagrams, preconceptions, a succession of disasters and mistakes, false perspectives and redundancies. I got sick of it, that's all. And screw the future.

And where could I earn my salt from the sweat off my brow? Where, without being cremated in the cold oven of timetables and meetings? These are such barbarous times! as Attila would say.

I choose to be 'gay'. The most explosive gaiety is mine; each stretch of the street, the city, is my stage, and I am the most sought-after starlet. I bury myself under a heap of sequins and mercury lights, I hope I don't perish under the weight of my own lights . . . That's why I adore bus stops, parks, shops and markets, lines at movie theaters. Of course, there's never been a public bathroom on my résumé. I'm too much of a hypochondriac and a romantic for that still.

What I like are flowers, music – Barbra Streisand is my idol – ice cream, and a sunny beach, the ocean spray and all the people, especially the people, good heavens! Really, practically naked. What a charming little country! It's the enchanted isle of gorgeous men. Everyone is beautiful. Everywhere I go, strong, young men of all shapes and colors encircle and devour me. They're mammoths who crush you with all their vitality. They encircle me – like 'a necklace of throbbing sexual oysters,' as Neruda would say – and yet so few ever belong to me. Watching isn't bad, but it's better to touch.

To touch: to perish. An instant, a wing-beat and then swift flight, on the back a relentlessly epidermic era. What a way to inflict damage! But anyway . . .

The fact is that I stop in front of the mirror and always look at myself and end up asking, 'What will become of this queen? What am I going to do with you, Leslie Caron? Why did I have to be like this?' I've tried to change, but I can't manage to find anything that truly interests me. Not anything or anyone. The majority of people I just feel sorry for. They're empty, so fake; they just move through the narrow margins of the designs imposed upon them. I chose this bondage. I didn't choose myself, but I accept the cards I've been dealt and play my deadly game just like anyone else. It's like eye color: I don't like mine, but since I need to see there's no choice but to use the eyes I've got. And oh, the things I've seen and still see!

I've seen a father who works too much and has 'meetings' even more; who when he's not off fishing with his work buddies runs around with other women; a father who has never remembered his children's birthdays.

I've seen a mother who works like a dog; who imprisons herself within her own cold-cream-slathered skin; who, when she's not suffering the macho antics of her husband, sets her son to brushing her wigs and then goes off to forget her woes. I've seen a sister who marries a guy just because he has a house in Miramar and a VCR and an exceedingly long et cetera; a sister who goes and leaves her queen brother with no trousseau, practically naked. And how everyone envies her! Yes, I see it all clearly.

And I'll see a poor, crestfallen fairy, all wrinkled and lonely, with no family, no friends to speak of, perhaps surrounded by a few cronies as old and ostentatious as he is. A fairy hoping to someday see the end of this daily chain of deaths she has been subjected to. I'm not committed to the future and I'm not being dramatic and I hope to God it won't really be quite like that. But what is to be done? What miracle could change the course of these visions?

And sometimes I say screw my fear of wrinkles and I let myself charge an exorbitant amount and (believe me) I cry and cry like a baby. Yes, I wake up cold and rainy, and that's how I take my revenge on the perfect backdrop of a warm, sunny day and sadistic realities.

And if someone were to ask, 'Why is Leslie Caron crying?' the only answer would be, 'Because life's a bitch.'

TRANSLATED BY LISA DILLMAN

The Voice of the Turtle
Guillermo Cabrera Infante

A story my mother-in-law told me

caguama: the biggest known species of marine turtle, weighing in at
up to forty stones, though its meat is inedible.

Cuba on Hand, 1936

When I first met my mother-in-law she was called Carmela, but she
hadn't been born to that name. At the age of four she went missing
for several days and her mother made a vow to the virgin of the
Carmen: if she were found alive, Carmen would be her name. On the
third day they found her on an island the other side of the river,
where crocodiles still swam. As a child I had seen manatees in the
same river and it was as wild as ever. Carmela now swears she was
carried across the river by a lanky, long-haired man who walked on
water. The whole family thought it was no lesser a person than Jesus
who had put her safely on the island. Ever since my mother-in-law's
been Carmen, Carmela.

She told me another story that was no less incredible. It happened
before her tenth birthday. A village boy had fallen in love with a local
beauty and his love did not go unrequited. They wanted to marry but
he was very poor. And so was she. Everybody in the village was poor.
But he didn't even have a job. Despite their hopelessness, they lived
on hope. Not knowing what to expect, they had their expectations.
One day he realized there was no future in a village which lived in the
past and decided, with his best friend, to go in search of fame and
fortune. Ironies of fate, he found one but not the other, although for
a moment he believed he had really found both. The only source of

life the village knew was the sea – and off to the sea he went.

But he didn't take to the sea. He suggested to his friend that they should explore the coast and together they headed for Los Caletones, in the opposite direction to the bay and the river. On the then deserted beach of Los Caletones an enormous whale had appeared one day, become beached and had died. When discovered it was already putrefying (people learned of its existence from the large gathering of vultures, a strange sight, because scavengers don't usually venture seawards) and the village entrepreneurs braved the stench and managed to extract from the carcass a great quantity of spermaceti which fetched a good price in the capital. Los Caletones seemed full of promise.

But they scoured the whole beach and found only flotsam and jetsam. Despondently they decided to go back to the village, the boy who wanted to marry more downcast than his friend who didn't want to get married. (Or, at any rate, not immediately.) On their way back to the village, scrambling out between two sand dunes, they saw a caguama. They already knew something you don't know about caguamas.

caguama.

The caguama is a reptile and like the crocodile moves well in water (rivers, seas) but poorly on land. It is in its element in the sea, where it can spend hours underwater, coming up for air very occasionally. Once a caguama, the Indian name for a giant turtle, reaches the sea, after making an ungainly exit from its shell, only the female returns to dry land, to lay her eggs. The male – it is known – never returns. The caguama moves slowly on land because her feet have turned into flippers for swimming and because she can tip the scales at two thousand pounds. Others measure two yards by three. A zoologist once said, 'carrying her shell as armour', the caguama has no need to be as swift as Achilles, or to furrow the waves like Ulysses. But the caguama continues swimming even when she is out of the sea and flaps her way over the few metres of beach to her nest. That is how she makes the return journey from and to the sea. Like all reptiles, the caguama practises internal fertilization and detecting her sex is no easy matter. In many species, on the other hand, it is possible to make out the sex of an adult animal. When the caguama has laid her eggs, her sex assumes a strangely human aspect. The belief has always been that the caguama sees little and hears less, though some species do have a voice, particularly when on heat. Those who have been in close contact with a caguama say it possesses an intelligence that is only possible in a mammal.

Both saw her at the same time and thought the same thoughts at the same time. The two boys bore some comparison, except one was good-looking and the other wasn't. But both were equally strong and often did identical press-ups, wrestled and executed other trials of strength for their own enjoyment. They were, in fact, the strongest boys in the village, only one was clever and the other wasn't. Now the cleverer of the two conceived an idea which he didn't have to tell his friend (they often had the same thoughts at the same time) but just resolved to put it into practice and his friend was only seconds behind in coming forward. He tried to get hold of the huge animal who was heading laboriously seawards. They would make a fortune from selling her meat (that was all but inedible), its tortoiseshell (though it wasn't a hawksbill) and the fat stored underneath her carapace, well known to be (only they knew this) better than chicken grease. 'Caguama fat, can cure all,' went the refrain which they knew and took to be truly axiomatic – although they didn't know what an axiom was.

The frightened caguama stopped in her tracks, not because she could make out one of the boys but because her feet had felt the vibration of the shoes running towards her. As often on her journey, the caguama sighed, not because she sensed the end was nigh (a caguama lives to be a hundred), but because she is a marine animal who always sighs on land. (Some people believe it is the release of breath left over from the energy needed to move over the sand, when she finally comes to a halt.) Be that as it may, in their excitement not one of the boys heard this land-locked siren's muted song. (Or perhaps one of them did.) They closed in on the caguama, shouting excitedly, enthusiastically, and at once got to work turning over a turtle paralysed by the hullabaloo. We know that a caguama on its back becomes helpless and requires help to recover its quadruped state. An upturned caguama is a dead caguama. Better than dead for the two boys: she is worth a fortune. Shouting each other on, with much heaving, more misspent heaving than ever before, they managed to turn over the animal, which flapped its legs in the air, as if air were water. The caguamas, they thought, aren't as intelligent as we are. Although only one of the pair was intelligent.

One of the boys or perhaps the other (they were indistinguishable) suggested going to borrow the travois from his uncle who lived in the nearby hillocks. Now you know what a hillock is when it's not being a hill, but perhaps few of you know what a travois is. It is a vehicle used by the Plains Indians and takes the place of the wheel they never knew. Though simple, it is a great invention. You need only to find three long poles, two act as converging axles where force is applied, and the third pole becomes a crossbar which can also carry a frame. The travois is pulled from the other end and can take a considerable weight. The uncle owning the travois apparently lived nearby. The other youth walked off through the sand dunes.

Meanwhile, the first boy watched over the caguama. He knew she was immobilized for ever and wasn't afraid she would roll over, though he wasn't sure she mightn't be stolen in that state of stasis. While he watched, the lad was thinking of the endless quantity of combs, clasps, jewel boxes and other luxury items to be made from such a specimen. The caguama would be a source of untold wealth in the village. If getting her there was a matter of muscle, selling the caguama required grey matter. His friend could drag it along by himself but only he could sell it, get rich and get married.

With these thoughts running through his head and feeling bored, he decided to take a close look at the caguama. The skin on her chest and belly seemed hard but was pale, almost white, and gave the already vulnerable animal a soft, silky aspect that belied its dark carapace. The lower covering ended in the flippers that were very strong and still plying the air, as if the animal didn't realize it was immobile in its armoured shell. Caguamas are stupid, thought the boy. Then the caguama stopped pawing to puff out air in a even louder sigh. The boy was alarmed by this almost human sound, this mixture of despair and resignation. But curiosity is stronger than alarm and he carried on inspecting. You stupid, stupid bitch. Then he made what he thought was a wonderful discovery.

The caguama's sex had suddenly come into sight. After her egg-laying, according to one naturalist, it is common – the result of the effort of laying dozens of eggs very, very quickly or perhaps down to a natural reaction – the caguama's vagina is left exposed. In this case to prying eyes. The caguama was now showing her sex that appeared virgin (turtles, unlike manatees, have hairless pubes) and the lad felt curiosity giving way to dour desire. He decided (or intuited) that he had to penetrate the caguama, a female for the taking. There and then. He took one shamefaced look round. Saw nobody. Los Caletones were always deserted and it would take his friend some time to drag the travois that distance. The youth walked once more around the caguama and the animal stirred a little as she sensed him, but then quietened down again. The boy returned to her pudenda that now moved in what he took to be a strong sucking movement. The softest areas of the depilated (or girlish) sex trembled. Driven by his own sex, the boy opened his rustic flies (no need to drop underwear poor people don't wear) and took out a big, fat penis whose darkness contrasted with the female whiteness (though next to the animal, his penis seemed puny.) He got close in, lay almost horizontal atop the caguama. With one hand (his left, being a left-hander) he clung to the carapace and, with the help of his right, inserted an anxious penis into the vast vagina, which swallowed it whole. He felt a pleasure that seemed extraordinary, perhaps because till then he had known only masturbation, but also because it was an animal pleasure: he was committing bestialism but he didn't know it. Ecstasy occurred a second before he in turn was penetrated, apparently, on all sides at the same time.

When a caguama is on heat (and the combination of egg-laying followed by sudden penetration had now created within her conditions similar to being on heat) she is subject to opposing but equally peremptory forces. One force is paralysis: the passivity of the female before her male attacker. The other is action to secure a coitus that is underway. Fornication always occurs out to sea, where the couple is weightless yet at the same time under tons of sea-pressure per square metre. Sometimes caguamas couple out in the Gulf Stream and are visible from the beach. Copulation is, then, often threatened by adverse elements. But nature, evolution or whatever has endowed the caguama with mechanical aids to union. The female of the species is equipped with an appendix of the same material as her shell, a sharp, curved point that she uses to hold on tight to the macho during coitus. This hook remains hidden as the male mounts the female and tries to maintain a penetrating position on the slippery, wave-tossed carapace, a precarious state the female immediately makes secure. The hook (or rather harpoon) is launched from its secret place within the female to catch its prey. The female literally nails the male from below and behind. Only the roughness of its carapace prevents the caguama, like the male praying mantis, from being killed by the female during coitus.

The other boy, meanwhile, was returning to the beach cheerfully pulling his heavy travois behind him, proving how strong he was. He was almost singing. When he left the hills and cleared his way through the overgrown coast, he saw in the distance what became an increasingly intimate couple as he drew near. He stopped suddenly not out of prudery but fear. He will never forget what he then saw. He moved nearer. He knew a caguama is a passive animal (tame was the preferred word) and although he didn't know what you know, he did see what he did see. The other boy, his friend, was rigid on top of the turtle and bleeding on all sides from under and over his trousers: from buttocks, legs, feet and calfskin shoes. A summary inspection revealed that the other boy had fainted (he wasn't dead yet though he had reason enough to die several times) and when he got as close to the other boy as fear, horror and the flow of blood making a puddle on the sand allowed him, he finally saw the unheard of weapon (or fragment thereof) with which the caguama had hoisted his friend. Had there been an autopsy, it would have shown how the animal's shaft had penetrated the intruding fornicator just above the coccyx, how the harpoon's curved action had transfixed the anus from top to bottom, twisted its hook into his rectum and drilled through it crossways, before shredding the prostate and obliterating both testicles (or just the one) until the end came to rest like another duct within a penis which was doubly rigid.

The other youth realized his friend was badly injured and certain to die if he stayed on the beach. He didn't try to extricate him or even to move him. Not from any intelligent inhibition or sense of pity, but because he was increasingly terrified. Now he wasn't sure whether to fear the inevitable death of his only friend or the dangers of the caguama, which now seemed an awesome apparition. He had an idea that in other circumstances would have been his salvation: the travois would do the job it was intended for and drag his friend and the caguama to the village. With more strength than skill he pushed the two axles of the travois over the loose, soft sand and inserted them under the sides of the beast. When the artefact was in place, he secured it with the ropes he had brought with him. He tied down the caguama and his friend, who was now livid, a deathly pale. The pallor emphasized the perfect features that now seemed etched on his rustic face. Unhappily he began to pull his happy burden.

How the other boy managed to drag the couple the eight leagues to the village is as extraordinary as the tragedy inspiring his feat. He finally reached the village after midday and was met by the usual indifference. But as ever in villages, the extraordinary presence immediately assembled a public that was too shocked to react to the horror confronting them. It was like a fairground. But among the last to arrive was the would-be fiancée, on a day whose horror had its limits. Obviously she immediately recognized her boyfriend. What she didn't see was him half-opening his eyes at the hue and cry.

Nobody saw that because right then the caguama, immortal like all turtles, let out a kind of scream that seemed to emerge not from the beast's mouth but from the open lips of the fiancée before her betrothed. Still atop the turtle, the boy closed his eyes and for a moment imagined he was dreaming of his wedding night.

TRANSLATED BY PETER BUSH

Someone's Got It All Licked
Ricardo Arrieta

It's a real bummer arriving in a room packed with intellectuals and having to search for some space. Luckily I'm a guy with great vision and between two blocks of chairs I discover an inviting aisle. A free trade zone. I sit on the floor, right in the middle of the room, and it seems like a good idea because a whole load of people immediately descend on the aisle and sit down.

It's all a trade-off: a couple of accessible-looking chicks settle right beside me. Just within arm's reach. I can describe them and make it sound utterly mundane; no, best limit myself to acknowledging that the nearest one has a pair of exuberant breasts, just within tongue's reach. She's the type that if you pay a little attention you can make out, one by one, all the energy lines of her biomagnetic aura and even the vestigial signs of her previous incarnation. My incontinence is thus proven. I ask her if she's heterosexual and, quite the comedienne, she answers no, she's bisexual. An Aristotelian response. I laugh at her joke with a reassuring, fixed smile.

But women are not everything in life, even the big-breasted ones, so I turn to my mates and start saying hello and that kind of thing.

I'm pleased to see Dennys in a corner, I wink at him just as he's winking at me, and ruffle David's hair who's sitting in front of me. How's it going, man? David is a great guy.

For example:

David is in front
of you.
You say hello to him.

David gives you
a lighted cigar etc.

and besides, he's one of the few people around who acts natural. It stands out a mile: these days everyone's sporting a ponytail – at least everyone in a place like this – except for David and Dennys, who wear their hair loose and any old how.

My spatial situation is truly privileged. From every point of view. Because of big tits and because from here I can oversee even the tiniest detail of what goes on in the room. Now they're discussing that business about the park on G and 23rd. A woman in a prewashed dress has started on an incoherent speech defending street art. A disaster. There are people who mean well who don't know how to dress. I ask big tits if she means well. By way of an answer, I suppose, she gives the most delicate little smile and presents me with a marpacífico she got from who knows where. This is going well. Desiderio is saying that performances have nothing to do with an exhibition in a gallery and that they work better as ephemeral events with different scenographic possibilities.

Example of a possible performance:

A girl with the most delicate smile presents you with a marpacífico. Let's imagine she's an especially attractive girl with incredible tits. You accept the marpacífico and enthusiastically set to pulling off the petals, or should I say deflowering it. The operation completed, you go over and ask her if she's really interested in sex. As was to be hoped, she will reply in the affirmative. And, original guy that you are, you'll give her back what remains of the flower that is, the pistil and stamen etc.

Of course, women don't usually understand performances. As the poet would have said: '. . . On cold Stockholm evenings, you don't see doves fly.' Luckily, sometimes someone says something of interest and you can listen in, especially if you've had no luck with your performance piece and need to save face. Right now they're discussing some journalist who apparently made two or three idiotic remarks about young artists and to cap that she didn't come to the debate even though she was invited. I don't see why there's so much fuss about the poor woman, she probably never had time to iron her dress.

However the debate is getting interesting again because one man, who hadn't spoken until now, is taking a stand against these boys who, he says, are playing into enemy hands with this stuff they call art, and in fact the boys in question are unconscious hypercritics; he understands them because they're young and they have to rebel and all that, it's just they don't know what they're rebelling against; what we should do is help them, give them some direction, that's what the Writers and Artists Union is for, isn't it, and those other organizations. Someone else replies that that's not a problem, at least in art, so long as there's no decline in quality. And now things are hotting up with this declining-quality business and the other problems of art in general as if this were the only one, until it occurs to someone that it's best to ask the boys in question. And then it turns out that the problem is space.

Space. Half the people don't understand. What does space have to do with art? At this point someone stands up deeply worried about the level of culture of these new generations who haven't studied the life and work of Picasso; he says he's a painter and until now the only thing he's ever needed is a crummy little studio in his house, he hasn't needed and doesn't need to ask anything of anyone . . . so what's all this about needing space? Big tits bursts out laughing. Evidently her friend's told her some frivolous joke. As for Dennys, he's absorbed in the debate because now Desiderio's speaking; his arm's draped round a blonde who's not half bad herself. Dennys is lucky when it comes to blondes. Desiderio finishes his speech, handing over to Mosquera, the one who's worked most directly with young artists.

(Critics can be very special people. Some of them. They're capable of putting their hand in the fire and then coming out with some theory on the fragile, explosive nature of guys who build bonfires.)

Milay has just arrived. She comes in holding hands with some guy, so my whole day's screwed.

Milay, as casual as can be, greets me with a peck on the cheek of the I-see-you-every-day kind, introduces her friend and as if it were no big deal they sit down behind me. What's more the guy's called Rubén. I will never get along with the Rubéns of this world, although this one looks friendly enough with his ponytail and all. Bugger. My situation's totally buggered again; now I won't even be able to talk to big tits because Milay might think I was doing it to get even with her. I remember that Ronaldo is always harping on about how easy it is to make a fool of yourself. I'm better off listening to the debate: at least five people are talking at once and no one can hear. I'll have to go out for a while and smoke a second cigar from David's box.

Outside I have two options. Either I get horribly depressed or I find someone I can spill my guts to about whatever. And luckily, as I go out, Nilo's coming in and I persuade him to hear me out a while. Nilo is amazingly odd. He's liable to tell you that bleeding gums is an illness that afflicts intellectuals and the best possible happening is to go down to Coppelia with a tape recorder round your neck and the whole brass band dancing behind you in single file. A surreal idea. Nilo can't imagine how helpful he's being; it's a shame he's bound to notice my face indicating art in decline. Yup. He asks me what's wrong, and what's more does so with the expression of someone hoping to be told nothing's wrong, so I answer nothing really, nada, women trouble.

'Brilliant!' He almost jumps for joy. 'Now you can have an existential crisis.'

I tell him not to piss about and I laugh at the joke, but only briefly because I'm really quite upset and Angel's just come out saying he can't take any more, these people are hopeless, they haven't even heard of the death of art aesthetic. This is my chance to lift my crestfallen spirits with a joke. I ask Angel what is all this about the death of art. Angel makes a disapproving face and advises me not to be tautological. Luckily the face was easy to make and I do one back.

My black mood is returning. Nilo notices and tells me the good news. He says today is Yeny's birthday and they're going to get a crowd together with alcohol and everything, they just don't know where yet. This is comforting. At least the night is smiling at me. How poetic! So I arrange to drop by Dennys's house and with an imperceptible gesture I take my leave. Or rather I slip away secretly as if carrying stolen goods. It's true, in a way I'm making off with the night and I don't want anyone to snatch it from me; so hardly a chao and I'm off.

What Angel and Nilo must see is a guy walking away, his head bowed, staggering down the street.

Things I need with some urgency
an electric kettle
Macbeth with a good cover to muck up
Macbeth with a leather cover
some pale-coloured paint
to caress the hands of a girl
with big eyes
listen to *Philip Glass*
drink methylated spirits
with distilled water and extract of strawberry
caress a girl with big eyes
tell Milay she's a bloody fool
see *The Wall* twice a week
it's an obsession
jump and shake my head
in a frenzy
if they put on *Philip Glass*
be a minimalist musician

You can get to know Yazmin in many ways. You can meet her anywhere like I met her after that afternoon. There's nothing particularly distinctive about Yazmin except maybe her hair twisted messily into a bun or the particular way she looks at people or rather looks at nothing, because her gaze disappears beyond your eyes.

I got to know her anyhow, meaning it wasn't anything special. It was just like meeting anyone as you turn a corner. I was on my way to Dennys's house. I was trying to imagine what the party would be like or constructing it in my mind, full of all my mates in a big room with me in the corner chatting to big tits. I was also pondering the poem I'd written the night before, one of those things you write just to splurge but which might merit serious interpretation, a kind of auto-interpretation of my drunken state objectified in the most anti-poetic verses, like the one about drinking meths.

The thing is that as I was tweaking big tits' nipple while divesting my poem of whatever neorealist influence it possessed, I rounded some corner or other and came across a girl who called out to me from the low wall of a launderette with an extremely abrupt 'hey' to ask for money. I'm not at all mean, so I gave her what I had, which was one peso, and without much conviction told her she was pretty and she gave the kind of stupid answer about not being pretty so she was even more grateful. Women are disastrous communicators.

I talked to her a while and learned various things. That her name was Yazmin, that she wasn't interested in coming to a party with me that night and anyway she couldn't because she had things to do, among them getting some money together, which she was going to ask from whoever walked by so she could wash a great bundle of clothes and while she was at it get herself something to eat.

In general she turned out to be very chatty, pleasant even; only her eyes worried me, lost in something I could never fathom. There was a whole world inside her that she kept in as if trying to make sure no one discovered it. I thought that then and still, when I see her sometimes, her veiled expression is so disconcerting I barely say hello for fear of shaking her from her deep absorption.

In any case I had to go. I said goodbye to Yazmin and went on my way, concentrating hard on my objectivist super-poem, not that it was important except to occupy myself and not have to imagine Yazmin putting the clothes into a gigantic washing machine or buying some crap from the corner café.

dance like a half-wit
go round the room get sad
bump into someone
who is also dancing like a half-wit
drink strawberry cordial with alcohol
a large piece of plywood
for a few things
make concessions paint
the wall a pale colour
see Nilo dance
acknowledge that Milay is extremely intelligent
and in a way it suits her
the haircut Aldito just gave her
acknowledge her
at least while the Robert Plant cassette is playing
with Robert Fripp
$^1\!/_2$ King Crimson + $^1\!/_2$ Led Zeppelin
a small almond tart
bitter chocolate in the tea
without sugar the way Fatty has it
bite a Czech girl's nipple
hear Teresita say she's a feminist see
her sketches or diagrams
or conceptual projects
I need a record player to listen to The Animals

Not bad. The house they found is huge, with loads of rooms for
scoring with a sure thing. Big tits is here, with three of her friends
and a revealing T-shirt that looks delicious on her. The acoustics are
fantastic, even in the hallway, where people are piled in with Frank
Zappa playing so everyone knows that this is no ordinary party, that
there's a huge amount of alcohol, an acoustic-ethylic club, the bass
reaches unbelievably deep tones, bounces off the neighbouring
houses, slides through twisted pelvises and dies out. Not at all bad.

When I arrived no one there was sober so I take it upon myself, along with Dennys, Chachi and Vizcaíno, who were all the last to arrive, to catch up with a big glass of alcohol with slices of fruit and the Joshua Tree that Dennys was carrying in his rucksack, *this is the edge*, and me escaping the edge to fit into this world of sweaty bodies and a heady drunkenness even U2 couldn't have dreamed of. Me on my own with my second glass of alcohol and Bono, Clayton and then another glass, big tits opposite me, spraying sweat over me in a violent head movement, someone starts jumping and we all jump ritualistically, U2, *this is the edge* man, they pass it to me so I take three drags and have to pass it on, I can't keep it but I'm moving like never before, almost vibrating with all this acoustic power; harmonics have their uses after all. I head for the living room nearer the music and throw myself into the dance or more like the mass that's sprung up and here's Chen and sweet Adriana, who passes me a slice of pineapple in her mouth, I swallow and taste pure alcohol plus cigarette, and Milena too with her usual blonde drunkenness and Yeny whose birthday it is only she doesn't know which one because she's so sad, part of that craziness which sometimes makes her laugh at nothing and then she rolls on the floor first in convulsions and peals of laughter and then in rhythm with the music coming from the speaker right next to her ear, until she gets sad again and tears fill her mouth and the salty taste makes her laugh uproariously and she's splitting her sides laughing lying there on the floor. I feel sorry for her so I get on top of her and cover her with kisses and ask her insistently what's wrong and it turns out the only problem is that Adriana, her soulmate, wouldn't talk to her all day; the crazy cow.

I go out to the hall to talk to big tits' group of friends and Rafael who's stolen the initiative from me and begun to play at passing the fruit slices from mouth to mouth with the girls. It seems to be a little house game. I join in the orgy until I'm bored and suggest we play Separated at Birth. The game consists of Rafael hiding a piece of fruit somewhere on one of their bodies and then I have to try and find it, colder, getting warmer, and then swallow it, so it's Rafael's turn to play detective. A fantastic game which would have had great potential if Rafael had not suddenly started kissing big tits so the game collapses, along with my sexual fantasies. I guess you can't win them all.

I accept defeat and make for the corner where Adriana is. Everything seems to be awaiting my arrival, including Adriana, who signals to me to sit next to her and passes me her glass with the ease of a bar-room sailor. I take a swig but don't say a word. She says nothing either and we stay like that until only the slices of dried fruit are left. Only when I come back with two full glasses do I ask why she won't talk to Yeny. It's not that it matters to me but I had to start somewhere and that was the only thing that occurred to me as I crossed from the kitchen to where I am now with Adriana. She answers that it's a delicate matter and she doesn't want to talk about it and just when I'm beginning to think my attempt at dialogue is truly thwarted she asks me if I'm bored. I didn't really understand at first, I thought she was referring to her company and I say no, that's normal, and since we hardly know each other . . .

'I mean generally, aren't you bored?'

'No,' I answer roundly, 'why would I be bored?'

'I don't know, you don't belong here, you're on loan in a way. Like an object that's out of place, haven't you noticed?'

'No, I haven't noticed.'

'God, you're slow,' she says and goes off, taking the drink with her.

I did not dare watch her go but I'm sure she went off to sit in a corner. Yeah, I think what Adriana needs is solitude. Like me now, staying where I am and emptying my glass and trying to think about something but the only thing that comes to mind is Yazmin washing her immense quantity of clothes, Yazmin getting herself a bit of cold sausage to eat, Yazmin so different to Milay, Yazmin putting up with the rude comments of whoever stops to give her some money.

The only thing that comes to mind is Yazmin and on top of that Milay too, whose face is now transforming into Adriana with her unexpected belligerence, her inexplicable solitude. I realize I'm feeling a bit sick and that staying here at this juncture isn't going to get me anywhere. The horizon looks bleak. I escape from my corner which was previously mine and Adriana's and make for the living room, where everyone's dancing and so am I, I jump and shake my head because they're playing Grand Funk. *We are the American Band.* And I'm leaping about and everyone's leaping and twisting and throwing their hands in the air, Dennys is pretending he's playing bass then drums and jumping and shaking his hair on his shoulders. Adriana stands in front of me and tells me this is how it's done, this is how Aquarians dance. I ask her how she knows I'm Aquarius and she answers you can tell, so is she, and she puts her hands on my shoulders, I grab her round the waist and we start jumping together and spinning round or everything's spinning around us like pure drunkenness.

The music stops and I go and sit on the sofa. Adriana sits down beside me and strokes my hair. At first I'm not aware of anything but the fact is the speakers are amplifying Robert Plant's voice, *this is the song heaven*, and beside me I have a girl with a happy face and thick eyebrows and I'm swept away by her charm, I kiss her on the lips and on the cheeks then another long kiss, I play with her tongue for an eternity until the stairways to heaven end and we pull apart to look at each other and study the other's reaction. A show of strength in which both sides proclaim themselves victorious.

Adriana excuses herself a moment and disappears amongst the dancing, sweaty bodies. But only for a moment because soon she returns, grabs my hand and takes me to a room and we shut ourselves in, away from the music, the din, people's laughter and madness, we are isolated, me alone with Adriana. Adriana alone.

'I'm lucky, I always make love with the guys that interest me,' she says and takes off her clothes to reveal the naked body of a starlet.

I'm left wanting to ask her if I really do interest her; but all I do is take off my clothes and lie down beside her. This is how the rite begins. A quiet inspection: we touch each other, establishing frontiers, closing in on the other's body, projecting ourselves in sexual caresses that make me feel like a well-oiled machine and I imagine the same thing's happening to Adriana, although the silence is broken more than once by a groan that finally makes me forget all my rational impulses to concentrate on her, on her knowing tenderness and her effluvia. I take hold of her sex and make her convulse under my powerful tongue which responds only to my excitement, her sensuality and exposed flesh. I had not thought of that. I have Adriana under me and it's as if I was having all women at once. As if I had any woman concentrating all her strength in the tension of her thighs, squeezing her pelvis against my erection and me playing at dominating her, kissing her everywhere that gives pleasure, sometimes automatically. And Adriana could be Yazmin and Yazmin anyone else I'm penetrating straight away as if wanting to show myself in all my virility, but in this case I won't be able to. There are things that go round and round in my head and suddenly I saw Yazmin in Adriana, not hallucinatory but real, silent beneath me, and then I couldn't do it.

I apologize to Adriana and she hugs me very understandingly and tells me it doesn't matter and there'll be another time, she kisses me repeatedly and strokes my hair as a mother would. But I can't take it. I stand up and with incredible speed get dressed and take refuge in the living room.

Here's Dennys, drunk as a thousand demons, entwined with Yeny. He gives me a swig of his drink, which I hardly sip. The taste isn't what I was expecting, it tastes more like stale water. Things never taste the same. Nor do they stay still; at least that's how it is with me. I give Dennys his glass back, ruffle his hair and go, almost fleeing the house with its whole orgiastic vision and Adriana alone in a bed.

I need to sleep
eat the tart
tell my neighbour to stop bugging me
as I'm caressing Milay or her friend

it doesn't matter and it's not my fault
if these people are shouting at one
or more in the morning and what's worse
jumping and shaking their heads
I need an alcoholic drink
to get away from here or sleep
for today

On my way back I was thinking a hundred things and none of them coming close to my objectivist poem born of last night's madness, just an enormous confusion of voices telling me incoherent things, half heard without my being able to place them because sometimes Adriana was saying them using Milay's voice or sometimes it was Dennys's voice mingling with another and in the end not saying anything logical. In fact I was feeling terribly sick. I remember I tried to walk along the crack in the pavement, an impossible game because the crack was twisting all over the place and then forking into two lines and then three and after it was just one and I wasn't exactly on top of it. The state of me. Wouldn't it be great to write a book on an eternal theme the way Burroughs does. Anything but the depression I felt that night. Luckily, and what I was least expecting, was that coming back I came across Yazmin, sitting on the same low wall as in the afternoon. It was the same image. Everything in the world had changed but her; with her bundle by her side, this time of clean clothes, and her hair in a dishevelled bun. We said 'hi' and so on. I asked her how she was like someone asking a nun the time, and the only thing she could do was give me a Japanese daisy from a bunch she was holding.

'What's this?' I asked her, referring to the flower twirling between my fingers.

Yazmin had collected a fair bit so as to have money left over and since she was no longer hungry and had no more clothes to wash, she had bought herself a bunch of daisies that she was now giving away to anyone who came her way.

At that moment I felt half lucid and really wanted to stay with Yazmin a while and even be able to help her in her enterprise; but I did not dare. I was afraid, with my clumsiness, of jolting her out of her solitude, her (congenital) introspection. Better to leave her staring into nothingness with her bunch of daisies for passers-by.

When I walked away I wasn't playing with the lines on the ground any more or wanting to be a writer with delirium tremens, I was just thinking useless thoughts and at some stage before getting home I remembered that the following morning there was the second part of the debate on art.

TRANSLATED BY LULU NORMAN

Don't Tell Her That You Love Her
Love Scene
With Paul McCartney At The Window
Senel Paz

Arnaldo let everybody know I'd be sleeping with a woman that night.
He didn't tell them it was Vivian, but they aren't that stupid at my
school. So I waited till they'd all had a wash and when they'd gone
and nobody was around to harass me, I went in feeling quite relaxed.
I gave myself a good hard scrub, got soapsuds and lather everywhere.
I thought she'd probably smell me here and there and touch me, I'm
not sure, she was bound to touch me and I wanted to be clean and
smelling fresh and I went back to the places where I was bound to
kiss her, where I *had* to kiss her, according to Arnaldo, so she would
never forget me, never forget her first time with a man, with me.
Arnaldo had explained three or four things you had to do to women,
emphasizing that I should never, never tell Vivian I loved her, not
even at the supreme moment, David, because if a woman knows you
love her, well, she'll make you go through hell right away. I was
singing, feeling great. I shampooed my hair, I tell you, I had a smart
shave, brushed my teeth and tongue. By the end I was sparkling,
feeling really pleased with myself and whenever I caught sight of
myself in the mirror, I waved like some Charlie Chaplin because I
knew what was going to happen, and it was my first time, and it was
with Vivian and, I swear, I tried not to think of anything, not to
anticipate events, but you know how our minds work, because you
can tell your mind not to think about something and it will reply,
'OK, OK, I won't think about it.' All lies, it's what you think about
most of all, and then I realized what was racing through my mind

because, you know, it was stirring down there, I was looking up at the ceiling, and in the end I grabbed hold of the wash basin, concentrated and thought of something totally different: 'James Paul McCartney was born 18 June 1942 in Walton General Hospital, England; John Winston Lennon was born 9 October 1940 in a maternity ward on Oxford Street, Liverpool, England . . .' I didn't have to get as far as Ringo, I got over it. Don't conclude from all this that I don't masturbate. I masturbate, but not thinking about Vivian, and especially not that afternoon. I now knew what I had to do, Arnaldo had explained everything. When the girl's a virgin, it's a delicate business. You don't get much pleasure but that's not the point. You go into the bedroom and you pretend you didn't realize that you are alone and that there's a bed there. You're in good spirits, you don't get too close, and swap jokes and other pleasantries. That's to get her relaxed and it'll take you about ten minutes. Then you go over and start kissing and caressing her above the waist, gently, not demanding anything she doesn't want to do. Every so often you stop and whisper a few affectionate little words, like, 'You're the only girl for me', 'When I'm with you, nothing else exists', 'Will you give your sweetheart everything he wants?' That's a softener to warm her up and then you tell her you'll be faithful. You'll be standing up or sitting on the bed, whichever she prefers. Every so often, in the middle of an embrace, you'll sigh, so she can see you're a sentimental type and easily carried away. Now and then, you extricate yourself and walk around the room, wringing your hands so she can see you struggling against your animal instincts, but then go back and kiss her passionately because her beauty and the love you feel are stronger than you are. This convinces her of your love and your moral sense. After a while, you switch the light off, any excuse will do, and you continue caressing her, kissing her, putting your hands under her clothes, always above the waist, and start undressing her very slowly, not violently, whatever she agrees to. Once she's naked, she'll inevitably get into bed, under the sheet and turn to the wall. But that doesn't put you off and you get undressed. You make a slight noise as you drop your clothes on the chair or something of the sort so she knows you've stripped off, and then you sit on the bed. You don't pull back the sheet, but go on kissing and cuddling, very passionately now, but all above the belt. That's the magic frontier, for that's how you show your high-mindedness, that although you're naked and alone in bed together, you've got honourable intentions and she can stop playing the game whenever she wants. But no chance of that, dear; you've reached the point of no return and any interruption would be an affront to your manhood. What's more, you've still not touched her with your tool or let her handle or see it. You've got to keep her totally in the dark about its size. She's crazy to find out and that's what will make her give way. That's the way, boy, soon she won't be able to stand it any more and will beg you to start the action. You won't answer with words but by groaning and moving your hips; you'll act as if you're not reading her messages; on the contrary, you'll intercept her hands when they go after your cock and you'll fondle and kiss her fingers. More softening her up to show her how inexperienced you are, but it also gets her worked up, and she'll end up trying to get you on top of her. When her demands gets insistent, you'll accept her invitation, be a good little boy. That's very important, because if there are problems later on (big bellies or dreams of marriage), she'll blame you for what happened, but in her subconscious she'll think that she was responsible because she lost her self-control, and that gives you an advantage in any dispute. OK, the moment's come, you get opposite her knees, pull her legs apart and without more ado put your head down and kiss her thing. You do that with all your heart, as if you were dousing your head in a pond on a hot day. Then she'll understand you think there's nothing more precious than what's she got down there, quite right too, and you can let out a few more sighs and moans (they'll come anyway), and you can say things like, 'My God' or 'This is heavenly.' That's the most difficult moment because apart from the fact that you're as stiff as a rod and wanting to get into the breach, when you smell it, feel how warm and wet it is, you may be thrown by a raging passion that turns you into a wild animal. The wolfman, the beast out of *Beauty and the Beast* and Frankenstein are babes in arms compared to you. You need some self-control. You smear her juices over your face, your ears, everywhere, and get up and kiss her, rub yourself against her face and kiss her so she can smell and lick herself. Then you'll be like two wild animals on the bed. Now, brother, the moment of truth has arrived. You get back where you were, kneel between her thighs, that she can't, doesn't want to close, you take your thing in your right hand, got that, your right hand, show her the tip that slips in easily. No pushing, turn it round a bit, widen her out, and the battle's won. But take care, there may be a last-minute hitch. That's just when a small, fortunately a very small, percentage of women takes fright: they think they won't be able to bear the pain or can see it's extremely unlikely you'll marry them afterwards. A few ask you not to do it, they can't go home without their honour, their fathers are machete-wielding brutes, Party members who have to set an example. But now you couldn't care less. In you go as hard as you can and the more blood the better. Let her feel the size of it, at least a good bit of it, and if she cries and claws your back don't be afraid or get upset. It means mission accomplished.

I was thinking about Arnaldo's advice when I had to grab hold of the wash basin. I'd mentally rehearsed his lesson several times, but never involved Vivian, although I was getting ready to go with her. We're free to choose what we want to think about our girlfriends, I thought. Vivian isn't Esther. In fact, Arnaldo hasn't ever been in love and no woman has loved him, though several have liked him. I didn't want Vivian to bleed a lot, or to be hurt, and if we were unlucky and she got pregnant, we'd get married or I'd give my blood for an abortion, whatever she wanted. I never told him, of course, nor did I ask him why you had to grab it with your right hand. 'Must be a tradition,' I thought.

So there I was lying in the bath, so happy, feeling those emotions I felt when I thought about Vivian, I'd finished and was gleaming when

I opened the door. Hell, they were all waiting for me, so quiet I hadn't heard them. 'Yippee!' was the bandits' welcoming cry, and pillows and kicks rained down and the Beatles blasted away at top volume. 'So, who was going to make a man of himself and not tell his mates, then?' I tried to shut the door. 'Get the perfume on him!' They got hold of me and lifted me up on a chair. 'Shall we shoe-polish his balls till they shine?' 'No, gentlemen, we certainly won't, that would take too long,' Arnaldo intoned. 'What about a squirt of toothpaste to the armpits?' They decided I would look smart in my best shirt. Keeping it to ourselves, were we? What about the lilac sweater that Jorge brought you from Czechoslovakia. Have you had your Atlantic oysters? They poured five kinds of deodorants and perfume over me, forced me to eat a peppermint to take away my bad breath and 'cause it's got other uses, kiddo, and planted me in front of the mirror. When they got tired of combing my hair, they reckoned there wasn't a handsomer film actor than me, I was brother chip to Alain Delon, but with a frog in my throat. They checked my wallet and added a whip-round from the club. They were leg-pulling, friendly, envious, but it was almost three o'clock, gentlemen, getting on, so off they went. The Beatles were singing 'She Loves You' and Arnaldo explained again how I should act so they wouldn't see I was a novice. We'd already been and booked the room, the man on the door was a friend of his, and he wished me luck, lots of luck, when I got back, I should wake him up and tell him how it went, even if it was late, and not tell Vivian that I loved her, for it was pretty obvious I might fall into that trap, please, David, take some notice of me. He said that because one day I'd told him that when I saw Vivian I saw sparks, fireworks, flowers, got the whole works in my head and thought I was riding on a merry-go-round. 'Don't fuck around, David. Listen to this guy, gents. Don't talk to me about merry-go-rounds. You pant like a horse, stick your tongue in and cling to her so she can feel your bulge.' I tell you, I still had my doubts. Now I had more doubts than ever and got really nervous. I wondered whether I was right, if I'd acted right when I put it to Vivian the way I had: 'I'm a man, we go to bed or it's all over, you decide.' Was that really the way I loved her? But there was no going back now, you understand. What would Arnaldo think? What would Vivian think? And now the others were all in the know. Unless I suddenly had an attack of appendicitis, but I'd never felt better, and when I reached the hostel she came out dressed in black. A blonde dressed in black is the prettiest thing out. As soon as I saw her beautiful smile I realized she hadn't got appendicitis either and hadn't got bad news from home either, though her grandmother had just been ill. So what had to be, had to be. 'You're cold,' she said, kissing me on the lips. 'The sea mist. Perhaps we shouldn't go out, it's going to rain.' 'I want you to take me to see a film called *Red Desert*.' And I couldn't back out because of some political commitment. The year before I had been selected as a *Model Youth* but I didn't make it as a member because they said I wasn't mature enough, and they gave me six months to work and mature, read the newspapers and get up to date with the international situation. And I did all that, till Vivian joined our class, and then I didn't get even nine votes in the mass meeting to choose the Model Youth. They spent an hour criticizing me, saying that I'd gone backwards, and what did I think, because the most important thing for me to do was to accept their criticisms, to 'internalize' them, as the comrade from the Communist Youth put it; and I said, of course I accepted them and internalized them, but I made a mental note of all those who didn't vote for me. Then Arnaldo told me that putting on a front was worse, told me to admit I didn't care a damn about the world and that I spent my whole life trailing after Vivian. So what kind of Communist militant could I ever be? Arnaldo and I were talking at the back of the patio, beneath the eucalyptus, and someone was playing the Beatles. They'd ordered him to work on me politically, I realized that right away, and I was sorry because he was like a brother, but the assignment was turning sour on him, until he said, 'You know what's up with you, my friend? You've got a problem with Vivian.' 'What problem with Vivian? Forget it. I haven't any problem with Vivian, no need to stick your oar in, brother.' I don't usually talk that way, but you had to talk that way at high school, and I was forestalling Arnaldo because I knew which way he was heading. 'Yes, compañero,' he softened his tone, 'Vivian's a very demanding woman, and your relationship has reached a point, how can I put it . . . Well, you've got to get her into bed.' 'Wait a minute. What kind of woman do you think you're talking about? I respect her and she respects me. We respect each other.' 'You respect each other, but you should get her into bed, or you'll never be a Party member. Besides, and this should shut your trap, our country is in constant danger. Wouldn't it be a fine thing if the Americans invaded tomorrow and you fell in battle, just like that, and you hadn't had an eyeful?' He threw his arm round my shoulders and we started to walk. We were alone under the eucalyptus and the Beatles were singing, I've told already you that very softly because it was forbidden for us to listen to them; they represented bourgeois decadence, were an example of degenerate youth, and we were being forged as Communists. 'You know what's happening?' Arnaldo returned to the fray. 'It's not like it used to be. Under capitalism when you got to thirteen or fourteen your dad or a brother took you to a brothel and off you went. Now it's different, because that was a social blight that had to be eliminated, obviously, I agree entirely. But, do you know what, we were left in limbo. Nobody had thought it through. They should have left one brothel, a teaching brothel for us students, don't you think?' I looked at him, trying to guess where he was leading. 'So now you have to bed your girlfriend, David, and no second thoughts. *The Communist Manifesto* says love is free under socialism.' 'Is that in *The Communist Manifesto*? I must read it.' 'Yeah, read it, and it's not the only thing you'll find there.'

Vivian wasn't like the girls he had relationships with. I couldn't turn up and say to her, 'I'm a man. Go to bed with me or it's all over. You decide.' So I thought it through. The politics of it, I mean, and I decided that there weren't going to be any more problems over my social attitudes. Hadn't the Revolution done things for me and my

social class? I was going to do things for the Revolution and I was
going to get my Party card. I could be in love with Vivian and worry
about the world, perfectly easily. Of course, I wasn't thinking about
this when I went to get Vivian that day. I was thinking about her and
trying to stop the small change jangling in my pocket as we walked
along. I gazed into the sky that was getting more and more overcast.
I remembered our conversations, rehearsed those conversations, our
never-ending conversations in class, in the library, in the breaks,
when we talked and talked about our teachers, school, our families,
what we wanted to study. When we exhausted one topic, we'd begin
again and never got bored. I told her all I knew about what it meant
to be a man, how we developed, how my nipples hurt like crazy at
twelve or thirteen and how much a kick to your testicles hurt and she
said the same with breasts, that she first menstruated at twelve and
that you pee through a different little hole. Don't you talk to your
girlfriend about those things? We do, we'd write to each other on the
last pages of our notebooks, on mine, that is, because she was very
protective of hers. Hers were covered and each cover had a
photograph of Che. We sometimes looked at Che. 'Where can he be
now, David?' 'He's around in South America.' 'Sometimes I think
something will happen to him.' 'To Che? Don't be silly, impossible.
Justice always triumphs, he's fighting for people to be free.' And
while we chatted, we looked in each other's eyes, I looked at her
mouth, Vivian has such a nice mouth, and we held hands to see if
they were cold or warm, to see whose were bigger and mine always
were, and to study our life and death lines. So, what did all this have
to do with the way I asked her to make love. Arnaldo thought it did,
that it was all to the good, but that way of falling in love bordered on
the platonic, which was disastrous. It wasn't true. We often went to
the cinema and the theatre, we liked walking the streets of Havana
and sitting in the parks and on the seafront to watch the sun set, but
when we went back to school we had our special place in the shadows
of Cubanacán, a little spot under a weeping willow, a tree I'm really
fond of, and we kissed there. I'd touched her breasts with my hand,

with my mouth, I opened her blouse and felt her breast against my body and heard her moan to my caresses. One day her hand came across something hard and she said, 'Look what I've found,' and I laughed and she laughed, and perhaps right then I should have grabbed her hand and pressed it against my hard-on, undone my trousers, but it didn't appeal, I preferred things to happen by themselves. 'That's all very well,' said Arnaldo, 'but then along comes someone else without a thought in his head and eats her alive and he's the one she'll remember for the rest of her life. You must talk to her this week, for your own good and even for hers.' 'OK. I'll talk to her on Friday.' 'Wednesday,' he insisted. 'And let's shake on it, you're a man now.' I'd do it during the break, in the patio with the almond trees, on the bench that was our bench, and Arnaldo would be on hand to make sure I didn't beat a retreat. And when we got to school that Wednesday morning everybody was lined up in the main playground. People were silent, which was quite out of character there. I looked out for her, wanting to tell her that we were going to talk about that important question I'd mentioned to her, did she remember? But her eyes were asking me, 'What's the matter? Do you know what the matter is?' And then I too realized that something was wrong. Our teachers were under the almond trees and they knew what was wrong. Some of the women teachers were crying. The principal got up on the platform and looked at us, as all our eyes glued on him. There was little doubt that something serious had happened, but what? An American invasion? Richard Nixon was President of the United States. Our principal tapped the microphone nervously, though it worked perfectly well and didn't need to be tapped, the fact was he couldn't get any words out, until out they came in a rush. 'They've killed Che in Bolivia, we are going to the Plaza de la Revolución on a memorial march, everybody must be very orderly, now off to your classes.' That's all he said. Vivian leaned on my shoulder and I heard her sobbing. 'I knew that might happen,' she said, and we went to our classrooms feeling sick, seeing Che's face and smile everywhere, hearing his voice saying *You can't trust imperialism one inch*. Esther joined us, Arnaldo joined us, and Esther said, 'Oh Vivian, oh David!' and the four of us hugged each other. Her notebooks looked so sad. She took the covers off and put them quietly away in her bag. In the end she said she didn't believe it, she couldn't believe it, no way was it possible. 'I wish you were right, Vivian, but come on, don't be crazy.' At any rate we cherished a few hopes, until we got to the Plaza, and the saddest Fidel you can imagine said it was true, they'd killed Che in Bolivia, but we couldn't give up because of that or anything else, and we went back to school, holding hands, and I didn't talk to her about the other business that week, or the next one, not that I remember.

When she arrived the other day she was wearing the black dress I told you about and we went to the cinema and it was such a beautiful night when we left the Payret. It had been raining and there were lights, colours, lots of people and it was damp and Vivian was walking next to me, hugging me, her hair loose. 'What's the rush? What did you think of the film? Let's discuss it.' And she started telling me her opinion, its slant on society, man's alienation brought on by capitalism, something of the sort. I wasn't listening to her, I hadn't watched the film and couldn't care less about capitalism, my heart was beating fit to burst because in the cinema I'd suddenly remembered how they say some couples can't make it the first time: it doesn't react, and nerves get in the way. 'I bet it will still be raining when the film finishes,' I thought. But it wasn't raining. 'Don't let's head for school,' I said when we were in the street. 'Where then?' I hadn't mentioned the business to her since we'd talked in the patio with the almond trees. 'I'm a man, we make love or it's all over. You decide.' She looked down, went quiet and finally grabbed my hand, squeezed it tight and averted her gaze and said, 'All right.' If my nerves didn't react, I'd slaughter them. 'Here we are,' I said. She looked and understood. We quickly went into the building, I spoke to the doorman, I had to pay again though I'd already paid when I came with Arnaldo, we walked past door after door after door, the key

wouldn't open, it wouldn't open, then it opened, and we went in . . .
I leaned against the wall, listened to my heart beating. 'Dear Paul
McCartney, help me, you the fifteen-year-old who lost your virginity
in far-off Liverpool.' The light was on and she took a couple of
steps inside, stopped, switching her handbag from one hand to the
other, as usual. It was an ugly room with a high ceiling, number
thirty-nine, disgusting, what's the point of going on to you. There
was a small wardrobe with no door and wire hangers that were all
bent. An unvarnished table with a washbowl and water, a tin jug, two
Soviet glasses, a roll of toilet paper and small tablets of scented soap.
The yellow light projected our shapes on the walls, where there were
drawings and obscene words. 'Kike and Puchitas did it here', 'I want
cunt and down with the government.' She went over to the open
window, and over her head I could read, in the distance, half hidden
by her hair, that red sign which says somewhere in Havana *Revolution
is Construction*. I read it five times. I could also see clouds scudding
across the moon and suddenly I calmed down. I know you shouldn't
stare at the moon, that's being romantic and sentimental, but it
looked really beautiful, I can tell you, and Vivian turned round. She
really dazzled me. More than ever. She was so beautiful, so beautiful.
'This isn't a hotel, is it?' she asked pathetically. I was going to say it
was, a tatty, two-star affair, but I told her the truth. 'No. It's a rented
room.' She turned her back on me. 'My mum's right when she says
I'm a bad girl who can't be trusted. She thinks I'm working quietly
at school and here I am in a lodging-house with my boyfriend.' 'We
did talk about this . . .' 'It's one thing to talk, quite another to bring
me to a room with holes in the walls.' It's true, there were holes in the
walls, and we clammed up. I was a good way from her, but I couldn't
think of any jokes to tell. I began to feel uneasy as well, to
understand her situation. But I remembered what Arnaldo says, you
can't feel sorry for women because they won't appreciate it at all.
'Couldn't you find anywhere else to take me?' 'No. I couldn't. I'm no
expert on these places.' I was upset she talked to me that way, that she
didn't understand me. 'If you want, if you're not keen, we can go

and no ill-feelings, I won't get upset.' 'Don't let's get upset,' she said after a while, 'it's just a pity we've got to do it in an ugly spot like this.' I hugged her, to help her not to feel guilty, besides I was the guilty party, and trying to say to her that she was there with a man who really loved her, *the* man in her life as she was *the* woman in his, so the place wasn't that important. She gave my top half a good hug, and I was back opposite the open window and I read the slogan again *Revolution is Construction*. Then I switched off the light, and it sounded as if they were playing the Beatles in the room next door. Everyone says John Lennon is the cleverest of them, but Paul McCartney is the friendliest and it was McCartney's song. She took her clothes off. You can't imagine how beautifully she took her clothes off and how good the Beatles sounded, and then she sat down on the bed. The moonlight through the window beamed brightly on her. I took my jumper off. I heard my jumper falling on the floor and felt pleased I'd put my black trousers on and not the other pair, because the black ones have a zipper fly and I really liked hearing the zipper zipping, I felt so manly undoing it in front of a woman, and realizing that she'd heard it as well, and we were both naked, alone in a room, with the Beatles, yellowish in the light, and reddish, not really knowing what to do next. We were afraid the door would open, that they'd shine a torch on us and the school principal, her mum, the Minister of Education, a militiaman would walk in, and her mum would shout, 'Holy God, Heavenly Virgin, Almighty God, look what my daughter's doing. If her father catches her, he'll kill her!' We waited and waited but nobody turned up. We could hear only the Beatles, and McCartney saying, 'Let's play for them,' and I sat down on the bed next to her, and she looked at the wall. I ran my fingers through her hair and caressed her back. I felt her skin burning and I caressed her shoulders, and then her breasts. She turned round, her lips inviting me. They were warmer and moister than ever, and I realised I wasn't going to have an attack of nerves and I embraced her with all my heart, but I didn't think I'd hugged her enough till the flowers appeared. There were dewy flowers all over the room:

they carpeted the floor and the bed, hung from the ceiling, stood out above the windowsill. McCartney said, 'Now!' and they blasted off, and spurred by our kisses and their music I eased her into the centre of the bed and soon we were so together that there weren't two of us and we didn't belong in this world and we started seeing the same things: two children running though a field of sunflowers at dawn, disturbing the butterflies, and further on, the four Beatles dressed in black, jumping and laughing. The girl was carrying a parasol, he had a drum and a sword; they were dressed in white and were holding hands. And when the rain suddenly blew in through the window, they threw themselves on the sunflowers, but didn't sink, they floated on the surface and began spinning round and round, driven by the wind, gathering speed, like a merry-go-round, until they suddenly felt they weren't moving any more and she opened her eyes. She saw they were under a huge tree, the Beatles were sitting on the branches and playing, she saw the light pouring through the leaves, and saw him rear up and he saw her on the greenest of grass, arms open wide, smiling at him, and he raised his sword, and she felt him killing her, felt he was killing her, and he kissed her, but he too was dying a death that was so sweet and that music again, spinning round and round, climbing in a whirlwind of leaves, seeing and pronouncing all those words: rose apple, royal palm, beach, cave, obelisk, rabbit, gourd, ring dove, fresh cream . . . And when the last possible word separated out and vanished, Vivian and I were dying elsewhere, or right there, in the rented room, very distant or very near, and we saw, or felt, the children cross over us. She forgot her parasol and he forgot his drum. She said goodbye to her, he said goodbye to me, moving further and further away, and the four Beatles sitting by the window, except Paul, standing with one elbow resting on John's thigh, and they looked at us, and when they saw that the children were no longer there, Paul said, 'That's us done for today,' and I rolled off Vivian, and she moaned gently, I sat up, looked at the window, *Revolution is Construction*, the jug of water on the small table, the walls, the wardrobe, Vivian. I saw her hair spread over the pillow, her lips, her breasts, her eyes that were open but closed, glowing, gazing at me, and though I remembered Arnaldo's advice, I couldn't stop myself from saying those words. I said *I love you*, kissed her, and a great flock of birds flew up from my chest, whoosh . . .

TRANSLATED BY PETER BUSH

South Latitude 13
Angel Santiesteban

Behind us, on the horizon, all we could see was the black smoke coming from the lorries. The plane had disappeared and we were afraid it would come back to finish the job. Rushing off scared, we still managed to rescue one of the wounded, but it was useless trying to mend the radio, we were out of touch with command, the operator said. There were eight of us soldiers and the company captain who had decided at the last minute to come with us on the mission, something he must be regretting now. He ordered us to march in an attempt to return to our unit.

Medina, who's dragging a wounded leg next to me, hands me a cigarette; I give it a drag and it passes from mouth to mouth until the heat burns our lips. Suddenly I realize that they have missed out Argüelles the Violinist, but he doesn't protest.

He's interested only in his violin which he carries beneath an arm bleeding from a wound. I remember we were walking in front of the lorries and when we heard the sound of the plane we threw ourselves under the bushes, thinking only about saving ourselves, dumping everything except our weapons. I pressed my AK to my body. Others put them over their heads as they bit on their identity tags. I don't do that because I know they are not going to kill me here. Before leaving to come here my grandmother gave me this little charm against all danger. At first, because of all the jokes and comments, I didn't want to take it, but it's small and doesn't weigh anything, so she persuaded me. And here it is. But Argüelles hugged his violin like an idiot while his AK hung on his back, getting in the way.

Sometimes I feel sorry for him, because I think he's fucked in the head. Some people weren't happy when he joined our group because they see him as a spoiled brat. Nobody talks to him and I don't think he wants anyone to.

The moon comes upon us as we walk. We camp on the banks of the finest trickle of water. The few tins of food that Crespo saved in his knapsack are shared out. Soon we smell something that begins to make our mouths water. In total silence we watch the ritual of the tins. When it's finished, on the captain's signal, we walk over to collect our share. The Violinist does the opposite, he sets off walking and disappears, coughing like a white shadow among the trees. But nobody pays any attention. We are still hypnotized by the smell of the rations. Then, carried on the wind, and from an indefinable spot, we hear sad, beautiful music, low and distant at first, gradually growing more intense. We look at each other, not knowing what's happening. Suddenly, we stop eating or moving and look up into the depths of the immense darkness that covers us, that makes us beg for the dawn to break and to know that all this has been a nightmare. We stay like this for several seconds, motionless, until Eladio complains, he doesn't understand why they let such an oddball take part in a mission. But Eladio is stubborn and we all prefer to keep quiet when he talks. The cook says that the Violinist never eats anything but the best and only with a napkin because he can't taste anything in his mess tin and that's why he is like he is, thin and yellow: just spectacles and violin. They laugh, and I say he was the same in camp. I couldn't help noticing him, he's just like that. Someone else interrupts because the injured man doesn't want to try the food, he's delirious with fever and warning us about the planes. Everyone, around the stretcher, watches him come back with his violin over his shoulder and sit in the same place as before, as silent as ever. He gives the impression he's never moved from that spot.

In the morning we decide to carry on in whatever direction to find a village. We don't know what is preferable, where we would endanger ourselves least, whether here, lost in this jungle, watching out to stop cobras getting into our boots or our trousers while we try

to sleep, or to look for hospitality in some kimberio* full of wachas†
waiting to ambush us with knives and bullets. We carry on walking,
using up the last of our energy; tiredness enters through our pores,
with every breath, with every thought. Always the same tiredness, not
the one they gave out in Cuba when we left nor the one we
experienced on board ship. We got this only when we disembarked in
this black-magic land; it entered our bodies like a virus, and there is
more saved up in every pocket for the worst moments.

Our steps are shorter and more indecisive. The trees cast off their
last leaves of the season and the branches, moved by the wind, seem
to be laughing at us. This is a labyrinth where foresight would drop
seeds at every step in order to find a way back, and I reckon if I got
the chance I wouldn't stop until I was back in bed with my mum,
asking her to punish me as she used to, not letting me go and play war
with my friends in the neighbourhood, for these aren't children's
games, they're adult whimsy. I am never going to buy my children
pistols or rifles. And I look behind, searching for seeds but see only
bullet shells and battered, rusty tin cans; in the end our enemies, or
ourselves, their enemies, it makes no difference, are but Tom
Thumbs trying to defeat the monster that we are ourselves, who give
birth to these scenes.

We have been walking for hours without seeing another human
being, a sign, a whiff of the most minimal civilization. I catch the
foul smell of Medina's leg, already turning blue, which drags
desperately along, leaving a trail on the path behind, like a slug's trail,
provoking disgust, pain and laughter in me which I try to hide. I look
behind, there are several stragglers, I turn my head back, very
violently it seems, and I feel dizzy, I'm going to lose my balance, I'm
going to fall, when once again that music that came from the sky
before now erupts with magic force from Argüelles's violin, and I
stop, breathe deeply and begin to sweat with fatigue. Crespo looks at
us, as if now was the time for musical tunes! But everything begins

*kimberio: Angolan word meaning a village or group of houses.
†wachas: Angolan slang for UNITA rebels.

to change strangely, because we feel our feet tremble slightly, move this way and that, my balls tighten and I am aroused as my legs rub together, and the rest of the troop begins to stretch along with him. We are back together again. Nobody has looked at him or has said anything to him either. We carry on walking because that's the order, walk to the next place . . .

No one points it out, we see it but are scared it's an hallucination. Still unsure, we approach the fence of the house. The wood's eaten away. Under orders, we surround it and he closes in on the door and knocks. He's greeted by a two-barrelled shotgun pointed at his head. The first thing I think is that's another one of us they've fucked. I prepare to reply with a burst of fire and get my two remaining magazines ready. Then the captain slowly lets his rifle fall and raises his arms. He talks, moves his head, gesticulates and signals. The shotgun withdraws and we can breathe. The captain returns, gets us together and tells us it's a half-mad Portuguese family. They can help us with a few vegetables, bread, water and the kimbo* at the back. They don't have any medicines, although there's a man dying. They'll lend us a black to put on mud and leaf poultices. 'And whatever else God wants,' I say out loud but nobody looks at me. I remember I'm a militant and militants don't believe in God. Then I spit in the air and sign myself with the cross. The captain says finally, 'Everything on the condition that we leave as soon as possible because they don't want problems with wachas.' The chief's clothes remind me of an empty and wrinkled wax-paper cup. I want to tell someone that but everyone is watching the Violinist, who has split off from us in order to watch a flock of white birds migrating to the north. Eladio touches me on the elbow, saying these are the things he can't forgive, he's interested in any old shit apart from us. And there he stands, nailed to the ground by his knees, staring at the spot where the birds disappeared, waiting. All that remains out there is emptiness.

*kimbo: small Angolan native house.

We are in the shade under a window, remembering our final parting words, working out the best moment to be betrayed by the women left behind, from which very few are spared. Prisoners always think of amnesty, we think of a peace treaty and going home. He comes back coughing and interrupts us. He crouches down on the ground and we all budge over on the wooden boxes to leave a space which nobody occupies, but he has already closed his eyes like a cat, in order not to be grateful. Medina hums a melody, I think in order to take his mind off the pain in his leg. We look at him, waiting for his reaction. But he remains immutable. We budge back and close up the space on the box. I can read in Eladio's face the desire to spit on the Violinist's skin, cracked and fine like the desert.

We lie down in the granary. Outside, Crespo is preparing what will be called lunch the best way he can. Suddenly, we become aware of a music that consumes us, slowly takes possession of us, covering everything like a caress we can almost feel. Sweat clouds over some eyes because the music makes us so sentimental. No one moves. Our eyes close, watching our dreams gallop. And not knowing why, in spite of everything, we smile.

Now the Portuguese calls the captain and invites him to the house. The chief declines to enter and they stand talking at the door. They argue until the angry man goes back in. The captain looks at us and wipes his hand over his moustache. He comes over, stops and stares at the violin in Argüelles's arms. He tries to go back but he's stopped by the look of the Portuguese staring at him through the window. He looks at Medina's blue leg, which is no longer a leg, and at Luis's stained bandages. Then he says to the Violinist that the Portuguese is prepared to accept his little guitar in exchange for the necessary medicines to cure these two men's infections and his own arm, five tins of meat, two bottles of home-made aguardiente and cigarettes. All of us approach him and nail our gaze on every dirty part of his body. The Violinist, backing off, returns our stares. The captain says he's sorry because he knows what the violin means to him, but it is a difficult situation. That much he should understand. Silence is his worst reply.

The chief continues prodding him until he manages to get him to his feet and stops him right in front of those of us covering the captain. 'Would you let your rifle go?' Argüelles says. The chief hesitates a moment. 'No, never, it's my life support, the guarantee I will get home.' The Violinist smiles: 'I suppose everyone thinks the same way,' he says, looking us over. 'I prefer to give up my rifle.' The chief shakes his head: 'You don't want to understand.' The Violinist looks down, his eyes moisten beneath his glasses as he grasps his violin. 'NO,' he says, 'NO'. No one moves, we go on staring as if he had not yet said anything. He looks at Luis's bandages, stained with blood at first and now with a greenish liquid. Also at the flies on Medina's leg that had appeared with his first shakes of fever. He sees birds of carrion flying where the birds of the north had crossed before. His voice trembles. 'Is it an order?' The chief nods. Then, indecisively, he lets the violin drop to the ground and says 'Shit,' turns his back to us and walks away.

He's been there ever since. Four days have gone by and he's not tried the tinned meat or the aguardiente, or looked at us. But we know that if he did, it would be with hate, because we don't want him with us. The chief has decided to walk on. And we leave that place, drag our bodies through this sterile land. The house is already out of sight, but there is always some nonconformist looking back. The Violinist follows us like a dog. His presence annoys us. If only he'd get lost. We wouldn't waste time looking for him; what use is a man here who does not talk about his country, or the people he left behind, or doesn't tell lies. Now we have walked several kilometres and the order is to rest. Maybe with the violin we would walk a little more. We stay quiet, someone spits, someone kicks a stone. He sits apart, not saying a word. He accuses us with his presence, with his silence. Someone says that to carry on walking without provisions is suicide. They look at him looking for support, but he continues to ignore us. We have three wounded. There's only one sacred watchword: survival. Now he has his back to us. 'War is war,' says somebody else. The captain talks about principles, nobody takes any notice and he is reminded that there are degrees of desperation. We know that sometimes, in the middle of gunfire, we forget why we kill: because they wear another uniform, nobody knows; some want to find a canteen full of rum, others look for pornographic magazines or just comics . . . The chief asks if everyone is agreed on going back. We get up with AKs at the ready. We wait for Argüelles, he ought to go ahead, but he stays seated. With the point of his rifle he has written THOU SHALT NOT STEAL in the dirt. Eladio tells him to go to hell and that we are going back. And no one listens to the orders of the captain. There is no attention or dismissal. No squad or soldiers. We've ripped off our epaulettes and badges. Just a group of desperate men who enter the house and, surprising the Portuguese, push him and take away his shotgun. The black wants to stop us, he shouts out that Angolan comrades are tired of helping Cuban comrades. And my reaction is my response, because I hit him with the butt of my rifle and leave him on the ground. We go to the kitchen and then the pantry and the girl's bedroom and recover the violin.

When we return he's making lines in the dirt with the point of his rifle. It is a strange landscape, neither here nor there. He keeps on doing it, completely ignoring our presence. Then the captain shouts at him, 'Attention!' and pushes him and his rifle sticks into the ground. The captain shouts that we are sick and tired of putting up with his attitude, his lack of sensitivity, his laziness, his sourness towards his comrades. He can punish him for mistreating his rifle and even shoot him for desertion . . . So he'll discharge him from everything because he doesn't care about anything. He'll decommission his rifle, now he'll be fucked, now he's going to have to shoot with his shitty violin. And the chief throws it on the ground, spits and takes off . . . He looks at us doubtfully, bends over and looks at us, he hesitates and grabs it and looks at us, he cleans it on his shirt sleeve. He goes. And leaves us here, hating him.

TRANSLATED BY STEPHEN WILKINSON

Shadows on the Beach
Carlos Victoria

For Luis de la Paz

Because it was one of those hot, clammy August days, when people pack the beaches and darken the sand and water, César walked on along Collins Avenue to Haulover Beach, where he thought he'd find a more peaceful spot. Although he always preferred peace and quiet, avoided the bustle of crowds, on this occasion there was another reason to seek out a solitary corner: he was with his aged mother, who shared her son's secret hatred of the madding crowd.

Was it fear, shyness or a mysterious kind of selfishness? Their singular dispositions made it difficult to give a clear answer. In the mother's case, love had dissolved into the sterility of disillusion; and in the son's, perhaps as a result of this failure, a strange intensity ruled his relationships with other people, something he tried to hide at all costs, but which remained latent in his contacts with strangers; a secret vehemence threatening his movements.

The Haulover strip of beach displayed a fine sample of bodies from one end to the other; but, after walking some way, the unlikely pair made do with an empty space next to a dilapidated lifeguards' hut. The mother spread out the towels in its shadow and carefully arranged the freeze-box with the cold drinks, as if she were setting the table for Christmas dinner, or straightening out the bed where an important guest was to sleep that night.

She had always done things that way; but by now family meals really belonged to a distant past, to the days of her youth in Cuba, and for many years only her son had slept under her roof. Then with some difficulty she sat down fully clothed on the towelling, as if resting on a park bench and not on a beach, and looked inquisitively around, pleased to see she was a long way from the bathers. Laughing at his mother's refusal to put on her costume, César ran to the edge of the sea.

The moment of entry into the water gave him great pleasure, and once in Guanabo fun-loving students had rippled the waters with their friendly rhythms. His college friends had surrounded him, waved their arms, and in a second several pairs of hands dragged him down into the deep, where his feet couldn't touch the bottom, for they all knew the boy hadn't learned to swim and enjoyed giving him a fright. He had struggled to break free from their hands, and finally let himself be carried along, with the salt burning his mouth. But by now Guanabo was a faded name, a leaf on the wind, and the hands that grabbed his body had departed as if they'd signed a silent agreement: today he had no need to struggle to remove them. Besides, in the meantime, César had become a competent if not outstanding swimmer, the story of every area of his life. He swam over the crest of some breakers and waved at the old lady watching him, protected from the sun by the shadows from the hut.

In one of the photos she'd kept from her time as a young schoolteacher, his mother was stretched out on the sand next to a beautiful girl; a portly man kept looking at them, with the stubbornness of still images we try in vain to capture in the movement of life. The place had been carefully written on the back: Playa La Concha, Habana. With the date underneath: *1948.*

But when César visited La Concha, it was already Braulio Coroneaux, rebaptized by the revolutionary government, relentless in its enthusiasm for change. And that beach brought a sombre memory to César's mind: it was there he'd seen a drowned man being pulled out of the water. It was October and the beach was deserted; Nora, shaking her hair, asked him not to look. But morbid curiosity made him study the bluey, deformed face of that ageless corpse, whose anguished expression later resurfaced in César's dreams.

'Let's be off,' said Nora, 'Drowned men bring bad luck.'

For Nora everything brought good or bad luck: she was simple-minded, superstitious, and her nipples stood out beneath her almost transparent blouse. That afternoon they bade each other a bad-tempered farewell; César kissed her coldly on the cheek when the bus arrived.

But the dead strangers are different to the dead one has known in life, and while he swam César remembered how Ernesto had died two months ago, when he was coming back on the Palmetto Expressway after a night of alcohol and marijuana, the steering wheel driven into his chest by the impact of the crash. Whenever César was floating on the swell, his mind wandered to death, and it made him neither fearful nor anxious, but rather pleasurably idle.

He lay down on the sand next to his mother, who rubbed cream over his back and whispered, 'That man's just like him.'

Him, in the language developed between mother and son over thirty years, with its whimsical words and frequent good humour, alluded to César's father, who had abandoned them both when his mother gave birth. The passage of time meant that mention of *him* was no longer painful, only inadequate, like a rude expression in a polite conversation between people who hardly know each other.

On the other side of the hut, a fifty-year-old man, with grey hair and a prominent chin, was covering a boy in sand, probably his son, enjoying his labours as if he too were a youngster.

'Alike in what way?' asked César, who had never met his father but had seen photos of him and could make no connection with those battered features.

'I don't know,' his mother answered vaguely. 'But there's something of him, particularly around the nose and mouth.'

'Don't start getting sentimental,' smiled César, gearing himself up to return to the water and avoid a dangerous conversation. But as he walked past the man he took a sly glance and thought how right his mother was: there was something of his father in that face. At that moment the stranger said loudly, in Cuban-accentuated Spanish, 'Once I slept for a whole afternoon in the sun on a Varadero beach, and they had to take me to hospital with sunstroke.

I spent a whole month peeling alive.'

'Expect you were drunk,' the boy tittered.

'You dare call your father a drunk?' the man said, throwing a handful of sand into his face. 'Is that how you show respect for your father?'

The young lad wriggled out of the hole, and they both began to lark around, swearing and laughing. César walked slowly on, keeping his eyes on them, and for a time couldn't forget the edge to the old man's voice.

Now in the water, a question worried him and wouldn't go away. What might his father's voice sound like? Over recent months he had been obsessed by two voices he'd listened to thanks to recording magic. One belonged to a friend on a tape sent from Spain, whose particular timbre he'd not heard for ten years. This friend had played a special part in his youth. Recognizing the voice on the cassette recorder, a beloved voice now almost forgotten, brought back memories of nights talking on the roof terrace of the house where they both lived, and this scene came back so vividly that for many hours he thought that if he opened his window he would see Havana and its blend of light and shade, framed by the darkness of the sea.

The other voice belonged to the husband of the woman he was presently in love with. The man was still in Cuba, hoping to join those in exile, like so many others, and reaffirming these hopes in the tapes he sent her. Initially César had refused to listen, for he was afraid of feeling jealous of that unknown voice, but then he realized as he listened to its serene words that things valued by the person one loves – for he had even fallen in love with this woman – should not create embarrassment or bitterness. And now a new question mark joined this chain of confused thoughts: the voice of the father he had never known.

On the seashore, the group of friends were trying to open bottles of beer with their teeth; the shacks of Santa Lucía shimmered beneath the sun. When César came out, gasping for breath after diving deep, he found Jorge spitting blood on the sand, his gums lacerated by the serrated edges.

'Serves you right for being so stupid,' said César, emptying a beer over his hair.

'Guess who didn't pay for the beer,' Tito shouted, and suddenly there was a flurry of dust on the embankment, as if warning holidaymakers of the end of the season. Every Santa Lucía summer ended that way, the wind blowing between the trees, empty beer bottles and a slight taste of blood on the lips.

But now the boy was astride the old man; you couldn't hear what they were both shouting. As he watched the man playing with his son, César remembered how on one occasion he came to Haulover with a friend from work, a likeable, rowdy youth who brought a raft, and in the middle of the struggle to board, in really deep water, the youth suddenly kissed him on the neck. César looked at him in surprise, for he had no idea his friend was that way inclined. But the lad's expression made him think perhaps it was a joke. Then they swam powerfully along the quayside. A naked woman bather canoodled with her lover next to a rusty boat, seemed to float off, slowly, rhythmically, boat and couple.

It's true, thought César, eroticism was disturbing. He had chosen an opponent skilled in the struggle, a cunning rival. During his last bout of alcoholism, which lasted more than three months, César went into a dingy dive one night, drunk and bleary eyed. Women were stripping off on a raised platform near the bar, and one of them, rolls of flab but with a fascinating face, was stroking the heel of a shoe through her pubic curls, while the jukebox blared out Fleetwood Mac's latest hit. That figure on the platform, her sinuous movements, and the suggestive backing music worked him up to frustration point and he left immediately, feeling hot, inadequate, vaguely wanting to humiliate a body. He ended up in the arms of a prostitute who stole his money and abandoned him unconscious in a sordid room in a backstreet hotel.

By now the pretend fight between father and son had come to an end, and while he devoured scraps of cold chicken, César suddenly felt the impulse to talk to the old man. But fear this might upset his susceptible and prickly mother meant he held off. Then he stretched out on the towel to get tanned. Hours by the sea went quickly, he thought; they were unlike those spent working or restless, or waiting for what never comes.

With the heat of the afternoon on his face he didn't notice when Caridad sat down next to him; feeling her hand on his mouth, he succeeded only in biting her delicate fingers, where a ring recalled an ancient promise, made in haste, under a leafless tree. Then she lay on top of him, pressed her breasts against his face, stifled him. Night fell on the fishing port. Guitars strummed behind the saltpans and the mangroves.

Now his mother was saying, 'He's not that like him.'

César looked at the stranger again, thinking how love usually makes people look alike: in spite of the years gone by, his mother had not forgotten the only man she had loved. But her face smiled peacefully and César allowed himself a joke, 'If it was him, I don't think you'd like him any more.'

'I'm too old now to think about that kind of thing', laughed his mother, and peered out of the cabin window to stare at the array of boats anchored in port, waiting for the order to leave. The water in Mariel bay whipped violently against the vessel, whose toing and froing led to seasickness. The bodies of the emigrants were pushed against each other, worn down by nights of waiting, in shameless exhaustion.

As he looked askance at the stranger, César remembered how on his eighteenth birthday he had decided to visit his father, and got his address via a distant relative. He didn't know the Santos Suárez district; he walked hesitantly down calle Juan Delgado. Tree roots had cracked the pavements, broken through the cement with their deformed, moss-covered limbs. The façades shielded the insides of the houses as a wall defends a fortress. In the silence of midday his footsteps had a sinister ring.

Years later, sitting opposite a friend in a Miami restaurant, he'd confessed to him that when he reached the door to his father's house, he hadn't knocked.

'I'm pleased you didn't,' responded his friend, and César was moved by the sincere tone of his words, for it was the first time he'd mentioned this to anyone, and he didn't regret choosing as a confidant the youth looking at him so warmly while he rested his white, well-shaped hands on the table. As César listened to him, he felt a desire to reach over and hold them in a gesture of friendship. But at that point where two people meet up at the end of a sea crossing, gestures are unnecessary; a nod is perhaps enough.

As dusk fell the sea swelled hugely. Waves towered like prison walls and the boat packed with refugees ran the danger of sinking in the Straits of Florida. The water runs differently by the coast; nearby a father plays with his son, a mother dozes in the shade from the old hut.

The father knows this day is at an end. Night advances across the reddening horizon, dotted by migratory birds in flight. As he calls to the youngster his voice sounds both impatient and tender, and César's mother neatly folds their towels as he enters the water for the last time.

On the beach at Santa Cruz del Sur he is one of the few bathers taking a swim at that time of day near the seafront littered by the debris from the cyclone of 1932. Only a handful of fishermen now remember. For César the mess of sticks covered in seaweed looks like the result of oversight rather than catastrophe.

Water streaming down his hair, César walked over to the clothed figure by the hut, surprised to see his mother's lips move as she stared at the sand. He could easily imagine she wasn't rehearsing any ordinary soliloquy or prayer learned by heart. As the evening sun dipped down into the verdant sea, his mother seemed to sense an unknown harmony and was perhaps saying as much to herself. Or voicing her wonder. Or giving thanks.

TRANSLATED BY PETER BUSH.

The Recruit
Fernando Villaverde

He took to work at a very young age, not so much out of conviction but because it afforded him precocious, enjoyable access to the girls in his poverty-stricken neighbourhood.

It was a low-profile job in terms of money and position; a kind of jack of all trades in a hotel set aside for the exclusive use of foreign visitors; an errand boy on the payroll but in practice also a lift operator, waiter, even a trash-collector to meet the needs of any given moment. Such apparently banal, varied work gave him fluidity of movement, allowed him to be everywhere, in the right place at the right time, so he was always the first to get his hands on a pair of almost new socks a German technical adviser had left on an unmade bed on his departure, a watch forgotten by the poolside and later – too late – hunted out by its Argentinian consultant-owner, a French tourist's sunshades put aside in the bar, crumpled shirts an American businessman abandoned to make way for bottles of rum and boxes of cigars in his suitcases or even a piece of hand luggage containing a little bit of everything mislaid by its Polish owner in the rush to leave; articles the wily employee requisitioned, then stashed away in the secret corner of a remote locker. The boy wrongfooted his bosses, who attributed his willingness as a factotum to inborn diligence, and those guests who, seeing in him a model of industriousness, imagined him like that since childhood, and made a point of mentioning him in their conversations in the hotel foyer as the perfect worker, a shining example of the new world.

They were mistaken. His had been a short apprenticeship in both visible and hidden trades. Sure, as a child, almost without thinking he had pocketed the odd stray sweet or items from mislaid errands;

but until that first job in the exclusive hotel where visitors from every species of friendly or enemy country combined in a small band of wealthy aristos, he had never gone in for pilfering on the grand scale that was now a regular habit.

A sign of the times. Shortages and uncertainty, weighing on the island as the calm before the storm, followed on year after year in a permanent twilight of semi-starvation; fear of waking up one day destitute ensured that every neighbourhood had its diligent layer of population painstakingly devoted to theft; people of diverse stripe for whom changes in the way of life had blurred the edges of crime, making it an everyday activity as necessary for survival as breathing.

That's why the boy had nothing to learn. Stealing came as naturally as beginning to walk or talk, an ingredient in his upbringing for which no lectures or classes were necessary, for he was young enough to have known nothing beyond that murky night. In a forlorn world where people led lives of waiting for the state distribution lorries to drop off their never very abundant offerings in shops and stores, to speak of watches or even cast-off shoes was to enter the big time. On a black market more prosperous than the official scene, the most basic battery radio guaranteed spectacular rations of select items of food, and a gold-plated bracelet of whatever carat would stretch to several legs of pork or the start of a wedding trousseau. However, guided by the natural priorities of youth, our lad did not yield all his takings up to such conspicuous consumption, as was the wont of most adults, who could be seen never-endingly scouring the streets, dangling a shopping bag, ready to turn over rubbish or barter, their lives devoted to roaming the streets. The youngster kept for himself select products from his labours, a silver ring which fitted his finger or aftershave lotions, touches of elegance which marked him out even at night from the adolescent crowd of threadbare shirts gathering on the sidewalks to idle away the time. And driven by the energy of youth, he also devoted some of his precious stolen goods to a system of barter even more secret than the one practised by his elders.

A small bar of ordinary soap wrapped in paper or a half-empty bottle of perfume was all he needed to reach the quiet, shady corners created by opportune water tanks on the flat terraced roofs, where, in exchange for the present of a stolen jewel, in between kisses he could fondle the breasts of a young next-door neighbour, touch her firm, tight buttocks, or press her with his whole body against the solid cement of a water cistern, allowing the spurts of love brought on by such tasty rub-rubbing to trickle down his trousers.

In spite of his apparent worldly wisdom, he was a good soul, naïve to the point of accepting twice out of every thrice the excuses of virginity, periods or even modesty proffered by streetwise girls wanting to surrender as little as possible in the exchange. And although sometimes he groped their best protected places, he often fell for the corniest excuses invented by his neighbours, as he was incapable of being pushy or using force to sell his presents at the price he would have liked. In the end, what he got wasn't the asking price, but it made him happy enough. The youth's lack of persistence was also due in large part to the fact that he had his eyes set on a particular prey: for some time he'd been entranced by a neighbour whose slanted eyes cheekily looked him over, and although he was older, he dared invite her to his trading terrace only at dusk on a day when his booty was plentiful.

They both went to the tried-and-tested terrace, its flagstones long cooled by the shadows from the cisterns, and sat down to study the morning's ill-gotten treasures. The main jewel and pretext for offering this particular invitation to slant eyes was a gold ring he had found in a hotel corridor, engraved on the inside with an initial that matched the enticing neighbour's name.

This time, sustained by the present of such a valued object, our odd-job man managed to overcome his shyness, sidestep obstacles, fend off excuses, until their betrothal was sealed at nightfall: her finger bore the valuable, exquisite gift that would make her feel the princess of the neighbourhood despite her fourteen and a bit years, and he also wore another little ring, not its first time out either but

new enough to win him over and carry him into an equally princely
delirium. He stood behind his bowed young friend, contemplating in
awe her bejewelled hand. The couple were shielded in their embrace
from neighbourly gazes by the voluminous circular tanks. And the
exultant bootboy watched in full-blown happiness the sun setting
behind the terrace roofs of an Old Havana that was shored up, worn
out, crumbling, its fractured balconies falling lethally from time to
time on to the street, where a routine downpour was enough to
provoke a string of collapses.

The lad was progressing in giant strides, over the moon with his
girl from next door, now a grateful recipient of bracelets and
earrings, perfumes and make-up, and at the very moment when he
was feeling on top of the world, they called him up to do his military
service.

At this point a dark vein surfaced, invisible till then, and he
strenuously rebelled against the conscription order, rejecting it as
something unexpected and unacceptable. However, in spite of his
excuses, the one repeated ad nauseam being his keenness to carry on
working at the hotel, he went the way of everyone else: he had no
choice but to respect the order and go off to the army.

As the neighbours watched him leave, they concluded that all in
all, his frantic bid to avoid service in the ranks had been nothing out
of the ordinary, perhaps only slightly more emphatic than anyone
else's. Unparalleled and extreme, on the other hand, was the mulish
rage which, within a month of donning the uniform, led him to run
away from the barracks, having had his fill of early rising, machete-
wielding and stinking latrines, preferring the certainties of
marginalization and punishment such an unacceptable revolt would
bring to the possibilities of a comfortable future guaranteed by a few
years of passive resignation as a conformist recruit.

At this first escape plausible explanations for his behaviour began
to fade. The local layabouts who found a hiding place for the fugitive
at a non-compromising arm's length commented in amazement to
each other how, although he immediately asked after his twilight

girlfriend, the youth seemed only slightly upset to discover she had moved base to the dangerous hallway of a tottering shell of a building where she looked a picture of health now she was sharing her twilights with the guy on the make who ran the corner store. The fugitive's return to his own neighbourhood, thick-skinned sloppiness on his part, enabled the authorities to catch him in a matter of days; this childish naïvety was given as the reason why his superiors treated him with a certain kindness and diagnosed him not as an impenitent counter-revolutionary but as an ill-advised, confused kid, not beyond the pale; they winked and called him a piss-taker behind his back. Consequently, his lunatic walkabout did not rate a jail sentence or a dishonourable discharge, only a dose of remote sugar-cane-cutting that tanned his hide and calloused his hands, in the course of which he learned some new tricks, when he observed and later participated in sharp practice over provisions and meals, vanishing sacks of rice, clandestine deals with the local peasantry. And in the implacable vandalism, whether chance or deliberate, to which the sugar cane fell victim, inexpertly macheted by recruits or volunteers without a drop of rural blood, the ill-treated plants were damaged for ever, sentenced to stunted, diseased, deformed lives.

Once the harmful sugar harvest was over, the disciplined troops returned to barracks, having made up for past impetuosity or foolishness, like the youth's desertion, with months of forced labour. But the retired hotelier, clearly impelled by an uncontrollable allergy to his uniform, didn't mend his ways but sought the first opportunity to clear off again.

This time he did not act rashly or simple-mindedly. He spent months loafing around, prowling in the background and occasionally linking up with pariahs of similar ilk. His sister's zealous righteousness led to his capture. Unthinkingly he had trusted her and, alarmed by the idea of being compromised by her younger brother, she shopped him without hesitation. All of which hastened the inevitable dénouement: the recruit's strange behaviour, his obstinate silence when questioned by superiors trying to find an explanation for his phobia, finally provoked an equally entrenched reaction from shocked superiors; instead of throwing him into a cell and then on to the hue and cry of Cuban streetlife, they were so put out by this apparent rebellion without cause that they insisted on curing their ward's wayward frenzy and put him back in the ranks, after a healthy dose of filthy dungeons and exhausting forced labour, the only point of which was to sap his strength of mind and body.

But nothing could deter him. The last and longest of his escapes took him to mountains far off the beaten track, where he ate handfuls of raw food, sought solace in solitude from lost animals he then sacrificed, sometimes sleeping on a bough of a tree, and surviving a passing cyclone in a cave.

If anyone could have seen him in the last few weeks of this rustic life they would have intuited at a glance the extent to which months as a hermit depressed his spirit and were getting the best of him. He spent days wandering aimlessly, lightheaded, not even on guard against those chasing him, forced to play with himself and his thoughts in that benighted haven, trapped impassively in a mind-softening routine. In the end, his persecutors caught him mid-conversation with a jungle rat he had half bludgeoned to death.

His otherworldly appearance, dirt up to his eyeballs, and troglodyte nakedness barely hidden by ravaged remains of olive green, the stench he gave off, meant that they treated him on his return more as a madman on the loose than as a deserter, and this babbling apeman aspect lay behind the decision taken by his superiors – with no right of appeal – with a certain amount of legal and medical sleight of hand: he was declared a lunatic and confined to an asylum for treatment and care.

Only specialists could have studied and dealt with such an indefinable case; amid bursts of alienated behaviour there were moments when the youth's unhinged actions verged on the unreal, were unmistakably theatrical. Due to this ambivalence, some reckoned he was mad while others were convinced the rebel had exhausted the escaping game and was now trying a new trick. The recluse had contorted fits, shook and trembled for no apparent reason; he acted capriciously and the day he was admitted took advantage of his nurses' oversight to run and shut himself inside a stuffy cupboard, out of which soon came via a crack under the door a jet of glinting urine, a discharge they were also unable to attribute unanimously to fear, cheek or contempt, to an unfortunate deviation or defiant madness.

Neither these nor other absurd scenes made an impact on the numerous sceptics, who contemptuously put them down to airs of a prima donna and supported their views by pointing to the extent a person as hard-headed and tenacious as his record showed him to be could sustain over months a farcical imitation of incurable paranoia. They rested their case on a recurrent mania that might be a symptom of regression to childhood but which they attributed to irrepressible shamelessness: the internee seized on any lapses in supervision to unzip his trousers and show himself to a female nurse full-length, in a tempting come-on. It was impossible to describe this action as totally stupid, when discovering the outcome of each episode depended on voluntary charges laid by the woman under siege.

At any rate this indefinable stage was short-lived and ended when they began to apply the most favoured official treatment to the disturbed patient. It was routine, well rehearsed, easy and soothing. In a short time, they inflicted on the renegade conscript half a dozen electric shocks.

Even the cleaners could see how these lashes were having the desired effect; after each one, the failed recruit's rebelliousness and edginess declined, as did his irritability, exhibitionism and vital spark. The youth went droopy, it made no difference whether he looked at a nurse or at the wall. He would soon be an incomplete social being, albeit pacified and acceptable. The debate about whether his fits were real or fake lost all meaning and soon sceptics as much as disbelievers, used to seeing him in a perennial state of blankness and abulia, admitted him with a catch-all diagnosis as one more cretin in their institution. The electric bombardment which his brain suffered gradually transformed his grey matter into a kind of amorphous porridge, filling up the cerebral nooks and crannies which, according to the specialists, generated his abnormal rejection of discipline, exaggerated his indomitable denial of military order. It flattened the zones which graphically had earned him the sobriquet of mulehead and where slowly the desired docility and vacuous, constant passivity gained ground. After each visit to the room where diligent doctors and nurses administered his regular supply of electric, he emerged in a gentler frame of mind, the desires he might have had were calmed, as were the escape plans he might have conceived, more contrite, evidently attached to his bleak little room and the white corridors, more compliant and uncomplaining to the nurses, male and female, who brought and carried him at will, regulated his life night and day, cleaned his sheets and pants like a baby's when late reactions to the electric shocks sometimes provoked a nocturnal diarrhoea which filled his smelly bed with sticky liquids or when the sleeping tablets were too much for night-time emergencies and he urinated on his mattress while dreaming of stables. He let men and women shift his filthy body, arse and balls, tickled perhaps by a long scratchy painted nail casually grazing his scrotum, a playful move that excited no desire, or only perhaps titters when they kept him standing naked for a while, as, cursing, they changed his bedlinen; and sometimes it was cause for jest and entertainment when during one of these early morning ablutions he had an inexplicable erection and his useless prick, which judging by their hilarity in no way attracted the nurses, swayed in the air like a stray puppet, which he too contemplated in surprise, not knowing how to respond or what to do until one of them, either to draw the entertainment to a close or give the others more laughs, grabbed it and, in tones of mock gravity, tucked it forcefully away between his legs, telling him to show more respect.

In the long run, the desire for control took the doctors too far. Their charge's nervous system had been totally becalmed; but rather than let him be in a pacified state, they prolonged over the odds the sessions of electric therapy, attacked with relish the theoretical site of his cerebral disorder, bent on silencing for ever their patient's antisocial behaviour, not realizing it had been purged some time ago. And so excessive zeal caused the treatment to fail.

The sick youth's general mood was clearly one of absolute placidity. He had only to be assigned a chore and he would strive to realize it to perfection; he despaired, trying to attain utopian goals. When he and another three inmates were told to clean the main hall, they would leave him with a mop and damp cloth, and after a while would find him polishing and repolishing the same patch, trying to give an impossible sheen to the same set of four tiles, determined not to abandon his little corner till it gleamed entirely to his satisfaction. The misfits who shared the task with him were annoyed, for once quite logically, when they saw him poised over his little square, not contributing to the common task, but they had learned to bite their tongues; they knew him better than the specialists and knew how their companion in captivity would greet benevolently and tolerantly anything except being distracted or upset when he had given himself over to a task, always undertaken body and soul, with a microscopic attention to detail; within their general unawareness, they understood any protest from them would only stir the youth up, make him uncontrollably aggressive; a single word distracting him from his work could lead to real rage, which would be calmed only by a strait-jacket and a couple of quick-action pills.

The relentless bombardment the doctors inflicted on the recruit's brain had certainly cleared out the rebelliousness, but the insistent electric charges finally sparked off a cerebral deviation, a deep fissure in the matter hidden till then, a fire which could be doused only with difficulty, whenever they tried to disturb his deep self-absorption, and somebody, on purpose or mistakenly, interrupted his tantric labours. And though his habitual state was one of simple-minded docility, that bit of his stupefied brain shaken but not incinerated by yet one more wave of electricity, a flame still hiding under the cold, grey ash, turned out to be decisive for his future, for those intermittent fits meant his file was included among the dossiers of madmen who were still a touch dangerous and that became crucial at zero hour, the hour of Mariel.

At that moment of destiny, all lunatics considered dangerous, whether a little or very, were gathered together: the ones locked away for almost a lifetime who at the first opportunity lacerated their skin, scratched out their eyes or bit their tongues, pulped and sliced them, and the ones for whom, isolated as trash, the presence of another was an unbearable provocation they sought to eliminate in any way they could; or those in need of an environment of perpetual calm in order to maintain their own and who, at the slightest quiver, the lightest vibration, spewed out torrents of rabid foam and required a contingent of hardy, well-built nurses to contain their unleashed fury; or those, like the renegade recruit, who never went into a murderous rage but occasionally abandoned the peaceful course traced across their dulled brains by the perpetual flow of medicine, and like whining dogs were capable of unconscious misdeeds; all were herded out of the lunatic asylum and as soon as they were in the buses to take them to the port of departure, their guards jumbled them up with the legion of citizens in their right senses bound on the same journey; an hallucinating package dispatched north in the Mariel boats, with no medical histories or diagnosis, carrying the same identification as normal folk, condemned to the absolute madness of being received and treated as sane.

The flotilla had been under way for barely two weeks when the ex-recruit was dispatched, drugged and befuddled in order to pass for normal, so unnaturally and deeply tranquillized that neither the change in landscape nor the lurching over the waves, no aspect of the disquieting venture, perturbed him; he wasn't even upset at having to travel standing up between two ex-jailbirds, a couple of kids whose sole entertainment on the nerve-racking crossing was to make as much fun as possible of his obvious impassivity, seen by them as pansy behaviour, touching his buttocks or scaring him as the waves buffeted the boat with endless predictions of imminent shipwreck.

When they arrived, his idiocy was just too obvious and he was sent off with the loonies; but, unlike other loose screws, he wasn't definitively locked up, his journey to the hospital being only a momentary setback.

As soon as his Cuban relatives found out about his untimely trip they alerted whatever distant or close family connections they had in Florida with a desperate insistence not shown hitherto in their care for the unhappy fledgeling. For once the youth sailed with Lady Luck, in spite of his burden of awesome lunacy. A distant aunt reacted immediately to the pleas from the family left behind by the boy, though they had always had few good words to say about her, praising more her fortune than her good self; a woman who had left the island in the first days of the revolution, she adopted the refugee nephew as an act of charity, welcoming him precisely because he was retarded; for judging by the scorn she poured on the new emigrants in telephone or personal conversations with numerous friends of similar chic, she would never have given a helping hand to the sane and healthy, being afraid that such togetherness would serve only to trick her, to pull the wool over her eyes, to end up in the lap of luxury at her expense. The aunt had been unable to get her wealth out of her country of birth, but she managed, like lots of high-class exiles, to make a new pile of money. Now her persistent efforts, well oiled by a grasp of the two languages, quickly enabled her to cut the endless red tape, and with well-rehearsed politeness, prudence, familiarity, flattery, pleas and more or less veiled threats, depending on the situation and the person, her forays soon managed to open the doors of the American asylum and bring her nephew under her responsible wing, in a sensibly out-of-the-way little room inside her ample residence.

With the change of air the sick lad's prescriptions changed. His new doctors, used to beefier norms, prescribed a generous but completely different diet whose higher doses of energy got him going more than strictly Cuban dishes; they also showered him with pharmaceuticals, supplied in such quantities that in the first weeks of adaptation, he was knocked out for days on end, immobilized, mouth gawping, looking even loopier than ever, seated in his sad little room. These personality ups and downs baffled everyone and in an attempt to free him from his dazed, bewildered state and to amuse and control him, they also prescribed the newcomer a portable radio; as they predicted, it hypnotized him for days on end and from time to time unleashed an unexpected dialogue, initiated hours of animated chat between lunatic and loudspeaker. These conversations crossed corridors to reach the lounge where his bountiful aunt met lady friends on most afternoons, from where they listened to the endless flow of monotonous gabble, streams of conversation that became more frequent by the day. For no apparent reason, the madman engaged in a perpetual monologue, like an endless tape recording, difficult to halt without resort to better stimulants, more captivating distractions.

The lad spent weeks in his peaceful residence doing nothing out of the ordinary, engrossed in his foolishness, tittering stupidly for no obvious reason, mumbling and chatting, in between periods of normality, betrayed only by the giveaway imbalance born in the sanatorium, a kind of lack of coordination between his means of expression, as if his eyes cried while his mouth laughed or vice versa. On other occasions his aunt found him sweating, standing up against a wall like a punished schoolboy, tetchy and scowling; he moved his legs without taking a step, as if, following the routines of the military training he'd always rejected, he wanted to release dangerous, unpredictable energies via his feet. When he sensed the presence of his relative, he turned round, mouth pleading, attempting a smile, but able only to painfully screw up his lips. He agreed to sit down, then timidly explained how it upset him to think that, in a remote corner of his chilled brain, an idea lay dormant, wanted to burst out; beautiful or melancholy but impossible to shape or touch, to know whether it was to be desired or feared. Then he had shaking and sweating fits, and struggled miserably as best he could against the impulse to smash and batter his head against the wall, to split open his skull in order to dip in, to seek out with his own hands that hidden concept, that feeling submerged in the sordid, brackish waters of his brain. Stormy days held special horrors for him. A crack of lightning led to expressions that worried even his pragmatic aunt, as when, after a particularly loud clap of thunder, he would say such a din might breach the heavens; and in effect, whenever one of these blasts came, he would slump to the floor, as if struck down, crawl on his knees over to a window and look upwards in search of the celestial hole.

These perennial variations of rushes to the brain hardly delighted his aunt, intent as she was on introducing her relation, madness notwithstanding, as a healthy exception to her negative interpretation of the recent exodus. She did not like his perpetual life of leisure, did not accept this lethargy as a sensible solution. This was why, after observing her nephew over time, noting the manic way he kept his room and affairs in perfect order, and registering the boy's obsession with cleanliness, she was persuaded, by his permanent docility, that he had falsely been labelled as potentially dangerous on the island; combining generosity and love of hard work, she gave her adoptive son the exclusive job of cleaning and looking after her museum. Thus she would save a servant girl's wages and allow the youth the undoubted satisfaction of knowing that he was at least in part earning his keep.

Her treasure was an all-embracing collection of Cuban bric-à-brac that stubbornly and against all advice she had refused to allow to become specialized or be influenced by value judgements. An Aladdin's cave of souvenirs, an archaeological store, where the Cuban origin of the exhibits was the only pre-condition the collector imposed. This loose common denominator was clear from first impressions: a 1920s dressing table from a Havana furniture store, painstaking imitation of the international styles of the time and made from rare, attractive woods, she'd adorned with a table lamp found in a hotel on Miami Beach, whose genuine 'made in Cuba' label revealed the interest a post-Second World War North American manufacturer had had in taking advantage of cheap island labour, but with its lack of local style, it merely recalled the décor of any 1950s Californian motel. Both objects were preserved, one on top of the other, with identical affection by their owner as equally priceless items rescued from previous, better times.

A blouse brought in a suitcase from Cuba, its collar and buttonholes embroidered with elaborate lacework, was kept in a drawer next to a pair of ordinary men's nylon socks with no printed trademark, their authenticity guaranteed by the paper label stuck to the material and identifying them as the product of a well-known cheap manufacturer. Things were heaped in a total jumble in one room after another on the side of the house devoted to these ancestral treasures, a wing till then forbidden to the youth and which was opened to eyes other than their owner's only on special occasions. The walls of room after room were covered in watercolours showing rows of royal palms, carts, hillocks, wooden huts, beaches, fighting cocks, ink sketches of narrow cobbled streets, façades with wrought-iron grilles, colonial stone fortresses, contemporary and folkloric street vendors, eighteenth-century alleyways, caricatures of well-known characters, posters and leaflets advertising a circus, a public dance, a bargain auction or the smiling, numbered face of a politician standing for public office; tables were packed with rococo figurines of romantic lovers next to more common plaster statuettes of prancing horses, still lifes, elephants or images of popular worship. One corner was piled high with bongos, pistols, bells, cowbells, drums and a multitude of Cuban maracas and Andalusian castanets, though these were made on the island and decorated with miniature tropical landscapes and English phrases welcoming tourists; one table was buried under cases, wallets, purses and shoes in various shapes, sizes and colours of crocodile leather, a piano lid was stuffed with musical scores, various shelves packed with cartons of cigars, some full of makers' labels, next to empty boxes of a variety of brands of cigarettes manufactured in Cuba, excluding any after 1959, since the woman chose that ill-fated year as the cut-off point for her collection; fine silver spoons crammed into small drawers, their handles distinguished by polychrome coats of arms of provinces, cities, clubs, associations or hotels; bookshelves filled a whole room stacked with albums of exclusively Cuban stamps next to family photo albums, hers and many others belonging to total strangers, rare editions, bestsellers, ancient and modern, political, society and literary magazines, and a discreet, locked bureau reserved for pornographic publications, often profusely illustrated; glass cases exhibited silk fans with hand-painted representations of national monuments, by the side of glasses with transfers advertising provincial hotels; a cupboard with glass doors displayed medals from veterans of the Wars of Independence, military and civil decorations from colony and republic, and small medals given as school prizes to pupils best at spelling, history or catechism, straw hats made in Havana so old they were difficult to touch without their falling to pieces and also baseball players' caps with the colours of teams long since gone; transcriptions of sessions from the abolished Republican Congress, copies of speeches given in that chamber or at important party conferences by old leaders, exiled like her, but less fortunate, whom the collector had lent a welcome hand by purchasing those historic documents; notes from over two centuries, the most recent signed twice by ex-Ministers of the Exchequer, who had inscribed their rubric in pen right over the identical printed stamp; and a room like an abandoned boutique where a large set of dummies had been dressed up in different uniforms: from the army general with his hat, sash and medals, to the everyday wear, from tie to toe, of pupils from a prestigious private school. And this was only a minimum selection, the tip of the iceberg, of the multicoloured, potentially infinite collection, giving the impression that the roof of the woman's house bore the spout of an enormous funnel coming from the island.

Her nephew's somewhat imbecilic rapture when he was first allowed to enter those rooms and contemplate her motley bazaar, much of which he didn't recognize since, to corroborate his traditionalist aunt's sombre visions, they had been swept from the island by social upheaval, convinced the woman that her intuition was correct, that she could entrust the care of her collection to this youth. The sick boy's attentive hands bore no relation to his mental torpor and the manic routines which his low IQ plunged him into would be an advantage when it came to tending and helping preserve her treasured collection.

The doctors gave their go-ahead to the plan, although as they had detected flashes of furious disquiet at the back of the boy's brain, they would have been slightly worried to see the brusque, bossy familiarity which the aunt sometimes employed towards the simpleton, certain it was the best remedy for his stupidity and would in no way disturb his idiot passivity.

She was right, till one day.

The woman went into a room her nephew was cleaning, where there was perpetual gloom no matter how many lights were switched on inside; the dark mahogany absorbed any luminosity. It was just another room in that peculiar museum, bursting with scraps from a precise geography and history. Nineteenth-century landscapes and portraits or more recent, experimental pictorial efforts, capriciously hung on walls by the side of cinema posters, front covers of defunct magazines and publicity material for a restaurant which, if it survived in Havana, would have another name and another menu, lived cheek by jowl with a lobster trap and a home-made fishing net stretched over one corner, both surrounded by plastic or glass crabs and lobsters, brought from the island's ports, where they'd been used to advertise fishmongers' stalls; not far away, a guitar made in a workshop in Sancti Spiritus rested silently by a linen jacket and a sisal hat; a whole sideboard was devoted to exquisite hand-painted fans, colourful, opened, next to paper, palm frond and real or even cardboard fans with faded coloured photos of dogs or children, advertising chemist's shops.

The boy stood with his back to her in front of a distant bookcase reserved for cards, where various albums had been placed in a set order, as if in a display. Next to leather-covered volumes of collections of postcards, landscapes or island scenes photographed over the previous hundred years, there were more modest examples, covered in fake leather or even cardboard, wrinkled and soiled by years of handling, collections of little children's cards, bits of coloured paper sold in Cuba with biscuits or chocolates or chewing gum, which narrated in a numbered series the adventures of characters popularized by comics or the radio, homespun or international heroes, Indian spies, cowboys from the Cuban outback, and also collections of plants or animals from the world over, episodes from the Wars of Independence or effigies of South American heroes. Her curator was trying to arrange these differently sized volumes in a perfect line and had been working at it for more than an hour, shifting them a centimetre at a time, concentrating, intent on the slow business of lining them up in an exact parallel to the edge of the shelf.

After striding in as masterfully as ever, his aunt hailed him, shouted in the familiar fashion that some people found amusing, mixing the playful, the bossy and the rude. The boy gave a frightened start and, in doing so, knocked the album he was trying to arrange, upsetting an order he'd spent many minutes trying to impose instantly. As he saw the pack collapse, the simpleton let out a low-pitched bellow, a kind of guttural moan the woman had never heard before. Giving her no time to react, to control his stress for better or worse, the addle-brained youth grabbed a bronze bookend, the head of some Caribbean literary great, which he didn't throw at the woman as she evidently feared he would, judging by the alarmed way she raised her arm and lowered her head, but in a crazed gesture he scraped it hard against the gilt-fitted, polished-wood dressing table, showing an unmistakably deep desire to inflict an incision, as if it were a carpenter's chisel and he had been engaged to carve a delicate pattern.

When the woman recovered and finally got near him, she spoke, first calmly and affectionately, but then, seeing he took no notice, she shouted peremptorily, trying to paralyse him and snatch away the demolition weapon, but the unbalanced youth lifted it up and banged it so hard against the curved dressing-table mirror, in such a frenzy, that at the second or third bash glass splinters began to fly through the air, endangering the aggressor and forcing the woman to retreat several paces and restrain her impulse to pin down the once more rebellious nephew. He kept on hammering and after he had shattered the bevelled mirror, he began to mumble a bitter, threatening litany, an incoherent recitation spurting and gushing from his mouth; it was then he noticed, perplexed, the blood pouring from his hand and arm, from skin encrusted with gleaming splinters of glass. The woman could stand the disastrous spectacle no more, in an instant she lost the public cool she had kept for so many years and walked out of the room distraught, screaming indecencies.

After a while, she calmed herself and returned to the devastated room, politely, gently, with a soothing glass of water on a plate next to several pills.

But when she saw the state of the room, she could not retain her composure. Impossible to expect her to be serene and understanding when faced by that hecatomb. Impossible when she saw albums wrenched from their bindings and, on the floor, century-old tinted photos torn to shreds, the bottom ripped out of the lobster trap, the fishing net and guitar strings cut, pictures and drawings gouged by the same destructive scissors, engravings pulled from their frames, posters and photos torn up and scattered to the four corners of the room, amid the seeds from maracas which were just then being sundered, split open like skulls smashed berserkly against the wall, in a tumult of vandalism that unhinged the woman, unaware in her desperation that she was confronting a dangerous lunatic, that her insulting wails were only winding him up even further.

But her flushed nephew was too far gone to be worried by her and was totally absorbed in his demolition job. Once he had destroyed the first room to his satisfaction, he hurled himself into a second gallery of the Cuban museum, vented more of his anger, took no notice of the insults of total loony his aunt was winging his way. Terrified, she saw him go into the other room, the one with sofas and hammocks, the wardrobe of pillows and sheets, many still wrapped in the factory cellophane that bore the addresses of working-class districts in Havana or of some small town from the provinces, the Louis XV meuble containing enough sets of layettes to supply an orphanage: hand-embroidered linen braces worthy of a prince, dozens of brightly coloured baby-gowns creating a rainbow formation, shoes and boots worn to different degrees, some gleaming white, others cracked, others stiffly gilt and preserved, plastic bibs with an infinite array of prints on the towelling – balloons, flowers, clowns, teddy bears, characters from centuries of children's mythology – and in a tiny drawer, a collection of first curls and cords cut from the newly born, lovingly kept in small, labelled bags of transparent plastic, tied up with coloured bows.

She could stand it no more. She ran to the telephone and dialled the emergency number, asked for everybody's help, police, firemen, telling them a raging lunatic was loose in her house, explaining that he was breaking everything, demolishing the lot, that her life was in danger, not failing to invoke at the end of her every phrase the magic word that would bring them running, speed up help, and set the sirens wailing through the streets; the word that put the authorities on red alert, marielito.

Her screams of alarm were so loud she couldn't hear the wrapping paper being torn, the embroidered sheets being ripped, or the lad's berserk heel-stamping, which irreparably dented the silver handles of the small hand-turned forks, or the mathematical precision with which he shredded multiple items of children's clothing. She returned in time only to see the ravages, to see the stuffing from the furniture scattered round the room as if there had been a Siberian avalanche, for her nephew, whose talent for demolition seemed to be gathering apace, now launched himself into another room leaving a trail of useless debris. She decided not to try to stop him, for she detected in his demented agility an irresistible determination to override any obstacle in order to continue the débâcle. Nor could she bring herself to survey the trail of destruction for fear of weeping, fainting, going mad as well, even absurdly joining the destructor in his lethal enterprise, only able mentally to compare the ruined remnants of her treasure with other historic ruins which had maintained their dignity and value despite cracks and mutilations, and consoling herself with the thought of years dedicated to careful restoration and renovation.

The youth pursued his painstaking labours in the third room, after smashing en route porcelain figurines that were perhaps outside the collection. He reached the corner where stacked on shelves by an antique gramophone were hundreds of records of danzones, sones, guarachas and rumbas preserved in unique recordings, circus and music-hall acts from the turn of the century sung by whites painted black and mulattos talcummed white whose photos appeared framed on walls or on items of furniture, and the varied sonorities of the collection began to fuse into a single sound, were transformed into a similar cracking noise, as the records were thrown through the air by the furious Attila and smashed in smithereens, flung festively, cheerfully you might almost say, from one end of the room to another, followed contentedly in their flight before they shattered and joined the pile of debris beyond recall.

The last records were breaking as the shriek of police sirens blotted out the sound of the gramophone lid and hinges being wrenched apart, the whelp of loudspeaker filters being broken into little pieces by her nephew's powerful hands, thrown to the ground or sent flying with carnival glee. When she heard the patrol cars, the woman ran to the door and locked him inside, in a silly attempt to keep her nephew in, to stop him from escaping, as if he were a thief. She rushed to let the police in, got flustered, babbled out what was happening, gave a detailed report on the bespoiling of her museum, urging them on, never forgetting in her fury to wind the spring, by repeating and repeating the word Mariel, Mariel, weaving round it the alarming words of dangerous and lunatic, at which the policemen reached for their holsters without a second thought and, Hollywood style, went into the room guns blazing.

TRANSLATED BY PETER BUSH

Prisoner In The Horizon's Circle
Jorge Luis Arzola

He woke up by a trail of blood on the stone path. It was the first time that it had happened and he didn't know what to think, now he wasn't so drunk. He stared anxiously at the stains and, while he left the guard hut behind, on his way home, tried to remember. He thought he had received a visit late at night; someone vague and quivering, somewhere between reality and fantasy. The best thing was not to think about that ghost or about the suspicious trail of blood, because he was innocent and had nothing to do with the incident. Anyway, he was in no fit state to remember anything.

They came to fetch him about midday. His frightened wife let the man in and the guy slammed the window open. The sunlight hit him roughly in the face and he sat bewildered on the edge of the bed. It was the police. Some turkeys had been stolen from the farm.

The policeman found nothing in the house, but the stains of blood on the stone path indicated that the thief could move about freely in the farm, he was someone who worked there, or at least was known there. The policeman assured him that there would be a trial within a week.

The rude guy left. Smiling maliciously, she stroked his head and said something about having hidden the turkeys in a safe place and in the evening would cook wonders with one of them, just wait. He didn't listen, or listened but didn't understand because his hangover made him stupid and he was snoozing off again.

His wife woke him up at six. It's as if you're ill, he heard her saying, and he opened his eyes and felt the shadows of twilight passing over and through his head, and he stared at her and smiled, he was going to get up, he said, don't worry, he wasn't ill.

He washed and sat down to eat as if new. There was turkey fricassee and he piled the slices into his mouth because meat was a special occasion at his table and his wife knew that glory lay exactly above his tongue . . . She cooked well and that was one of the few things he liked about her. She was docile and fat, a bit dumb and ugly, but she could cook a great rice with black beans and an exquisite turkey fricassee, with loads of potatoes and sauce.

He ate thinking about nothing, and for a while didn't want to ask her where she had found the turkeys. He felt good and had no wish at all to move his mouth.

He threw himself on his bed. He didn't have to work until six the next evening and fell asleep again and didn't hear his wife call him for breakfast, and when he woke at ten in the morning he had to make a huge effort to disentangle himself from the sheets, worried that he had slept so long.

For lunch there was cold turkey, with lots of garlic and tomato sauce. He worked around the house in the afternoon, changing the washers on the cooker and grinding the knives.

At five he was ready to go to work, and at half-past he ate.

This time he was not really hungry and quarrelled with his wife. There was turkey soup and roast turkey. As his way of saying goodbye, he asked where did you get the turkeys? She didn't have a clue, she said, looking at him with her large innocent eyes and shrugging her shoulders; he should ask himself that question.

He sat on the bench in the guard hut thinking vaguely about turkeys, of those he'd eaten, of course, because better not to think about the stolen ones. He was innocent.

He kept guard suspicious of every shadow, noise or owl, and at dawn went quietly home. Now he had a clear conscience!

He slept a little and well. He chucked his lunch portion of turkey into the yard and ate three decent fried eggs with bread. Later, he ordered his wife to pick up all the turkey bones in the yard and make them vanish.

Even then he didn't feel right. He strolled around the yard

searching for incriminating bones and again asked his wife where she got the turkeys from. But she answered him with tall stories, lying to him, saying that he had stolen the turkeys the night he went tipsy to his guard duty because he had drunk up the last twenty pesos of the month with some bloke over there.

He felt giddy with rage and wanted to drink something strong to clear his throat and warm his heart. He couldn't believe he had got caught up in such a mess. It couldn't be, and shouldn't be, because he was not a despicable thief and a few days before he had been about to argue with a drinking companion who had offered to do business with him over the farm turkeys, a man calling himself Juan who he bumped into every now and then at the bar, a jerk who had only to look at him before he began telling him it wouldn't be difficult to do a good job, turkeys, a shit he had to be firm with, let it be, friend, because lately he couldn't find him there without being bugged by his heavy jokes, and because he joined in the jokes he caught himself thinking a quick job would relieve him for a few days from money miseries and an empty stomach.

So let his wife repeat that crazy accusation, if she dared, and she'd soon feel his slap on her face . . . She was careful this time. She said that the night he was drunk someone had woken her at four in the morning, had placed three turkeys in her hand and left without a word.

She didn't seem to be lying . . . but she had to be lying, because that story was too absurd and he knew it, she was playing a dirty trick on him, so let her clear up who that man was who had come out of the blue to bring turkeys to a married woman in her home, a woman with a husband who loved her and went off trustingly to do guard duty, she must clear this up, because he was no turkey thief nor had he ordered anyone to bring stolen turkeys to his wife.

So she was a little tart, who'd have thought it? And now she comes up with a story about a man who appeared with turkeys at dawn and, thanks to her pretty, stupid little face, had given them to her as a present.

He watched his chaste, most beloved wife cry, and felt like gagging her. She could turn so ugly, even uglier, poor thing, and she howled in an ugly way. He didn't beat her up, because he realized that this time she was not crying because she hated him, or had been humiliated; but because she loved him, and he knew it, that fat, sexless and unhappy woman was in love with him, and knew that she had given him something he had long been waiting for, a beautiful, shiny fit of jealousy.

And so, with knitted brow, like a truly outraged husband, he watched her cry and patiently waited for an explanation, something that would convince him and restore the confidence he had always had in her.

But what could she explain if the man had placed turkeys in her hand and had left before she could ask him who had sent them. She thought he had sent them, she said, her darling husband, drying her tears, her love, and he sat her on his knees and kissed her tenderly, lovingly, he would forgive her. He wanted to finish with this once and for all. He accepted her reasons as kindly as he could and sat in the doorway.

The weather was lethargic and stagnant, and he thought of going to bed, but he wasn't sleepy. He still wasn't sleepy at night, although he was tired and his head and all his body ached. He fell asleep towards dawn and woke at midday, hungry and angry.

He didn't eat anything. He shoved his breakfast aside, an omelet and white rice, and went to sit in the doorway. His wife knew that when he decided to sit in the doorway it was best to leave him alone and postpone the reconciliation for later.

She tried to patch things up all evening. She showed him a new shirt that she had just bought and embroidered. She offered him sweets and even tried to comb his hair, or kiss him . . . He remained indifferent. Nothing tempted him, he said, while he meticulously surveyed the yard.

He left for work earlier than usual, leaving behind a wife worried by how little he had eaten and slept. He bought two pastry snacks in the village bar and ate them on his way, his left hand in his trouser pocket, fingering an enigmatic and worrying bone he'd found in the yard.

He spent his guard duty with the bone in his hand, examining and playing with it until he got bored and chucked it away in the dark. His eyes were burning and he was tired and sleepy, but he couldn't sleep, nobody would steal a damn turkey from under his nose. The bone was hard, like a pig's or a cow's or a horses's, but he had a hunch (without knowing exactly why) that it was a turkey's.

Then when he was fed up with struggling against tiredness and sleep and boredom, he grabbed his torch and began to search for the bone, slowly, methodically, anxiously, furiously, desperately. He had to find it at all costs to make sure that it was a bone from a pig, from a horse, from some cow and not a turkey bone, because turkey it couldn't be and surely wasn't or else he, poor, innocent man, was in danger of falling into the hands of (in)justice . . . Who knows how many of these bones the police might find in his yard? Thousands, he said to himself, millions of pieces of God knows what species of chaste little animals, innocent little animals that had died who know how many years back or decades or centuries before those dirty farm turkeys whose remains his wife had conjured away from the yard.

The bone did not appear and he handed over his guard duty to his replacement trembling with desperation and a longing to drink something, and returned home and began sweeping the damn yard, looking for bones, collecting them like an archaeologist.

When his wife got up at seven in the morning, she found him dragging himself around the yard on all fours, excited by the idea of finding the last fragment of bone in order to leave the yard free of suspicion.

He forced her to help him and she threw herself to the ground without a murmur. She knew her husband well. She didn't dare offer him a glass of cold water and a tranquillizer. Between the two of them they collected seventy bits of bone, which he thought were innocent because they were black and inoffensive.

He washed himself cheerfully, ate lunch at two, chucked the bones into a cartridge case and hid it under his pillow and lay down to sleep. He didn't have nightmares or sweet dreams. He slept blissfully and only woke up at seven in the morning. He was voraciously hungry and ate his breakfast fried eggs as if he had just got over some serious illness. Then he shocked his wife by making love to her slowly and violently, he did it for himself, unaware that she screamed with pleasure and was ugly and fat, a little thick, and he devotedly despised her.

He ate lunch without appetite and in the evening didn't even touch his food. He was tired of eating fried eggs with rice. He hated all laying hens and all the rice paddies on earth and celebrated the memory of the five heroic turkeys that he had eaten days back. His pay would not allow him to survive the month in a decent way and he was an honourable man. Never in his life had he stolen from the State or from anybody, but life was hard and what he earned bought very little.

At five in the afternoon he lifted up his pillow, grabbed the cartridge case with the bones and went off to guard duty. In his pocket he had thirty pesos that his wife had just handed over and while walking he fondled them in a rage, asking himself what he could do with them, whether to blow it all on a conciliatory drunken spree.

He left his home behind, free of bones and guilt, and a screaming, unpleasant woman who he had just hit because she had accepted money from strangers, he told her, and on top of that, for arguing with him, for saying no sir, the man who brought the turkeys and the money was no stranger, but a friend of his and she had seen them together once, drinking rum somewhere, the two of them implicated in the stolen-turkey mess.

But he was innocent and sick of his wife, of the bones, his work and everything and that's why he hit her, for all that and for not letting him be crushed by pessimism, to lift his spirits.

He was innocent and if they insisted on taking him to trial

(something he thought not possible, now that he was thinking clearly, because he had not been called to sign the records and they had no proof, no witnesses, nothing, shit) he would put on the most naïve face in the world and ask the police to check the yard at home where they wouldn't find even a splinter of a bone. He would say that and much more and the police would get intimidated by his insolence, which would make their insolence seem trifling. And if he didn't say that his wife had had an affair in exchange for two or three turkeys and some cash, it wouldn't be necessary in order to prove his innocence.

He pulled a chair from out of the guard hut and leaned it against the doorframe. He said to himself, forced himself to believe, that the night was quiet, full of stars and few worries. It was promising for thinking good things and pure abstractions, and he thought without remorse about the meanings of the words honour and innocence. He was honourable and innocent and because of that was ready to kill the scoundrel who tried to break into the farm to steal turkeys.

He was there on the watch because it was his duty, eyes wide open, sitting in the doorway when he saw him approach along the stone path. Then he rushed inside, lifted down the shotgun and pointed it at the intruder. 'You'd better push off,' he said.

The guy, scared, looked at him from the other side of the fence, paralysed by the black barrel, like saying it's me, don't you recognize me, and as he pushed the barrel almost against his chest, of course he knew who it was, he knew it too well, a wretched turkey thief who had come to steal turkeys, and screw an innocent man like himself.

He sized him up, he studied him, like something he was hunting. He looked like a rabbit and shook like a rabbit. It made him sick, and he wanted him to turn around and disappear from view for ever, or, better, not to have ever spotted him.

'Beat it,' he told him, 'because you are not going to steal one more turkey.'

The guy tried to smile, said something about a waiting car, what a crazy idea! He felt the trigger. His finger was shaking and for a second he thought he would shoot him, but he restrained himself. He shivered like a leaf. He had almost killed a down-and-out, a wretch who was fed up with eating badly and was looking for a way to make a few pesos. Then he felt the lump in his pocket and had a brainwave. He felt sorry for the man who at the time was literally a shit held up by a gun, and gave him the thirty pesos as a present, he should take them and scram before he changed his mind, the wretch needed the money more than he did.

But the man did nothing to pick them up and was prolonging the ridiculous scene too far, saying but but, so that he had to chuck the money at him to keep his two hands free and threaten him, force him to leave for once and for bloody all in this murky situation.

'Shove off, Juan,' he told him, 'because I recognize you and nobody is going to pay you.'

The man, the screwed-up bloke, went off, picked up the money and finally left, in a hurry, turning his head around every five or six steps. He breathed a sigh of relief and, while he watched him go off, asked himself who the hell would believe that such a low form of life could be with someone's wife. He didn't know how he could have concocted such a naïve story. Nobody would believe him. The police would laugh at him.

He sat down again and felt like crying. The shotgun slipped off his lap and fell noisily on to the flagstones in the doorway of the guard hut. He was lost. There was no point hiding it from himself. The cell awaited him with its prison bars open to give him a last embrace.

He imagined himself on the stool and said to himself it was better that way. Let them lock him up, let them screw him because he tried to find some pesos and eat some grub, let them condemn him for that and for all the robberies there had been in that farm. Let them leave him to rot in prison, your bastard honour, poofy public prosecutor.

They did condemn him. The prosecutor asked for two years, but in the end the judge thought two years too lenient for a turkey thief and sent him to the firing squad, to be killed on the spot, then and there, and if they didn't carry this out it was because, suddenly, somebody said that the accused was innocent, something that could be proved right away.

He picked up the shotgun, went back inside the hut and hung it on its hook. He searched for the cartridge case that he'd left in the desk drawer, turned on all the lights and carefully scattered the bones over the desk top. He couldn't let himself be crushed by this, he was innocent. He lovingly examined the bones one by one. He looked at them from every angle, lowered his head, stepped back, always concentrating on them . . . until he had no doubt that there were bones from many different animals and none from a turkey.

He fetched the chair in the doorway and sat at the desk, leaned his chin on it and contemplated his beautiful, beloved bones. There were black ones, less than black ones, others were white, iridescent, green, purple. One looked like a Turkish scimitar, another was covered in pores like a sponge. Staring at them made him feel good, sure of himself, free; he even felt tender towards them, or maybe a sweet gratitude: he thanked them deeply for being bones from a cow, a horse and a pig and not from a turkey. Those bones were the ultimate proof of his innocence.

He examined them once more and put them back into the cartridge case. Then he had the bad idea of going to sit in the doorway and remembered that he had chucked a bone into the dark two nights before and that didn't seem to be a fowl's bone but could have been, and more than some fowl's, a turkey's.

Suddenly he had to find it as quickly as possible to hide it in the cartridge case next to the other inoffensive bones . . . (Because he knew that the bone was as inoffensive as the others, he knew it belonged to some small animal, but he needed to find it as if it were a gold coin.)

Armed with a well-sharpened machete he cut a perfect circle in the place where he had seen the bone fall, cleaned it of weeds and swept the earth carefully with a broom. Instead of his tiny and insignificant bone he found two bluish-black ones that looked suspicious.

He was relieved at six and had to stop his search. He was very tired, having spent the night combing for his house key, which he had lost there.

He slept badly. He had guilty nightmares that revealed a terrible secret. When he woke up he began contemplating the two bones that he'd found in the circle. So that his wife would not bug him with meal and bath times, he made her think he was angry with her and didn't want to see her. Shocked and sad, he spent hours meditating on them.

The next day he went to his guard duty thinking of nothing. He dragged his feet, had rings round his eyes and felt weak, and those who saw him thought he had died and that the person on his way to the farm was only his ghost.

He carried the two bones in his shirt pocket, after tirelessly comparing them with the phalanxes of his fingers, always hoping they might be smaller or larger. But they were about the same size.

When he tested this for the first time he felt a shower of cold water rush up his spine to his head, and from that moment he had done nothing but search and scrape the earth and dig holes where he probably wouldn't find anything but more earth or, worse, where he might find the remains of a human skeleton whose bits he would collect together and make them disappear, crushed into amorphous dust.

He began to dig with a good pick in his hands. He still hoped that he was hallucinating and was seeing two phalanxes where in fact there were only two small cow or pig or God knows what animal bones . . . Just then he found a large, flat bone that seemed like a shoulder blade and then a tibia and then a jaw with fine dentures and an extremely white skull, split open like a sweet.

Then he wished he'd been dreaming, or could jump back two days in time to that moment when he hadn't handled the machete or marked out the circle or found the first fatal bones; he wanted to jump back not two days but an hour and a half, find himself again in that recent, beautiful minute when the nightmare was still a suspicion, a foreboding.

However, it was too late. He had scraped and found the damn bones, and went on digging and finding, and each new bone made him yearn for his simple and carefree life of two days before, of two hours back. He let himself collapse into the hole and cried for everything that he had lost, his childhood, his naïvety, his true life. Ah, how wonderful those times long ago when he thought he was done for stealing some turkeys.

He dug without respite, and the deeper he went the more he found complete skulls, vertebrae, breast bones, shoulder blades and countless nameless little bones. He piled them up carefully around the hole. He should work hard, find the last fragments and then incinerate them, pound them into dust and fill the hole up before the next guard arrived.

He felt guilty, knew he was guilty, but wanted to save himself and could still save himself. There were three hours before dawn, and three hours were just what he needed.

But soon the depth of the hole began to irritate him and hinder his activity, and he had to begin to open it out towards the horizon. Then he understood that there was no salvation because the earth itself was pregnant with bones and the horizon was a prison, his circular prison.

He went to the guard house, drank two glasses of water, rested five minutes and began work again in a more tranquil mood. He knew with absolute certainty that he would not escape that cell and that eternity was not enough.

TRANSLATED BY JASON WILSON

The Ivory Trader And The Red Melons
Zoé Valdés

'. . . like an angel created by man, leaping forth upon the joyous and
meandering sands then disappearing into the torrid royal blue seas . . . .'
Cintio Vitier

She wasn't over-ample, nor especially wide-hipped, not even exotic-
ally brunette. Her eyes were not exactly Egyptian and her breasts
wouldn't squeeze into her neckline. She was eighteen years old and
– as her closest confidante the Pole would tell her – merely the soft-
touch lover of a fifty-nine-year-old bureaucrat. The 'tit fetishist' (in
Cuba, an ageing chaser of young girls) rented her a room containing
a Russian-manufactured colour television; promised her a video on
his return from the next foreign trip; and went to collect her in his
Lada from school, until she decided to abandon her studies. She
decided to abandon them in order to come closer to the legendary
BB. BB always acted contrariwise, when everyone was marrying, she
was divorcing, and now that everyone was divorcing, she wanted
matrimony to set the seal on her serious relationship. She'd read as
much in the latest *Paris-Match* the Pole had lent her.

She spent her days and nights alone. Her mother had given up on
her ever since she found out that her youngest daughter was sleeping
with her boss, with whom (in parentheses) she herself had
outrageously flirted, strictly in the interests of providing her
offspring with a better life. The old man took it upon himself to
convince her that her mother's spite was quite logical given her

double humiliation, as both mother and lover. Some future day she'd get over it, as time would tell, as it did so much. So she just kept reading and reading the books lent by the Pole. On his constant trips to Eastern Europe her Old Man only brought her cotton frocks, the cheapest make-up and unfashionable shoes. The Pole made fun of her, wondering where on earth she'd dredged up her fancy man.* The lack of a father might afford some explanation. The Pole never understood why she always acted so contrary, since amorous relations (in inverted commas) with bureaucrats had gone out of fashion; they didn't deliver and delivered less than ever now that there were cars but no petrol. And from one day to the next, they'd put their hands in the till, they'd get their marching orders, until bye-bye trips, and keep your pyjamas buttoned.

Her one and only friend was the Pole, her confessor and confidante. Now their game was called 'taking in laundry' and it meant finding a foreigner to marry. For the Pole this was easy, she'd studied and was a writer (although no one had ever seen a book by her), and she spoke English, Japanese, French, German, Italian, Hungarian, Russian and Esperanto, because you have to be ready for anything. One whiff of an Italian and the Pole was there. The French are very romantic, that's true, but they deliver up their Paloma Picasso, their two meals with oysters, then a look to leave with. The Spaniards sugar the pill with chorizos from the dollar shop. The Germans consider that the best form of payment is to perfect your accent. The Japanese massage your neck and press a photo album on you as they leave – the most generous adding, by way of ineradicable souvenirs, some of the most technologically advanced equipment on offer and some ear acupuncture to soothe anxiety. The English are all married and broke, and forever riddled with guilt. The Canadians go for the beach. Those from the former socialist camp were still unexplored territory, still no good at playing

---

*There's a Cuban saying, supposedly addressed to young girls, which onomatopoeically runs, 'Busca un temba que te mantenga' (Get yourself a forty-plus old lag to support you).

games. The Italians constituted a case apart. Yes, they married without preliminaries, a direct approach and without false promises of a Venetian palace. The Pole spoke from experience of numerous close friends who, after taking in laundry, had scaled great heights with the authentic heirs of Dante.

She was called Beatriz. She didn't want to stir, didn't want to do anything. She loved the Old Man, although she occasionally wished he were dead. She still didn't know what she did want. She slept a lot. It's true she was charmed by the taste of the chocolates the Pole introduced her to, the Baci, meaning in English 'kisses', each one wrapped in a verse from a different poet. Within a month she learned that the verses were repeated, but she also discovered many poets she'd never previously read, like Rimbaud for example. And she read and read, without preconception or pretension, which is the best way to read.

They were making a film about slavery in the Cathedral Square. The blacks, the heavyweights for over a quarter of a century, were endowing too great an authority on their role of slaves. Meanwhile, the fair moustachios, while intent on graduating in the Engineering Faculty, sabotaged the delicate minuets of their creole performance with rock and roll and coffee-stained pages of arithmetical calculations.

The blacks had no more notion of being slaves than the whites of playing masters. On top of everything, they'd gathered to learn how to move to a different rhythm. The Producer puffed herself up, twitching with nerves – the one thing no producer should ever be allowed to suffer from – dressed in period in order not to jar with the rest, frustrated over and over again with the repeated clambering up and down into the carriage, hand extended, very much the grande dame, striving to explain to the extras, the blackest in the city, how a nineteenth-century Andalusian lord would behave when confronted by the refined young lady who was preparing to descend, smothered in mother-of-pearl appliqué.

From there the rest absconded to an assembly of lunatics where they devoured frozen black beans. Others fled, ostensibly to a fictitious guard duty, in truth to a session of rum and dominoes.

It was now midday and the Director desired that at all costs the noontime tropical heat be converted into deepest night. To achieve this, she penned the actors up in a chapel and wafted sandalwood smoke around the place. The Assistant Director suffered a detached retina, and the place moved into a Leningrad June night, scented with antibiotics and decomposing cane liquor – emerald in its vase blown of Venetian glass.

Meanwhile Beatriz got dressed any-old-how. She pulled on a pair of boring Swedish clogs, gathered up thirty musty twenty-centavo coins, bunged the litre-size cut-glass perfume bottle into a Bally's shoe shop plastic carrier, and set off in search of yoghurt. And that was how she made her entrance, dressed in cotton stays and a skirt some five inches above the knee, her toenails painted a pearly white (one of the tit fetishist's requirements), her feet incarcerated in their northern wood, a strip of office cloth tying back her scraggy ponytail, bearing an old carrier bag, relic of a remote and expensive European furriers (the Pole always presented her with the wrappings to the presents she received); inside the carrier bag, having bribed the dairy assistant and jumped a queue that went the length of the block – the litre of curdled milk was in the process of reheating. Thus in the most fin-de-siècle style she could muster, Beatriz entered the slavery stage set without even noticing; and of course, being there, fucked it up.

'A present-day – blonde – Chinese . . . ?!' screeched the Director, panicking wildly.

At this point another sandalwood cloud erased Beatriz from the naturalistic scenery required by the actors' state of trance. The Producer rapidly crowned her with a shiny, frizzy black wig, coated her in brown stain, flung a white smock over her and even shoved a cigar in her mulatta's refined mouth. The bottle of yoghurt went from hand to hand and ended up hidden behind a bunch of green bananas, supposedly attached to the estate in that other period where mildew and machete strokes had implacably withered them.

Which was when, further on and seated at an ivory table resting on its bronze base, furiously meditating on her cup of lemon tea, Beatriz encountered the scruffy image of a fellow contemporary, chin cupped in the palm of a semi-open hand and elbow pressed into the eternity of a page. Beatriz registered that they resembled siblings or, more likely, those lovers who, with all that loving come to resemble one another, thus ending up loving themselves most of all, and eliminating the need for mirrors. Such a situation could never happen to the Old Man. No way.

First Beatriz lightly lifted her right foot from the verge of nothingness, then took a leap into durable reality. She fled beneath the waterspout of the fountain, casting off the trappings of the mestiza outfit. Nobody observed her departure, or maybe they thought it was merely an exquisite exit premeditated by the eye of the genius behind the camera lens.

Beatriz focused on the Contemporary, but realized that the most important matter in hand was to collect the yoghurt. She opened up her shawl and crawled on all fours towards the greengrocer's, where, taking advantage of the general uninterest, she seized her flask and once again slunk cat-like back to her epoch.

The Contemporary rested his eyes on the young woman dressed in filthy rags, now creeping towards his table with a Bally shoe-bag in her hand. It occurred to him to rhapsodize, 'What natural pearl is this in the sand!' and to note it down on the paper napkin stained with the tea sweating at the base of his cup. And he experienced a compelling desire to be invited down to the beach.

The young woman scrambled to her feet and spat out a small stone. She decided that the most sensible thing would be to put the litre of yoghurt on the table, sit down beside whoever was going to be her new friend and invite him to have a drink of it. Beatriz surprised herself at the rapid realization of her plan. The Contemporary refused her invitation with disdain. He made a suitably sweeping gesture, as if to say that neither tea nor yoghurt were the kind of fluids he enjoyed. Again, no way. Beatriz studied the pronounced 'r' of the Contemporary and it occurred to her that she'd struggled with that rolled consonant ever since childhood: 'R as in cig*a*r, R as in *barr*el; the *carr*iages *r*un *r*apidly on the *r*ailway tracks.' Her aunt had obliged her to recite the refrain through a mouthful of stones because she believed that vicars' r's could be cured just like stammering. The upshot was that Beatriz was left with the sensation that she was infinitely striving to spit out a wayward pebble which was preventing her from saying what she wanted.

She began to wax lyrical. Through reading she discovered the visionary trails laid open by words. She caught at images, romantically assuming that they could have been written for her. She had intermittently been bitten by the writing bug, but here again the Pole was way ahead of her, and so she pretended to forget about it, confusing even herself. She could never have been someone in another century who confused the state of being with the role of being. Being, against all odds, seduced her at least as much as surrendering to the possible in that unwonted terrain, egotistical and profound, of love and art. But she was definitively not an artist and had never fallen in love to the point of slicing her jugular. She loved the Old Man like she loved her mother, because he had been put there, there in her life. Putting herself in the precise position of a clairvoyant, she got it right second time around and proposed a trip to the seaside to her Contemporary.

They walked smartly over the cobbled surfaces of old-fashioned streets, seeking out the taxi avenue. They still hadn't figured out how to cope with walking side by side, still less when combining it with strenuously attempting to recount something sufficiently fascinating to rush them headlong into a profound mutual understanding.

He impertinently paraded his gift of being a foreigner, brandishing his jetlag in her face, rubbing in the ease with which he criss-crossed frontiers. He reported on the tragedy of a pistol duel with his best friend in one of Europe's most beautiful squares. That was what Beatriz wanted, a best friend. To play once more in a patio scented with the fragrance of scorched jasmine. He replied without a yes or a no. The Contemporary was hell-bent on marinating his lungs in the sea

air, bronzing himself 'in lost climates . . . swimming, walking
barefoot on grass . . .' He was quoting himself. Without exactly
meaning to, he spoke as though about to fall in love. Nor, for her part,
did Beatriz pursue him with this in mind. But a certain curiosity as
to who knew if . . .

'Are you married?' she asked calculatingly.

'I can't remember . . . What has that got to do with us?'

'I've got an old man. When I'm old, then I'll have a young one . . . '

'That's hardly original. You'll just be one more . . . '

'I know I'll always just be one more.'

'At last I've discovered someone I can exchange idiocies with.'

A chasm of interruptions swallowed up the magic of their
conversation. People were turning to look admiringly at this new
couple, even asking the time in order to fathom whether they were
tourists or not, checking out their accents. After this once-over, they
followed on another twenty metres behind, demanding peppermint
chewing gum to freshen their breath. Beatriz sealed their ears with a
strategically soft whistle, as though from a strangulated porcelain
doll. The frequent absence of intelligent conversation was rendering
her stupidly childish, artificially ingenuous. She had furthermore
observed how deliberately coming out with stupidities could be an
intelligent game. They were aware of the aroma of tilapia fish giving
rise to a distinct moistening of their lips. Between that smell lodged
in their clothes and the open rundown tenements, the dusty street
came to an end and they emerged on to asphalt and a fresh
dimension, sparkling with beer bottletops encrusted there over the
decades. The Contemporary attempted to hail passing taxis.

'Those are the "specials", they won't stop. Hold out a twenty-
dollar note – we call them draculas – and "specials" will appear out
of the blue, ready to take you to the ends of the earth. Or so says my
friend the Pole.'

'I don't have "draculas". Mine seem to be all "frankensteins".'

'Ah, so you have the hang of our slang. Brilliant,' Beatriz said
coldly. 'Get out your twenty dollars and you'll see.'

A minute later they were on their way to the eastern beaches, their complex currency stowed in the pocket of his linen trousers and the yoghurt fermenting in its plastic bag. The taxi driver agreed to take them on the clear understanding that he never got mixed up in business with whores. After a while he asked the Contemporary if he were a troglodyte. Beatriz, all too familiar with that kind of mistake, agreed that yes, her friend was a polyglot.

'In any case, it's all the same . . . you get my drift . . . you're in the business . . . ' and humming 'La vie en rose', he left them to discuss the weather and the remotest possibility of violent rains.

The taxi coasted the beach at full speed, running on adulterated bitumen. They felt the silent incandescence in their bones and the day slipping away without a move made. Beatriz listened quietly and the Contemporary moved only his lips, imperceptibly. Sweat flowed between breasts and groins. The taxi driver folded his hanky in four and, with one hand liberated from the steering wheel, he tied it around his neck, Mao-style. Super-macho, boldly daring, he at least was making moves, his shirt unbuttoned to the navel, displaying his hairy chest, thrusting it out to impress. Sweat had sapped the starch from his uniform, which (as he told them) his wife ironed and ironed like a workhorse for him. He felt sticky and spat out the brownish spittle of his last gulp of coffee.

Beatriz took another look at the Contemporary, but he was studying the countryside, grimacing as if refusing to acknowledge so much beauty all at once. They selected the beach furthest from the city and squealed to a halt there with a screech of rubber. The taxi driver apologized for exceeding the speed limit, reminding them that he could not go hungry all day long, without so much as warming his guts. There he dumped and overcharged them, and with one slam of the door sprung the intimation that on an island adventure is godlike.

Beatriz wanted to know more, but it troubled her to keep asking. She wanted to get on and get to bed, since in bed you can discover so much. They walked beneath the palms, collecting seaweed streamers and snail shells. Eventually they sat down on the seashore and she stripped off, exploiting their juvenile crisis. She was bent on converting this interlude in their lives into a black-and white film, scripted by Cocteau.

'I'm not undressing to be provocative, it's so you'll notice how my real beauty lies within . . . so that we may talk and wrestle with our thoughts, not with our bodies . . .' (She also delighted saying the opposite of what she was thinking.)

'That's sheer provocation, then,' he said, without appearing in the least nervous.

The Contemporary was either the desired presence or else a glass image, particularly constructed to reveal her secret, the reason she felt herself to be an historical attribute. And he was moving closer to her, without once registering the existence of her splendidly ambiguous body.

'Do you enjoy making love with an old man?'

She nodded hesitantly. 'I know you only get *half* the pleasure. Not during penetration, only when your clitoris is sucked. I know that you're still unaware of your body and of your desires.'

'When will I know them? What do you see in my body? You don't frighten me staring at my private parts like that.'

To him it wasn't private and he recounted in dissolute tones how he had burned out his emotions early on, with the single intention of avoiding compromising responses. He also told her how he had written the material essential to forging his soul in the most ardent proof of solitude, deciding not to single out any one object for his verses, burying them in their own rhythms. He decided to sell a role to himself: that of being someone else inside himself, in order to escape into his inner self, travelling with the reflexes of a champion who experiences the intimate pleasure of the boxer who ejaculates after knocking out his opponent. And Beatriz actually believed for a moment that she had captured an angel, only then the image of the Pole came into her head. Today she would try to be like her.

'Talking of ejaculation, I'm an expert in procuring them – with my mouth.'

He wasn't into that, to waste his seed fronting the sea and discovering a sucker, albeit one of fragile nakedness. He was voyaging to shake out the last ray of sunlight and to enter that fateful and blessed slumber of destiny there on the beach. Beatriz had confused making a friend with the perfect shaft of conquest. For her, perfection was a matter of first fucking and then loving. Without mercy. That much she'd learned from her Old Man.

'I'm thirsty,' he announced, looking for a café in the distance.

'D'you think I should study? I left school . . . '

'You study a lot, you spend your whole time reading. That's obvious from the wrinkles in your fingertips. Those who are self-taught clench their fists and sleep in a foetal position with their hand in their crotch and . . . surround themselves with older companions . . . the reason is the lack of teachers. You don't belong to the classroom but to the world . . . You see? I find it intriguing to play the imbecile . . . I'm thirsty!'

The yoghurt in its plastic carrier had been forgotten in the car and there were no signs of tourist oases in their surroundings. The world seemed a worse place for those obliged to be irredeemably traversing it, and the Contemporary remembered his time as a bum when he ate leftovers from the rubbish bins of the rich, inhaled damaging substances and slept under Parisian bridges in a state of bestial inebriation. The girl was sucking her middle finger, causing saliva to wet his lips. But not even this technique, apparently intelligently undertaken, managed to move the Contemporary in an erotic direction, given his further consideration that a kiss delayed the pleasures of caresses and that gentle friction was the prelude to an imminent erection.

'You're one of those women without a man, because you behave like a man, and that scares men away.'

'Are you homosexual?'

'You see? Ardour and impulse will forever complicate your chances of communicating with others. We're too boring a planet for that kind of question.'

'I think I'm bisexual but I've never done it with a woman . . . the very thought makes me all jittery! The Old Man suggested it once, but . . .'

'Please. There are things one doesn't discuss.'

'I haven't any friends, that's why I'm telling you all this. I spend days on end without speaking to anyone. In peace, solitude and dumbness.'

Beatriz began to whimper quietly, taking up fistfuls of sand and throwing them angrily away from her. The Old Man had forbidden her to go out with her lifelong friends, arguing that they were too effeminate and that he didn't want to see them there in that room he paid for out of his own pocket. As for fag hags, you should know them for what they are, cruising, upfront dykes, and it didn't suit him to be associated with such a trendy group, he was too old for all of that.

Anyway, one noon – the Old Man made love at noon because he was on a diet and never swallowed a mouthful during the morning – one noon, in the midst of a hysterically sadomasochistic destruction of Beatriz's fresh young body with pinches, bites, scratches, slaps and blows (his revenge on old age), the Old Man whispered a request so disconcerting about inserting her finger and calling him a whore that she could only uncomprehendingly reply with, 'Pardon?'

'Stick in your finger and call me a whore . . .'

Beatriz flung him off her, both feet together kicking him in the belly and in the direction of the mirrored wardrobe.

'So that's how you inform against my friends, you bribe them into becoming informers, driving them away from me, and now you're asking me to fuck your arse and call you a whore! Yes, that's it, you're no better than a whore, an old whore, how d'you like that?'

Beatriz was still more surprised when he didn't react; on the contrary, he kept his face pressed up against the mirror, as though wasted by the pleasures of urinating, he sighed and his cock sputtered a feeble dribble. She cried and cried. He went over to her, embracing and kissing her gently on the forehead.

'Thank you. You've achieved what no one else has managed in a long while, made me come like that on my own, just with insults . . . I'd like it if you hit me from time to time . . .'

Beatriz cried harder. No comfort was at hand since, worse still, the Old Man closed the conversation with the following words in a menacing tone, 'And let there be no mistake, I'm a real man, a proper macho.'

Beatriz cried and cried, for she realized the extent that most important people's brains are full of shit. And instinctively the one thing she did not want was to have her brains full of shit.

She stopped silently crying when she saw a figure pushing a cart off in the distance. Beatriz made frantic signals and the Salesman approached hastily towards his one aspiration: a sale.

'Red watermelons!' the Contemporary called out euphorically.

To which the Salesman added, almost mechanically, 'And tamales too, underneath the melons,' he explained, looking around conspiratorially. 'If you buy the tamales, please eat them discreetly, you know how things are, the whole hassle about the maize and where I get it, then the hassle about the pork and where I get *that* . . .'

The Salesman had the eyes of a cat and a skin like you see only in the photos in Italian fashion magazines. He was a classic macho beauty. No mystery, only beauty.

Contrary to the Contemporary's reaction, when the Salesman caught sight of Beatriz's nakedness, only semi-covered with sand, his candour was aroused and the smoothness of his looks dissolved in an excess of prophetic grimaces that went from the swelling of the veins in his neck to *that age-old skyward throbbing of the traitor below*. The Contemporary let out the most horrible guffaw and the crest dived for the floor. Not that amid all this the Salesman would admit defeat, but stood as ecstatic as a Greek bronze. It was then that Beatriz knew she could use him to catch her friend. But jealous intrigues didn't work with the Contemporary, who with all his worldly experience, already fully recovered from his fright, sat himself indolently down on her shirt and began devouring melons.

'Does nobody want a tamal? Give me one of your cigarettes,

French, they'll have to be French if you are . . .' The new-found presence was asking, shamelessly.

Chewing on the black melon seeds, the Contemporary poked around in his pockets and retrieved three proud filtered Gauloises. It was the first time she had smoked and she couldn't deny the intensity of the sensation.

'You, what's your line of work?' the Salesman asked Beatriz's friend.

'I'm not sure what you'd call work . . . I'm an ivory dealer.'

The other man's face lit up like the expression of a cat before a mirror; he kept exhaling mouthfuls of smoke and turned unpleasantly to Beatriz ominously, as if to inflict punishment, an air of warning that intimated, 'You're fucked, I'm going to devote my afternoon to this, I've spoilt your romp.' Then he continued, overbearingly interrogating the other. The other had entered a state of ecstasy, sucking noisily on the skins of the luscious fruit. The Contemporary answered him with actions and, feeling overladen with liquid, he lifted up his cock and pissed at the luminous heavens.

'So far and so high, with the pardon and absolution of the heliotropes . . . ' he finally pronounced, sighing deeply.

The Salesman couldn't concur in someone else peeing higher than himself, so he strained and failed, then hid his face against the burning sands and put the valour of his reputation as the conqueror of forbidden and frigid maidens into mourning.

Beatriz observed the sea with funereal laments, crushing the voluptuous temptation to coil herself around the waves. The sea appeared as an error, meaning death. She began to imagine she was an actress in the process of designing a new reality beholden to this existence. She stood and watched the sea and then, with renewed reluctance, those two midday bodies: one of which rejected her without knowing why and the other dying for the chance to touch her. She left them resigned to the sea air. Walking towards the water, she defended her premonitions.

This was what would be truly new for her, happening for the first time, even though it was sure to be repeated one day. Submerged to the top of her crown, she breathed alternately through her nose and her mouth, until instinct propelled her to the surface once more, coughing phlegm from between bruised lips. Nobody noticed her poor acting, or perhaps to put it more simply that she was such a weakling. Suicide is not accomplished with such deliberation, still less before two spectators of like calibre. Once recovered from reacting against the reflection of what she herself called her mediocrity, she swam underwater. She liked to think while she swam. Why was she still panting after love with the Contemporary? Why kill herself so theatrically? She swam until she hit a pair of knees blocking her passage. Brought up sharp against them, she emerged clutching that pubis, the chest, and the face of the Contemporary. His eyes were closed and he was laughing ironically.

'Bathe me, arouse me . . . I'm so weary of big cities, of stigma . . . . *merde*! Even the breeze causes me anguish, and still I live on inert, feeling more than ever the lack of a heart, as though it were a leg that they'd amputated . . . Valour is a bourgeois ruse, you put on a brave front and you're ready to kill. Give me a postmodern world to contradict them with . . . I'm weary, I want to write, sell red watermelons, to love . . . The fact is that I'm happy with weariness, that way I feel perfect, unique, envied and powerful. It's a lie: I loathe power, I loathe all of it! And a fist in the face by broad daylight is what they deserve. That's what I'd like to give them right now. I'm preoccupied with hating too much to feel love. I don't need to go gently, curses on all politicians and I'll never, never be happy . . . Melancholia is my protest . . . Bathe me, arouse me!'

Beatriz was scared by all this sounding suspiciously like anarchism, like nonconformity with the system, like voluntarism, but a few seconds later she reflected that perhaps it was his way to win over a woman. Beatriz stepped back just far enough to land him an indecisive punch.

'So why are you stripping off then?' the Salesman whispered to Beatriz, having silently swum up and caught her unexpectedly from behind. The Contemporary embraced them, sobbing theatrically, but suddenly his crying dried up in unleashed guffaws. This rapture so infected the others they threw him broadside into the waves, then pursued him, racing against each other, into the sparkling indigo sea.

Once detained, the Contemporary embraced them both again, first kissing Beatriz on the lips. Meanwhile, the Salesman licked his chops like the cat that got the cream. Then the Contemporary stared fixedly into the feline eyes of the Salesman and kissed him fiercely on his clenched, resistant lips. When he was himself once more, his opponent squared up to him and flung him a punch straight in the face. The Contemporary's nose streamed blood, darkening a rough, complaining sea. The Salesman grabbed the girl with one hand, pulled her away and issued a direct warning: 'Watch out, you'd better not trust this one. In your place, I'd call the police!'

Yet another one out to deceive her. Why not take it all transcendentally?

'Whoever told you that if one man kisses another it's necessary to inform the police? And don't the Russians kiss each other on the mouth? I've seen Gorbachov on television . . .'

'Ah, no, no! I never had too much time for our Soviet comrades, and now they're down, don't even mention either them or Gorbachov! My thing is the melons and tamales; he's your problem, and as for me, I'm off!'

The Salesman swam like lightning, then disappeared with his little handcart through the curtain of trembling palm fronds.

The pallid arm covered in light freckles stretched out and drew back a veil of sudden clouds. A storm of sewing needles impudently stitched a double horizon.

They waited, cut off on the shore, fearful of attracting the electricity of a lightning bolt through the contact of their feet with the shells. The cloud's silhouette was that of a cannon-ball and sped energetically along. The sky, and of course the sun's viscosity reappeared. The waters washed the wound. The sea green diluted over the Contemporary's face, accentuating his vanity. The girl invited him to return, tugging his hair, and he replied with a wave, although mentally paralysed.

'Let yourself be loved,' pleaded Beatriz.

For him to let himself be loved implied allowing himself to be dominated, and his aim was to profile the souls of others with an authoritatively bloody finger. The girl squeezed out her hair and knotted it at the base of her neck. She shrugged her shoulders and left him standing. She too then set off in the direction of the Victor.

Vertigo was suffocating the Contemporary. He celebrated his solitude in the middle of the sea, beating very gradual breast strokes in Beatriz's wake. When he reached her, he found her dressed and saltily sticky.

'I appreciate your homage to Kabuki. I too enjoy living theatrically. It's the best way to assume a double morality. For example, always indulge in a game whereby when someone says something to me, I switch it around so that I can more or less get the gist of what they really believe.'

'Do you need the truth?'

'Yes, it's a defect of mine.'

'I don't belong to this era and I urgently need to return to my own,' he muttered, gasping in the brine, his hair slipping over the blisters on his shoulders.

'Don't worry about it, and if one day they get around to interrogating me, I'll tell them it was all a dream.'

'And if it all was?'

'Then I'd be free of the interrogation. Who's interested in dreams?'

They walked towards the bus stop.

'Beatriz, it was a pleasure to accompany you to the beach and to get to know you.'

'You don't know me. For me too it was a pleasure. It's the first time I've seen a poet's face. They hardly ever – almost never – appear on television.'

Once it arrived, the crowd swept them hungrily down the bus, fighting for space inside. The human tide found in their favour and they clambered horizontally on board through the window. In the blink of an eye they were squashed in like sardines in a tin, crushed beneath sandy armpits and greasy jaws. The doors concertinaed around the last passenger's back, who, although he wasn't deaf, found it necessary to blow his mind with a transistor on at full volume pressed to his ear.

'Tell me if you found in my past . . .'

The Contemporary attempted to explain: 'Poets are afflicted with an endemic disease. When invited to appear on television, they become invisible before the cameras, just like vampires before mirrors, no one can bear confronting the invisible. It'll be the cause of the next war. I arrived courtesy of the dreams of the film director . . . I'm a tourist of chance, of the imagination.'

'A reason for forgetting or for loving me . . . '

The sound of the undulating sweet sugar-cane field released scented memories of crinkled baobabs. Beatriz didn't hear the Contemporary's voice, bellowing in her ear, 'I don't belong to any particular space . . . I dare to set about revolutionizing the world too precociously . . . revolutionizing the world through the verses of an inspired adolescent. Who would have thought it!'

Astounded by the indifferent response he'd precipitated in intellectual circles, he then retired to Africa to trade in ivory. Beatriz longed to boast: 'These things happen. Look at Rimbaud.'

'That's me. The other. That was when time exploded in my brain.'

Benny Moré,* the one and only, sang on soothingly, beguilingly, insinuatingly.

'You ask forgiveness . . .'

In the future someone would dream of transporting him with a load of slaves to the set of a film being made on a deluded island. The Cinema Director's dream had been so authentic that the punishment dictated by rheumatic visions was to fail in its

---

*An enormously popular romantic balladeer and dance singer of the 1940s and 1950s.

consecration, fragmenting its impact by scattering the characters across different centuries. Why did he always have to be defending himself?

'That's why I transgressed another dreamlike desire: yours.'

'The Cinema Director maybe, but me, what have I in common with you if all you tell me is true?'

'Curiosity. Knowledge.'

'*If it suits you . . .*'

Compelled by impulse. Cursed be he who puts a break on an angel's dreams. Beatriz knew that she had something in common with him in at least one respect: the two of them were ambitious and poorly regarded among others who are neither clear-headed nor over-concerned as to where their ambitions are heading. Overly metaphysical. Beatriz felt she was going for the dealer like the last hair on a bald man's head, a point of no return. The Contemporary was so flesh and blood, he strode across the paving stones with such energy, that he cut the breeze, and it occurred to her that perhaps the Cinema Director and she only existed in his dreams. Tourists from the past passing through the mind drugged by the desire to peer into the far beyond.

On the other hand, the dead had never appeared to her as they had to the Pole, who frequently told her of it. But in the here and now she trembled with a fierce aversion to squandering the opportunity to catch hold of an affair, because whichever way, one of them must be the other's dream. And what was it she wanted? Love or adventure? Naturally there's no difference, this much she knew thanks to the encounter. But never with him. Nor with the Old Man. Lately things had been happening to her, that from there on in, she thereafter couldn't share with anyone. Life was becoming a big secret. She was going to be alone after all.

And why do we rush around here and there, forever looking for love? Never again, that was what she wanted to think: never to be thought of again. Only two things were clear to her: did she understand love, did she understand death? Was it necessary to understand or was it simply something that occurred some time after an immediate and terrible now? And why was she worrying over understanding, she who had never attempted to understand anything? If the Old Man had found out about this, he'd have flayed her alive, not for having gone off to the beach with someone else, but because that someone else was a foreigner, and above all because he couldn't stand women who thought for themselves.

'*Don't call what you have a heart . . .* '

They got out of the bus and retraced their steps to the film set. The guy with the radio followed closely behind them.

'Does it also bother you they dragged it out of you that you've virtually no past, that you can only express yourself when life's daily violences force you to?'

'Beatriz, people are entirely composed of their pasts.'

'In which case, what the hell is the future?'

'A fabrication to distract us.'

'You depress me.'

They had arrived. The Cinema Director opened her notebook and wrote the most exquisite last page.

'*You ask me about my past, what it was like . . .*'

The Contemporary also jotted his final sentence down in his notebook. Then he shut it for ever, not one line too many between its covers.

'*Before loving you have to have faith . . .*'

The same present-day characters masked with the past welcomed them in a sandalwood haze. Serene and ambiguous slaves let their masters' arms slip around their hips. Laced in their stays, aristocratic ladies indulged beneath the crushing bondage of their corsets. Under duress.

'*Surrendering life for love . . .*'

The Contemporary handed his notebook to Beatriz. She read its title with surprise: *Mauvais Sang*. And the dedication: *For Beatriz, who is me, solitary and future.* And his enigmatic signature. And a date from the past.

'It's for your eyes only. Just like with television, anyone else who looks at its pages will find them blank.'

And he smiled. The Cinema Director gave the order to get on set and everyone scurried to their posts. The Producer swelled up, fearing a lack of respect from outside the epoch. The Assistant, suddenly aroused by a mouthful of salad dressing, grunted loudly on finding that someone had cut down on the mayonnaise in his tea-time sandwich. And life ground into gear, without dreams, without . . .

'*Without dying, that's caring, that's something you don't possess . . .*'

Beatriz gave her friend a shove in the back, a gilded postmodern foot assailing a vertical reality.

'*To love I don't need a reason . . .*'

Beatriz by now no longer wished to let herself be loved.

'Another contemporary. Cut!' shouted the Director, her feet on the ground.

As reality advanced, more members were lost in the admiration of angels. And he took the lad by the hand, extricating him from his slave make-up. Seated together at the marble table with its bronze base, he there erased it with a drop of tea, as easily as unpinning the wings of an angel.

'*I'm overwhelmed, so overwhelmed, my heart.*'

The Contemporary stood petrified within the Fantin-Latour portrait, utterly hysterical, uncomprehending, repenting of his return. Only Beatriz could see him.

Beatriz witnessed a fabulous ambition. She extended her arm and pulled the cloud aside. She readied herself to approve the obligatory subject. Double Standards. She'd never been a good student. It all left her pretty cold. But at heart, at heart she knew it was important to derive the maximum possible from it.

She flipped back her seat and made out she'd only just noticed that she'd escaped to the cinema with the money intended to buy yoghurt. That was why she loathed money, it always rendered her guilty. She pretended to leave the cinema humming a tune that had nothing to do with the film. Or maybe it did.

She began to feel or to make believe she felt a need for something trifling and bought herself an ice cream. She was alone, sweaty and blameworthy, and the seaside didn't suit her. She convinced herself that she was seeking a thousand pretexts for going into a bookshop, or for listening to the entire classical repertoire of the planet, to go and see someone, to dance, or even return to the cinema.

She kept chewing it over. Love. Love. Forgetting that love couldn't exist because nobody had a quiet spot to look themselves in the eye any longer. Lost because of a dream, because of a film, because of reality. Because of herself. She made as if she repeated this last phrase to herself because it was healthier to develop awareness and a spirit of self-criticism.

She chucked aside her ice-cream cone. Plenty of people were watching her despite the fact that she had cast it aside calmly, thoughtfully, in slow motion. Beatrice pretended to be looking for a way out. Out of herself or out of where? She affected to be looking for the answer in herself.

In any case, loneliness was the Old Man making love with a pornographic magazine between them, the constant and impatient anxiety. Loneliness was avarice, not ambition. Even a foreign fan was loneliness.

She went into a café, bought cigarettes, smoked in order to be even more bored with herself, to feign the passing of time, as though she were watching its flight. She couldn't even let the Pole in on what had happened. She'd only make fun of her: a fuck for a book of poetry, hilarious! The Old Man would have to be informed that his lover had been in contact with a bisexual Frenchman, and a writer at that! They would oblige her to answer for herself. To flee. She wouldn't respond. And she wouldn't flee. Now she would learn the full extent of her strength. Putting it into operation wasn't a game. It could break her. No.

TRANSLATED BY AMANDA HOPKINSON

Wunderbar
Jesús Vega

He woke up suddenly frightened by the sound of a can, filled with water, hitting the ground. A faint light was filtering in through the cracks in his room. It must already be late if the sun was reaching that far up the wall. And after he'd told his aunt to wake him up at eight o'clock that morning.

He could hear the rattle of cans, and people talking, coming from outside. The daily hustle and bustle of Old Havana's arid backstreets. He stumbled around in the gloom and found his trousers. He pulled them on in one go and put his trainers on. He opened the door and looked at his watch. Half-past twelve. He belched and the bitter taste left in the back of his throat reminded him that he'd overdone the rum the night before.

He ran to the wash house and, ignoring the protests of two old women doing their laundry, plunged his hands into the first tub he came across to wash his face. He went back to his room and dried himself with the towel hung on a peg. Just at that moment in walked Auntie, carrying a bag of chives, and opened her volley of abuse. No, she hadn't woken him up because he should mend his ways and find himself an honest job, she'd had enough of him pissing about, he was twenty-three years old now and what would his mother say if she were alive to see what a layabout he'd turned out to be. It was the same old sermon as always, which he cut short with an abrupt, 'I'm goin' out.'

He left without even looking at Auntie, putting on his Atlanta University T-shirt as the old women carried on like a scratched record behind him. 'Just my fucking luck,' he said to himself. The day had got off to a bad start. He set off for the San Juan de Dios park, almost running the two blocks it took to get there. He came out by the hospital in Empedrado. No sign of Jábico. He got fed up with waiting for him and headed for the Bodeguita.

He walked towards the cathedral, and as he neared the Bodeguita the smell of pork scratchings reached him and went straight to his stomach. He hadn't even had a coffee with his aunt going on at him like that. Inside the bar guitarists were already playing and the clamour increased as the spirits began to take effect. Jábico would be in there, waiting for him, with the money from the deal. Three hundred and fifty dollars, half. Hopefully, and then he'd invite him to have lunch.

He went into the Bodeguita and searched among the tourists, all crammed together into a small space with whores and their pimps. He looked over the bar towards the packed restaurant and saw him walk in very slowly, followed by a deadly serious-looking man. He tried to catch Jábico's eye, but he kept staring straight ahead, as if he was trying to tell him that something was up.

'Shit, they've caught Jábico!' he said, lying low in his corner, as they bundled him into a police car that hadn't been parked outside earlier, when he'd got to the Bodeguita. Crap luck, Jábico banged up and he didn't have a bean on him. He hid in the crowd as soon as he spotted Jábico's escort, who had come back in, as though he was looking for someone else. 'They never give up,' he thought. 'They're addicted to nicking people.' Suddenly the man began to head in his direction. At least he gave that impression. What if they were looking for him? There was no escape.

Without warning, a woman's voice whispered, 'Sprecken zi doytch?' He turned towards her as though she were his last port in this storm. She was an incredibly fat and ugly woman with dyed blonde hair obligingly flashing a set of gold-capped teeth his way. He had no choice but to answer her in broken English, picked up on the street, until the policeman left again by the front door.

The woman was German and she handed him a mojito while she introduced him to two other women the same age. 'Ernesto, glat to meyt yu,' he responded primly. They all laughed when they noticed his guardian angel was stroking his brown biceps and exclaiming, 'Wunderbar, wunderbar, marvellous!'

He was focusing his mind on getting out of there even before he had completely recovered from the shock. They were on their third round of mojitos and his head was already starting to feel like a basketball. But it was the old women touching him and laughing that was really pissing him off. And still no sign of lunch. And the restaurant smelt better than ever. 'Old cows,' he thought. He took a decision and quickly got up from the bench, ready to leave with any old excuse. But his move was aped by the tourists, who apparently didn't want to let him go. His newly acquired friend paid, while the other two took him by the arm, inviting him outside for a photo.

Ernesto reluctantly consented, planning, as a last resort, to make a quick exit via Empedrado with one of their purses, to compensate for Jábico being arrested with his money. He didn't like stealing but at that moment he had no alternative; he hadn't eaten a square meal since Auntie had sounded off at him. He looked to see where he'd find the most lucrative purse and looked over to the swing door to check the situation outside. He pulled away from one of the German women so he could make an easy escape. A group of Italians was obstructing the doorway. The German woman rummaged in her bag for her camera. He should grab his chance. He'd at least get the Nikon, if not the purse.

He tried to get in front and bumped into one of the Italians out on the street. A perfect moment for creating confusion. But his sixth sense told him it was dodgy. He looked above the crowd and spotted two policemen lurking at the end of a cobbled alley. He clutched the German woman's arm more tightly and they all posed for a nice group photo.

Still blinded by the flash, he started to walk slowly, not hearing, just listening to what the fat old German woman, who had gone back on the attack, was saying about Munich, about the cathedral and the heat. They finally reached a hired car which they clambered into amid laughter and comments in German. They turned into Empedrado and went in search of the Malecón. The old girl whispered to him that they were off to Playa Hermosa. He was so hungry his head was spinning. With a bit of luck he might get a lobster bake and a can of beer out of it. Or a pair of jeans or, at the very least, a bottle of whisky. After fucking the old dear, of course.

Anyway, he could always escape before they got to the tunnel. If they stopped he would open the door and make a run for it. But they went through the tunnel at about a hundred and twenty and he couldn't make his move. No one escaped the old girl alive.

He leaned back in the seat, closed his eyes and prayed to the saints, oblivious to the chatter of the old women who had momentarily forgotten he existed. Next to him the fat old girl was repeating 'Wunderbar, wunderbar' as she stroked his nose with her finger.

He drifted off into the land of the just, as they say, wondering what the hell the old girl meant by all that vunderbaring. After all, Jábico would be having a worse time down at the station, or the Special Investigations Department.

TRANSLATED BY CLARE HASKINS

Ask The Good Lord
Marilyn Bobes

Damned woman, if you really want to know
all the misery you've put me through
lift your eyes up to the skies
and there, at heaven's gate, ask the Lord
ask the good Lord about my pain.
a Cuban song

I

Iluminada Peña got to know Jacques Dupuis during a night of disappointments on Havana's Malecón esplanade. Her eyes were weepy, her make-up smudged and she was wearing a Lycra dress that daringly exposed her back. It was a special dress for her: its yellow hue showed off the coppery tones in her skin and her pitch-black ringlets; the hugging cut of the cloth permitted you to visualize her slender figure, with its solid hips and finely turned and tuned extremities. Despite everything her grandmother had spent to obtain the garment from a black-marketeer, Bebo still refused to show willing to take on Iluminada as his regular partner on the dance floor at the Tropical.

II

Yanai, I've been in Tulus for four days now and I miss you more than I would have dreamed possible. It's very pretty here but I'm bored, yes, I'm really bored. Last weekend Jacques took me to a church to hear music for the dead and I fell sound asleep. Then we went on to eat, but the restaurant didn't have a roof over it and I nearly froze. Jacques says that if I'm feeling the cold now, over the summer, he doesn't know what'll become of me when winter comes. Yesterday I met Nadin, the woman who used to be Jacques's wife. We went to dinner with her and her new husband. Jacques doesn't find anything wrong in being friends with a woman who went off and cheated on him. He even treats that Fransua quite normally, and he was the guy she cheated on him with. If my Mum, finds out, she'd say that it proves how depraved all the French are. Better not to mention it to her. Not this or any of the other sordid details I reveal in my other letters. During that famous dinner I tried to talk French, but I couldn't. They served such small portions of food that I was still hungry afterwards. I asked for a beer to go with it, because the wine over here gives me a bellyache and a strange sensation of heaviness, but Nadin said that bier was a funny custom among Germans mal eleve. Well, I know that mal eleve means badly brought up and although she mentioned Germans it seemed obvious to me that she was saying so on my account, so I shot her a sidelong look. Immediately Jacques placed his hand on my thigh, as though shocked at my rudeness.

III

Jacques Dupuis quietly approached the sea wall and, after gazing out to sea, asked Iluminada Peña about Ze Castle of ze King Tigairs of ze Morro. She had hesitated before replying: she resented the whole business with foreigners even more since that horrible experience at the Hemingway Marina.

IV

It was my own fault that a porcelain vase got broken this morning. Madame Dupuis had such an attack of hysteria that after jabbering on in her incomprehensible French, she retired to her room to weep. Jacques spent the afternoon attempting to stick the pieces together and then had a go at me because he says that I'm always rushing down the stairs. Tonight I saw Lady Diana on television. You know what all the magazines say about her, she acts as if butter wouldn't melt in her mouth, gives herself the airs of a proper lady and pretends like she's walking on eggshells, I swear. Madame Dupuis tracked me down to tell me, the old fart face, 'Tu regard? Si com sa.' I almost wished her in hell. And to cap it all, I've been dreaming about Bebo. I don't know why he appears to me, now I'm living here in France. Jacques is my husband and he's a good man. His one defect is that he lets his mother dominate him. But my own mum and my grandma – the people who love me most in all the world – say I made the right choice. And I think they're right.

V

Before getting to know Jacques Dupuis, and accepting his first invitation and the caresses that came with it, Iluminada Peña had had only one foray with someone from overseas. It happened one day when Bebo left her in the lurch in the middle of a power cut. Consumed with boredom, by the light of an oil-lamp, she listened to her mother and grandmother complaining of the lack of food – and then Yanai's invitation arrived. Her friend appeared with a couple of Spaniards in a rented Toyota which took them all the way to the Hemingway Marina. There Iluminada discovered how on that very yachting wharf, to the west of Havana, an old North American writer had fished for eels back in the 1950s. Yes, it was Hemingway. Iluminada had read a bit of *The Old Man and the Sea* during her second year of secondary school, before wearying of all those books. But now the Hemingway Marina was filled with hotels, discotheques and tourist shops.

According to Yanai, the Spaniards were a couple of slavering fifty-somethings who shouted at one another, flushed with rum and the beachy sun. Iluminada felt uncomfortable from the start and on the stroke of eleven o'clock, tired of dodging the bulk of a lecherous barrel-belly assiduously promising her skin creams and bath soaps in return for a few hours of bliss, she decided to fake a toothache and abandon all the booty to Yanai. She returned alone to her flatlet in the block called Neptune and his Trident. The resumption of electricity was just then being hailed by a crowd applauding and whistling. She was satisfied at simply getting in to see the closing scenes of the Saturday night movie: the one where Glenn Close, in a resurrection worthy of Christ Himself, suddenly emerges from the bath, knife in hand, ready to defend *her* bliss.

VI

Yesterday I received your letter and it made me really happy and also really sad. As to what you were saying about keeping my patience with Jacques's mother, you just don't know her. That woman is a total disaster zone, Yanai. After she'd seen I only wore the clothes Jacques bought me in Havana and not the old rags she'd put in the wardrobe, she turned up today with a parcel. 'Vuala, she said, zis iz for you since you dress az a clochard.' I looked up clochard in the dictionary and it means a tramp. You should have seen her there, she was shameless. I couldn't stand it any more, so I grabbed a scrap of paper and wrote seven times over: Adele Dupuis, Adele Dupuis, Adele Dupuis, Adele Dupuis, Adele Dupuis, Adele Dupuis, Adele Dupuis and put it into the freezer. So she wouldn't fuck me about again. If you can please go and ask my godmother Clarita what else we can do to neutralize her. Preferably something simple, as I'd find it really hard to get hold of black hens, coconuts or cooking plantains. The only plantains you see around these parts are the ones you eat raw. Tell me if all you lot at home are now eating well on the money I'm sending back. Don't you think it comes easy. Over here people are really stingy and spend their lives saving up. You're right not to tell grandma all about what's going on here. I know how to look after myself and the situation is far worse for them over there. Don't forget to go and see Clarita and let me know what she says as soon as you can.

VI

The night they met, Jacques Dupuis invited her to the Divine Shepherd, a restaurant that Iluminada Peña could never have entered even in her wildest dreams. They sat down at a table from where they could view a large slice of the city. He improvised a map on the napkin and showed her exactly where they were. Iluminada then understood why she could now see the Malecón as if from a boat: from the sea to land, rather than looking outwards from the sea wall. It was the first time Iluminada had contemplated Havana, or at least the Havana on all the postcards. There was the hillside of Zulueta and the hole into the tunnel, and the peeling buildings adjacent to the resplendent Spanish Embassy.

VIII

I'm writing because today is the holy day of Our Lady of Charity of El Cobre and I'm feeling quite desperate. Jacques is away on a trip and I'm so bored. From time to time I go out and look at the shops, without even daring to go inside. This country is full of racists and most of them are shop assistants. I only have to approach their wares and they park themselves alongside them as if I were about to commit a robbery. It's different when I go out with Jacques, but when I decided to go to the cinema alone last week, two policemen pulled me up and went through my handbag paper by paper. Do you remember how Bebo reacted when there were those scenes in the Tropical and the police went in demanding everyone's identity papers? Well, that's nothing to what they get up to here. Here you keep to the straight and narrow, or else. If you so much as scowl, they'll cart you off and even beat you up, most of all if you're foreign. An African woman who lived around here was thrown out of France for good for having a go at a cop. And I've heard it's as bad, or even worse, in Spain. That's why, Yanai, I'm telling you, think carefully about what may happen to you in the future if you marry a Spaniard. In any case, don't waste too much pity on me, Jacques is a good man who treats me with respect. When I compare him with Bebo I realize that he only wanted me for you-know-what and never gave me a thing. Make sure you write back at once and tell me about everyone at home.

IX

Jacques Dupuis and Iluminada Peña first made love in a splendid suite at the National Hotel. It was good for her, if not quite as good as with Bebo, but more gentle. Although he came quickly, he embraced and held her against his body for a long while. In time, Iluminada was to learn that this was called tendresse. It was what she most liked about Jacques: la tendresse.

The Sunday before he departed, he asked her to marry him. They were relaxing under a beach parasol, after a succulent meal on the sands of Varadero. Iluminada brought him home to meet her family and, affected by the lack of so many consumer goods in their home, Jacques made strenuous efforts to provide them with whatever he could manage to find.

On the flight back to Toulouse, Jacques never for a single instant stopped fingering the final settlement on those decisive holidays in his battered briefcase, a bald statement on which could be read: Received from Jacques Dupuis the sum of seven hundred and twenty dollars for the procedures of marriage and naturalization. Havana, 28 December 1991.

X

*My friend, I did everything you said regarding Clarita's advice and here
are the results. I put lily petals in the bathwater and threw eggs at the door
through which the old woman had to enter. She was really worried, in her
deliberations about who could have made such a cochinerie, but since she
doesn't know anything about African gods, it never crossed her mind I might
have been behind it. Lately I've been spending a fair bit of time alone with
Madame Dupuis. Jacques is travelling a lot. You know he's a rep for an
agency which takes tourists over to Cuba and I can't always go with him.
Underneath it all I'm delighted, because every time I go to one of those
business dinners I feel like a bull in a china shop, and I have endless
problems with the place settings and all that French etiquette. And after
every one of those meals, Jacques ends up going wild. So it's better if I
don't go along any more. He's also after telling me that I need to lose weight.
I'd always thought he liked me the way I am, you know you can tell these
things in bed, but then when we frequent all those places where I keep seeing
Frenchwomen thin as broomsticks, I can tell it makes him uncomfortable to
see me attracting so much attention.*

*Now to my news: in December, we're coming to Cuba. That's news to
keep me awake at night. Sometimes I even dream that Jacques and I will
be coming to live over there. The other day I hinted at it to him. I thought
he'd be pleased, considering that he was a revolutionary in the days of that
Revolution they had back in '68. Some hope: I merely mentioned the
thought of our going to live in Cuba one day and he pulled such a terrifying
face that I froze over completely. And to tell you the truth, I wasn't exactly
pleased. If Cuba had more goods and they could get rid of the power cuts,
it would be a place a thousand times better than this Tulus, crammed with
wicked and selfish people, who look down on you according to what you've
got, not for what you're worth. And on top of it all, they're a boring lot,
don't have any decent beaches, don't know how to dance, never say what
they mean and are stingy to boot. You'll find out when you get to know
them, Yanai, if you marry your Spanish boyfriend.*

XI

Iluminada Dupuis is on Havana's Malecón once more, her eyes once more brimming with tears, wearing a flowery dress with velvet sleeves and gossamer across the low neck over a wide, black skirt. Yanai is at her side, also laughing and crying and praising Iluminada's elegant clothes and new hairstyle, you're so beautiful, you're a real queen and with a Frenchman in the palm of your hand, crazy about you, yours and yours alone, that much you can tell, my friend. How lucky you are – what luck! Iluminada Dupuis smiles with ineffable sadness. Yanai, at least, can't comprehend it, takes great pains in spreading a scarf out on the damp cement so her friend won't damage her clothes, her lovely and elegant clothes, while Iluminada runs her eyes across the twilit barrio and learns that Bebo is now in prison, they caught him stealing cotton wool from a hospital. Other young women are flagging down the tourist cars passing along the Malecón and a lump rises in Iluminada's throat when Yanai tells her that the Spaniard never returned, he sent me twenty dollars as a Christmas present in with the card, just imagine, twenty dollars, and Iluminada weeps without knowing whether it's for her friend or for Bebo or for her grandma or for her mother or for the room they've kept empty, except when it's sporadically let to Yanai's foreign friends.

XII

Yanai, I'm leaving for Havana on Tuesday. My friend, I've never before in my whole life felt such a jumping in my chest, such longing to see my people. My God, Yanai, I can't even tell you. You'll be thrilled with the blouse I'm bringing you. Oh, how I love you, Yanai, how I love all of you so much.

XIII

Iluminada surveys Havana again. The spray from a wave splashes her and the lustre of the Morro fortress inundates her body with its raw brilliance. The dark sea spread before her. Iluminada watches it in silence, looking out from the still-dark city. A few metres away from the wall, entangled and stumbling, two drunks sing and bawl abuse at a hooker, inviting her on an impossible voyage to the very heavens. 'Ask the good Lord, ask the good Lord,' chorus the drunks' wavering voices. Yanai looks at them and winks. Iluminada shivers. 'I'm leaving tomorrow,' she announces flatly, and her friend hangs round her neck and Iluminada smells her cheap perfume, suffering that this scent will no longer belong to her.

TRANSLATED BY AMANDA HOPKINSON

Epilogue

Explosion of Emptiness
Severo Sarduy

I

The senses transcended, *obscured*. Also understanding: 'All that the imagination can imagine and the understanding can receive and understand in this life is not, nor can serve as, a means of union with God.

Only by blinding oneself to all paths can one see the *ray of darkness*, a ray whose illumination the subject transmits unawares. 'And thus it is that contemplation, whereby the understanding has the loftiest knowledge of God, is called mystical theology, which signifies secret wisdom of God; for it is secret *even to the understanding that receives it*. For that reason Saint Dionysius calls it a *ray of darkness*. The prophet Baruch says (3.23): *There is none that knoweth its way, nor any that can imagine of its paths*. Clearly, then, the understanding must be blinded to all paths open to it in order to unite with God.'

San Juan de la Cruz, *Ascent of Mount Carmel*, Chapter 8, paragraph 6, tr. E. Allison Peers.

II

Written in exile, when I can't sleep: So many books that nobody has read, so many meticulous paintings – bringing me to the edge of blindness – that no collector has bought nor any museum sought; so much ardor that no body has calmed.
'My life' – I tell myself, deliberating pre-posthumously – 'has had no *telos*. No purpose nor destiny has unfolded in its passing.'

But immediately I correct myself: 'Yes, it has. How can one not see in this succession of frustrations, failures, illnesses and abandonments the repeated blows of God's hand?'

III

Simple-minded and stubborn, we pray to the gods to abandon their detachment and to reveal themselves. We long for miracles, ecstasy, the gift of inexplicable objects, fragrances, resurrections, a sense of His presence. Or simply a harmony, a reason.

Naïve mysticism. The divinity's being is *precisely* what is not manifest, what does not have access to the world of phenomena or to perception. Not even as an immaterial presence or 'intuition' of the mystical. We ask them, finally, to renounce their essence and to *be* in ours, which is our gaze.

But it's useless.

They never abandon that night, that black hole that devoured them forever.

IV

Despite everything, I still believe in God. Whom else can we call upon to curse our enemies? Even though God is so indifferent to human language that He can give me only a generic Blessing.

V

Morandi: those whitewashed bottles, those mute vases reach us, in a sense fall from the night of the non-manifest. They have put aside for a moment their firm reticence toward the visible, their absolute principle not to appear.

Soon they return to their chaos, battered by that brief residence in the gaze, refracting the day's screeching glare, the definition of every line, the explosion of color. The light.

VI

A work of art, exceptional or not, requires brilliant adjectives, syntactical surprises, the invention or play of words: a display of techniques whose finality is to dazzle the reader.

The sublime work – which does not bestow *night* for an instant but rather leaves the trace of its long sojourn in non-being – is rudimentary, incompetent, streaked with rough spots, faded, always flat.

Thus San Juan's *Spiritual Canticle* contains the most repellent cacophony in the history of the Spanish language, *un no sé qué que quedan balbuciendo* – a stammering stuttering God knows what.

It doesn't matter. God, who dictated the other verses, erased that babble. With one blow.

VII

Marcel Duchamp, John Cage, Octavio Paz: they all worked with the imitation of nature. Not its appearance of course – realism's naïve project – but rather its *functioning*. Exploit chaos, invoke chance, insist on the imperceptible, privilege the unfinished. Alternate the strong, continuous and virile with the interrupted and the feminine. Dramatize the unity of all phenomena.

Forget the rest. But there is no rest.

VIII

Cioran – we must acknowledge – is disillusioned with everything. Disenchanted. Back from it all. Fed up with Man and his criminal initiatives, with Literature and its tricks, with the Parisian crowd and its intrigues.

He lives alone. Never sees anyone or gives interviews. Publishes very little. When he is spoken to he's very friendly but never eloquent.

Even so, when you read him attentively something is unequivocally evident: the quality and propriety of his style, the elegance – inspired by the French eighteenth century – of his sentences, as if those brief aphorisms that constitute his work were carved out of insomnia and out of the perfection emanating so frequently from him, refined time and again. Something persists, then, beyond total despair: a faith. In language and its faculties. In the word.

It is in this light that we need to interpret the final silence of the Buddha.

IX

When the sun returned, it was already late. Late in the day though not in his life, he managed to see that light he had desired so much. And the sea. And the naked castles. And perhaps in Collioure, an open window.

X

Defended, walled up by solitude and silence. Last hope: to refrain from becoming embittered with remorse, desires for revenge, yearnings for survival or annihilation, recapitulations, fears.

Take the step without any backdrop, without pathos. In the most neutral way. Almost calmly.

XI

Fires shining for San Juan de la Cruz. Maybe that's what death is: burning, turning to ashes, being blinded by the crackling sparks of that light. As if someone were stirring the flames both within and without our body, until it's consumed.

Burning. Ardor.

In order to enter another light, to become that light. An immaterial light, impenetrable to vibration, weightless, colorless, alien to the sun and to the iris. Uncreated, edgeless, with neither beginning nor end.

Light: San Juan (Book II, Chapter 9) quotes David (*Sol*, 17, 10): 'He set darkness under His feet. And He rose upon the cherubim, and flew upon the wings of the wind. And He made darkness, and the dark water, His hiding-place.'

He points out, some paragraphs later, that among the fantasies or imaginings to which the understanding lends credence is *considering or imagining glory as a beautiful light*.

XII

Radical conclusion, extreme negation. Fog closing in. Senses and understanding blockaded against everything which can deviate from the unknown, unrepresentable road, inaccessible to any enunciation or glimmer of anything else, the road to the inconceivable, to that absence of attributes which language's vulgarity might refer to as *Union*.

Unknown then both goal and path: 'In order to arrive at that which thou knowest not, Thou must go by a way that thou knowest not.' (*Ascent of Mount Carmel*, Chapter 13, 11.)

The *Ascent* can thus be read as an obstinate repetition of recommendations, warnings, advice, precautions and even alerting against any and all distractions:

> It now remains, then, to be pointed out that the soul must not allow its eyes to rest upon that outer husk – namely, figures and objects set before it supernaturally. These may be presented to the exterior senses, as are locutions and words audible to the ear; or, to the eyes, visions of saints, and of beauteous radiance, or perfumes to the sense of smell; or tastes and sweetnesses to the palate; or other delights to the touch, which are wont to proceed from the spirit, a thing that very commonly happens to spiritual persons. Or the soul may have to avert its eyes from visions of interior sense, such as imaginary visions, *all of which it must renounce entirely* (*Ascent*, Book II, Chapter 17.9. Emphasis added).

XIII

He had already been forced to eat all of his papers as fast as he could in order to save them from the harassing eyes of his inquisitors.

They locked him up for nine months in Toledo, in a cell six feet by ten. He had no water, no light: to read the Gospels he had to climb up to a tiny skylight in the wall near the ceiling.

On bread and water and an occasional sardine. His back rots, festers, lashed by the whips of the Carmelites, to make him renounce his Reform.

He's forced to cohabit with the pail of his own excrement. He's overcome by vomiting, dysentery and perhaps even regrets and guilt.

In that hell he conceives, learns by heart, sings, on his knees and even at the top of his lungs, the first verses of the *Canticle*.

As if to ascend to the absolute and to know dissolution in the One it were necessary to descend to putrefaction, touch the most foul, lose himself in revulsion and corruption.

San Juan de la Cruz, *Complete Works* (I), Alianza Editorial, eds. Luce
López-Baralt and Eulogio Pacho.

XIV

One day I say to Gombrowicz – I think it was in Royaumont, in
any case we were under a tree – 'I am lost and alone, I write in
Spanish, or rather in Cuban, in a country not interested in
anything that isn't its own culture and traditions; here it's as if
nothing were newsworthy any longer, as if it were completely
assimilated and no traces were left of an author's past identity, as
if it hadn't existed.'

With his usual touch of irony, his discreet but sarcastic smile, and
that asthmatic panting that cut off his sentences, he comes back with
a cutting reply: 'And what would you say, my dear boy, about a Pole
in Buenos Aires?'

XV

Everything formed is disconnected and dispersed, everything
assembled dissolves, everything created disappears. The body and its
components – hair, skin, blood, semen – the mind and its will,
projections, memories, regrets, loves and rejections.

What is called *I* or *being* is merely an assemblage, an ensemble of
physical and mental elements that appear to act in concert as if
interdependently, in a flux of momentary changes, subject to the
laws of cause and effect, in which there is nothing permanent, nor
eternal, nor exempt from change in the totality of universal
existence.

There is no subject, individual soul, consciousness of oneself or
I. There is thought but no thinker. Neither is there – if we believe in

the categorical responses of Milinda to Nagasena – a cosmic consciousness, a universal being.

If there is no *atman* – being, I, subject, soul – what can be reincarnated after death?

If there is no *brahman* – universal soul, cosmic consciousness . . . – into what do we dissolve?

Given the leap, how will we hear the *explosion of emptiness*?

XVI

Paris, May, Montparnasse
I get up very early and throw open all the windows.

The transparent light of day flashes upon me. Barely blue. How far from the blue of Matisse – a butterfly's wings – which nevertheless he painted near here!

It's possible, I say to myself, submerged in contemplation, as if I were witnessing a miracle, that everything can be reduced to and formulated as a function of vibrating phenomena, as adaptations to the human iris etc.

It's also conceivable that this light is the reverse, the residue, the double, the 'fall' of another light.

Or its distant, seemingly alien metaphor.

Or a brutal *epiphany*, but of what?

XVII

Even knowing perfectly well that his commentaries on readings – or his pretentious aphorisms – will remain unpublished, or will be published under the sinister rubric of *posthumous*, a *true* writer continues writing them.

Very early in the morning he gets up and, beside the window, with day's first light he writes down some lines.

Why? What for?

Perhaps because the only way of responding to the absurd – and death is the absurd par excellence – is an even greater absurd: writing *for nothing*, with neither motive nor goal, without theoretical proofs, plots, fictions, readers, or esthetic or literary efforts.

In the supreme freedom of *total gratuitousness*.

XVIII

Solitude, sickness, depression, silence.

Wherever the gaze rests it discovers dust, larval filth, slovenliness, stains.

The protocol of everyday life starts turning into a constant vigilance, at times into a mitigated hell. Accepting the degradation of things, the relentless progress of disorder, would be like one more invitation to death.

After all, though, it is normal for everything to collapse, down to the very last detail . . . .

If life, which is the most essential, most precious thing, has been taken away, how could anyone not expect to find breadcrumbs on the floor?

XIX

Indifference, provincial aggressivity, collective rejection and mockery finally chip away at a writer's work. Also flattery, excessive praise, exaggerated eulogies spoken to his face, promoting him to the status of hero.

The former undermines his confidence in himself, makes him doubt what he's creating, the usefulness – or transcendence – of all possible creation.

The latter's explicitly fictitious nature is also destructive. No one believes in those apotheoses, neither the person who utters them – and who knows very well what the appropriate criteria are – nor the person who receives them – who immediately detects the emphatic emptiness, the total or at least banal gratuitousness of such inopportune inventions.

Backstabbers and backslappers: equally ominous for an author.

What would be the *moral position* of a true reader? Where is the threshold of discretion that must not be crossed?

The true reading – discreet, ideally silent – is as far from the sting, the insult, as it is from blatant frivolity.

(I endured these two vilifications, which I shall never forget.)

XX

He abandons his native country and adopts a distant land whose sky is always gray and whose people are harsh.

In exile he constructs laborious fictions whose chiseled sentences and skillfully wrought Baroque volutes are seductive, though, when the end comes, everything dissolves into oblivion.

These models of perseverance are published and tolerated by readers, ignored somewhat sarcastically by the multitudes and suspended in that respectful limbo of university dissertations and translations into unfathomable languages.

He has begun to plan the summary, the final cycle of his inventions, when he's struck down by a strange irreversible disease.

He protects himself with converging manias: morning readings of the mystics, a need for emptiness, and the project of finishing paintings, detailed down to the last millimeter with the final strokes of red calligraphy, emphatic though discreet, ostensibly Eastern.

He divests himself of dusty books, summer clothes, accumulated letters, faded drawings and paintings.

He surrenders, as if to a drug, to solitude and silence.

In that domestic peace he awaits death. With his library in order.

TRANSLATED BY SUZANNE JILL LEVINE

Notes on the Writers

ARAGÓN Uva de, aka Clavijo Uva A. (Havana, 1944) has published nine books including two short story collections, *Ni verdad ni mentira y otros cuentos* (1976) and *No puedo más y otros cuentos* (1989), and *Alfonso Hernández-Catá. Un escritor cubano, salmantino y universal* (1996), a critical essay on the Cuban novelist and short-story writer who is her maternal grandfather. A graduate of the University of Miami, Uva de Aragón is assistant-director of the Cuban Research Institute at Florida International University and writes a weekly column for *Diario Las Américas*. She has lived in the United States since 1959.

ARENAS Reinaldo (Holguin, 1943–1990, New York) came from a poor rural family. He studied at Havana University and worked for various cultural bodies including the José Martí National Library. His talent as a writer and storyteller was soon spotted by José Lezama Lima. However, he suffered because he was homosexual and voiced critical opinions. After a long, bitter period when he was ostracized and imprisoned, he went into exile at the time of the 1980 Mariel exodus. In the United States he co-founded and edited the cultural magazine *Mariel* (1983-1985) and collaborated on other literary Cuban exile publications. Many of his novels and short stories are available in translation including *Singing from the Well* (1967), *The Palace of the White Skunks* (1972) and *Farewell to the Sea* (1982). His memoir, *Before Night Falls*, was published in 1993.

ARMAND Octavio (Cuba, 1946) was born into a family that would be exiled twice: once, in 1958, under Batista, and again under Castro in 1960. For many years of the second exile he lived in New York City; at present he resides in Caracas. Armand's first book of poems,

Horizonte no es siempre lejanía, was published in 1970. Since that date he has published six other collections of poetry, the most recent of which is *Origami* (Caracas, 1987), *Superficies,* a collection of essays (Caracas, 1980). He has also published translations of poems by Mark Strand (*Mark Strand: 20 poemas*, Caracas, 1979) and edited an anthology of Latin American poetry (*Towards an Image of Latin American Poetry*, Durango, Colorado, 1982). In 1978, he founded *escandalar*, a literary journal that he edited until 1984, in which he published works by writers from Spain and Latin America as well as many European and North American writers in Spanish translation. In English translations by Carol Maier, Armand's work has appeared in numerous literary journals and in *Refractions* (Lumen, 1994).

ARRIETA RICARDO (Santiago de Cuba, 1967). My mother was from Santiago and my father from El Salvador and the States. I have lived in Havana from the age of two. I started to work as a secondary school teacher when I was seventeen. I then started to study Physics and History of Art at Havana University but finished neither course. I started writing whilst I was studying and belonged to El Establo, a noninstitutional literary group. Between 1988 and 1990 I won several national prizes thanks to which some stories have been published in magazines and anthologies. My book of stories *Someone's got it all licked* (the David Prize, 1990) is about to be published and was written in collaboration with Ronaldo Menéndez.

ARZOLA Jorge Luis (Jatibonico, Sancti Spíritus, 1966). I spent my adolescence in the countryside a long time after the long-haired guys from the Sierra Maestra had had proper shaves and haircuts. I always felt I wanted to be a writer but had little opportunity to read. A few classics, mainly thrillers, came my way. The first book which I ever read was *The Promise* by Friedrich Dürrenmatt. I owe a lot to the Russian classics, to Dostoievski, and then to Kafka, to Poe and all North American literature, to Borges, Cortázar and Juan Rulfo. But this all came much later, after abandoning my studies (I fled from what we call rural school in an act of rebellion that hurt me more than the state of things against which I was reacting). I spent my childhood and adolescence thinking about things which are now vague memories, including perhaps the inadmissible desire to let my hair grow long (as a child obsessed with action and meditation I got really worked up about frequent haircuts). I started to publish a few small pieces before I was twenty, started to think of myself as a writer and participate in literary bohemian life and an infinity of seminars organised by the Alejo Carpentier Centre, UNEAC and the Cuban Book Institute. This story was published in 1994 in my only book bearing the same title. Other stories have been published in anthologies in Cuba and abroad. I belong to that generation dubbed 'los novísimos' by Cuban critics and which is now getting very old. I am just finishing my first novel about a taciturn, rebellious adolescent who doesn't want to be devoured by the vulture of History whilst he contemplates the bones of the nation turning white in the sun.

BENÍTEZ Rojo Antonio (Havana, 1931) was born into a well-off middle class family and spent his childhood in Panama where he became fluent in English. He studied business and won a year's scholarship to continue his studies in Washington. He worked for the Cuban Telephone Company and then for the revolutionary, nationalized version. It was only in the mid-'60s that he began to write stories and link up with the world of culture. He was director of the Casa del Teatro in Havana (1966–67) and editor of *Cuba Internacional* (1968–69). He went on to head important sections in the Casa de las Américas, the Centre for Literary Research (1970–71), the Publishing Department (1974-80) and the Centre for Caribbean Studies (1979-80). During these years he suffered periods of 'disgrace', partly because his wife and children moved to Boston in search of medical care for one of their children and he wanted to visit them. The director of the Casa de las Américas and veteran of the revolution, Haydée Santamaria defended him and his defection became one of the reasons forwarded for her suicide on 26 July 1980.

He has published four collections of stories, two novels and three screenplays. One, *Los sobrevivientes*, based on the story in this anthology, was directed by Gutiérrez Alea and shown at the 1979 Cannes Festival. He defected from Cuba in 1980 when on an official visit to Paris and now teaches Latin American literature at Amherst College. He is writing a series of essays on Caribbean culture.

BOBES Marilyn (Havana, 1955) is a journalist, poet and short-story writer. She won the 1995 Casa de las Américas Prize for the collection, *Alguien tiene que llorar*. She is co-author of the anthology of women's short stories *Estatuas de sal* (1996) and vice-president of the Cuban Writers' Union.

CABRERA Lydia (Havana, 1900–1991, Miami) lived in Paris from 1922 to 1939 where she learned French and started her research into African folklore. She studied Yoruba mythology and wrote the *Cuentos negros de Cuba in* 1934. Francis Miomandre translated them into French and they were published in Paris in 1936. The stories came out in Cuba in 1940. She returned to Havana at the end of the Second World War, began research into Afro-Cuban culture and *El monte* (1954) is a main source of information on the stories, rites and beliefs of *santería* as are her books on the secret society of the Abakua, the marine deities, Yemayá and Ochún, and *Anago*, the Yoruba that is spoken in Cuba. Lydia Cabrera left Havana after the revolution to live in Madrid and finally settled in Miami.

CABRERA INFANTE Guillermo (Gibara, Oriente, Cuba 1929) was the son of founder members of the Cuban Communist Party and experienced as a child the twists and turns of Stalinist politics: his parents were jailed by Batista; two years later they were electorally campaigning for him on party orders. In 1941 his family moved to Havana and the city's labyrinths have absorbed him ever since. He wrote his first story in 1947 and in 1952 was imprisoned and fined for the crime of publishing a story containing English swear words. In

1954 he became editor of the cinema section of the magazine *Carteles*. In 1959 he was momentarily director of the National Council for Culture and assistant-director of the daily newspaper *Revolución*, founding and editing the cultural supplement *Lunes de Revolución*. After a political-literary polemic over the banning of his brother's film *P.M.* the government closed down the supplement. In the same year he divorced and married the actress Miriam Gómez. His official exile was initiated in 1962. Through periods of poverty, nervous breakdown and the bitterness of exile, he has written and published fictions, essays, screenplays, film criticism and memoirs. His international literary reputation was established with the publication of *Tres tigres tristes* in 1965 – *Three Trapped Tigers*, translated by Suzanne Jill Levine (New York, 1971). Since 1966 he has lived in London where he is now a British citizen. When *Holy Smoke*, his first book in English was published, the *Times Literary Supplement* called him Cuba's answer to Conrad and Nabokov.

CASEY Calvert (Baltimore, 1924–1969, Rome), son of an American father and Cuban mother, travelled to Canada, the United States and Europe from a very early age. He worked as a translator for international institutions. One of his first short stories, *El paseo*, published in *The New Mexico Quarterly*, won a prize from Doubleday in New York. One day, while he was in Rome, he had a kind of vision as if he were in the streets of Havana. 'My voluntary exile ended that morning', he commented, 'I had to go back to the landscape where everything is given and there's no need to explain anything . . .'

Faithful to his vision, he made his way back to the island. With the advent of the revolution, he joined the new wave of writers and intellectuals. He wrote feverishly for several publications, including theatre and literary reviews for the controversial *Lunes de Revolución*. He also wrote for the *Casa de las Américas, Gaceta de Cuba* and *UNION*. His anthology of short stories *El regreso* (Barcelona, 1962) including the present story, was followed by *Memorias de una isla*, a collection of articles on Cuban culture. In 1966 while working at the Casa de las Américas, he was terrified by the repression of homosexuals, escaped via Hungary and returned to Rome where he continued work as a translator. In 1969, he committed suicide, exhausted and in despair at his enforced exile. He wrote a novel originally in English which he burnt completely except for one chapter that he left to the Spanish writer, Rafael Martínez Nadal, who translated and published it after Calvert's death.

CARDOSO Jorge Onelio (Las Villas, 1914–1986, Havana) was the son of a *mambí*, an independence fighter against Spanish imperialism. He submitted his first short story to a competition at the age of twelve but was disqualified for poor spelling. He grew up in the countryside and later worked as a rural school teacher where his experience of rural poverty and an interest in writing led him to dedicate himself to literature. He tried his hand at photography, pharmaceuticals and ironmongery to earn a living and support his short-story writing. In the 1940s he established a literary, theatrical group, the Club Umbral, with friends in Santa Clara. He won the Hernández Catá prize in 1945 with 'The Charcoal Burners' which was to inspire the 1955 critical documentary film, *El Mégano,* by Tomás Gutiérrez Alea and Julio García Espinosa. His first collection of stories was published in Mexico in 1945. He broadcast for the Cuban radio company *Mil diez*. After the revolution he worked at the Cuban Film Institute and wrote the script for the film *Cumbite,* directed by Alea, about the struggles of Haitian immigrant workers, land and *santería*. He was a leading member of the Cuban Writers' Union, cultural attaché in Paris and in Peru.

CASAL Lourdes (Havana, 1938–1981, Havana) left Cuba for the United States in 1961 and taught Psychology at Brooklyn College, New York and then Rutgers University, New Jersey. She was a founder member of the magazine *Areíto,* the Circle for Cuban Culture and the Institute for Cuban Studies and wrote numerous articles on the Cuban revolution and Cubans in the US. She is the author of *Los fundadores: Alfonso y otros cuentos* (Miami: Universal, 1973) and *Palabras juntan revolución* (Havana: Casa de las Américas, 1981).

DESNOES Edmundo (Havana, 1930). *Where I Stand*, when I arrogantly titled this story thirty years ago, was a commitment to stay in Cuba till I was buried, or better, cremated and flushed down any island toilet. Now *where* is here in the United States where I live and write, if I ever bother to do something I no longer trust, mostly screenplays in English. Yet I was born in Spanish. And I no longer stand but sit and drive. Above all I only feel at home on the road, travelling through the urban monotony and the overwhelming natural beauty of America, watching television at night and plunging into sleep in timeless motels. Here there is no more religion – which I once called historical materialism; I had and have a weakness for absolutes. There is one thing left – the passion. The intensity, the destructive macho embrace of revolution. To see everything turned upside down is shattering, gave me a 'rush', as the young here/there now refer to meaning. That has remained with me and makes everything taste trivial. The passion of the revolution has spoilt consumer pleasures. I have only death to look forward to, as I crumple up and rot. (Only the love of a woman has kept me driving.) But maybe it will be a flat whimper when it comes – compared to the big bang of the Sixties. I sometimes squander my time cutting out ideas and sensations in old magazines, mainly porno glossies and pasting collages dominated by the circle. Last year I became a United States citizen and painfully enjoy being invisible in this country, since I want nothing more, don't ever want to go back, to see Cuba again. Decapitate Patriarchy and bring up the womb. Davenport, New York, 1997.

Desnoes was educated in Havana and in the United States. During the 1950s he lived abroad in Venezuela and then in New York where he wrote for the magazine *Vision*. He returned to Cuba to work for the National Book Publishing Company and the Revolutionary

Orientation Commission. His novel *Memorias del subdesarrollo*, *Memories of Underdevelopment*, was published in Cuba in 1962 and became the basis for Gutiérrez Alea's film of that name.

HERNÁNDEZ-CATÁ Alfonso (Aldeadávila de la Ribera, Salamanca, Spain, 1885–1940, Brazil). One of Cuba's most powerful short-story writers during the first third of the century, he was one of the first authors from the island to be translated into many languages. His stories follow the line of Poe and Maupassant and are known for their pychological insights and crafted modernist style. Recent critics have emphasised his foresight in the treatment of such themes as racism (*La piel*, 1923), homosexuality (*El ángel de Sodoma*, 1929) and dictatorship (*Un cementerio en las Antillas*, 1933). Although he cultivated every genre, it is his short novels and stories where he gained most recognition. Collections of stories include *Cuentos pasionales* (1907), *Una mala mujer* (1922), and *Manicomio* (1931). The present story is from *Piedras preciosas* (1927). He served Cuba as a diplomat and died in an aeroplane crash in Brazil where he was Cuba's Ambassador.

LEZAMA LIMA José (Havana, 1910–1976, Havana) is best known for his masterpiece of Cuban baroque, erotic fiction, *Paradiso* (1966), but there is an unknown – because untranslated – realm of his writing that includes five short stories which were published in literary magazines between 1936 and 1946, essays and poetry. Lezama created an original poetic language from his intimate knowledge of the languages and cultures of Cuba and an encyclopedic knowledge of literature and culture from China to Europe. His extensive essays and letters are as likely to include references to Nietzsche, Hegel and Eastern mysticism as they are to José Martí. He was also a key figure in encouraging the development of Cuban literature through such journals as *Orígenes* whose pages attracted contemporary writers on the island and leading writers from abroad. Lezama's translations from the French include Saint-

John Perse's *Lluvias* (1961). After gaining a doctorate in law he worked in the 1940s as a civil servant and in the Ministry of Culture from 1945 to 1950 when he lived for a period in Mexico and Jamaica. After the Revolution he occupied various posts in cultural bodies but was relegated to the status of invisible master when eroticism, homosexuality and poetic writing had to be sidelined for the benefit of the social realists. His name was rarely mentioned; he had become a non-person and anyway made a point of avoiding public events. Anecdotes abound related to rare sightings or mentions of him on television. Life at the family home became increasingly melancholy when the departure of all his close relatives left him alone in 1961 with his mother. She died in 1964: his novel was, among other things, an epiphany to her memory. Currently, their old house is being restored as a Lezama Lima museum and *Paradiso* is a favourite name for tourist locations. Lezama suffered from asthma and liked to joke that his best writing — long sentences without pauses, complex imagery and symbolism — came in the sleepless reaches of the night as he sucked on his Havana cigars.

MONTENEGRO Carlos (Puebla del Caraminal, 1900–1981, Miami), son of a Cuban mother and Spanish soldier stationed in Cuba, lived in Galicia till 1907 when the family moved to Cuba. His father lost the family fortune and they were forced to move to Argentina for a year. Carlos hated his Catholic Cuban schooling and went to sea from 1914 to 1918. He loaded bananas in Costa Rica, mined in New York State, worked in a munitions factory in Pennsylvania, lumberjacked near Ottawa and did odd jobs in New York and Albany. In 1917 he was charged and imprisoned for arms dealing in Mexico. In 1918 in the port of Havana he got involved in a fight and mortally wounded an assailant. His subsequent twelve years in the Castillo del Príncipe prison turned him into a writer and he published numerous stories in magazines and daily newspapers. He met (1927) and married (1929) Emma L. Pérez whilst in prison. He remarked, 'My wedding and relations with Esther Emma Luis Pérez González were the stuff of legend. Consider the social and family prejudices that confronted my wife. Her mother moved heaven and earth to prevent our union. This included a visit from the secretary to the president to persuade me not to marry Emma: "You are an intellectual, but . . ."' Cuban and Spanish intellectuals and the general public signed a petition that led to his release and he received an unconditional pardon in 1931. He joined the Communist Party in 1933, was general editor of their newspaper and sent reports back from the Spanish Civil War. In 1938 he published *Hombres sin mujer*, a major Latin American novel based on his experiences in prison and centred on the obsessions, rituals and homosexuality of prison life. During the 1940s he contributed to magazines but only began to work on a second novel in the early '60s in Miami where he reached via Costa Rica after leaving Cuba in 1959.

NOVÁS CALVO Lino (Granas del Sor, Galicia, 1905–1983, New York). His family moved to Cuba from Spain in 1912. He worked in the catering trade from an early age through economic necessity and later moved on to journalism. He wrote for the weekly *Orbe* as its North American correspondent. He later visited France, Germany and Spain where he worked as foreign correspondent in Madrid from 1931 to 1936 and wrote on the Second Republic and the first months of the Civil War. On his return to Havana, he taught French and continued writing short stories. In 1942 he won the Hernández Catá Prize for the story *Un dedo encima*. In 1960 he sought asylum in the Columbian Embassy, convinced that Fidel Castro was going to enter an alliance with Russia. In exile, he continued writing and taught at the University of Syracuse. Novás Calvo wrote in 1932 that the present story 'was inspired by things seen and heard some years earlier. A well-known writer told me he thought it was rather mannered. But don Fernando Vela, don Antonio Marichalar and don José Ortega y Gasset liked it and published it in the *Revista de Occidente*. I am not sure, but I think it represented an innovation in Spanish American writing.' (*Maneras de contar*, Novás Calvo, New York, 1970).

PAZ Senel (Las Villas, 1950) grew up in a poor hamlet in rural Cuba. A scholarship boy of the revolution, he went to Havana to follow his secondary and university educations where he was inspired by his teacher and writer, Eduardo Heras Léon. As a result of his defence of the latter when he was accused of writing anti-Cuban fictions, he himself was expelled from the official youth organisation and exiled as a fledgling journalist to a remote corner of the island after graduating with a distinction. His short story *The Woods, the Wolf and the New Man* which is a continuation of the present story won the Juan Rulfo Prize awarded by Radio France International in 1990. Both stories were elaborated by Senel Paz into the screenplay for the film *Strawberry and Chocolate* directed by the late Tomas Gutiérrez Alea. The original screenplay has been published in Italy, Spain and the UK (Bloomsbury, 1995). The film won the Critics' Silver Bear Award at the Berlin Film Festival and was nominated for an Academy Award for Best Foreign Film in 1994. Paz is currently finishing his second novel set in contemporary Cuba. His first novel *Un rey en el jardin* (1984) explores the world of children. He also works as a screenplay writer for the Cuban Film Institute and for European film producers.

PIÑERA Virgilio (Cárdenas, Matanzas, Havana, 1912–1979) was a poet, novelist, dramatist and critic. He was secretary to the magazine *Ciclón* edited by José Rodriguez Feo, a leading Cuban critic, and collaborated on Lezama Lima's *Orígines*. His theatre was absurd before Ionesco and existentialist before Sartre. He emigrated to Buenos Aires in 1946 where Borges read and published his work. He also participated in the collective translation of *Ferdyduke* by Witold Gombrowicz. His first novel was written in Buenos Aires in 1952 – *La carne de René* – and was followed by *Pequeñas maniobras* (Havana 1963) and *Presiones y diamantes* (Havana, 1967). He worked there for ten years as a Cuban consular official and returned to Cuba before the revolution. He wrote for *Lunes de Revolución* and *Casa de las Américas*. He directed the publishing project Ediciones R

(Revolution) in Havana until it was closed down. His homosexuality and political and literary non-conformism soon led to his marginalization which involved lengthy police interrogations and clashes with the censorship until his work was banned.

PITA RODRÍGUEZ Félix (Bejucal, Havana, 1909–1990, Havana) first won a reputation as an avant garde writer of poetry in 1927. As an adolescent he had travelled extensively in Central and South America and lived in Paris. His left-wing opinions led him to participate in the Spanish Civil War in 1936 and in the Congress of Anti-Fascist Writers in Madrid, Valencia and Barcelona in 1937. On his return he began to write for radio and a short story of his won the Hernández Catá Prize in 1946. After a period living in Caracas and Buenos Aires in the 1950s, he came back to Cuba in 1959. He was then president of the Writers Union, travelled to Viet Nam and what was the Soviet Union and Eastern Europe.

RODRÍGUEZ Luis Felipe (Manzanillo, Oriente, 1888–1947, Havana) began writing as a youngster for local newspapers and literary journals such as *Orto* and *Alma Joven*. He moved to Havana where he wrote for the magazines *Bohemia*, *Carteles* and *Letras*. His collections, *La pascua de la tierra natal* (1928), and later *Marcos Antilla* (1932), initiated a literature that focused on the landscape and hardships of a sugar-cane economy: rural tales – *el cuento guajiro* – that soon came to symbolize national identity and fall victim to a host of imitators.

SÁNCHEZ MEJÍAS Rolando (Holguin, 1959) is a poet, *Derivas 1*, short-story writer, *Escrituras* and editor of an anthology of Cuban poetry *Mapa imaginario*. In 1989 he won the *Hucha de Plata Prize* in Spain for short stories and in 1993 and '94, the Cuban Critics' Prize. In 1993 he created the GRUPO DIÁSPORACS to explore alternative approaches to writing.

SANTIESTEBAN Prats Angel (Havana, 1966). I belong to a generation born after the Revolution and which approaches the writing of Literature by stripping away the marked ideological influences that have so damaged Cuban literature over past decades. We are trying to rescue the necessary, vital autonomy of Literature in turn-of-the century Cuban writing with all the risks and challenges that implies. I discovered my passion for literature in 1985 and was fortunate to get to know the leading Cuban short-story writer, Eduardo Heras León, who guided me along my literary path. After reading widely I find myself attracted by the techniques of Hemingway, Rulfo and Babel, my three presiding deities. My third story won a special mention in the Juan Rulfo competition sponsored by Radio France International and my next won first prize in 1990 in the National Literary Workshops Competition in Cuba. In 1992 and 1994 I was a finalist for the Casa de las Américas Prize and finally in 1996 I got the National UNEAC prize for my book, *Dream on a Summer's Day*, an anti-heroic vision of the Angolan war, which remains, and, will indefinitely remain, unpublished.

I have finished a new book of stories where I deal with contemporary Cuban reality and am writing my first novel – about the Cuban prison system.

SARDUY Pérez Pedro (Santa Clara, 1943) is an Afro-Cuban poet, writer, journalist and broadcaster resident in London. He is the author of *Surrealidad* (Havana, 1967) and *Cumbite and Other Poems* (Havana, 1987 and New York, 1990), coeditor of AFRO-CUBA: An Anthology of Cuban Writing on Race, Politics and Culture (Melbourne/London, 1993) and co-author of the Introduction for the anthology *No Longer Invisible/Afro-Latin Americans Today* (London, 1995). He has finished *Journal in Babylon,* a series of chronicles on Britain and a first novel, *The Maids of Havana* (both unpublished). He finished *Afro-Cuban Voices: On Race, Representation and Identity in 1990s Cuba,* a book based on interviews with Afro-Cubans living on the island – forthcoming 1997 with Ocean

Press. The recipient of several literary awards, writer-in-residence at Columbia University, New York (1989), and Rockefeller Visiting Scholar at the University of Florida, Gainesville (1993). The present story is unpublished in Spanish.

SARDUY Severo (Camagüey, 1936–1993, Paris) went to France as a voluntary exile in 1960. He was a close friend of Roland Barthes and Jacques Lacan and an influential member of the *Tel Quel* group. He published six novels, several books of poetry, essays and plays, hosted a radio show and, as editor at Editions du Seuil, published an array of new Latin American writing. One of the most outrageous and baroque writers of the Latin American boom, he created texts that revel in transgression and the transvestite, are exuberant adventures in language mingling Maoism and Tantric Buddhism, drag and drugs, the playful and the intellectual. In 1995 Dalkey Archive Press published *Cobra* (1972) and *Maitreya* (1978), translated by Suzanne Jill Levine who with Carol Maier translated *Christ on the rue Jacob* (1987) (Mercury House, 1995). The meditation-epilogue is his last text, written as he was dying of AIDS.

URÍA Hernández Roberto. I was born on 6 August, 1959, in Havana the vain city, that bewitches. One 6 August the North Americans dropped the first atomic bomb (1945), on Hiroshima; in 1959 the illustrious Comandante Fidel Castro ascended to the throne, the one who grew his beard under a lucky star, who has worked so hard for the happiness of all Cubans, yet never got there: an era, like any other, when life was difficult. From childhood, to avoid the rough edges of reality I took refuge in the invented realities of literature and art. I'm a voracious 'professional' reader; but only an amateur writer. I always write manually, with paper and pen, to enjoy more keenly the pain of the struggle between language and the world. Sometimes I feel I have reached the nirvana of complete freedom, that I'm hostage to nothing or to nobody, that I am the living word. But it's a short-lived physical joy: 'The moment's up', I say to myself and then I read passionately

Jorge Luis Borges. Finally in 1995, after numerous Kafkian, that is, very Cuban processes, and thanks to the good graces of Castroism, my ravenous bones landed in Miami, the 'other' Cuba. Translated, not defeated, I now live in the real world. And as I can't stand too much reality, I return, like the prodigal son, to my true land: the night; and dreamlike, to a book, my constant love. I believe in God, in the riddles of the universe, in the labyrinths of love, in Here and Now, solid, flowing, and in silence . . . For the moment I'm an optimistic sceptic.

VALDÉS Zoé (Havana, 1959) is a poet, novelist and short-story writer. She worked for many years at the Cuban Film Institute and then for several years as a member of the Cuban delegation at UNESCO in Paris where she resides and writes. Her novel *La nada cotidiana* deals with the life of a girl from birth during the triumphant revolutionary workers' demonstrations in Cuba 1959 to the struggle to survive the recent 'special period', the years of severe rationing and power-cuts. She was a finalist for the 1996 Planeta Prize in Spain.

VEGA Jesús (Havana, 1954) is a writer, poet and critic. He has written occasional poetry from his teens and his first attempts at literary criticism appeared in *El Caimán Barbudo*. He has penned essays and reviews on literature, art and film in every possible Cuban publication as well as *Babel* (Venezuela) and *Cinémas d'Amérique Latine* (France). In 1994 his book of short stories *Wunderbar, maravilloso* was published as a joint project by the Cuban Book Institute and Argentinian publishing houses. The stories and style vary from a kind of realism to poetic experimentalism. The main subject is the inner reality of the writer reacting to the harsh, sad realities of Cuban reality. In 1995 the Cuban Writers' Union published his *Zavattini en La Habana*, a chronicle of the visits to the island of the Italian neo-realist *cinéaste*. He has travelled to Germany, Argentina and the United States where he lectured and read his poems and stories in several universities. In 1995 he defected and obtained political asylum while on a tour of American universities. He now lives in Miami where he writes and edits for several Hispanic magazines. Some of his stories recently appeared in an anthology of Cuban stories published in Italy. His unpublished books include: *Illegal Productions*, a second collection of short stories, *The Return of Calvert Casey* and *The Cuban Film Poster*.

VICTORIA Carlos (Camagüey, 1950) in 1965 won the short-story prize offered by the magazine *El Caimán Barbudo*. In 1971 he was expelled for 'political deviationism' from Havana University, where he was studying English Language and Literature. In 1978 he was arrested by Cuban State Security officers and all his manuscripts were confiscated. In 1980 he left the island via the Mariel-Cayo Hueso crossing and ever since his stories have appeared in literary anthologies and magazines in the United States, Spain, France, Germany and Latin America. In 1985 one of his stories was included in the annual selection published by *Le Monde*. He has published a book of short stories *Shadows on the Beach* (1992) and the novels *Puente en la oscuridad* (1993) and *La travesía secreta* (1994). He has just published a second collection of short stories *La ruta del mago* and is working on a new novel. He is a journalist on *The Miami Herald* and has received two prizes for his work, *Cintas* and *Letras de Oro*, a national literary prize for works written in Spanish in the USA.

VILLAVERDE Fernando (Havana, 1938) worked in Cuba as a screenplay writer and film producer for the Cuban Film Institute (ICAIC) from its inception in 1959 until he left the country in 1985 after ICAIC decided not to distribute his last two films, *Elena* and *El Mar*. In Europe and later in New York he worked for the theatre and produced independent, experimental films. His fiction and criticism have been published in literary magazines and other publications in the US, Cuba, Spain and elsewhere; in the '80s he was a literary critic for the Miami Spanish daily *El Miami Herald*. He has twice won the Letras de Oro prize: first for the play *Cosas de viejos* and secondly for the short stories *Los labios pintados de Diderot*, which have both been published in Spanish in the United States. He has also published the book of poems *Cuaderno de caligrafía and Crónicas del Mariel*. He has just finished another play, *Esos mares de locura* and has another volume of novella about to be published, *Las tetas europeas*.

YAÑEZ Mirta (Havana, 1947) studied Spanish language and literature at Havana University where she was awarded in 1990 a Ph.D on the work of Esteban Echevarria, supervised by Roberto Fernández Retamar. Her early interests centred on *nahuatl* and the literature of the Aztecs. In 1935 she was appointed Assistant Professor at the university where she had taught since 1977 but she abandoned her academic career in 1988 to devote herself entirely to creative writing after winning the Critics' Prize. She has published three collections of short stories to date: *Todos los negros tomamos café*, 1976, *La Habana es una ciudad bien grande*, 1981, *El diablo son las cosas*, 1988, a novel *La hora de los mameyes* (1983), one of the few novels published by women in post-revolutionary Cuba, and a collection of essays *La narrativa romántica en Latinoamérica* (1990). In 1991 she published a memoir, *Una memoria de elefante*. Her most recent book (co-edited with Marilyn Bobes) is an anthology of Cuban women short-story writers, *Estatuas de sal. Cuentistas cubanas contemporáneas* (1996). She contributes regularly to literary reviews in Cuba and has lectured throughout Latin America and Europe.

Notes on the Translators

BASSNETT Susan is Professor of Comparative Cultural Studies at the University of Warwick, where she teaches Translation Studies at postgraduate level. Her involvement with translation began when she first learned to talk, and through her peripatetic childhood where there was always at least one other language somewhere in her head. From her first professional work as an interpreter and translator of everything from medical treatises to B-movie screenplays, she moved to translating literary texts: poetry, plays, in particular several plays by Pirandello, and novels. Her translation languages include Italian, Spanish, Latin and French, and she co-translated a collection of Polish women poets with Piotr Kuhiwczac. She is the author of the best-selling *Translation Studies*, and with the late André Lefevere co-edited *Translation, History and Culture*. She currently edits two series of books on translation: the Routledge Translation Studies series and the Multilingual Matters Topics in Translation series. Her latest project is a collection of her own poems and the poems of Alejandra Pizarnik in translation, entitled *Exchanging Lives*. She has four children and now lives in rural England.

BUSH Peter is Professor of Literary Translation at Middlesex University and a freelance literary translator. He has translated the work of Juan Goytisolo, Antonio Muñoz Molina, Juan Carlos Onetti, Senel Paz and Luis Sepúlveda whose *The Old Man Who Read Love Stories* won a 1995 Best Translation Award from the American Literary Translators Association. His most recent translations are Juan Goytisolo's *The Marx Family Saga* and Juan Carlos Onetti's *Past Caring*. He is a member of the General Council of the International Federation of Translators (FIT), edits the journal *In*

Other Words of the Translators Association (UK) and coorganises the Institute of Translation and Interpreting International Colloquia on Literary Translation. He is currently leading a European network of literary translators funded by the European Commission in an Ariane project, 'The Translator as Reader and Writer: Training and Literary Translation'. He is now translating a selection of essays by Juan Goytisolo, *The Eye of the Imagination*, and Carlos Montenegro's *Men without Women*.

CAZABON Maria J. had a traditional bilingual education in Havana with American nuns. Before leaving her native Cuba for the US in 1983 she had worked extensively in designing and implementing programmes to train English teachers and translator/interpreters, and also as a translator and conference interpreter. In the US she first taught Spanish at Harvard University while freelancing as a translator/interpreter and Spanish-language textbook writer. In Miami, where she has lived since 1986, she has taught at Florida International University and is now a staff interpreter for the Federal District Court.

COSTA Margaret Jull has translated novels and short stories by Spanish, Portuguese and Latin American writers including: *Obabakoak* and *The Lone Man* by Bernardo Atxaga; *All Souls, A Heart So White* and *Tomorrow in the Battle Think on Me* by Javier Marías; *The Witness* by Juan José Saer; *The Mandarin* by Eça de Queiroz; *Lúcio's Confession* and *The Great Shadow* by Mario Sá-Carneiro and *The Snow Queen* by Carmen Martín Gaite. She was joint-winner of the Teixeira Gomes Portuguese Translation Prize in 1992 for her translation of *The Book of Disquiet* by Fernand Pessoa and was shortlisted for the 1996 Prize for her translation of *The Relic* by Eça de Queiroz. Current projects include translations of Bernardo Atxaga's *Esos cielos* and a collection of short stories by Javier Marías.

DAVIES Catherine is Professor of Spanish at the University of

Manchester where she specialises in Modern Spanish and Spanish American literature. After completing her studies at the Universidad Complutense, Madrid, and the University of Glasgow, where she was awarded a Ph.D in 1984, she took up lecturing posts at St. Andrews University and Queen Mary and Westfield College, University of London. She has published various articles on nineteenth and twentieth-century Spanish and Spanish American poetry and film, with special emphasis on women's writing and Galician literature. She is author of *Rosalía de Castro no seu tempo* (1987), and *Contemporary Feminist Fiction in Spain* (1994), editor of *Women Writers in Spain and Spanish America* (1993) and co-editor (with Anny Brooksbank Jones) of *Latin American Women's Writing. Feminist Readings in Theory and Crisis* (1996). Since 1990 her research has focused on women's writing in Cuba where she spent research leave in 1990 and 1992. She has published several articles on the subject and has recently completed a book *Inventing Spaces, Finding Time, Women Writers in Twentieth-Century Cuba*.

DILLMAN Lisa was born in 1967, in Washington D.C. and was raised in Los Angeles. Growing up in California led her to become interested in Spanish, which she studied at the University of California, San Diego and at the Universitat de Barcelona. Her attraction to translation originally stems from experiencing culture clash at a linguistic level while abroad for the first time: frustration at being unable to make people laugh at jokes in Spanish, bewilderment at the translation of film titles. In 1991, she began a Ph.D. in Spanish at Emory University in Atlanta, which she quit after two years, having obtained a Master's Degree and decided to pursue translation. She moved back to Barcelona, where she studied Catalan and had little luck as a freelance translator. In 1995 Lisa moved to England where she is currently working on an MA in Translation at Middlesex University. In addition to translating, she writes poetry and lectures in Spanish at the University of North London. She lives with her partner in North London.

FRANK Miriam, born in Spain of German and American parents, grew up in France, Mexico and New Zealand. She graduated in medicine and became a senior lecturer and consultant at a London teaching hospital. The author of many scientific articles and chapters in medical publications, she discovered the work of Héctor Tizón during a lecture tour in Argentina, and translated his novels, *The Man Who Came to a Village* and *Fire in Casabindo*, published by Quartet in 1993, and short stories which appeared in *The Guardian* and *Index on Censorship*. She has since translated works for Spanish and Latin American anthologies and a film script for the Argentine director, Miguel Pereira. She is now writing her own work; her first short story was published in a collection by Serpent's Tail.

HASKINS Clare was born in 1973 in Wiltshire and now lives in London. She graduated from Middlesex University with a BA in Spanish and History of Ideas in 1995. She has lived in Costa Rica and travelled and studied in Central and South America. Clare is currently working towards her Masters in the Theory and Practice of Translation. She works for an alternative trade organization; a company which seeks to improve terms of trade for small-scale farmers in Latin America and Africa. She hopes to continue her work in literary translation.

HOPKINSON Amanda is a literary translator and a curator of photographic exhibitions. Latin American titles she has translated include *They Won't Take Me Alive* (1988) and *Family Album* (1990) by Claribel Alegría, the poetry anthology *Lovers and Comrades* (1989); *The Miracle Worker* (1993) by Carmen Boullosa and *Sacred Cow* (1995) by Diamela Eltit. Recent exhibitions have been *The Forbidden Rainbow*, photos by Julio Etchart and catalogue introduced by Eduard Galeano (The Photographers' Gallery,1992), *Desires and Disguises*, work by five Latin American Photographers, catalogue introduced by Elena Poniatowska (The Photographers' Gallery, London 1993); *A Hidden View: Images of Bahia*, by four Brazilian photographers, introduced by Jorge Amado (Barbican, 1994); *Black Butterfly: photographs of death* by 25 Mexican photographers (National Gallery, Scotland,1995). Amanda Hopkinson also contributes to teaching undergraduate and graduate courses on Latin American culture and media; contributes regularly as a critic to both press and broadcast media on Latin American subjects, and edits work on literary translation, art and photography.

HURLEY Andrew is Professor of English in the College of Humanities at the University of Puerto Rico. He is the translator of the novels of Reinaldo Arenas's 'pentalogy' as well as other works by Arenas, and has also translated short stories and novels by Ernesto Sábato, Fernando Arrabal, Gustavo Sainz, Manuel Puig, Juan Carlos Onetti, Heberto Padilla, and the Puerto Rican writers, Ana Lydia Vega and Eduardo Rodriguez Juliá. Most recently he has retranslated the complete fiction of Jorge Luis Borges (nine volumes), which is scheduled for publication in late 1997.

LEVINE Suzanne Jill is Professor of Latin American Literature at the University of California (Santa Bárbara). She was born and raised in New York City, in a culture within a culture, in an 'assimilated' Jewish family in which her mother spoke Yiddish to her father when she wanted to ensure her daughter didn't understand. She lived in the old part of Madrid by the Ronda de Segovia in 1965 and 'the macaronic colourfulness, the cities of the lottery ticket vendors, the smell of olive oil frying recalled the ethnic of (then Jewish, Irish and Italian) New York neighbourhood of my childhood.' She found the familiar within the exotic, seemed to be striking out to a Yiddish land from which she had been exiled. Her book, *The Subversive Scribe* (1991) recounts her journey of personal and professional translation, in particular her creative, collaborative translations of the work of Guillermo Cabrera Infante, Severo Sarduy and Manuel Puig whose biography she is currently completing.

MACDONALD Olivia read Latin American literature at university and then worked for many years as a translator and interpreter of the Spanish language. She became involved with Latin America, its history, culture and literature in several ways: firstly through association with human rights committees in the seventies and a brief period at the Latin American Bureau; then she was married to a Venezuelan musician and lived on the island of Margarita where she taught English; later she worked and studied in Lima, Peru taking a particular interest in indigenous music; and then worked in Cuba as a translator on the Cuban newspaper *Granma*, where she took responsibility for the cultural pages. On her return to the UK she was the Nicaraguan Embassy administrator. She was recently involved in the translation of another anthology of Cuban writing *AfroCuba* and has worked on several Latin American and Cuban films, the last of which was the tragic story of Brindis de Salas, the Cuban violinist.

MAIER Carol is Professor of Spanish at Kent State University (Ohio), where she teaches in the Department of Modern and Classical Studies and is affiliated with the Institute for Applied Linguistics. Other translations of work by Octavio Armand include *With Dusk* (1994). She has also translated Rosa Chacel's *Memoirs of Leticia Valle* (1994) which won the MLA Scaglione Translation Prize for 1996. Her current projects include translations of Chacel's *La sinrazón* and María Zambrano's *Delirio y destino*. She is also co-editor, with Anuradha Dingwaney Needham of *Between Languages and Cultures: Translation and Cross-Cultural Texts* (1995). In addition she has published essays on translation theory and pedagogy, gender issues, reviewing and contemporary Hispanic literature, especially the work of Ramón del Valle-Inclán.

McCARTHY John was born in Merthyr Tydfil in 1960. After leaving school he lived in London for a year before leaving the country to travel. It was while abroad and working as a fruit-picker, house-painter and labourer that he discovered an interest in and an aptitude for languages. This discovery came as something of a surprise, he says, for at school he'd earned a dubious notoriety and the respect of his male peers for his consistent and spectactularly poor results in the widely considered effeminate subjects of French and Welsh. As a mature student he completed a degree in Spanish and Theatre Studies, and from there went on to the MA in Translation at Middlesex University which he is on the point of completing. He likes the challenge of translating texts which upon a first reading are all but incomprehensible. Such apparently difficult texts help his development as a translator. John McCarthy hopes to begin a novel-length project imminently and to continue translating challenging shorter fiction from all over the Spanish-speaking world. He lives in north London with his Spanish wife and young son.

NORMAN Lulu is a freelance writer and translator from French and Spanish. She went to University College, London and trained at the London School of Translation Studies, and began to translate professionally after gaining her Diplomas in Translation. Her literary work has comprised profiles, reviews and travel writing which have appeared in national newspapers, magazines and literary journals. Her translations include the work of Egyptian writer, Albert Cossery, Renaissance women's poetry, and most recently new titles from the French Embassy/Translators Association French Book Scheme and the songs of Serge Gainsbourg. She also works occasionally as a freelance photographer and is currently studying Arabic. She lives in London.

STUBBS Jean spent nineteen years in Cuba, where she researched Cuban history and contemporary development. She is currently Professor at the University of North London where she lectures on Caribbean and Latin American history. She is the author of various articles and books on Cuba, *Tobacco on the Periphery: a Case Study in Labour History 1869-1958* (CUP,1985); *Cuba:the Test of Time* (Latin

AmericaBureau/Monthly Review, London/New York) She co-edited with Pedro Pérez Sarduy *AFROCUBA* (1993) and co-authored with him the introduction to the anthology *No Longer Invisible / Afro-Latin Americans Today* (1995). She compiled with Lila Haines and Meic F. Haines, *Cuba: World Bibliographical Series*, Clio Press (1996)

WILKINSON Stephen has a degree in American Studies and a Masters in Hispanic Studies. He is editor of *CubaSi*, a quarterly magazine of Cuban current affairs, and has travelled widely in Cuba since 1986. He is currently at Queen Mary and Westfield College, London, researching a Ph.D thesis on the subject of Cuban detective fiction. Among the other works he has translated is a Cuban detective novel, *Máscaras*, by Leonardo Padura Fuentes, which will be published in 1997.

WILSON Jason was born in Mauritius in 1944. He is Reader in Latin American Literature at University College. As a translator he has introduced, abridged and translated Alexandre von Humboldt, *Personal Narrative of a Journey to the Equinoctial Regions of the New Continent*, for Penguin Classics, 1995. He translated four Argentine writers for *Translation, The Journal of Literary Translation* (Spring 1987), poems by Octavio Paz for a BBC *Bookmark* programme on Paz (26 October 1988), an essay by Paz for *The Times Literary Supplement*, 1989, and four Poems by Paz in Octavio Paz, *Between Sweden and Mexico*, Adam Poets: London 1990. He has also translated Enrique Serna's 'An Artist's Sustenance', in *Storm*, n.7-8 (October), 1992, and Enrique Murillo, Ignacio Martínez de Pisón and Pedro Zarraluki in Juan Antonio Masoliver (ed.) *The Origins of Desire, Modern Spanish Short Stories*, Serpent's Tail, 1993. His most recent translation is Mario Gradowczyk, *Alejandro Xu Solar*, Harry Abrams Inc. and Ediciones Alba: Buenos Aires and New York,1966. He is currently translating Spanish American surrealist poems for an anthology.